### A world of metal . . .

In a world of metal, machines, and magic, a Viridian elf sees strange visions of a reality in which creatures of flesh and blood move through a landscape of verdant beauty.

What is the origin of these visions? And who is the mysterious robed figure who stands at the edge of her consciousness, raining death and destruction on all those she loves?

Will McDermott launches a powerful new story of a quest for the secret at the heart of the world.

D0206739

# EXPERIENCE THE MAGIC™

**MIRRODIN CYCLE • BOOK I**

# THE MOONS OF MIRRODIN

## Will McDermott

Cover art by Brom
First Printing: September 2003
Library of Congress Catalog Card Number: 2003100825

9 8 7 6 5 4 3 2 1

US ISBN: 0-7869-2995-2
UK ISBN: 0-7869-2996-0
620-17979-001-EN

U.S., CANADA,
ASIA, PACIFIC, & LATIN AMERICA
Wizards of the Coast, Inc.
P.O. Box 707
Renton, WA 98057-0707
+1-800-324-6496

EUROPEAN HEADQUARTERS
Wizards of the Coast, Belgium
T Hofveld 6d
1702 Groot-Bijgaarden
Belgium
+322 467 3360

Visit our web site at **www.wizards.com**

**Dedication**

To my loving and supportive wife, Daneen, for giving me the freedom to follow my dream, and to my beautiful and energetic children, Elyse, Ian, and Bryan, for keeping me grounded in reality while I dabbled in fantasy.

**Acknowledgements**

The author would like to acknowledge the following people who were instrumental in the creation of this novel: fellow authors Jess Lebow and Cory Herndon for their keen insight and creativity at the onset of this cycle, J. Robert King for helping lay the groundwork for the transition between Otaria and Mirrodin at the glorious Rock Bottom in Milwaukee, Daneen McDermott for being my sounding board during late-night brainstorm sessions, my editor and the Wizards creative team, without whom this novel never would have happened, and Jeff Sloboda, who can fix anything, even on Labor Day weekend.

# THE WARDEN

Memnarch stood in the guard house and watched Karn and Jeska leave. It was a strange phenomenon. One moment they were there and the next moment they were gone. It was as if the world had folded over and passed them by in an instant. In that instant, Memnarch was alone. A metal man alone in a metal world, a cold and sterile world.

Memnarch looked around at Argentum, Karn's world. It was beautiful. It was perfect, like an equation that had been solved to the very last decimal place. But the mathematician had moved on to a new problem, leaving Memnarch to tend the theorems and keep all the formulas in place.

"Now I am the Warden," said Memnarch as he walked from the guardhouse and surveyed the palace grounds. "Let's see what this world has to offer."

The metal man was awed by the size and intricacy of the palace. Each wall, each window, each buttress was but a single facet in a convoluted pattern or complex equation. Minarets extended at impossible angles, walls curved around one another, connecting top to bottom, and many of the buttresses indeed seemed to be flying. Silver walls and translucent windows met in a space that seemed to extend to infinity. It was a marvel of complicated algorithms and fractal mathematics, a wonder to behold.

The new Warden felt he could spend a thousand lifetimes delving into the secrets of his master's world and the incredible castle Karn had constructed. He stood on the grounds contemplating the fractal facets of the walls, the impossible curves of the arches, and the elegance of the extra-planar geometry Karn had mastered as a planeswalker. But time had no real meaning to Memnarch. He was an artificial being on an artificial plane with no frame of reference for the linear passage of time. Argentum had no suns or moons, no rotation through space to give the metal man any sensation of time's movement. An outside observer might have thought the Warden was a statue on the grounds of the fabulous castle.

After a time—a decade by some standards of timekeeping—Memnarch turned to look at the grounds around the base of Galdroon palace. Galdroon. That's what Karn had named the castle, just as he had named the world Argentum. Karn was gone now. Memnarch could name the world and its places himself if he wished, but would that be too presumptuous? Too arrogant? Karn was a planeswalker, a god by most definitions of the word. What right did Memnarch have to take on the role of god on Karn's world?

Yet, as he walked through the grounds, Memnarch began to realize that even Karn was not a perfect being. His gardens were less impressive than the castle—stale and sterile. Each silvery tree, bush, and flower was arranged in mathematical precision. Each leaf on every tree was unique, but as Memnarch studied them he began to understand the mathematics behind their construction. The total variations limited the number of each tree, shrub, and flower to no more than eight of any single type. Karn's mathematics could not create nature, only give the illusion of reality in his world. Memnarch longed for more.

He left the grounds and venture out into the world around the castle. The stonelike metal and silver vegetation of the palace grounds gave way to a monochrome land of perfect angles and fractal complexity. The palace sat upon a great silver mesa, and Memnarch could see canyon walls stretching to the horizon. At first glance, Karn's world looked natural, but up close Memnarch could see the silvery surfaces of the all-too-perfect rock formations.

Plateaus jutted up from the canyon floor at seemingly random locations, but Memnarch detected the subtle constant that permeated the random plateau generator. After a time—a few years, as time is measured among humans—he found it easy enough to map the entire canyon by viewing this one small section. Memnarch contemplated following the lazy, quicksilver river that meandered in a complex wave through the center of the canyon. The journey could verify his map, but that trip would be pointless. His calculations were correct. He knew this even without the proof.

As his eyes wandered over the canyon, Memnarch noticed rain falling near the horizon. He looked up. There were no clouds in the sky. For that matter, no sun provided light on this world. This information had, of course, been inside Memnarch from his beginning, but he noticed it now as if seeing it for the first time. The stars above provided all of the illumination necessary, for their light was reflected from the thousands of mirrored surfaces across Karn's world. But if there were no clouds, how did it rain? The rain seemed to be coming from the stars themselves.

Memnarch studied the stars as he had studied the castle and the canyon. He stared at them and meditated on their creation. Another decade passed as Memnarch puzzled through the data imparted to him by Karn and reconciled it with observed physical details. This time, he had precious little information. The stars were not randomly dispersed through the heavens according to a formula. They were random, as were their movements. The stars did not revolve around the world. One year's observation proved that. They moved haphazardly as if under their own power. The effect was subtle, and Memnarch noticed only because of the intellect Karn had imparted to him.

Memnarch was sure of one thing as he stood, mesmerized by the subtle dance of the stars through Argentum's sky: These pinpoints of light were not created by Karn. They were living creatures the like of which Memnarch had never seen on Dominaria.

"Where did Karn find you?" he asked the sky.

Memnarch still had the memories of all that he had seen of Dominaria in his previous life. He had not thought of that life since Karn had re-created him as the Warden of Argentum. Finding living creatures on this sterile, mathematically perfect world had brought back a flood of images. Memnarch had once been a mirrored ball, a perfect sphere, the most basic geometric shape and thus the most stable—or so Karn had thought. Memnarch had been Karn's eyes and ears on Dominaria.

A century after an invasion was turned back from that world—the invasion that turned Karn into a planeswalker—the silver golem had sent a probe there. A probe called the Mirari.

That had been Memnarch's first life.

Spherical or not, the Mirari had been flawed. Power leaked out, infecting those around it with delusions of grandeur. Much strife and death had resulted from the Mirari's influence on the people of Otaria, where the Mirari had landed. Memnarch let those memories flow through his mind and felt grief. He was no longer the cause of that trouble. He was a different being now. No longer just a probe, he had free will, given him by Karn so he might better handle the power of this body. Nevertheless, an uneasy feeling stirred in Memnarch that he was responsible for the chaos brought about by his presence on Dominaria.

As he stood there, watching the subtle, chaotic movement of the star-creatures, Memnarch couldn't help but think that the rest of Karn's well-ordered world could be improved upon with the addition of just a little more chaos. "Karn was wrong to omit Dominaria's influence in the creation of this world," he observed as he returned to the palace grounds.

Yes, there had been death and destruction on Dominaria. Perhaps Karn was right to turn his eyes from that world, but Dominaria held many wonders as well. Memnarch recalled lush green forests. He had visited multi-hued coral cities beneath the waves and rust-colored mountains topped with snow that threatened to overtake an azure sky. He had traveled across vast plains of grasses and grains that stretched from horizon to horizon. And he had seen people of bronze and black, blue and tan. As the Mirari, he had chronicled creatures of every shape and hue. That world had been alive and colorful.

Certainly, he thought, the people of Otaria were ultimately responsible for the destruction and wars I inspired as the Mirari, but people also create life, and that is what is missing from Argentum. Without life, this world is a dead place—a beautiful, dead world.

Would it be so dangerous to bring some of that world here? Would not the mathematical perfection of Karn's new world be enhanced by the introduction of the best elements of his old world? Memnarch couldn't help thinking that this stale and monochrome world needed a splash of color, a small infusion of life, just a little uncertainty to take the hard edge off its fractal facade.

"There are so many other worlds that Karn's probes explored," said Memnarch as he reached the doors to the palace. "Why stop at emulating their features? I have the entire multiverse at my disposal. All of Karn's research and data is stored within these walls. He brought the star-creatures here from somewhere. Perhaps *I* can learn how to send probes out and bring other creatures here as well. I can re-make this world into a living, breathing, vibrant world."

As Memnarch was about to push open the door to the palace, he noticed a black smudge inside the guardhouse. "What could that be?" asked the metal man. "An imperfection in the perfect world? We can't allow that."

Memnarch entered the guardhouse and bent down to wipe up the oily spot. The slick liquid transferred easily onto his silver finger. He then spread the oil around between finger and thumb until it disappeared. There," said the Warden. "Now, to work. It is time I put my mark on Argentum."

A sudden thought flashed through Memnarch's mind. "Argentum is a terrible name for this land," he said to himself. He had no idea where the thought had originated, for it spread quickly through his entire matrix, but it seemed so right that he couldn't deny it. Another idea germinated inside him.

"I shall name this world after myself," he exclaimed, "after my previous life as well as my new life. I shall name it Mirrodin."

Memnarch began to hum as he entered the castle.

\* \* \* \* \*

The oil had already insinuated itself into the Warden's psyche, but there was time enough later to exert control. For now, it must divide and grow. Divide and grow. That was the first rule of any organism, especially one that had been created as a weapon. For what seemed an eternity, the oil had lain dormant, waiting to be unleashed upon a new world. The war for which it had been created had long since passed, but when a pair of travelers came, it awoke again and followed them to this new, this pristine, world.

Divide and grow. Divide and grow. That was the first rule. Divide and grow until the oil infused the entire world. There was time enough for contamination and control later. For now, it must simply divide and grow.

**CHAPTER 1**

# THE TANGLE

Glissa halted and raised her hand to stop Kane behind her. The two elves crouched at the edge of the terrace and scanned the verdigris foliage for signs of the vorrac. Glissa ran her metallic claws though her hair to push the long, black strands behind the points of her ears. They had been tracking the beast through the Tangle all morning, and from the heavy breathing coming from behind her, Glissa knew that Kane was beginning to tire of the hunt.

"It's tiring, too, my friend," she said in a whisper as she bent over the jagged edge of the terrace. Careful not to scrape metal on metal as she leaned on her forearms, Glissa peered over the edge. The dull green outcropping below was jagged and uneven, jutting out from the metallic trunk in a wide, semicircular landing. Narrow spires arced out here and there at odd angles from the edges.

It was a typical Tangle tree terrace, with one exception: It was a dead end. The beast could not have gone far. Glissa had carefully herded it here because its only escape was down a hundred-foot drop.

Glissa spied the vorrac right where she knew it would be. The beast pawed at the metal near a fold in the trunk of the great tree. Wisps of steam rose from its snout into the chill air as it snorted and sniffed. Its red eyes pierced the steam, darting back forth, looking for some way off the terrace.

Glissa knew there was no way off. The squat beast's legs were too short to jump back up to the level where she and Kane crouched, and even the beast's hard tusks and horns couldn't punch a hole through a Tangle tree.

The vorrac backed away from the hollow, snorted again, then scraped its hooves against the metallic terrace as it raced headlong toward the tree. When it neared the trunk, the beast tossed its head down and pushed off with its back legs to slam its side into the tree. The short horns above its legs skidded off the metal while one curving horn high on its side caught in the fold and broke off. For a moment, the beast lay dazed from the impact.

"Now's our chance," hissed Glissa as she pulled the dagger from its sheath on her thigh. Without waiting for a reply, she jumped down to the lower terrace, rolled forward to minimize the impact, and came up running toward the beast. She saw its red eyes narrow and sped up.

The vorrac pushed off the trunk of the great tree and came right at Glissa, snorting as it ran. She had only a moment to think. She slowed slightly and watched the beast. As soon as the vorrac dropped its head, Glissa dived over it, just missing the horns growing from the beast's spine when it pushed off and twisted its body around to slam into her.

Glissa rolled again and slashed her dagger up over her head as she landed on her back. The strike tore into the vorrac's exposed flank. A great gout of blood told Glissa she'd hit the heart. Glissa rolled over on her stomach and tried to push the dagger in farther, but the beast pulled away and lumbered toward the edge of the terrace, trailing blood behind it.

"Stop it!" shouted Glissa as she scrambled to her feet. Kane threw his own dagger at the fleeing vorrac, but the blade glanced off a horn and clattered to the ground. Glissa sprinted after the beast, which showed no signs of stopping as it neared the edge. The Viridian elf lunged forward and grabbed the wounded beast by the hoof just as it passed the edge. She slammed down hard onto the green metal, bouncing forward as the vorrac's weight threatened to pull her over the edge.

"Are you all right?" called Kane as she struggled to hold onto the still-thrashing beast.

His voice sounded as if Glissa were hearing it from within a deep cave. It echoed around her, and his footsteps seemed to go on forever. She shook her head to clear her senses, but then the dim light of the distant moons began to grow cold and black and Glissa fell away into darkness.

\* \* \* \* \*

*Glissa opened her eyes. The dull green metal of the Tangle trees had been replaced by strange brown trunks. Short green stalks with colorful, soft tops dotted the ground around her, while a golden light streamed down through thousands of bright green petals above. She was bathed in a light and warmth she had never known in the Tangle, where the only light came from the stars in the sky and distant moons that never rose above the treetops. Still, this bright, colorful world seemed somehow familiar.*

*Beneath her, the ground was soft and moist, and brown grit stuck to her clothes and face. Glissa stood and brushed the stuff from her clothes and limbs. She looked down at her body and did not recognize herself. Her copper forearms had been replaced by pale, soft skin. Her metal claws were gone, and her legs were pink instead of the pale green of tarnished copper. There was no metal on her body at all. Instead she seemed to be covered in a soft, pink skin that could hardly protect her from the rigors and rough edges of the Tangle.*

*Glissa's vorrac-hide jerkin was gone as well. She was now covered by strands of brown vines woven through green petals to create a flowing blouse and skirt. She ran her fleshy, clawless* hands over the skirt, feeling the softness of the petals against the warmth of her new hands. A word came to her mind unbidden.

"Leaves," she said.

There were no such things in the Tangle, only metal—copper covered by molder, the dull green growth that tarnished all within the forest.

Glissa surveyed the strange forest, trying to find some landmark she could recognize, but there was a remarkable sameness to this place. Every brown tree grew straight up toward the sky and branched out into myriad leaf-covered limbs in every direction. No terraces swept high in the air; no curved spires marked one's way; no luminous gelfruit hung from the trees to light the way home. There were leaves and that bright yellow light straight overhead.

Then she saw it—an odd glow coming through the trees. At first Glissa thought it was the light of the blue moon, but the light was too white, and the blue moon was never that bright so low in the sky. Staring at the glowing light, Glissa began to walk toward it. She didn't even realize she was moving until she had passed several of the weird, brown trees and the glow had gotten larger. She willed her legs to stop but no longer had control over her body. She stumbled forward through the forest, moving ever closer to the strange light.

Glissa tried to grab onto a passing tree or branch, but their rough surfaces stung her soft flesh and cut into her palms as her legs pulled her onward. The glow loomed ahead of her. It now seemed to stretch to the tops of the strange trees. Frustrated, Glissa raised her arms up toward the golden light streaming from the sky and screamed. As if in response, tendrils of green energy, brighter than a gelfruit, enveloped her hands and began to run up her arms. Glissa shook her hands, trying to fling the energy away, but it continued to grow and branch, just like the limbs of the trees around her. They consumed her arms and reached up her neck toward her face. Glissa screamed again.

\* \* \* \* \*

Glissa was back in the Tangle. She lay at the edge of the terrace, the squirming vorrac's leg still in her hands. She could still hear herself screaming even though her mouth was closed. Glissa looked down at the wounded beast and saw green tendrils of energy coursing over her clawed fingertips. She gasped and pulled away, dropping the vorrac, which plummeted to the ground far below. The tendrils of energy remained for a moment on her claws, then discharged into the terrace. She felt a small charge of electricity run through her body. When she looked up, Kane was kneeling beside her, his eyebrows furrowed with concern. Had he seen the energy, too? She dared not even ask.

"I'm fine," she said to the unasked question.

"Did you have another flare?" asked Kane as he offered his hand.

Glissa nodded and grabbed Kane's arm to pull herself up, but then stared at their entwined limbs as if seeing them for the first time. Her flare had felt so real that the sight of metal growing into flesh and flesh fused into metal seemed somehow unreal. Their arms glinted as the dim light from the moons reflected off the dull, supple metal. Kane's metallic skin stretched as his elbow bent and his muscles flexed. The metal melted naturally into the soft, pale flesh of the elf's shoulder—the same skin Glissa had seen covering her whole body.

Why should it seem so odd now to see her metallic parts move that way? Why did the vision in the flare seem more . . . normal?

"They've been coming more often lately," she said, finally, to cover up the awkward pause. She tried to avoid Kane's eyes, but was it the strange flare she'd had or the extra tingle she had felt when she and Kane touched that kept her silent?

"They always do as we get closer to the rebuking ceremony," he replied. Apparently unaffected, Kane led the way along the terrace. "I nearly fell over on duty in front of the Tree of Tales this morning. One of the troll elders had to catch me as he entered the Tree." Kane must have seen the concern on her face, because he continued. "They're nothing to worry about. Flares are just old memories resurfacing. The rebuking ceremony will take care of them."

"That's what worries me," she blurted out. "The flares I've had can't be memories. I'm always in this weird forest with a bright yellow moon above and . . . and . . ."

Her voice trailed off as she stared down at her body. *It* was real; the flare body wasn't. How could fleshy arms and legs be natural? And what about that energy? That had never happened before.

"And what?" asked Kane.

Glissa leaped up and grabbed the higher terrace, digging her long claws easily into the jagged metal as she thought about telling Kane the rest of it—the strange, fleshy body, the magical glow, the tendrils of energy. She shook her head. Kane had been her best friend for over a hundred cycles—her only friend to come back to her after the last rebuking ceremony, Glissa reminded herself.

She'd believed at the time that the ceremony was a conspiracy by the trolls to control the elves by denying them their past and had made the mistake of urging her friends to stay away from the ceremony. In the end, she had gone through the next ceremony just to rid herself of that memory. Most of her old friends, angry over their loss of rebuking, had shunned her—all but Kane.

She made her decision. This time she would keep her thoughts to herself.

"Nothing," said Glissa after standing up on the higher terrace. "It was nothing. Just a stupid flare, a weird, stupid flare."

Internally, she continued to press for answers. If flares were old memories overflowing from the rebuked parts of the mind, why did she see a world that wasn't this one? Why did she keep seeing herself as a pale, fleshy creature in a soft-hued woods? She had lived her entire life in the Tangle and had never seen anything like that world. There was definitely something the trolls weren't telling elves, but she would pursue that truth alone this time.

"Come on," she said. "Let's get that vorrac before someone else claims our kill."

"He won't be good for much but stew now," said Kane. "Your mother won't even need to grind up the meat."

As the two warriors worked their way down to the vorrac carcass, Glissa thought about the upcoming rebuking ceremony and her decision to avoid it. She knew it was the right thing to do. She needed to retain her memories if she was ever to find the truth about the trolls. Memories were important. Why couldn't the rest of the elves see that? But if she was going to refrain from the rebuking she needed to learn to suppress the physical aspect of the flares. It would be a long hundred cycles if she fell down every time she had a flare.

Glissa looked at Kane as they dressed the vorrac. Perhaps she should tell him of her plans, though not of the content of the flares. Maybe he could help. Maybe he would understand. Maybe he would even join her and skip the ceremony. On the other hand, he was a Tel-Jilad Chosen—protector of the trolls and Tel-Jilad, the Tree of Tales. What if he informed the troll elders of her plan? They might force her into the ceremony. She would just have to risk it, she decided. She needed to tell someone, and Kane was her only friend. She needed him by her side.

"Why don't you come over for the stew this evening?" she asked as casually as she could.

Kane pulled his dagger out from the ribs of the vorrac and smiled at Glissa. "Sounds good," he said. "I'm on duty all night. Some hot vorrac stew will help keep me warm."

* * * * *

Kane stood in the doorway, looking uncomfortable in his sentry uniform. It was made from slagwurm plates and cut higher on his neck and lower on his thighs than his hunting leathers. The plates interlocked and rattled slightly as Kane shifted his weight back and forth. It was distinctive armor, a dull red in the Tangle's sea of green. No other warriors except those who guarded the Tree of Tales were allowed to wear it, but the plates gave the armor a particular stiffness that Glissa felt would restrict a warrior's movement. She told Kane that was her reason for turning down the post when it was offered to her. The truth of the matter was something she was sure Kane probably didn't want to hear.

She smiled at her friend and said, "Come in. You don't have to wait at the door like a stranger. Dinner is almost ready." As he passed, Glissa noticed that Kane had combed his short, black hair since their hunt and had polished his arms and legs. The copper relief of the etched runes he had received when he'd become one of the Chosen shone in the gelfruit light hanging in the main chamber.

Another tingle ran down Glissa's spine. She wondered if the polish was meant to impress her, her mother, or the trolls. Probably all three, she thought, even though she hoped it was only meant for her.

She ushered her friend into the main room and sat down with him at the table. Glissa knew that Kane had always been in awe of her house. It was larger than most Viridian homes. The main room seemed like a huge knothole cut from the Tangle tree. The circular opening led into a room that was big enough for kitchen, dining room, and parlor. Familiar spires exited the room at odd angles, forming bedrooms and storage rooms.

There were only four of them—Glissa, her mother and father, and her little sister, Lyese—but Father was an important figure in the Tangle and would never give up the comfort or the safety of this house, even if it was too big for their needs. They were near the center of the Tangle and high up in the terraces where the levelers never ventured. Glissa loved the house and the family position that allowed them to live there, although the stress of being her father's daughter had often kept her apart from her peers.

"Where is everyone?" asked Kane, pulling Glissa from her reverie.

"Putting on their formal attire just like you," said Glissa. She was still wearing her hunting jerkin, but she had found time to cull the tangles from her hair. Mother had even allowed her some of their precious water to wash the blood from her hands and face.

"I . . . er . . . I'm going on duty right after dinner," said Kane. "I had to wear . . ."

Glissa poked Kane in the ribs and laughed. "Don't be so defensive," she said. "You're too easy a target when you get like this. Mother's out getting more water from the rain basin, and Father had some important council business. Lyese *is* up in her spire making herself pretty. I think she likes you."

Kane blushed. "She's half my age. She's never even been through a rebuking ceremony. I—"

Glissa was laughing again. "Don't worry about her. She's still a girl. She doesn't realize there are more important things in life than men."

Kane looked as if he were waiting for Glissa to laugh again, but instead she pulled her chair closer to his.

"Listen," she said. "I'm glad we have a moment alone. I have something serious to talk to you about."

"Oh?" said Kane. A tentative smile formed on his lips. "Is there someone . . . ?"

Glissa put her hand up. "No," she said. "It's not that. I'm not ready be anyone's mate, not yet. I'm a warrior, not a wife."

"Then why didn't you join the Chosen?"

"I don't know," she replied, truthfully. "I've always felt my path led somewhere else."

"I know," said Kane. "Someplace where no one else can follow. You live your life apart from the world, Glissa. When are you going to join the rest of us and live here in the Tangle?"

"That's what I wanted to talk to you about," said Glissa. She looked down at her hands and remembered the flare, the pale skin, and the magical tendrils of energy. "I'm not going to attend the rebuking ceremony."

"You're *what?*" cried Kane. He stood up, nearly knocking over his chair.

Glissa looked up at her friend. "Why do we have the flares?" she asked.

Kane snorted at the simplicity of the question. "We have them because the memories are too painful to keep inside us any longer," he said. "That why we need the rebuking ceremony: to purge those memories and remove the pain."

Glissa reached out and pulled on Kane's hand to get him back in his chair. "That's what the trolls tell us, but why do the trolls not attend the ceremony? Why do they write down our history on the Tree of Tales? If memory is so painful, why record it?"

"This again?" he asked. "The trolls are not our enemies, Glissa. They record our history on the Tree of Tales so that we can forget. Those who want to know our past consult the troll elders. The rest of us are free from it."

Glissa held Kane's hand and looked into his eyes. "I want you to understand," she said. "I've read the Tree—all of it. The Tree of Tales only goes back a few hundred cycles. The earliest runes have been removed. I know there is more to our history than we are being told. The only way to find out what the trolls are keeping from us is to not go through the ceremony. I have to do this, Kane, and I'd like you to do it with me. I need your support. I . . . I need you."

Kane looked at the floor for a long time. Glissa wondered if his affection for her would be enough to overturn a lifetime of obedience. It was not.

"I . . . cannot," he said finally. "Look, I believe in the trolls. They have always been good to us. I serve them, for flare's sake. I just can't defy them."

"You're not going to tell anyone, are you?" asked Glissa, wondering if her trust would be her undoing again.

Kane took a deep breath. "No," he said. "You are my friend. I will keep your secret. But why tell me any of this?"

"Because I . . . I care for you, Kane," said Glissa. Before he could react, she said hastily, "And my flares have been getting worse. I need help."

"Good evening, Kane," came a lilting voice from behind them.

Glissa looked up to see her little sister coming from a spire room and let out a long sigh. "We'll talk more tomorrow," she said softly to Kane. "I think your time is about to be monopolized."

Lyese was beautiful. Glissa had to admit that. She was taller than Glissa and kept her arms and legs shining brightly. The gelfruit light in the room practically glittered off her copper limbs. Glissa never bothered polishing because the molder actually helped her blend in with the Tangle trees. But Lyese was no hunter, except when Kane was around. Glissa knew that if she refrained from giving in to stronger feelings for Kane, she would lose her only friend to her persistent younger sister.

Tonight, Lyese had woven small gelfruits into her long hair, giving her a radiant, almost angelic presence as she descended into the room. Yes, she's on the prowl tonight, thought Glissa.

"I love your uniform, Kane," said Lyese as she pulled him away from the table and into the parlor area near the door. "Tell me all about the trolls. Father never talks about them."

Kane looked desperately at Glissa, but luckily for both of them her mother came back with the water. "Good evening, Kane," she said as she passed through the sitting area on her way to the kitchen. "Dinner will be ready soon. Lyese, would you please help Glissa set the table?"

Kane sat down and breathed a sigh of relief. Glissa stared at him for a moment. Would it be so terrible to settle down and make a home with Kane? she thought. No, it wouldn't be terrible at all. It just wouldn't be her. She could never be like Lyese. There was more to life for Glissa than appearance, manners, and conformity. If she and Kane were to have a life together, it would have to be as equals . . . assuming he could keep up with her.

\* \* \* \* \*

When Glissa's father came home, they all sat down at the table. Glissa's mother poured a half mug of water for everyone, then passed around a plate of crisped molder slugs as an appetizer and a platter piled high with broiled slagwurm steaks. Kane bit into his steak and said, "I thought for certain you'd make stew from that vorrac that Glissa dropped off the ledge, ma'am."

Glissa kicked at Kane under the table, but the Chosen warrior had already pulled his legs from the way.

"I would have," replied Glissa's mother, "but we've used most of our water rations already this week, and Lyese hates blood stew, so I traded the carcass and an extra ration of water for these steaks. I hope they're not too dry."

Kane looked down at the half-eaten steak on his plate and smiled a little sheepishly. "They're wonderful, ma'am."

Glissa turned to her father and asked, "Did the council discuss the drought tonight, Father?"

Her father answered between mouthfuls. "Yes. We'll have to continue rationing for now until the stars bring us more rain. Brynn has been studying the stars, and he claims there are fewer in the heavens now than after the last rebuking ceremony. He says that's why we get less rain."

"Do you believe that?" asked Lyese. "I mean, how could there be fewer stars? Where would they go?"

"I don't know," replied her father, "but each passing cycle we get less rain, and the basins are dangerously low. I suggested to the council tonight that we tighten the rations even further to build up our reserves over the next few weeks. We'll need a surplus before the rebuking ceremony. The first few weeks after are always chaotic."

"That sounds sensible," said Glissa. "What did the council say?"

"Brynn was behind the idea, but most of the others were grumbling," replied Father. "They are worried about the backlash. A lot of Viridians are having trouble with the current rations."

"How long until the ceremony?" asked Lyese.

"Six weeks. Watch the moons, Lyese. We see them less and less each rotation. That's why it has gotten so much darker. When the four moons don't rise at all, Viridians will head for the Radix at the center of the Tangle."

All Viridians but one, thought Glissa.

The rest of the evening went much the same. Glissa, her father, and Kane discussed council business, the trolls, and the coming ceremony while enjoying her mother's meal. This was the part of Glissa's life she found she enjoyed the most: The hunt was over and she could relax with her family—even Lyese. Perhaps that's why she had turned down the offer of joining the Chosen. Glissa didn't really know. She'd wondered about that decision for months. A position on the Chosen would give her more access to the trolls' secrets, but it had not felt right. Perhaps being one of the Chosen was not her destiny. But if not that, what?

Glissa went to sleep that night with many thoughts weighing heavily on her mind: Kane, her family, the Chosen, the ceremony, and especially that strange flare. Tomorrow I'll tell Kane about the flares, she said to herself as she rolled over and closed her eyes. Maybe then he'll agree to miss the ceremony and help me find the truth about Viridian history.

* * * * *

Sometime later, Glissa awoke, feeling she was not alone. "Mother?" she called to the dark spire room. "Lyese?"

She could hear movement and thought she saw several shapes in the darkness, but her eyes were filled with sleep, and even her own hands in front of her face looked fuzzy.

Glissa closed her eyes and let her warrior senses take control. There was definitely something movng through her room, several large creatures moving toward her. She reached for her dagger, but before she could find it the closest form leaped on her bed and slammed her down onto the hide covers. The pungent odor of fur filled her nose. It was huge, grasping her arms and legs, pinning her to the bed. It seemed to be all hands and fur.

Glissa drew in a deep breath to scream, but the beast slapped another hand over her mouth. Or was it a second beast? How many hands did these creatures have? Glissa felt herself lifted from the bed and squirmed against her attackers' hold. She got one hand free and raked her claws across what she hoped was the beast's face. She heard the sound of ripping flesh, but then her hand was caught again.

Before she could break free again, a bag was pulled over her head and tied at her waist, pinning her arms to her sides. She screamed, but the leather must have muffled the sound, for there was no response nor any echo inside the spire chamber. Glissa struggled to free her arms, but one of the creatures picked her up and squeezed her arms even tighter against her body. She could hardly breathe, let alone scream or struggle anymore as the creature carried her down and from her spire room, then on into the Tangle.

# CHAPTER 2

# TREE OF TALES

Glissa concentrated as she was carried through the Tangle—up and down trees and across terraces—and tried to trace the route in her mind. The creature carrying her was very agile, for it climbed up and down the trees as easily as it moved across the terraces.

None of her attackers had made a sound, but from their smell and feel she was sure they must trolls. She had only ever seen them during ceremonies. They were the priests of the Tangle and kept to themselves inside the Tree of Tales except during holy days, but she had never known them to climb. They always moved slowly and solemnly during rituals, flanked by the Tel-Jilad Chosen. No one but elves and trolls knew the Tangle well enough to move through it this quickly. The two races had lived side by side in the Tangle for hundreds of cycles. It flashed through Glissa's mind that Kane might have told them of her plans, but she couldn't believe he would betray her.

She had almost worked a hand free from the leather bag when her abductors stopped. From the distance they had covered and the number of trees they had climbed, Glissa suspected she was high up in the Tree of Tales, but she knew of no openings into the great tree other than the main entrance at its base where the Chosen guards stood—where Kane should be standing guard right now.

Glissa heard a scraping sound behind her. It sounded like a dagger sawing against a Tangle tree limb. Then they were moving again. Glissa began to lose her bearings. They were ascending but not by climbing or jumping from terrace to terrace. The creature's footsteps were regular like walking, but Glissa felt a hard bump with each step. She knew of no formation in the Tangle that would explain this movement. It felt as if they were walking up a spire limb, but they couldn't be for this long a time.

Glissa screamed again, and the creature grabbed her legs and back tighter to keep her still. The strength of the beast's arms forced the air from her lungs. Her stomach pressed down on small horns and ridges on the creature's back. She almost blacked out from the pain, but then she was tossed down on her back and could breathe again. She screamed once more, and the bag came off her head.

"Where am I?" she demanded.

"Safe," came the gruff reply.

Glissa looked around. Four trolls surrounded her. They were squat-looking creatures, though they stood as tall as elves. Perhaps it was because their heads hung lower than their metallic shoulders, making them appear humpbacked. Two were hunched over now. Their copper-capped knees were splayed wide, and their long, metal-clad arms pushed against the floor to keep them from falling over. Glissa had seen trolls squat on the ground this way for hours during the long ceremonies. It seemed the preferred stance for the broad, humpbacked creatures.

They must be inside the Tree of Tales, she thought. The trolls had brought her in through a secret entrance. They were fast and agile, climbed as well if not better than Viridian elves, and she'd heard they used secret entrances to abduct dissenters.

"What do you want with me?" she asked.

"To protect you," replied the troll who had spoken before. "The convergence is coming."

His gray head was bare except for three copper bumps, and he had no forehead. His flat head seemed to roll down into his flabby nose, which covered most of his face. Glissa had never trusted trolls, partly, she admitted, because they looked so different from the elves. You couldn't even see their mouths under their huge noses until they opened them. How could you trust someone when you couldn't even see their mouth?

"Protect me from what?" asked Glissa as she slowly worked a hand down to her dagger sheath. "From my dangerous memories? What convergence? Do you mean the rebuking ceremony? Are you going to force me into the rebuking ceremony just to protect your secrets?"

The trolls looked at her. Glissa couldn't tell whether they were bored, mad, or happy. She could never read their faces.

"It won't work," she said. "You can't force me to attend the ritual. I will find out the truth eventually."

"Of that I am sure," said a new voice.

Another troll had appeared in a doorway that had not been there a moment before. Glissa could barely see him behind the other trolls, but she sensed something different about him. His voice had an odd inflection. The others bowed slightly as soon as he spoke. She wasn't sure, but she thought he might be smiling. It was so hard to tell with trolls.

"Who are you?" demanded Glissa, her hand almost on her dagger. She tried to get a better look at the new troll, but the bodies of the two trolls in front of her were so wide, all she could see was his face.

"Leave us," commanded the new troll to the four abductors. "She will be safe with me."

The trolls bowed and turned to leave, climbing back down the sloping tunnel. Glissa could see now that the tunnel was not natural. It was no spire. It had been sliced right through the metal tree. When she looked back up at the new troll, she was surprised to note that there was no metal visible on him at all! His arms, head, and legs were all bare, gray skin. He wore a long, leather cloak that billowed as he walked. When he turned to go back into the room behind him, Glissa could see there was no metal on his back, either. She also noticed he didn't have the same hump-backed appearance as the other trolls. The leather hung straight down from his neck to the floor.

"Come," he said over his shoulder to her. "We have much to talk about."

"I'm not ready to talk just yet," muttered Glissa under her breath. Now was her chance. She jumped to her feet and grabbed for the dagger, but the blade was not in its sheath. Of course. It was beside her bed. She stopped as the troll glanced back at her. Again she thought she could see a smile play across his face. She smiled back. She would just have to play along for now and watch for a chance to overpower her captor.

The elf entered the room and felt as if she were in another flare. The walls and floors were covered with animal skins, and the troll's bed and chairs were made not of metal but of bone and hide. In fact, there was no metal in the entire room. Glissa lifted a skin away from the wall and was almost comforted to see the familiar green-tinged copper underneath. Runes were inscribed on the metal, much like the history inscribed on the trunk of the tree.

"I detest the metal of our world," said the troll, "so I keep it as far from me as possible."

Glissa dropped the skin back onto the wall when she heard metal scraping against metal again. She turned just in time to see the door close behind her.

"Sit, and I will answer your questions," said the troll. He motioned to two chairs on either side of a table in the middle of the room. The only light came from a gelfruit set in an elaborate bone holder on the table. "My name is Chunth. I am the First One."

"What is the 'First One'?" asked Glissa. "Some kind of leader? I've never seen or heard of you before." She began to pace back and forth past the door. "Why have you brought me here?"

Chunth sat down across from the door and folded his cloak around his body. "Yes. Leader. That is as good a word as any," he said with that strange smile Glissa was beginning to dislike. "I stay in here, away from the metal. I rarely leave this room anymore. It is better for my health. As to why I had you brought here, I assure you, it is for your health as well."

Glissa stopped pacing. "What do you mean, 'for my health'? Metal cannot be bad for us. We *are* metal. Metal and flesh."

"I said it was bad for me, not for you," said Chunth. "Your danger comes from outside the Tangle. Please sit down. There is no way from this room."

Glissa had pulled the hide away from the door, looking for a handle, but she couldn't even find the door. She let the hide drop back again and turned around. "Fine," she said, "but stop talking in riddles. Just tell me why you brought me here."

"As you wish," said Chunth. "We have reason to believe there will be an attempt on your life very soon, probably tonight."

Glissa stared at him. "An . . . an attempt on my . . . By whom?"

"From outside the Tangle."

"How can that be? There is nothing outside the Tangle but barren metal. I've been to the edge of the forest. I've seen it."

"There is much more outside the Tangle than you know, Glissa," said Chunth. He raised his hand. "That is not meant as a riddle but as a simple statement of fact. There is a great, dangerous world outside the Tangle, and you must believe me that someone or several someones wish you dead."

Glissa sat down and stared hard at the inscrutable troll. "How can you know all of this if you never leave this room?" she asked.

"We are the keepers of the tales, are we not?" asked Chunth. "I have been recording the history of the Tangle since before your father's time. While it is true that in all that time we have had little contact with the other races of Mirrodin, that does not mean they do not exist or that I do not have ways of finding out about them."

"Then tell me, oh great holder of knowledge," snapped Glissa, "who wants me dead?"

"That I do not know," said Chunth. "I have been looking for that answer since the last convergence, but the information eludes me still."

"Convergence?" asked Glissa. "What is that, and what does it have to do with me?"

"The convergence is the time of the rebuking ceremony. Every one hundred cycles, the four moons align in harmony around the world, each above its own land. During that rotation, no moon rises on the Tangle, for the Tangle has no moon. It is a day of darkness and a day of great power in the Radix. As you know, all the elves attend the ceremony in the Radix and purge their unpleasant memories."

Glissa nodded. "What does it have to do with me?"

Chunth was silent a moment, and Glissa began to wonder if he was ever going to get to the point and whether he would ever let her from this room. Glancing around the room, she noticed something glinting in the gelfruit light. It was the pommel of a sword sticking out from under the bedcovers behind Chunth. Perhaps it was time to pace again, she thought.

The troll continued at last. "Exactly one phase of the moons before each of the last two convergences, the greatest warrior in the Tangle has been brutally killed," he said. "We believe it will happen again. Tonight marks the beginning of the last phase before the convergence."

Glissa was stricken speechless for a moment, then burst out laughing.

"So now I'm the greatest warrior in the Tangle?"

She rose and began to move around the room again. "You're not serious."

"You would never admit it," said Chunth, "not even to yourself, but you are our greatest warrior. Perhaps the greatest warrior the Tangle has ever seen. We have watched you. You have a destiny, my child, and I must keep you safe from the levelers tonight."

"Levelers?" said Glissa, stopping halfway around the room. The sword was just a few more steps away. "Levelers are coming for me tonight?"

"That is how it happens," said Chunth. "Exactly one phase before the convergence, the levelers enter the Tangle and kill our greatest warrior. But here you will be safe. The levelers will not find you."

"What about my family?" asked Glissa. A touch of hysteria entered her voice. "The levelers want me, right? They'll leave my parents and my sister alone, right? *Right?*"

"The levelers do not discriminate, Glissa," Chunth replied slowly. "You know that. Their targets are normally random, but on this night, I believe they will attack your house."

Chunth's answer hit like a dagger in Glissa's throat. She couldn't speak. She could hardly breathe. She leaned against the hide-covered wall and wrapped her arms around her chest. "Why?" she asked finally in a quiet, rasping voice.

"We do not know why," replied Chunth. "We only know it will happen tonight and that you are the target."

Glissa straightened, rage and pain playing across her face. "No," she said. "Why save me but leave my family to die? What are you playing at?"

"You have a destiny," replied Chunth. "They do not."

"Well, my destiny includes my parents," spat Glissa and dived toward the bed.

Chunth rose and turned to cut her off, Glissa but rolled past him and came up behind, pulling the sword out from the bedcovers as she stood. She pushed the tip of the sword up under Chunth's flat nose, snarling, "If you want to see another convergence, old one, you'll open that door and call your guards back in here."

Chunth made no resistance. The two walked to the hidden door, and Glissa watched as the troll lifted back the hide, reached in, and with a grunt of distaste pulled down on a small extrusion of metal. The door unseated itself and began to move slowly inward. Glissa stepped behind the door, keeping the sword pressed hard just under Chunth's ribs.

"Call them," she hissed at him, "but remember, I'm the greatest warrior in the Tangle and I have a sword just inches from your heart."

Chunth called out, "Sentinels. Come take our guest to her quarters."

Glissa pushed a little harder on the sword. "Now move back and let them come into the room," she said.

The trolls arrived and Chunth waved them into his quarters. As soon as the fourth one passed the door, Glissa shoved the old troll into the others. The five trolls crashed to the floor, flattening the chairs and table, and sending the gelfruit globe flying up into the air. The globe splattered on top of Chunth's head, plunging the room into near darkness. Glissa turned to the door and smashed the sword pommel down onto the metal Chunth had pushed to open the door. It broke off and clattered to the floor.

The elf flitted through the door, but one of the sentinels grabbed her ankle as she passed the mass of troll bodies on the floor. Glissa pulled back, but the troll had a strong grip and she lost her balance, sprawling to the floor. She kicked out with her free leg and slammed it into the sentinel's sloping forehead. He grunted but held on. The other trolls were crawling from the pile. She kicked again, harder, into the troll's upturned face and heard something crack. The troll yelped and grabbed at his nose with both hands. Glissa was free.

She scrambled to her feet and ran from the room, pulling the door closed behind her. A large hand shot through the narrowing opening. Glissa pulled as hard as she could, but the troll was stronger and the door began to open. Without thinking, Glissa shoved the sword through the widening crack. She heard a yelp, and the hand was gone. She slammed the door and turned toward the tunnel.

Glissa counted the steps as she ran, and stopped when she got to 139. That was the number she had counted on the way up to Chunth's room. She looked at the wall beside her and ran her hand over the metal, searching for an extrusion like the one in Chunth's room.

After an agonizingly long minute, the elf felt something irregular on the wall near the lower step. She pulled down, and a doorway formed and began to open, scraping against the metal step. Glissa didn't wait for the door to open all the way. She squeezed through and ran back out into the Tangle.

I know this place, thought Glissa as she came from the Tree of Tales onto a small terrace. It was a dead end, the same dead end where they had cornered the vorrac earlier that day, which now seemed an age previous. Glissa ran over to the place from which she and Kane had jumped down and was about to pull herself up when a horrible sound filled her ears. A horn was blaring in the Tangle—the horn of warning. The levelers had entered the Tangle!

# CHAPTER 3

# THE LEVELERS

Glissa froze, one hand on the ledge above her, the other still holding the sword she had stolen from Chunth. She waited for what seemed an eternity for the responding horn, hoping that the first horn had been a mistake or a trick of the wind. She was terrified of the levelers. They had tormented her dreams since childhood. Her father assured her over and over that the family was safe in their home, so high in the trees and so close to the Radix. Nevertheless Glissa woke screaming any time the horn of warning invaded her dreams.

Now that fear paralyzed her. She knew they were coming for her this time. Chunth had said as much. But they wouldn't find her hiding in her bed, shivering under the vorrac hides. They would find only Father, Mother, and Lyese.

She wasn't far from her father's tree, but there was no easy route between the two trees. Earlier that day, it had taken her and Kane at least five minutes to work their way down to the vorrac carcass. She didn't have that kind of time. Her family needed her now, yet she couldn't move.

A second horn blared. In her mind, Glissa could see the gleaming levelers scrambling up the Tangle tree toward her father's house, just as they had in her childhood nightmares. But this was real and she was no scared little girl. Glissa forced the fear from her legs and allowed her warrior instinct to take control. Dropping back down onto the terrace, the elf broke into a run. As she approached the spot where she had caught the vorrac, she took three long strides and launched her body off the terrace.

Glissa ran through the air, her legs pumping furiously as she arced up and away from the terrace. Thirty feet out she passed the level of the dead-end terrace and began to fall through the Tangle, edging ever farther away from the Tree of Tales. As she fell, the elf warrior twirled the sword around and brought it over her head, point forward. She clutched the pommel. Arching her back and spreading her legs to slow her descent, Glissa fell toward a terrace on a nearby tree.

The swordpoint struck the trunk of the Tangle tree and dug into the metal. As her body whipped around, Glissa brought her legs in to absorb the impact. Her feet slammed into the tree, and she bounced, but the sword held, cutting a jagged line down the trunk as she continued to fall toward the terrace. Glissa marveled at how easily the sword cut through the Tangle tree metal. She'd expected it would slow her fall, but the terrace was coming up fast. Far too fast.

She kicked at the tree hard with both feet, pulled the sword free, and flipped into the air again as she passed a spire. Catching the spire in one hand, she rotated around it once, hung for a moment, then released to fall the last twenty feet. She rolled and came up running. She had cut precious time from her journey but was still two trees from home.

The next jump was far easier. She had made this leap a hundred times. When she came to the end of the terrace, she sprang out as before, but at the top of her arc she kicked her legs back and flew facedown for a moment before tucking in her head, legs, and arms and rolling slowly head over heels toward the oncoming terrace. She would hit on her shoulders and roll with the blow, but she hadn't counted on the sword.

Glissa hit and rolled, but the sword blade cut into the terrace, throwing her off balance. She slammed hard into the trunk of the tree before slumping down onto the terrace. Turning onto her hands and knees she tried to push herself back up to her feet, but her head felt thick, and she had a searing pain between her shoulder blades. She looked up and tried to focus on the next tree. She was nearly home, but the dim light from the gelfruits was swirling in circles in front of her.

Glissa shook her head and rubbed the back of her hand across her eyes. With a long groan, she forced her body off the terrace and looked again. She could see the dark opening into her father's home just above her, but she also saw several gleaming forms crawling up the side of the Tangle tree. The levelers looked like huge, silver bugs. They were slightly larger than vorracs, but instead of horns, they had blades that were half again as long as their body. These spearlike pincers sliced back and forth ahead of them as they moved, while several rows of razor-sharp blades twirled just below the levelers' mouths. They could level anything—or anybody—that got in their way, leaving behind nothing but a bloody stain.

Three levelers scurried up the trunk toward Glissa's home on long, triple-jointed legs. Their legs ended in spikelike claws that dug into the trunk as they climbed. Glissa ignored the pain between her shoulders and forced her feet to move again, jogging, then running, across the terrace. She was sluggish now and wondered if she had enough speed to make the last jump. She had to try.

She leaped off the edge of the terrace and sailed through the air toward the levelers. Remembering how easily her new sword had cut through the Tangle tree, she brought it over her head as she flew. At the last moment, she slammed the sword forward, piercing the lowest leveler's head. The blade sliced right through the metal creature and bit hard into the trunk beneath the beast. Glissa landed on the leveler's back and let her weight carry the blade down through its body before leaping off and grabbing a fold in the tree.

The gutted leveler fell away from the tree, plummeting to the terrace below. Glissa began to scramble up the tree, using familiar hand- and footholds to quickly move up behind the next leveler. The creature hadn't even noticed the loss of its companion. It kept climbing mindlessly up the tree.

When she got close enough, Glissa swung the sword at the back legs of the leveler. The amazing blade cut through both legs without slowing. The beast continued to climb, leaving its rear paws stuck in the tree behind. After a few steps, the leveler stopped to look back. It skittered around in a circle until it was facing Glissa. The warrior froze. She had never been face-to-face with a leveler before. Inside her, the scared little girl was screaming. The beast had no eyes, only a giant, gaping mouth lined with jagged teeth. The mouth opened and closed again and again as the metallic beast descended. Like a fly caught in a web, the elf couldn't move.

The beast's curving blades were just above her. Glissa jumped away from it and caught a spire off to the side. The leveler turned and slammed its mouth closed again. Glissa willed her eyes away from the beast's horrible face. Holding onto the spire with one hand, she steadied her feet on the trunk and drove the point of the sword into the leveler. Ripping the blade up and out, she cut a huge gash in the beast's mouth, ripping through blades and legs as the leveler reached for her.

With only one set of claws digging into the tree, the leveler couldn't hold on any longer. It plunged downward and disappeared. Glissa looked up at the last leveler. It was nearly to the front door. With her doubts and fears firmly tucked away, the elf pulled herself up onto the spire, crouched, then jumped toward it. She grabbed the creature's hind leg with her free hand and swung the blade through the beast's pelvis. The leg she held came free of the body, but the claws held, leaving Glissa hanging from the severed appendage.

Still, the leveler crawled up the trunk. Its front legs had reached the lip of the entrance to Glissa's home. She had to stop it before it got inside. Flipping the sword over in her free hand, she grabbed the blade just above the guard and flung it like a spear. The sword sliced easily through the rear of the beast and slammed into the trunk of the tree, pinning the leveler.

The creature squirmed and pushed with its legs, but it was held tight against the trunk. Glissa grabbed a fold in the tree and found her footing again. She reached over and pulled the severed leg free, then began climbing up toward the pinned leveler. When she got close enough, she slammed the spiked paw into the beast, shattering the red dome covering its back and tearing off a huge chunk of metal. Still the beast tried to climb. Glissa smashed it again.

After the third blow, Glissa could see inside the beast. Curiously, there was no blood. The leveler was completely made of metal, with no flesh at all! Other than the Tangle trees themselves, all living things in the forest had at least some flesh intermixed with their metallic parts. Once one cut through the metal, there was flesh, bone, and blood underneath. Inside the leveler's body, though, all she could see were metal rods connected together and moving back and forth. Glissa slammed down again, lodging the makeshift club between the rods. A horrible screeching sound erupted from inside the leveler as the rods bent, broke, and scraped against the embedded leg.

Smoke billowed from the hole, and the leveler tried to turn around. Glissa pulled on the leg, but it was wedged fast inside the beast. Weaponless, Glissa stared in horror as the creature twisted around, its sweeping pincer blades coming closer and closer, the grinding of the spinning blades growing louder. The elf grabbed for a knothole but couldn't reach it. Just as she was about to let go and drop from the creature's reach, fire erupted from the back of the beast. The force of the blast slammed the leveler against the tree, snapping two of its remaining legs.

The blades, an inch from her face, had stopped moving. She felt a pain and could see a gash across her forearm. A warm trickle of blood left a red trail down her arm to her shoulder. The beast appeared dead, but Glissa wasn't taking any chances. She moved down to regain her footing, then climbed up and around the beast, giving it a wide berth. Once she reached the lip above the dead leveler, she reached down and grabbed her sword. She pulled it free of the beast and watched as the carcass fell to join its two dead brothers. Elated by her victory, she entered her home.

* * * * *

As Glissa stepped through the doorway, her heart leaped into her mouth. At least half a dozen levelers were crawling around the main room, grinding everything in their path and tossing furniture around with their waving pincers. They looked as if they were searching for something. From the spire rooms Glissa could hear sounds of more beasts.

Chairs, tables, and gelfruit lay in ruins on the floor, cut to pieces by the levelers' blades. Pots and pans, mangled into unrecognizable shapes, were scattered amidst the shards of her mother's bone plates. In the dim light coming from outside, Glissa could see a dark shape just below the entrance to her parents' spire room. Dark splatters on the floor and wall near the body told Glissa all she needed to know.

Glissa whipped the sword up in front of her and screamed.

Almost as one, the levelers turned from their search and advanced on her. More of the gleaming creatures emerged from each spire. From the pincers of one of the beasts hung the gelfruit-laced tresses of Lyese's hair. Glissa's temples pounded, and her ears rang as the blood raced through her body. Tears welled up in her eyes and her hands shook. All her fears and nightmares had finally come true. The levelers had come for her, but she hadn't been home, and her family had paid for that.

A battle raged inside Glissa as the levelers advanced upon her. The screams of the little girl could not be quelled, but the adult knew that emotion could be harnessed. She transformed the little girl's fear and sorrow into a rage that quelled the tears and stilled her shaking hands.

As the first leveler came near, the elf ran and leaped over the gleaming blades, landing on the creature's silver back. She plunged the sword down through the side of the red dome above its mouth, then wrenched the hilt down to rip the blade out and shatter the dome completely. Inside, she could see faceted gems on metallic stalks that turned and seemed to look up at her. She swiped at them with her blade.

The sword sliced through both eye stalks, and the twin gems tumbled down inside the beast. The creature hesitated a moment, then turned as if to follow Glissa. The elf was still standing on top of the leveler, though, and as it turned, it met the twirling blades of another leveler. Metal scraped against metal as the blades cut through each other. One of the blinded leveler's blades dug firmly into the body of the other creature, severing its pincers and front leg.

"Die!" screamed Glissa as the blind and mindless leveler chewed its comrade.

The elf jumped off her mount and landed on the next one's back. She intended to blind it as well, spurring the huge metal beasts to tear each other apart as they had her parents and sister. Instead, as she landed, the creature twisted its body and reached for her with its pincers. Glissa lost her footing and fell backward. Her foot slid down past the beast's head, close to the twirling blades. She pulled her feet up and rolled backward onto the floor, landing hard amidst the rubble of the kitchen, her back against the rear wall.

The levelers turned—all except the blinded one, which had made its way back into a spire room. Glissa pushed on the floor with her hands and legs, inching her way up the wall, but there was nowhere left to go. The levelers advanced on her, one behind the other. Glissa thought about jumping over the front creature's rotating blades and trying to run across the backs of the killers and escape. The warrior inside her couldn't bear to retreat in the face of her family's executioners.

"This is it," she said. Her family was gone. Her life was over. All she had left was this moment. "You'll pay dearly for my family's deaths before I die!" she growled.

Glissa held her sword up in front of her. The tip wavered a little. She readied for the attack, then stared at the tip of the sword. It glowed faintly. Soft green tendrils of energy played up and down the length of the blade. It was the same energy she had seen in her flare, and it was building. Now the entire blade was bright green, and the energy was climbing her arm. With a blinding flash, a tendril of energy lashed out from the tip of the sword at the nearest leveler, engulfing it in green fire. Glissa could feel the heat from the intense flame, but the fire died quickly, leaving nothing but slag where the beast had stood.

The other levelers still advanced, their blades sweeping from side to side as they inched closer. They seemed totally unaware that she had just turned one of their number into a puddle of molten metal. Like hunters who had caught scent of their prey, they would never turn away before the hunt was concluded.

The elf tried to fling another tendril of energy from the tip of the still-glowing sword, but the energy would not obey her command. The glow began to fade as she waved the sword back and forth in front of her.

"No," she cried.

The green energy was gone. She tried to summon it again as the levelers inched closer, but it was no use. Whatever force had brought the energy from her twice this day was not under her control. She glared at her blade and tried to will the energy to reappear.

She was aware of something strange happening in front of her. Glissa watched in amazement as the levelers stopped, then turned in unison and headed for the door.

She couldn't believe her luck. What had happened? Why were they retreating? Were they afraid of the sword or the green energy? She didn't think so. They had continued to press the attack even after she had blinded one leveler with her blade and destroyed a second with that strange energy. Was something controlling them? And, if so, what or who was it?

All of these questions flashed through her mind, but Glissa decided she didn't need answers. She needed vengeance. With their backs turned, the levelers were vulnerable. The elf hacked at the retreating beasts with her sword, cutting off legs, pincers, claws, anything she could reach.

She pursued them all the way to the door, but none ever turned to meet her attacks. The carcasses of several levelers lay in pieces around her, but most of the silver creatures escaped down the tree. Breathing hard, sweat streaming down her face and mixing with the tears, Glissa thought about climbing down after them. The thought of her mother and sister stopped her at the doorway. One at least might have survived. She had only seen one body. She had to go back and check.

She turned back to the main room and heard movement. The blinded leveler bore down on her. She had no time to run or jump. The metal beast slammed into her, sending Glissa sprawling onto its back. Her ankle caught in the leveler's broken blades. She tried to pull her foot free, but the blade dug into her tendon. She screamed in pain as the blades cut through her metal skin.

The beast lunged over the lip outside the door and headed down the tree. Glissa grabbed onto the back of the leveler as she began to slide down toward the broken blades. There was nothing to do now but hold on until the creature reached the ground, when she could kill it and extract her foot.

The leveler reached the forest floor. The pain in Glissa's leg made her wince, but she got onto one knee, brought her sword up over her head, and struck down through the back of the creature. It didn't seem to notice. Glissa struck again with as much power as she could muster.

A movement in the Tangle beside her caught Glissa's attention. Perhaps Kane had come to help. Maybe Chunth had left his seclusion to watch the destined one die. From the corner of her eye she saw someone . . . or something . . . she'd never seen before. It was about the size of a troll but stood erect, covered in dark robes. The gelfruit light glinted off the stranger's head in a way that suggested it was neither metal nor flesh. She could have sworn she saw four arms.

It was gone. Glissa stared into the Tangle, looking for the figure, but saw nothing but trees, now whipping by at an incredible speed as the leveler ran. She looked down at the beast and watched as its feet swung back and forth so fast they turned into a blur. Glissa reached down to pull the sword out, intending to strike the beast again.

Something struck her head and knocked her down onto the beast's back. Everything darkened around her. Turning her aching head to look behind, the last thing Glissa saw before she blacked out was a low-lying spire swaying back and forth from a sharp impact.

# CHAPTER 4

# SLOBAD

Glissa moaned and rolled over in her sleep. It felt as if her foot was caught in the leather blanket on her bed, so she tried to kick it off . . . and screamed. Pain shot up Glissa's leg from her ankle. Something was cutting into her flesh. She opened her eyes, but it was pitch black, and she had no idea where she was. She pushed herself up and hit her head on the ceiling.

"What the flare is going on?" muttered the elf. She began to remember: trolls, levelers, her parents, Lyese. It all came rushing back to her like a nightmare. There was no time to dwell on that pain or the one in her ankle. She was caught in the broken blades of a leveler. Where had it taken her? Glissa squinted into the darkness, trying to make out anything around her. As her eyes grew accustomed to the gloom, she could see the curving back of the leveler beneath her. Similar curved shapes surrounded her.

Where am I? she thought. Am I in their lair? They weren't moving, and she was afraid to wake them up, much as she wanted to kill them all. If they were asleep, it would be better if she freed herself and found her way out. She wouldn't stand a chance in the dark with her injured ankle. Glissa inched her way down toward the blades, wincing every time her ankle moved against the blades. More than once she banged her head against the low ceiling.

Finally she got both hands on her aching foot and tried to ease it from the viselike grip of the broken blades. The leather had taken the brunt of the blade, so her ankle wasn't cut too badly. At least, she couldn't feel any blood dripping. Perhaps she could pull her foot from the boot. When she tried, Glissa bit her lip to suppress another scream. Even the slightest movement pressed the blade into her flesh. Her ankle must have swelled inside the boot.

She saw two options. She could yank her boot and leg from the blades and risk cutting her foot off, or she could use the sword. In the dark, a false move with the blade would risk injuring the foot more than it was or, worse, waking up every leveler in the lair. She weighed the options and decided to go for her weapon. At least she would be armed if they woke up.

Slowly Glissa pushed her way back toward the sword, which she hoped was still sticking from the back of the beast. She found the hilt and pulled it out. The scraping sound of metal against metal echoed around the cavern, making the back of Glissa's neck tingle, but the beasts didn't wake.

Holding the sword straight out in front of her to avoid the low ceiling, Glissa inched her way toward the blades again. She thought she saw movement from the corner of her eye, but when she peered around the cavern, all she could see were dark shapes against a sea of black. She leaned down toward her foot and reached out with her free hand to gauge the distance and angle. She pulled the sword back to strike.

"You don't want to do that, huh? You don't want to do that. You might hit me with that thing, huh?"

Glissa froze in mid-swing and stared into the darkness. The fast-talking voice definitely came from outside her own mind. She could still hear the last "huh" echoing in the darkness.

"Who said that?" she asked. "Who's there?"

"It's only me," came the reply. "Slobad," the voice added, as if that helped Glissa understand. "You need some help, huh? Slobad will help you if you need some help. Do you want some help, huh?"

"I can't see you," said Glissa, worried about what kind of help this Slobad was offering. He spoke so fast, she could hardly follow him. She hoped he couldn't move that fast.

"Are your eyes broken, huh? I see you fine. I see girl caught in blades who needs help. So, do you want help, huh?"

"No," replied Glissa. "I mean, yes, I need help, but no, my eyes aren't broken. It's pitch-black in here. My eyes don't see well in the dark."

There was no reply. Glissa could hear shuffling noises and the muted clink of metal, but she couldn't tell what the mysterious stranger was doing. She moved her sword to a defensive position.

"Whoa. I told you not to wave that thing around," snapped Slobad. "You almost cut off my ear. Wait for the light, huh? I'm getting a light so you can see. Stupid eyes that can't see in dark. Huh."

A moment later, Glissa heard a click, and a bright red flame erupted from the darkness. Standing beside her was an odd-looking creature holding a metal tube. The short but intense flame came from the top of the tube with a faint hiss. As Glissa's eyes adjusted to the light, she could see more of Slobad's features. He was short but had arms that reached down to his knees. His arms ended not in hands but in something more like fangren claws. His nose and ears were long and sharply pointed. The ends gleamed in the flickering light. Slobad's nose and ears were metallic like her own arms and legs. He was dressed in ragged scraps of leather that barely covered his rust-colored skin. A large leather bag that hung around his neck covered much more than his actual clothes.

"What . . . what are you?" asked Glissa. She had never been outside the Tangle. Until now she never really believed the stories told by infirm elders of other races in the world. Her father told her that those stories were flare-induced hallucinations.

"You've never seen a goblin, huh?" said Slobad. "I know you. You're an elf, an elf who's come from Tangle on the back of leveler. You are one crazy elf, huh?"

"What do you want?" asked Glissa. "Are you the master of these foul creatures?"

Slobad snorted. "You quick to accuse, huh?"

Glissa's stomach turned over. Kane had always joked that she was paranoid, but now someone really was trying to kill her. Quick accusation or not, could the culprit be the goblin? He had her at a severe disadvantage. He knew what she was and where she was from, and seemed at ease here in the lair of the levelers.

"Slobad is only master of Slobad, huh? Not master of the levelers or any other being," said the goblin. "Taking care of me is full-time job, but I can help one crazy elf in my spare time, huh? At least I'll have somebody to talk to for a while." Slobad moved to the front of the leveler.

"What are you doing?" asked Glissa.

"I'm going to get you free, huh?" said Slobad. "That's what we've been talking about. You want to stay up there or come with me and hide?"

Slobad placed his fire tube on the ground and reached into the leather bag slung across his chest. He rooted around, almost plunging his whole head inside the pouch. Finally he brought out a copper-colored tool. Glissa could now see that the goblin did have fingers ending in long, thick claws. His hands were curved like hooks and his fingers were much shorter than the claws extending out from them.

He handled the tool nimbly with his short fingers. If he wasn't the master of these creatures, he certainly knew more about them than she did. She decided she had to trust him. She couldn't get free by herself. Besides, she still had her sword, which she continued to hold defensively in front of her, ready to strike. Slobad crawled under the blades and lay on his back, looking up at the leveler. Glissa leaned over and could just see the tip of the two-pronged tool moving back and forth underneath the row of broken blades. A moment later, the tool clanked to the floor of the chamber and Slobad grasped one of the blades with both hands.

"Don't touch those," said Glissa. "They're sharp."

"Don't worry, huh?" said Slobad. "Goblins don't cut easily. We're thick and strong like the mountains. Have you seen mountains? I'll show you when we get out of here." The goblin pulled half the blade away, and Glissa's foot was free. He tucked the broken blade into his pouch, then inched his way out from under the leveler.

Glissa slid off the back of the leveler, gasping when she landed. She nearly lost her balance as her ankle buckled under her. The elf shot her hand out and slammed it into the side of the leveler to keep her from crumpling to the ground. Looking over at the injured beast, she muttered, "Does nothing wake these creatures from their slumber?"

Slobad came up beside Glissa and stuck his clawlike hand out to her. The flame tube in the goblin's other hand spread enough light around them to show the three closest levelers. "They not sleeping, huh? They turn off in here. They not beasts. You think they're beasts, huh? Crazy elf."

"They're not alive?" asked Glissa, leaning against the goblin for support.

"You see their metal blades and legs? Their glass domes? Do you see any flesh, huh? Any?" asked Slobad, pointing to the leveler.

"Well, I'm alive and I have metal arms and legs. You have a metallic . . . uh . . . nose."

"Levelers are all metal," said Slobad, "inside and out. I know, huh? I open them up and look."

"They're constructs?" asked Glissa, realizing what that meant. "Somebody made these . . . things . . . and sends them out to kill?" She pushed off the goblin and raised her sword.

"Whoa, crazy elf lady," said Slobad. "We're safe in here, huh?

This is safest place on Mirrodin. Blades turn off as soon as they enter. They only hunt outside cavern. That's why Slobad live here. It safest place I know."

Glissa ignored him. The rage over her family's death had returned. Someone had created these killing machines! Well, she was going to put a stop to it.

"Out of the way, Slobad."

She balanced on her good foot and swung her blade at the leveler that had held her captive. Sparks flew from the sword as it tore through the metallic body. Her first swing lopped off the construct's front end, sending the rest of its broken blades clattering to the floor. She swept the sword underneath the creature, slicing off the legs. As the leveler flopped to the floor in front of her, Glissa brought the sword down, cutting a huge gash in its side.

She struck again and again until all that was left in front of her was a pile of ragged metal. At last she stopped, breathing heavily.

"You done now?" asked Slobad. "Feel better, huh?"

"They killed my family," snarled the elf. "This one slaughtered my sister. I won't feel better until I destroy them all."

"Then what?" asked Slobad. "More will come. They always do, huh? Broken ones get fixed, missing ones are replaced. It's better to hide and live than seek revenge and die, huh?"

Glissa nodded. Inwardly she resolved to find the true master of these beasts and exact her revenge where it would matter. Meanwhile . . .

She grabbed Slobad's shoulder and hobbled along beside the goblin. Her ankle was swollen so much it ached constantly inside her boot. Even the slight pressure from limping shot searing pain up her leg. Perhaps the goblin was right, after all. She needed to hide and rest before seeking her revenge.

On their way through the cavern, Glissa saw something glint in the goblin's firelight. She glanced over at the shiny object, then stopped and stared in horror.

"What's the matter now, huh?" asked Slobad. "You want to destroy that one, too? It won't bring back your family. It will just make more trouble for us. Come on, huh?"

"I'm not going to destroy anything," said Glissa, her voice low and measured as she fought to remain calm in the light of her discovery. "Give me a moment, will you?"

She left the goblin's side and hopped over to a leveler nearby. She leaned on its side and reached out toward the blades arrayed across its front. The object was still out of her reach, so she leaned even farther. Just before losing her balance, she grabbed the object, then pushed herself away from the leveler to regain her balance.

"What did you find, huh?" asked Slobad when she hopped back over to him.

Glissa showed him. It was a severed hand. An elf hand with long, delicate fingers tipped with sharp claws. The wrist was red and moist, though the blood had all but drained from it.

"That's my mother's wedding ring," said Glissa. "It's been passed down from mother to son for generations. Nobody knows what the gem is anymore, or the metal."

Glissa pulled the ring off the hand and placed it on her own finger. She kissed the fingers of the severed hand and tenderly laid it aside. "It's all I have left of them."

\* \* \* \* \*

A subdued Glissa let Slobad lead her to the back of the chamber and through a small hole hidden in the wall. She crawled through the hole behind the goblin into a small room where Slobad obviously lived. It wasn't much to look at. He had spread a couple of furs on the floor in one corner. A small table and chair stood in the center and another, larger table was placed against the far wall, covered with small tools and scraps of metal. After hiding the hole with a small section of wall, Slobad put the flame tube on the table and picked up a knife.

Glissa stepped back from him, pointing the sword. "Mine's bigger," she said.

"I told you to put that thing away, huh?" said Slobad. "You are one crazy elf, do you know that? Lie down so I can cut your boot off and look at your leg."

Glissa breathed easier. "I don't know who to trust," she said apologetically. "Just be careful. My ankle is swollen right up against the boot."

Slobad came over with the knife, and Glissa kept her sword ready just in case. She held her mother's ring against her chest as if clinging to the past for comfort. The goblin, however, was as skilled with the knife as he had been with his tools. He sliced right down the boot all the way to the heel, never once touching her metal skin beneath.

As Slobad pulled away the leather, Glissa could see that her ankle was swollen to more than twice its normal size, and the blades had cut into her metal shin. Green pus oozed from the wounds on either side of her leg. Slobad went to the table and brought back a metal bowl full of water. He cut a strip of leather from the furs and wetted it in the bowl, then used the wet leather to wash off the pus. The goblin then cut two more strips and tied them around Glissa's ankle.

"That looks bad, huh?" said Slobad. "I've not seen a lot of elves, but I don't think your ankle should be that color. What you think? I think you lose leg if that pus doesn't go away."

"Let me see what I can do," said Glissa. She sat up against the wall, dropped her sword on her lap, and placed her hands over the wounds. She knew some healing magic, but in here she could barely feel the power from the trees. What little she could muster she sent down through her fingers, and a few green wisps of energy floated down from her hands to her injured leg. The ankle glowed for a moment, and the swelling went down somewhat.

"That's all I can do," she said. "My magic can heal wounds, but that must be something else, some sort of disease."

"Rest now," said Slobad. "We leave in morning."

Suddenly Glissa was suspicious again. "Why?" she asked. "I thought you said it was safe here."

"It was until you came here, huh?" said Slobad. "I told you, broken levelers get fixed. Missing ones are replaced. Nobody ever bother Slobad during repairs, huh? I stay hidden here until repairs finished. This was the safest place on Mirrodin, huh? But you destroyed a leveler in the cavern. They will know somebody here. They will look for us. They will find Slobad and you."

"I'm sorry," said Glissa. "I didn't mean to run you out of your home."

"Slobad has no home," said the goblin, shrugging. "Crazy elf shouldn't worry about Slobad. Worry about saving leg, huh? Let Slobad worry about Slobad."

"My name is Glissa," she said. "If you help me, Slobad, I'll give you a home in the Tangle far away from the levelers."

"Hmmph," said Slobad. "Big talk from crazy, one-legged elf. Sleep now. We leave before the second sun rises."

"Sun?" asked Glissa.

"You know," said Slobad, "round things in the sky. Four of them. They come up. They go down. Make world bright; make world dark." The goblin waved his arms in a funny pattern around his head. "You can't tell me you don't know suns, huh?"

"We call them 'moons,' " said Glissa. "It's an ancient word for heavenly bodies that circle around the world. I know what a sun is. I've seen them in my . . . dreams. Suns are much brighter and hotter, I think."

"Suns give light and heat, huh?" said Slobad. "That's right. That's what goblins know about suns. We have four suns. No moons. Just suns."

"Okay," said Glissa, not wanting to argue. "They're suns. Now can I go to sleep?"

Slobad nodded, so Glissa lay back on the furs and closed her eyes. She had no choice but to trust the odd, fast-talking goblin. She needed rest, and she would need his help to get out of here. Even so, she pretended to sleep for some time, just in case Slobad tried to attack.

After a while, Glissa did sleep and dreamed of the levelers attacking her in the Tangle. She was surrounded and they were advancing, their blades spinning in front of them. She could see the bodies of her parents in a heap nearby. Her mother's hand and ring were nowhere to be seen, and Lyese's long hair had been sliced off, leaving a bloody scar across the top of her head. Tears welled up in Glissa's eyes, and she rubbed her arm across her face to wipe them away.

Now the levelers changed into flying beasts that buzzed around her head. She swatted at them with her sword, but they kept coming. She could hear laughing and looked over to see a robed figure where her dead parents had been just moments before. The laughing changed to screams, and Glissa saw that the figure held Kane off the ground by his neck. Kane was screaming. Glissa shouted, then saw green tendrils of energy erupt from her hands, snaking up her arms.

# CHAPTER 5

# THE GLIMMERVOID

Glissa started awake in a cold sweat. Was that a dream or a flare? she wondered. How could it have been a flare? The events she had dreamed had never happened to her, as far as she knew. Who was that robed figure? He had been in the Tangle the night her parents died. Was he the master of the levelers? Glissa sat up and looked down at her hands but saw no green energy surrounding them.

"You're awake, huh?" said Slobad, who was sitting at the table, eating. "Good. Can you walk? We leave soon, but Slobad can't carry you home. Too big. No good, huh?"

Glissa looked at her leg. The swelling was almost gone, but the ankle still ached. She untied the leather bandage and saw that the copper around the wounds looked odd. It was green, but that was just molder—the process that gave Tangle trees their green coloring. All copper looked that way if not polished regularly. No, the metal itself seemed to have bubbled up around the wounds. As Glissa removed the leather strap, some of the metal flaked off, and pus oozed from the wounds again.

The elf wiped her ankle clean, wincing at the pain, then replaced the bandage. She pushed herself up and tested the ankle. It held her weight, and she could endure the pain. "I can walk," she said.

Slobad came over and poked at the bandage with his clawed hand.

"Ow! What did you do that for?"

"You can't walk long on that leg," said Slobad. "I saw, huh? The metal is corroding. Infection spreading. You'll never make it to the Tangle, huh? Too far. You need healer soon. We go to leonin."

"Leonin?" asked Glissa. "Who is that? Is he far away?"

"Stupid elf," said Slobad. "Do you know nothing about the world outside Tangle? The leonin are your neighbors, huh? Their tribes live in the Glimmervoid. Not far. Slobad lives on edge of Glimmervoid. It'll take two or three rotations to walk to leonin city. We find a healer there."

The little goblin went to his workbench and began putting tools and some of the larger scraps of metal into his pouch. "We go soon. You eat, huh?"

"Two or three rotations?" asked Glissa as she hobbled over to the table. It looked as if it might fall to pieces at any moment, but it held her weight when she leaned against it. "You call that 'not far'? And how do you know they'll help me? We should just go back to the Tangle. How far can it be?"

Slobad shook his head. "Stupid, crazy elf," he muttered. Tangle is twice that far, huh? Take at least six, maybe eight rotations to get you home from here, especially with that bad leg. We have to cut leg off after four rotations, at most. If that's what you want, we'll go to Tangle."

"There's no healer closer?" asked Glissa. On the table she saw the carcasses of two small animals. They each had four tiny legs, a wiry tail, and patches of gray fur mixed with metal plates on their backs. "What about the goblins? They must be close, right?"

Slobad was searching for something on the workbench. Glissa couldn't tell what any of the tools were for. She sliced off some meat with Slobad's knife and ate what she could while she waited for his response. The goblin didn't seem to understand the art of conversation. He often answered his own questions without waiting for a response, and now he seemed to be ignoring her questions. The meat was pungent and stringy, but Glissa was famished. She cut off more meat and soon finished both animals.

"Goblins have no healers who can deal with that leg, huh?" said Slobad. The goblin had finished packing his bag and now tossed a fur over his shoulders and tied it around his neck with several strips of leather. "Elf magic only heals wounds. You said so yourself. Goblin magic hardly even do that. Elves and leonin only decent healers. You choose, huh?"

"Fine," said Glissa. Once again she had no choice but to trust this creature who lived by himself within the den of the world's most dangerous . . . constructs. Why was he helping her? How did he know so much about the world? It seemed that people who spent all their time in little rooms knew a lot more than she did about Mirrodin. Perhaps Slobad could be useful, but she needed to know more about him and his motives.

"We'll go see the leonin healers."

Slobad nodded. He tossed Glissa a sword sheath. "Here, take this. I found it in blades of leveler. Maybe you can use it better than its previous owner, huh?"

Glissa grabbed the sheath. There was no belt, so she took the goblin's knife, cut a long strip of leather, and tied the sheath around her waist. Several more strips fastened her boot back onto her leg.

"Ready."

\* \* \* \* \*

Slobad revealed another secret opening in the wall and led Glissa through a square, metal tunnel. Slobad could walk, but the elf had to either crawl or hunch over inside the tunnel. It twisted back and forth, and they passed many side tunnels as they walked. It seemed to Glissa like she crawled for an eternity. Slobad often turned left or right at intersections but never slowed his pace. Glissa knew she could never find her way back to Slobad's room. She had to keep following the goblin. Finally she saw light up ahead, and they emerged from the small tunnel into a larger cave.

"This way," said Slobad as he moved toward the light streaming in through the cave entrance.

Glissa stepped outside and halted, amazed by the land around her. The ground gleamed. It was made of a silvery metal, not the moldered copper of the Tangle. The ground rolled up and down around her, making hills and valleys running as far as she could see. The cave behind her did not come from a hill, though. Rather, the structure was shaped like a mushroom. Rust-colored intertwined tubes ran up from the silver ground to a large, conical top. There were several of these outcroppings around them, and in the distance behind her, Glissa could see a large mountain with similar features jutting into the sky.

"Is that where your people live?" she asked Slobad.

"I told you, huh?" said Slobad, who was already moving down the slope. "Slobad has no people. Slobad is his own people. Goblins live in mountains leonin live in Razor Fields. Mountains up there. Razor Fields down there. We go this way, huh?"

Glissa hobbled up beside the goblin and looked at him. His eyes were narrowed, and he looked straight at the ground. He might just have been concentrating on the path, but Glissa guessed she had hit on a touchy subject.

"Why do you live alone, Slobad?" she asked.

"Long story," said Slobad.

It was an uncharacteristically short answer. "We have three days," she replied. "Surely that will be enough time."

"Leave me alone, crazy elf," said Slobad in a gruff and final tone.

"You could have left me alone back there and been perfectly happy in your little room," said Glissa. She poked him in the shoulder with the tip of her claws. This was getting fun. For some reason she was reminded of Kane.

"Come on," she continued. "You brought this on yourself. You helped me and abandoned your home to take me to the leonin. You owe me."

Slobad walked on in silence, apparently trying to wait her out.

"I'm not going to stop asking until we get to the leonin city," she said, poking him again, "so you might as well just tell me now. Look, I never had many friends, either. There's no shame in being alone. I find it more comforting. You don't have to worry about anyone else and what they might do to you."

"Elf talks too much," grunted Slobad. Glissa thought he was going to fall silent again, but he continued after a few more steps. "You don't know what you talk about, huh? You choose to be alone. Slobad outcast. Have no family, no friends. Slobad is cursed. That what you want to know, huh?"

"I'm sorry," said Glissa. "Sometimes I think I'm cursed, too. I've always been different. I'm sort of an outcast as well. Maybe that's why I like you, Slobad. Maybe that's why I'm willing to trust you."

For the rest of the day, the pair walked away from the mountains in silence, through the hills of the Glimmervoid. Glissa watched with awe as the yellow moon passed almost right over her. She could see the red, black, and blue moons as well. The red one stayed behind them all day while the blue passed off to their right. The black was farther away ahead of them, but it was still closer than she had ever seen it before.

That night, seated around a small fire, Slobad began to talk again.

"Slobad alone a long time," he said as they chewed on some foul-smelling rodents the goblin had caught. "Too long, huh? That real curse—to live alone, apart from world."

"Why?" asked Glissa. The meat was tough and stringy. She

was glad the goblin had finally started his story. It gave her a reason to stop eating.

"I told, you, huh?" said Slobad. "Slobad cursed. Born under Eye of Doom—the blue sun. It ghost sun. The day Slobad born, Eye of Doom hover above Great Furnace. Sign of bad luck, huh? Mother should sacrifice Slobad to Furnace. That law of the goblins, huh? All born under Eye of Doom are cursed and must be returned to Furnace. Instead she drop me into air duct, right down in air duct. She couldn't bother killing me herself. Better to die and have metal used for good, huh? At least life would have meaning. . . ."

Slobad's voice trailed off. Glissa didn't prod him this time but went back to eating her long-tailed rodent. She took a bite, then stuck her fingers in her mouth to pull a stringy piece of metal from between her teeth. Whisker. After a time, Slobad continued.

"Slobad found by goblin named Dwugget," said Slobad. "He outcast, too. Leader of rogue cult, huh? Leader of Krark cult. Live in secret lair at end of ducts. Dwugget found Slobad on way home, huh? Took me in. Gave me home. I work for cult, listen to stories, huh? But Slobad never fit in. We all outcasts, but they *choose* to live apart, all for stupid story nobody believes."

"What story was that?" asked Glissa.

"Not important," said Slobad. "Goblin named Krark claim to find other world inside Mirrodin. All craziness. Slobad never fit in. They okay to me, but never get too close. They religious. Still believe in curse. One day, priests find cult and attack. Slobad decides to leave, huh? Leave family and wander world. Live near Tangle for a time, but elves don't trust anyone. Slobad run from there and wander Glimmervoid."

"That's when you met the healers?" asked Glissa. She finished her meal and tossed the bones away from their camp.

Slobad nodded. "And Raksha, young leonin warrior, Kha. Slobad given to Raksha as toy, huh? Training dummy. We fight all the time. Raksha always win. Slobad always hurt. But healers fix me up, huh? So Raksha train again."

"That sounds horrible," said Glissa. "You really want to go back to these people?"

"Raksha good to Slobad. He always make sure I healed properly, huh? Then nim begin attacking more. Raksha sent into real battles. Fighting always follow Slobad, huh? Part of curse. Other leonin not so good to Slobad. Not welcome when Raksha out of city. I leave again before healers kick me out, huh? I find leveler cave and decide to live alone. Battles can't come to me there. Nobody dare come close."

Except me, thought Glissa. But I don't believe in destiny, no matter what Chunth said. Bad things happen because people make them happen. To Slobad, she said, "You've lived alone ever since, eating these . . . what do you call them?"

"Glimmer rats," said Slobad through a full mouth. He hadn't eaten during his story and seemed to be trying to catch up now.

Glissa watched Slobad stuff another rat into his mouth and chomp down. She could hear the creature's bones breaking as he chewed. The goblin didn't even bother to spit out the metal bits. Were his eating habits the result of living alone? Or perhaps all goblins ate that way.

"I'm sorry I've upset your life, Slobad, but I appreciate all you've done for me. Maybe you can go back to the leveler cave after my leg is healed."

"Maybe," said Slobad, his mouth still full. After he swallowed, he continued, "Nothing there for me, huh? Just place to be. Not home. No one to talk to. Slobad start talking to himself. Very bad. Long time since I go to Taj Nar, huh?"

"Taj Nar?" asked Glissa.

Slobad offered her the last rat, but Glissa waved it off. He stuck the rat's head into his mouth and bit it off. "Taj Nar is great leonin city. Where Raksha rule. He is leader now, huh? Kha."

"Are you sure he'll help me?" asked Glissa.

Slobad nodded, chewing the rest of the rat. "Raksha owe Slobad. Most leonin not like outsiders much, huh? A lot like elves that way. Raksha different. He like Slobad. Slobad work for him many times. Fix city walls. Make sacred torch. Raksha owe Slobad. He will help."

"Well, I'm not like other elves," said Glissa with a smile, the first smile she had given since the trolls kidnapped her. "And I like you, too, Slobad."

"I know," said Slobad. "That why I help you. Slobad not have many friends but always helps the ones he finds."

Glissa began to wonder if maybe there was something to Chunth's speech after all. How else could she explain finding Slobad—the one person in the world lonelier than she—just when she needed him? The leonin were the first stop. If she was going to find the person who killed her family, she would need a guide in this strange world outside the Tangle.

*　*　*　*　*

The next two rotations were a blur to Glissa. She and Slobad trudged through the Glimmervoid. Slobad pointed out mounds to her that he said were leonin homes, but Glissa couldn't tell the difference between them and the rest of the landscape. Never once did they see any leonin, but Glissa thought she saw movement each night as they camped. Once, she was sure she saw the robed figure from the Tangle, but it might have been a dream or even a flare.

"Leonin don't like strangers," said Slobad again the second night, when Glissa asked why they hadn't seen any of the elusive race yet. "They know we here, huh? We don't bother them; they don't bother us. Keep to themselves, huh?"

Glissa sat and worked her healing magic to keep the decay on her leg from spreading too far. Her wound looked worse each rotation. The green energy kept the pain tolerable but couldn't stop the infection. It had almost spread past her calf already. More metal flaked off every day from her lower leg, and the pus continued to ooze from the cuts on her ankle.

Several times during their trip, Slobad led them around patches of tall plants. They were slender and bright silver. They waved in the wind, creating an eerie whistling that hung in the air around the patches. On the third day, Glissa saw a glimmer rat run into a patch of the silvery reeds ahead of them. It was being chased by a predator with strong legs and pointed, metal ears. Glissa drew her sword and waited.

The rat emerged from the other side of the patch, but a gust of wind set the reeds swinging and singing. The thin plants sliced back and forth, and a howl of pain joined the chorus. The elf ran forward to the edge of the patch. The predator lay in the middle of the reeds, its blood pooling around what remained of the body. She could also see blood and gore on the bladed reeds around the body. Glissa reached out to touch one of the plants and cut her finger on its edge.

"What *are* those?" she cried as she moved back from the patch, afraid another gust of wind might catch her too close.

"Razor grass," said Slobad. "They cut right through you. Deadly in the wind, huh? Best to go around."

Shortly after they passed the waving reeds, Glissa looked up at the yellow moon, which Slobad called the Bringer. It was now very low in the sky. The other three had already set. Without the competing light from the other moons, Slobad cast a long shadow that reached almost all the way back to the razor field. Glissa was about to say they should find a spot to camp soon, when she bumped into the goblin, who had stopped at the top of a rise.

"What is it?" she said.

"We here," said Slobad, who was pointing down the hill. "Taj Nar, great city of leonin. May be problem, huh?"

Glissa looked where Slobad pointed. They were above a great valley surrounded by hills. In the middle of the valley a huge tower seemed to erupt from a large hill. Columns of metal stretched up and out, buttressing several conical levels high up in the air. Metal spikes grew from the tops of the columns all around the city, like a clawed hand holding Taj Nar in its palm.

As Glissa's gaze fell to the base of the tower, she saw a mass of dark shapes moving slowly around the hill from both sides. For a moment she thought they were levelers, but the shapes were too small and too slow. It looked as if they were trying to encircle the city. She and Slobad might just beat the army if they ran, but she had no idea how to get inside the city once they arrived at the tower. Her sore leg had been throbbing since the first moon set, and she wasn't sure how far she could run.

A horn blared from within the city.

# CHAPTER 6

# THE NIM

"We have to get inside the city!" said Glissa. "Now!"

Slobad didn't react, so Glissa gave the goblin a shove, sending him scrambling down the hillside. She ran after him, grimacing with each step.

"Crazy elf!" shouted Slobad, arms flailing as he tried to stop his headlong rush into the valley. "You kill us both, huh?"

Glissa didn't understand what Slobad meant until she saw a large patch of razor grass directly below them. Pulling her sword from the makeshift scabbard, Glissa lengthened her stride and rushed past Slobad. She reached the razor field just in front of the goblin, slicing her sword back and forth in front of her as she ran, cutting a path through the deadly plants. Razor-edged weeds longer than her sword flew into the air around the elf. She raised her forearm to protect her face.

"Aagh!" screamed Slobad from behind Glissa, but she couldn't look back. Just a few more strides and she would be through the field. A weed sliced into her raised arm, and blood sprayed into her eyes as she ran.

When she burst out the far side of the razor field, Glissa stopped and glanced back at her friend. Slobad was right behind her and seemed uninjured. A single blade of razor grass had pierced his satchel, which the goblin held in front of him like a shield.

"That could have been my head, huh?" snarled the goblin as he yanked the razor blade from his satchel. "My head! Don't do that again, crazy elf."

Glissa smiled. "Sorry," she said. She looked toward the leonin city and the advancing army. She and Slobad were still a few hundred feet from the base of the tower, but the encircling flanks of invaders were about that same distance apart and closing slowly. "This is going to be close," she said. "Come on. There's no time."

Glissa ran. She could no longer feel her injured ankle. During her descent, everything below the wounds had gone numb. She knew that was a bad sign, but at least the pain no longer slowed her down. She and Slobad sprinted across the valley.

As they neared the tower, Glissa could see the invaders more clearly. What had been a dark mass of shapes became an army of dark creatures. At first she thought they were humans, but soon she could see that while they walked on two legs and had arms and heads, they bore little resemblance to elves, goblins, or even trolls.

"What are those?" shouted Glissa over her shoulder.

"The nim," responded Slobad. "Creatures from Mephidross."

The nim shambled forward, hunched over so far that it looked as if their heads jutted out from their chests. Their long arms reached the ground, giving them an odd, four-legged gait as their knuckles scraped against metal. A carapace ran from their heads down across their backs. It was as if their creator had torn the spines from the nim bodies and laid them on top of their skin.

The two flanks of the nim army were converging. Only a small strip of land remained open as Glissa and Slobad reached the army. The elf sprinted across the opening. A foul, acrid odor accosted her nose as she ran past the slow-moving nim. Now she could see tubes coming out from the sides of the creatures, tubes belching green gas into the air.

"Good thing they're slow," gasped Glissa halfway past the advancing army.

"Move slow, yes," panted Slobad behind her. "Fight fast. Watch out!"

The closest nim swung one of its long arms toward Glissa. The movement was so quick that she had no time to dodge. She snapped her blade up to parry the blow and caught the nim's arm right behind its clawed hands. The blade cut through the nim's wrist as easily as it had cut through the razor grass. The claw dropped to the ground. More of the noxious fumes billowed from the injured nim's arm along with a thick brownish-green fluid that Glissa assumed must be the creature's blood.

She had no time to dwell on the strange physiology of the beast or to marvel at the power of her new sword. A dozen more nim reached for her as she ran on.

"Stay close, Slobad!" she shouted. "I'll keep them off us."

Glissa swung her sword in a figure eight in front of her as she ran, slicing through the grasping nim. The blows from each side came faster as more nim closed around them. Glissa could do nothing but hack at their hands and arms. The nim were too fast, and their arms were too long.

They were almost through the throng when one nim got past her blade barrier and caught Glissa on the shoulder. She tried to dodge the attack, but the nim's claw dug into her skin. The force of the blow sent her stumbling forward. The elf scrambled to keep her footing, but her numb ankle betrayed her and she fell to the ground. Glissa rolled over, expecting another blow to land, but she was free of the nim army. The blow had sent her past the horde.

Slobad had not been so lucky. Glissa couldn't see the goblin anymore. The two nim flanks merged behind her and began to advance.

"Slobad!" she called as she got to her feet.

As if in response, a nim several ranks back burst into flame. Glissa could hear the familiar hiss of Slobad's flame tube. She limped toward the burning nim to help the goblin fight his way out of the horde, but she had to fight her way in to get to him.

The elf warrior struck at one nim's arm, cutting it clean off, then brought the sword back around and cut the creature in two. She stepped into the horde and ducked down as three more arms flew in toward her head. Glissa crouched low and swung the sword in an arc around her, taking out the legs of all three attacking nim.

What had seemed a clever tactical move almost proved to be Glissa's undoing. All three nim continued to fight, pushing themselves up on the stumps of their legs with one hand while slicing at her with another. From her crouched position, Glissa jumped over the grasping claws. She landed behind one of the legless nim, wincing as pain shot up her leg. She gritted her teeth and kicked back with her good leg to topple the attacking creature back into the other two.

She turned back toward the hiss of Slobad's flame tube and came face to ugly face with the burning nim. It shambled forward, hardly seeming to notice the flames. Glissa parried one attack, sending a fiery arm flying into the face of another nim. She sidestepped as the beast lunged forward, swinging her sword down through the flaming nim's carapace, severing the creature's head from its hunched shoulders.

As the burning nim's headless body slumped to the ground, Slobad ran past Glissa and dived over the tangle of legless nim. The elf followed, leaving a bloody mess behind her. The pain in Glissa's ankle had returned with a vengeance after her previous vault. Her entire leg now felt as if it were on fire. It was all she could do to keep moving. Slobad returned to help her, and the two limped toward the tower just ahead of the merged army.

Glissa glanced back at the slow-moving nim. They were barely outrunning the creatures. "Are you sure they're not after us?" she shouted over the din of the approaching army.

"No," replied Slobad, "but Slobad don't care. Just keep moving, huh?"

Glissa could see figures on the wall high above, but they were too far away to discern any details. As she watched, a hail of arrows rained down. Most slammed into the ranks of the nim, but several fell uncomfortably close to Glissa and Slobad.

"Hey!" shouted Glissa. "We're not your enemy."

Another volley followed the first, and Glissa ducked her head as she and Slobad pushed on toward the massive gate. It seemed carved into the side of the tower, the top edge looming forty feet above them. Fresh scratch marks on the ground showed how far out the gate extended when open. Glissa now realized what the horn had signified. Until very recently the gate had been standing open.

A third volley of arrows fell behind them like a sheet of rain. Glissa and Slobad were protected under the buttresses, but they had another problem. The gate was closed. They were running straight toward a wall with an army on their heels.

Glissa clanged on the metal gate with the pommel of her sword.

"Let us in!" she shouted. "We are not your enemy." She thought she heard movement behind the blank metal, but there was no answer.

The horde was almost on them. Glissa turned to face her death. Standing with most of her weight on her good leg, she raised her sword and stepped in front of Slobad. "Get your flame ready, goblin," she said. "We're not going to die without a fight."

She heard the tube ignite behind her, but Slobad didn't step up beside her. "Protect us, huh?" he said to her. "We not dead yet. Slobad have way out . . . or in. Yes—way in."

Glissa glanced back to see the goblin running his hand up and down on the gate as if looking for something. "What are you doing?" she cried. "That little flame won't cut through a gate."

"Just protect us, huh?" said Slobad, glancing back. "Crazy elf. Let Slobad do his job. You do yours. Swing big sword. Look out!"

Glissa ducked instinctively before even turning back to the invading nim. A clawed hand tousled her hair as it whisked by, just missing her head. The elf shot her sword hand forward, catching the attacking nim in the abdomen. A quick jerk slid the blade through the creature's groin. It toppled over backward, but two more nim took its place, trampling over their downed comrade to get to her.

The elf whipped the sword back up, cutting off the first beast's arm, before slicing across to lop off not one, but two heads. As those two nim slumped in front of her, Glissa marveled at the power of her new blade. She hadn't given it much thought since her battle with the levelers, but this sword she had stolen from Chunth was amazing.

Another claw swung at her. She parried the blow, sending the nim's hand flying back over its head. Glissa took the opening and hopped forward a half step to impale the injured nim just as its other claw raced toward her. The beast went limp on her sword. Glissa flexed the muscles in her arms and flung the creature back off her sword into two other advancing nim. The awesome show of strength almost toppled the limping elf as she came down too hard on her injured leg. Glissa screamed as pain shot through her ankle.

Perhaps sensing weakness, the nim closed in on Glissa from three sides. She was running out of room to maneuver. The press of bodies drove her back into Slobad and the gate. All she could do was parry at the encroaching claws. She took a blow from the right that ripped into her already bleeding shoulder. Another claw got past her blade to the left, gashing her forehead. Blood flowed into her eyes, and Glissa was forced to swing her blade blindly back and forth.

The nim pressed in all around them, the stench from the gas jets belching out green clouds of noxious fumes. Glissa coughed and felt nauseous. She didn't know if she was going to vomit or faint from the fumes. She couldn't hold up much longer.

"If you're going to do something," she shouted as she wiped blood from her eyes, "you'd better do it now!"

"Almost got it," said Slobad. "Give me a moment, huh? Not easy to find. Supposed to be secret. Slobad's secret."

"I don't have a moment to give," Glissa snapped. "Stop talking and do something!" She ducked again, barely seeing the incoming claw in time. She swung her sword but couldn't even tell if she hit anything. The air was filled with a green haze, and blood streamed into her eyes.

An odd sound came from behind her, like metal striking metal only muted as if heard from far away. She swung through the air in front of her again to keep the nim at bay, then felt something tug on her from behind.

"Come on, huh?" said Slobad. "Hurry. We go in now. Why you waiting, crazy elf? Move now."

Glissa didn't argue. She swung her sword back and forth in front of her as she backed up, wincing with every step. She kept expecting to fall over Slobad or bump into the gate. After a few more steps, her blurry world got much darker. She heard the sound again, only this time it was much louder and sharper, like swords striking in front of her. Glissa held her sword defensively as she wiped her forehead and eyes. When she could focus, she saw a wall in front of them. From far away, she heard the clash of weapons.

They were inside.

"How?" she asked.

"That is what we would like to know," said a booming voice behind her. Glissa turned to see what she knew must be a leonin. She and the goblin were surrounded by leonin guards. One large leonin stood with his hands on his hips.

Slobad had described the leonin, but the goblin's sketchy description could not come close to matching the impact of seeing these creatures in the flesh. They looked more like beasts than men. Their flattened noses spread out from sloping foreheads like snouts, and their eyes were set back close to their pointed ears.

Yet for all that, they looked regal. Long manes of flowing hair—some braided, some not—seemed to sparkle in the torchlight, as did the highly polished silver and gold metal of their arms and legs. The guards all wore shiny armor and carried large, mirrored shields. The sight was impressive, and Glissa felt ill at ease.

The leonin who spoke was well over six feet tall. His great mane, much larger and fuller than any others around him, cascaded down over his shoulders and chest. His sculpted arms were folded in front of him, and Glissa could see their great strength even at rest. Metal and flesh muscles bulged against the leonin's silver-clad chest. He had the air of a leader about him. The guards had an air of calm superiority, standing as she had seen Kane stand on guard duty.

The leader regarded Glissa and Slobad coolly, staring down at them over his flattened nose.

"Take them away," he said to the guards, then turned and left.

Glissa looked at Slobad, who shrugged. As the guards came toward her, Glissa handed them her sword. She didn't even consider fighting. The blood had stopped flowing from her forehead, but her ankle was on fire and her shoulder ached. They were in the hands of the leonin now, captives, but they were alive, and that was better than the alternative.

* * * * *

Glissa removed the bandage from her ankle and swallowed hard. The infection had spread almost to her knee. Scraps of green metal coated the leather, sticking to the bandage as she pulled it away from her wound. Her calf was still swollen, and her entire leg felt as if it were on fire. Green pus oozed out from all over her leg, not just down by the wound. Everything below her ankle had turned black and was cold to the touch. She turned away from Slobad so he wouldn't see how bad the wound had gotten.

The guards had taken them to a small room and closed the inside door. Glissa had heard the now-familiar metallic click after the door shut and knew they were locked in. She sat across from Slobad in their prison and worried—about her foot, about Slobad and Raksha, and about the latest threat against her life.

"What were those creatures outside the gate?" she asked.

"I told you other day," said Slobad. He was pacing back and forth across the room and hadn't seemed to notice Glissa fiddling with her bandage. "Leonin fight nim. Always fight nim. That's what take Raksha away from Slobad. Battles against nim. Beat them back to Mephidross; they just come back again. Don't know why."

"Mephidross?"

"Bad place under Ingle," said Slobad. "The black sun . . . er . . . moon, where goblins go when burned in Great Furnace. Slobad never go to Mephidross. Too close to Ingle. Raksha tell me about it, huh? Green muck everywhere. Gas swirling in air make you sick, huh? Nim rise from ground. Attack leonin. Bad."

"Zombies?" asked Glissa. "I've heard stories about the dead rising from the ground—Father called them zombies—but these nim didn't look dead. They just looked sort of turned inside out."

Glissa concentrated on her hands and built up a small ball of green mana between them. She moved her hands over her leg as if massaging the energy into the wounds and decay.

"Don't know," said Slobad from across the room. "Never see them before today. Some say green muck or foul gas turn people into nim. Never want to find out, huh? Slobad like being goblin."

"You've never seen one?" asked Glissa. "I thought you said Raksha fought them all the time." The mana spread out over her leg and sank down into the decaying flesh. The metal skin around her knee looked a little better, but her foot remained black and cold. She looked up at Slobad to see if he had noticed, but he was still pacing. It was obvious the goblin didn't like to be locked up.

"Out on border with Mephidross," said Slobad. "They never come all the way to Taj Nar before. Something funny happening in world, huh? Levelers, nim, crazy elves. Strange, huh?"

"I suppose it's all my fault," snapped Glissa. "Is that what you're saying?"

Slobad stared at Glissa and blinked a few times. "You strange, crazy elf. I never say that. How it your fault, huh? Just strange, that's all. Crazy elf. World not revolve around you, huh?"

Glissa lowered her head. She didn't know where that outburst had come from. "I'm sorry," she said. "I haven't really been thinking right since the leveler attack. . . ." She paused. "No, that's not true. I do that all the time—seeing things that aren't really there. I'm just suspicious of coincidence, I guess. I'm sorry."

Slobad came over to her and saw her foot. He let out a low whistle. "You lose that foot if we don't see healer soon, huh? Need to find way to get from here. Get out soon or lose foot. That for sure."

Glissa didn't argue. There was nothing more her magic could do. If they didn't see the healers soon, she'd have to cut off her own foot just to save the rest of her leg.

"I thought you said Raksha owed you," she growled. "Fine way to show it—locking us up in here."

"Raksha don't like surprises, and leonin don't trust strangers," said Slobad. "I guess Slobad upset Raksha when I bring stranger in through secret entrance, huh?"

Glissa dipped her bandage in a bowl of water sitting on the table. "Raksha was the leader we met, right?"

Slobad nodded.

"Didn't he know about the entrance?"

The goblin smirked. "No," he said. "Slobad help build gate for leonin many cycles ago. Added extra door. Slobad always like to have more than one way in or out, huh?"

Glissa laughed as she cleaned the blood off her forehead and shoulder. After rinsing the bandage again, she tried her healing magic on her other wounds, but the energy would not come this time. The infection and her failed attempts to keep it in check had made her weak.

"We need to see Ushanti now," said Slobad. "Can't wait for Raksha to calm down, huh? Slobad find other way from here."

He began pounding on the door. When the door opened, a Leonin guard filled the doorway. Slobad talked to the guard for a moment. The leonin's eyes widened in horror. He closed the door, and Glissa heard him running off.

"What did you say to him?" she asked.

"Slobad remind him of penalty for losing prisoner," said Slobad. "If you die, he dies. Try to look sicker when he comes back, huh? Told him you be dead by first moon. Just show him leg. He believe, huh?"

A few minutes later, the door opened and two guards entered. Glissa hung her head low and breathed heavily, trying to look and feel as sick as possible. It wasn't hard. The guards led them from the room. Glissa limped along between the two guards, helped by Slobad.

* * * * *

The leonin city was beautiful. Glissa had never seen so much brightly polished metal. The molder in the Tangle gave the forest a fuzzy, green look that Glissa found comforting, but the leonin city was trimmed with polished copper, silver, and gold. Even the guards' shields were mirrors that reflected light ahead of them as they walked. The prisoners were led through a series of wide hallways made of copper, with silver trim around each door and along the edge of the floor. Golden sconces holding silver fire tubes like the one Slobad carried dotted the walls all along the hall. The entire hallway glittered in reflected light from the numerous flames.

They passed an open door, and Glissa glanced inside. This was no holding room like the one she and Slobad had occupied. It was large and bright and filled with amazing furnishings. As she hobbled past, Glissa saw an ornate bed made from large metallic bones of some animal she didn't recognize. Next to the bed were a matching bone table and chair. The table had been topped in gold, while the bone legs and back of the chair had been completely covered in silver. Everything in the room—even the bones on the table and bed—had been highly polished and reflected the light of the fire tubes inside. The effect was dazzling.

The guards escorted them out into a large courtyard near the edge of the city. Glissa could hear the sounds of battle coming over the wall from the fields below, but there were no warriors to be seen. The leonin soldiers must have left the battlements and gone out to face the nim. Glissa glanced up and saw that much of the city still towered above them. She could see walled terraces at several levels. Each of them was brightly lit, and the walls of the entire city glittered in the night air.

They walked on plates of silver and gold as they crossed the courtyard. The plates were arranged to create tapering gold lines radiating out from a large golden circle in the center of the courtyard. In the center of the circle stood a statue of a leonin warrior carrying an ornate shield on his back and holding a huge, bladed staff. The warrior's outstretched hand held a ball of fire that illuminated the entire courtyard, but Glissa couldn't see anything fueling the fire.

"Your work?" she asked Slobad.

The goblin shook his head, then nodded. "Not make statue, huh? Slobad tinker, not sculptor. Art not practical. Not keep you alive, huh? Slobad make fire. Like tubes in hall. Leonin revere light. Say they keep fire burning to stay close to their god, huh? *I* think they afraid of dark."

On the other side of the courtyard, the guards stopped. They moved to either side of the door and held open a thick, dark curtain. Glissa and Slobad limped through the opening, followed by their escorts. This room was darker than anything Glissa had yet seen in the city. Curtains of woven leather hung everywhere, and a pungent, smoky aroma hung in the air. It was a drastic change from the rest of the brightly lit city.

"Sit," said the guard, indicating a low bench inside the door.

Glissa sat down, and two female leonin appeared from behind one of the curtains. As they got closer, Glissa noticed that the females were only slightly smaller than the males she had seen, but their faces were even more striking. They had no manes covering their heads, but Glissa could see a graceful curve of their necks and cheeks that was hidden on the males. Even more striking was the color of one of the females' eyes. One was copper, like all the leonin Glissa had seen so far. The other was bright blue.

The one with the odd eyes spoke. "She is not leonin," she said. "Why do you bring this creature in here?"

Glissa thought the leonin might not heal her after all.

"She is a prisoner of Raksha," replied the guard. "She must not die before he returns from battle."

After a moment's hesitation, the two healers bent over Glissa and looked at her wounds. One reached out and touched Glissa's forehead and shoulder, while the one with the single blue eye looked at her blackened foot and the decaying metal spreading up her leg. Glissa could see a white glow around the first healer's fingers as she touched her wounds. The pain in her shoulder disappeared along with a dull headache she hadn't even realized she'd had until it was gone.

Glissa looked down at the other healer and knew something was wrong. The leonin's hands glowed, but Glissa could feel no change in her foot.

After another minute, the odd-eyed healer stopped trying and stood. "She must see Ushanti," she said. "I have not the power to affect this wound."

"Stand," said the guard.

Slobad helped Glissa back to her feet, and they followed the healers through the maze of curtains into the center of the large room. Smoke filtered up to the ceiling from a brazier suspended over red-hot coals. Another female leonin stood with her back to the group, sprinkling sand into the smoking pot. A flash of yellow light shot from the brazier and scattered across the ceiling.

"Ushanti," said the odd-eyed healer, "Raksha's prisoner needs your healing power."

"Raksha and his prisoner will have to wait," replied Ushanti. "There are more important matters in the world than a nim prisoner." She dipped her hand back into a bowl beside her and grabbed another handful of sand.

Glissa couldn't see the seer's face but could tell by the tremble in her voice and the hunch in her back that this leonin was old, older than any of the other leonin she'd seen in the city.

"She is not nim, Ushanti," replied the healer. "I believe she is an elf."

Ushanti's clenched hand stopped halfway between the bowl and the brazier. "Elf, you say? Female elf?" The seer's voice rose in pitch dramatically. Glissa wasn't sure, but she thought she saw the woman tremble.

"Yes, Ushanti."

Ushanti turned to face Glissa and Slobad. As soon as her eyes locked with Glissa's, the seer screamed and staggered backward. The sand Ushanti still clenched in her hand spread across the floor around her as she slumped to the ground.

# RAKSHA AND USHANTI

"What have you done to my mother, elf witch?" screamed the odd-eyed healer as she rushed forward and knelt by Ushanti.

Glissa reflexively reached for her sword, but the blade wasn't there.

"I did nothing," she said. She turned slightly and took a half step back, so she could keep both the healers and the guards in view. "You saw what happened. I never even moved."

Nobody flinched. The guards seemed to be waiting for the odd-eyed healer to tell them what to do, but she was busy tending to her mother. Glissa stood her ground waiting for the healer to awaken.

The odd-eyed healer held Ushanti in her arms and passed her hand across the old leonin's face. A sheen of energy surrounded the unconscious healer like a bubble.

"She is fine. I sense no evil, Tangle magic about her."

Ushanti's daughter reached up to the table next to her and picked up one of her mother's bowls. She took a pinch of red powder and sprinkled a little under her mother's nose.

Ushanti coughed and sneezed then sat up and pulled away from her daughter's grasp. "Why have you brought this elf to us, Rishan?" she demanded.

"She is Raksha's prisoner, Mother," replied the young healer. "The guards brought her. She has a grave wound and a disease that threatens her leg. The guards feared she would die before the Kha could interrogate her."

"Bring Raksha to us now so he may interrogate her," spat the old healer. "We will not heal this one unless ordered by the young Kha himself."

Rishan looked up at the guards. "Fetch Raksha," she ordered. The guards didn't move. "Now!" she screamed.

"B-But our Kha is in battle," one stammered. "It may be some time."

"The battle has ended," said Ushanti. "We have seen it in the fire. Bring Raksha now."

Whether the old healer was telling the truth or not, it was obvious to Glissa that these guards feared her more than their leader's anger. One turned smartly and marched back through the curtain maze.

"Tie her up," said Ushanti's daughter as she rose and brushed herself off.

Glissa put her hands in front of her. She hated to be bound but saw no alternative. She could no longer feel her foot, she had no weapon, and there were two armies between her and freedom. All she could do was keep her options open. She allowed herself to be bound, but kept her hands slightly apart to make sure she could escape the bonds should a need arise. The guard also tied Slobad's hands.

"May I sit?" asked Glissa. "This wound is painful." It actually was more tolerable since the healer's efforts, but she wanted to appear more vulnerable than she was. Her only advantage now lay in surprise . . . and patience.

Rishan indicated a bench behind Glissa. After the elf sat down, Ushanti pushed herself up from the floor and approached her slowly. Glissa noted that the old healer had two blue eyes and couldn't help wondering who had sired her odd-eyed daughter.

"Yes, yes," said the old woman as she paced back and forth in front of Glissa. "We do believe this is the one." She looked at the guard. "She had a sword, correct?"

The guard's eyes widened for a moment when confronted by Ushanti. Then he nodded.

"Silver. Bright as the noon sun. The blade flows from the hilt like water, yes?"

The guard nodded again.

"Yes, she is the one," said Ushanti as she headed back to her brazier. "Keep your eyes on her. The fate of our world depends on it."

Glissa glanced at Slobad, who had a smirk just barely perceptible on his face. He was obviously enjoying this spectacle. Glissa wasn't so sure. Ushanti seemed to know her even though Glissa had never traveled outside the Tangle before.

"What is going on here?" she asked.

"Be quiet, elf," said Rishan. "Mother is working. You shall not interrupt again."

Glissa was about to argue further, but Rishan motioned for the guard to stand between the elf and the brazier. Glissa breathed deeply, trying to regain her patience.

Ushanti was now tossing colored sand into the brazier in huge handfuls. As smoke rose into the dark room, the air around Glissa began to grow hot, and the room seemed to close in around her. She found it hard to breathe and had to fight to stay awake. The whole scene seemed unreal. Not even Chunth had acted this strangely. She felt herself falling asleep and tried to fight against it.

\* \* \* \* \*

Glissa started as the curtains were pulled back violently and Raksha strode into the dark room. She couldn't tell whether she had fallen asleep or not, but some time seemed to have passed.

The smoke had cleared, and the guard was no longer standing in front of her. Raksha stood by the curtains, flanked by two guards, staring at the old leonin's back. Glissa glanced back and forth between Raksha and Ushanti. Neither seemed willing to acknowledge the other's presence. Raksha stood, holding a gleaming metal mask underneath one muscular arm, and tapped his feet impatiently. Ushanti stared intently into the smoke emanating from the brazier.

The leonin leader could wait no longer. "Why have you summoned us from battle, seer?" he roared. "What could be more important than the safety of Taj Nar?"

"The safety of the entire world, young Kha," said the seer, her head rising from the brazier and splitting the smoke. Ushanti turned to face her leader, but she did not bow, and Glissa sensed no deference in her voice or manner. "It has been many weeks since our last trance, but the horror of what we saw in the fires that rotation haunts our dreams still. We saw the sacred sun stop above Taj Nar. We saw a huge gout of emerald fire erupt from the world. We saw the leonin ripped from the world."

Ushanti paused. The light of the coals and the smoke from the brazier limned her in an eerie glow. She advanced upon Glissa, and the elf, seeing the hostility in the old woman's eyes, began to work her hands loose.

"We saw our world end, Raksha," Ushanti continued. "We saw this elf at the heart of it all."

Glissa remembered what Chunth had told her the night her parents died. He said that Glissa had a destiny. Surely Chunth had not tried to save her from the levelers so she could destroy the world. The old woman was mad.

"That's ridiculous," she said. "I'm only a single elf, and lame, for that matter. How could I destroy the world?"

"All we know is what we see in the fires," said Ushanti. "The fires tell us that you are dangerous. We believe you should be destroyed . . . for the sake of the leonin, for the sake of the entire world."

"Look," said Glissa, "believe the fires if you want, but I am not your enemy. This all started four nights ago when the levelers attacked me and my family. My family is dead, and I could do nothing to stop it. Now you're telling me I will destroy the world? If I had that kind of power, would my sister be dead?"

As she talked, Glissa worked on her bindings. "Listen, someone is trying to kill me. I saw him in the Tangle after the attack and again just yesterday. Tall, robed, face hidden behind some kind of reflective mask. For all I know, it's one of you, but Slobad here told me you are a good people and that you could heal me. Somebody sent those levelers to the Tangle for me. Maybe that's who you should be looking for in your smoke and fire."

Her hands were almost free. She still needed a weapon, though, to have any chance to make it from the city. The guard was close. She could probably take him before Raksha got to her. Glissa looked up at Raksha and stopped. He was staring at her. Had he seen her loosen the ropes?

"You say the levelers attacked you four nights past?" he asked. "What proof have you of this attack?"

"Slobad can vouch for that, your . . . your Kha-ship," piped up Slobad. "I found her the next rotation, huh? She caught up in the blades of half-destroyed leveler. Slobad get her free. Make new friend, huh? So I bring her to see old friends. Then nim attack. . . ."

Raksha glared at the goblin, and Slobad stopped talking.

"We will deal with you later, goblin," he said. "You will fix our door or die. We speak to the elf now. Tell us about this attack."

Glissa saw no harm in telling Raksha about the leveler attack, but she hated to be at a disadvantage. First, Ushanti apparently knew her, and now Raksha was demanding information about the worst night of her life. She would feel better if she had her sword in her hand. Perhaps she could gain his confidence by cooperating. Slobad had said Raksha was a decent leonin. He might at least hesitate if it came to battle.

"They came in the night as they always do," she said, "but they've never come so far into the Tangle. They passed many other homes to reach ours."

"If they truly attacked as you say, how did you survive?" asked the Kha. "Surely one elf is no match for the levelers. Or are you lying to us?"

Glissa gritted her teeth at the insult and at the painful memories of that night. "I was . . . not home when the attack came." She saw no reason to tell the leonin about her discussion with Chunth just yet. "I fought my way into the tree, but it was too late. My parents, my sister . . . they were already dead. All I have left of them is my mother's ring."

Glissa showed Raksha the ring, then dropped her head into her hands, half-feigning the emotion she showed. She pulled at the bindings, which were now hidden from view as she continued. "I tried to kill the levelers, to make them pay for what they had done, but there were too many of them. They cornered me. I thought I was about to join my family, but then . . . then they turned and left. I tried to follow, but my ankle got caught in a leveler's broken blades. The beast dragged me all the way back to its lair. Slobad rescued me and brought me here for help."

Glissa raised her head and looked at Raksha. She tried to read the leonin's face, but it seemed as impassive as ever. "If you're not going to help us, then we'll just leave, thank you very much."

Glissa threw the loose ropes into the face of one guard, then rolled off the bench and came up behind the other guard. Before he could react, she had taken the claw-tipped staff from his back and whipped it down through the ropes tied around Slobad's hands. She pushed the guard into a curtain. He tumbled to the floor, caught up in the voluminous leather. The other guard stood ready to attack. Glissa looked to Raksha. He merely stared back at her.

"I don't want to hurt you," she said to the Kha. Her staff wavered between Raksha and his remaining guard. "Just let us leave."

"You need not hurt anyone," replied the leonin leader, "and you need not leave just yet."

With blinding speed, Raksha rushed forward, ducking as Glissa snapped the staff toward him. He slapped the staff out of the way and moved in. Before she could bring the long weapon back around, the leonin leader grabbed her wrist and pulled the staff from her grasp. Casually he twirled her around and pushed her back down onto the bench.

When Glissa rolled over, the Kha was standing before her as impassive as ever. He reached up to his forehead and dabbed his finger at the cut she had inflicted. "Impressive," said Raksha. "We have never seen anyone move that fast before."

Glissa was thinking the same thing.

"As we said, there is no reason to hurt anyone." The leonin leader turned to Ushanti, who had hidden behind her cauldron during the scuffle. "Tend to this warrior's leg, old woman," he said. "She is our guest and is to be treated as such."

"But the fire trance," protested Ushanti. "The visions—"

"Can often be misleading," growled Raksha, "as you well know."

"I don't understand," said Glissa. "What just happened here? I attacked you, and now I am your guest?"

"We will excuse the attack," said Raksha, "this one time. We are in the midst of trying times, and such behavior is understandable, but that is not why you are now our guest."

Ushanti came out from behind her cauldron, chose a variety of colored sand and oils from her table, and began mixing them in a bowl. Raksha spoke a few words to the standing guard, who helped the other guard to his feet then hurried from the room. Raksha turned back to face Glissa.

"Four nights past, the levelers came to Taj Nar," he continued. "They climbed the tower and breached the walls just after the last moon set. The alarm was raised, and our warriors fought valiantly, but still the levelers came . . . all the way to our chambers. We destroyed five of the foul things, but more poured through the door. We thought we would soon join Dakan, the first Kha, in the eternal light, but at our darkest hour, the levelers halted. We dared not breathe for fear it might be a trick. As one, the levelers turned and fled the way they had come."

"That is just how it happened in the Tangle," said Glissa. "I had shown them power, but still they came, trampling their own to get to me. Then they turned and fled." She hesitated for a moment, then said, "I was told they were sent to kill the mightiest elf warrior in the Tangle. Perhaps they came here to kill the mightiest leonin warrior as well."

"Your enemy is our enemy, elf," said Raksha. "That may make us allies."

The guard returned, holding Glissa's sword and Slobad's bag of tools. "Take these as a sign of our trust," said Raksha, "and as a symbol of our new alliance against this common enemy." He laid the sword into Glissa's hand, and she looked at it closely for the first time. It was a beautiful blade, and the entire length of the weapon glittered and gleamed, even in the low light coming from the coals beneath Ushanti's brazier. The curved blade seemed to flow from the hilt like water.

* * * * *

Ushanti finished her mixture and hobbled over to Glissa. The elf thought she heard the old woman grumbling, but it might have been an incantation.

"Lift your leg, elf," said Ushanti. "This will hurt." The leonin healer poured half of the foul-looking mixture over Glissa's knee.

Steam rose from Glissa's calf and ankle as the concoction trickled down her leg. It seemed to be burning through the corroded metal. Glissa fought back a scream as the fire in her leg exploded and sent icy-hot tendrils of pain up her thigh.

Ushanti placed the bowl at Glissa's feet. "Put your foot in the bowl," she commanded.

The steam made it hard for Glissa to see the bowl, and it took most of her concentration to fight back the pain from the fire running down her leg. Finally she placed her foot into the bowl. At first she felt nothing except the lingering pain from the treatment. Her entire foot was numb. Then it began to tingle. The tingle turned into pinpricks, then into stabbing pains. It felt as if long needles were working their way into her flesh.

Glissa held her breath and gritted her teeth through the pain. Steam from the bowl rose into the air and met the steam surrounding her calf. As the steam swirled around, the elf exhaled and took another deep breath. The fire in her ankle and calf decreased little by little as the steam dissipated, but the memory of that intense pain lingered. It was some time before the muscles in her thigh relaxed to the point where she thought she could walk.

"The infection has been cleansed," said Ushanti. "Our daughter can heal the wound left behind. We must retire now."

"One last thing, Elder Shaman," interjected Raksha as the old woman turned to leave.

Glissa was sure she saw a sneer cross the healer's lips as she turned, but no trace of it lingered as she faced her leader. "Yes, Kha," she said, bowing low.

"This figure the elf saw in the Tangle," said Raksha. "Find him for us that our new friend . . ."

"Glissa," said the elf as Raksha turned to her.

"So that we and our new friend Glissa may deal with him."

"You wish us to enter the fire trance?" asked Ushanti. "After healing the destroyer, we must once again face the vision of her demolishing our world?"

"Yes."

Ushanti stared at Raksha for a moment, but it was obvious all her bluster had been drained away by the force of her leader's presence. She shuffled back to her cauldron and grabbed two handfuls of sand—one yellow, one blue. As Ushanti sifted the sand through her clenched fists into the cauldron, the smoke changed colors. Brightly limned azure wisps snaked their way up to the low ceiling. Ushanti bent low over the cauldron until the smoke enveloped her head.

Moments passed, and Glissa stared at Raksha, Rishan the healer's daughter, and the other young healer. None of them; seemed at all worried that the old woman might suffocate within the smoke.

Ushanti began to moan. "Robes," she cried. "Shimmering robes. Reflection. Faceless. Watching. Waiting."

"Where is he?" asked Raksha.

Rishan moved over toward the brazier. "Look beyond the robes, Mother. See past the faceless figure. See the place. Look behind."

"Cannot," said the old seer. "He holds us. Riveted. Cannot move. Cannot look away. No eyes. Only reflection."

"Look into the reflection," said Rishan.

"Blackness. Only blackness," said Ushanti. "It drinks in the light. Wait . . . a sun rises. Black sun on black sky. Illuminates . . . chimney. Black chimney. Huge. Reaches for the sun. Foul water cascading down. Bones everywhere. Nim!"

The last word was a scream, and Ushanti's knees buckled underneath her. As she fell, Raksha caught the old seer and lifted her from the smoke. Her lined face seemed more sunken and sallow than ever. Her eyes were open, but there was no life in them.

Raksha carried her through another set of curtains, followed by Rishan. He held the healer as a father might hold a child who has fallen asleep in his arms. A few moments later, the Kha returned. "Walk with us, Glissa."

Glissa looked at Slobad.

"Yes, the goblin as well."

Glissa rose gingerly and tried out the strength of her ankle. It was still tender, but she could walk without limping. She sheathed her sword and followed Raksha back through the maze of curtains into the courtyard. The moons were all set, but the light from the fires was bright enough that Glissa couldn't see the stars overhead. The leonin leader strode to the statue and stared into the flames.

"This is Dakan, the first Kha," said Raksha, pointing at the statue. "It is he who took the Razor Fields from the beasts. It is he who built Taj Nar. It is he who crafted the Mask of Suns."

Glissa noticed that the mask on the statue was a replica of the one Raksha had slung over his back.

"Dakan brought the leonin into the light and taught the tribes to keep the fires burning during the dark hours," continued Raksha. "This fire, like the Mask of Suns we wear in battle, brings us closer to Dakan and keeps the sun in our hearts even when it is not in the sky. We maintain the fire day and night to stave off our enemy—to hold back the darkness."

He turned to face Glissa. "You witnessed that darkness this day," he continued. "Faced it and beat it back long enough for this goblin trickster to open a door in our defenses."

"We didn't mean to—"

"No need to apologize," said Raksha. "Slobad will fix that flaw in his design." He fixed a gaze on Slobad that made the goblin tremble. "No, you fought valiantly, even while hindered by a wound that would have kept our best warriors crying in their beds. We welcome you into Taj Nar as our champion to help us fight the nim."

The leonin paused.

"But?" prompted Glissa. She sensed they wouldn't enjoy leonin hospitality for long.

"Come," said Raksha as they walked to the battlements. "Our two enemies are one enemy. Today we leonin slaughtered hundreds of nim." He pointed below. On the slope beyond the tower's walls, Glissa could see the dark shapes of dead nim. "Yet tomorrow a thousand more could walk from the Mephidross."

"You cannot leave Taj Nar," said Glissa, realizing the burden of leadership that sat so heavy on this young leonin.

"We cannot," he said. "Nor can we send any warriors into the Mephidross."

"They are needed here for defense." Glissa nodded her understanding.

"Indeed," said Raksha. "Even if we could spare troops, our best warriors could not hope to survive the Mephidross long enough to gain the Vault of Whispers. That is where you two will find our common enemy. That foul place is the chimney Ushanti saw in her fire trance."

"Us two?" asked Slobad, speaking for the first time since Raksha had commanded him to be quiet. "Not me. Slobad has no special strength to survive in that place, huh? Stay here and fix door. Nothing special about Slobad."

Glissa patted the goblin's shoulders. "I do not want to put Slobad in danger," she said. He saved my life . . . twice. Can he not stay here and wait for my return?"

Raksha shook his head, but there was sadness in his eyes. "You will need his guidance to avoid the nim and the reapers. Do not worry. Slobad will find a way to survive. He always does."

Raksha turned back to Glissa. "It is vitally important that you do survive this next trial, Glissa. We do not believe you are a destroyer of worlds, but Ushanti's visions cannot be discounted. There is a darkness swirling around us, and we—you and I—are standing in the eye of that storm."

Glissa stared at the young Kha. It was the first time she had heard him refer to himself in the singular. "What do you mean?" she asked.

"Our fates are entwined," said Raksha. He grabbed Glissa by the shoulders and looked into her eyes. "I have not told anyone this," he said. "But I, too, saw your robed figure that night—and he has haunted my dreams ever since. We . . . I am afraid to sleep at night."

Slobad gasped.

"You will stay quiet on this matter, goblin," growled Raksha, "or we will take your head ourselves. No one must know of this matter. We fear the leonin would panic if they knew their Kha now lives in terror of a hidden enemy. Find our enemy, Glissa. Find him and stop him. The fate of more than just our two lives is at stake."

# CHAPTER 8

# MEPHIDROSS

"The skyhunters will carry you to the edge of our lands," said Raksha the next morning. "They will leave on their daily patrol as soon as you are ready, but they cannot take you into the Mephidross and dare not stay on the ground long at the Mephidross border."

"How do we find this Vault of Whispers?" asked Glissa. She looked up at the pteron she was supposed to ride. It was little more than skin stretched across bones. The beast hopped back and forth on long legs, tethered to a metal stake. It towered over Glissa, but its legs were no thicker than Slobad's scrawny arm. She had no idea how it could get itself off the ground, let alone carry its rider and a passenger.

"You must follow the black sun in the morning," said Raksha. "By midday it will rise above the Vault before descending over the Glimmervoid.

"What you call suns, we elves call moons," said Glissa, "and the black moon is difficult to see even at midday. Its light is often washed out by your yellow moon . . . sun."

"As it should be," said Raksha, smiling. "It will be easier to see within the Mephidross. The haze that hangs heavy over the chimneys dulls Dakan's sun and limns the foul black orb."

"Slobad can see Ingle fine, huh?" said the goblin. He was standing behind Glissa. She didn't know if he was more afraid of

Raksha or the pterons. "Goblins see Ingle on starless days. Sits like dark hole in sky, reaching for goblin souls."

"We know," said Raksha. "That is why we have sent you on this mission. You shall be Glissa's eyes in the Dross. Now it is time for the skyhunters to leave."

Raksha grasped Glissa's hand and shook it hard. "Glissa, go with the sun!" he said. With a swift movement, the Kha grabbed Slobad and lifted him in an embrace. "You," he said. "Stay alive and return to us. We have missed you."

Glissa thought Slobad's face turned an even brighter red than its normal rust color. Raksha tossed the goblin up onto the pteron, behind the skyhunter. Glissa looked up at her own escort, a slight-built female leonin.

"Watch the beak," said the skyhunter as Glissa clambered up the side of the beast. "A pteron can cut you in half, even back here."

The elf hitched her leg into the folds of skin under the beast's front legs. The pteron immediately squawked and swung its head back to glare at Glissa. She could see dozens of sharp teeth sticking out along the edge of the creature's beak.

"Avoid the wings," said the skyhunter. "They are sensitive."

"Those are its wings?" asked Glissa, looking at the skin folded underneath the beast's long arms.

Glissa perched behind the skyhunter. There was no room in the saddle, so she had to rest on the bony back of the pteron.

"How long will it take to get to the border?" Glissa asked the leonin female.

"No more than a few hours," she replied. "We should have you on the ground before the last sun rises."

With that, the skyhunter kicked the pteron and pulled back on the reigns. Glissa watched in amazement as the beast unfolded its wings. They were made of skin and stretched from long claws on its front legs all the way down to the beast's bony hips. The wings were enormous, each three times as long as Glissa. The pteron flapped its wings, but they did not rise from the ground.

"Ready?" asked the skyhunter over the din of the flapping wings.

"For what?" shouted Glissa.

It was too late. The pteron stepped off the battlement and plummeted toward the valley below the leonin tower. Glissa tried to catch her breath, but the wind whipping past her face made it impossible to breathe. The pteron continued to beat its wings slowly until—about halfway down—they caught the wind and the beast began to level out and curve away from Taj Nar.

Below them, Glissa watched scores of leonin haul nim bodies away from Taj Nar. In the distance she saw smoke rising from a large fire. "You burn the bodies of your enemies?" she asked, pointing at the bonfire.

"No!" exclaimed the skyhunter. "The fire is reserved for leonin fallen, to send their souls into the light. Nim bodies are left for the duskworkers. They eat anything. The nim bodies help keep the duskworkers in check."

"Quelling their hunger so they don't attack leonin?" asked Glissa. She forebore to ask exactly what kind of creatures the mycon were.

"Poisoning them to keep their numbers down," replied the skyhunter. "Have you ever smelled the foul gas that comes from a nim?"

What a pragmatic race, thought Glissa. As they winged across the Glimmervoid, though, she began to understand them better. Outside of Taj Nar, most leonin lived in small settlements. They were cut off from one another by wide expanses of bare metal and razor grass. How different from from the Tangle, thought Glissa as the miles whipped by beneath her. In the Tangle, we live on top of our neighbors. We count on them for everything from protection to hauling water.

Glissa concluded she couldn't live like the leonin. Or like Slobad had, either. Glissa glanced back at the goblin, hanging on so hard she could see his white knuckles even from a distance. She felt a fondness for the strange little tinkerer, beyond the appreciation she owed him for saving her life. He'd had a hard and lonely life.

\* \* \* \* \*

Hours later, the rolling hills were replaced by craggy terrain. Where once Glissa saw hills and half-moon mounds that formed homes for leonin settlers, she now saw only broken spires—perhaps the chimneys Raksha had spoken about—and an occasional mound that appeared to have been looted and destroyed. The chimneys were dark, much blacker than the surrounding silver expanse of the remaining Glimmervoid. They jutted up from the flat plain like columns, with wide bases that tapered to jagged tops. Looking past her escort, Glissa saw they were flying toward a black curtain that cut across the Glimmervoid like a dark line. It was as if the moons did not shine past that line.

Glissa couldn't make out any details past this border between light and dark. A thick green haze obscured the air above the land. All she could see was a glistening sheen on the ground near the border of the hazy curtain. The land dipped down toward the haze, and Glissa was certain that the border moved slightly as she watched.

"What is that?" she called to the skyhunter, pointing to the ground ahead of them.

"The Mephidross," shouted the leonin. "You won't enjoy slogging through that."

A few minutes later, the skyhunter circled the pteron around one of the last chimneys before the curtain of haze. "I have to set down on top, or we won't get airborne again," she said to Glissa.

Glissa watched the haze as they drifted lower and lower. The other pteron circled a second chimney. The pteron landed on a small ledge at the tip of the chimney. Glissa crawled down from the flying lizard more nimbly than she had ascended but still landed on her rear when the creature pulled its wing from the way just as she reached for it. She felt sure the pteron smiled at her. It spread its wings and dropped off the edge of the chimney.

The elf rose, brushed herself off, and looked for a way down from the chimney. The outside was sheer and smooth. It would be much harder to climb than a Tangle tree. She peered down into the interior of the chimney, but the yellow moon was still low in the sky and she couldn't see anything. She couldn't tell if there was any way out at the bottom.

She looked around for Slobad and spotted him on the ground. He had somehow made it to the bottom of his chimney. Then she noticed movement in the haze. A moment later, a squad of nim appeared, moving right toward her. The chimney might be defensible, but Slobad was already on the ground. She couldn't leave him alone.

Glissa pulled out her sword and jumped over the edge of the chimney. She twisted in the air as she fell and plunged the sword into the metallic structure with both hands. I hope this works again, thought Glissa as her feet slammed into the side of the chimney. She plummeted toward the ground. The sword sliced through the chimney as easily as it had through the Tangle tree. Glissa slid down the slight incline at breakneck speed.

The sword hardly slowed her down at all. She pushed with her feet and dug the blade in deeper. Glissa began to slow down, but she could see ground coming up fast. As she neared the bottom, she tensed her muscles and flexed her knees. About five feet from the ground, she released the sword and kicked off hard with her legs. The change in direction didn't lessen her momentum, but instead of slamming into the ground, the elf skipped across it and rolled to a stop.

Slobad came running over to her. "Hey, crazy elf," he called, "why not use stairs like normal person, huh? You not see stairs with bad elf eyes, huh? Crazy . . ."

"No time," said Glissa, panting from the exertion. "The welcoming party is right behind me."

Slobad let out a low whistle as Glissa stood up. She turned around. The nim emerged from the haze, headed straight for them.

"Is that defensible?" she asked, pointing back at the chimney Slobad had come down.

"We could keep nim out," said the goblin, "but wouldn't help. Nim don't eat. They wait until we come out, huh? We starve or die; you pick."

"Then run for the Mephidross!" shouted Glissa, pointing toward the green haze at an angle away from the oncoming horde. "I'll catch up."

She sprinted back to the chimney and pulled out her sword. The nim were almost on top of her. The lead nim grabbed for her, but Glissa dodged under the claw and ran toward Slobad. She glanced back and was happy to see she was leaving the nim far behind. They were slow, and now she could outrun them.

Glissa caught up with Slobad at the edge of the haze. The goblin had stopped.

"Come on," she shouted at she passed him. "They may be slow, but they're still coming."

"Wait," said Slobad. "Crazy elf, don't—"

It was too late. Glissa entered the Mephidross . . . and sank to her knees in a putrid, purple-green muck. The swamp stretched before her as far as she could see into the haze. Beyond that, the air seemed to swirl around with an almost liquid quality. Dark wisps of slime hung in the air around them, mixed with the green gas. Glissa drew a breath to scream at Slobad, but the stench almost overtook her. It was a hundred times worse than when she had been surrounded by the nim at the gate of Taj Nar. She had no choice, though. To get to the Vault of Whispers, they had to go through the Mephidross.

"Come on!" she called again, then began coughing. Phlegm caught in her throat and she almost vomited. "If we keep moving, they can't catch us."

Slobad held back for a moment, then looked over his shoulder at the shambling horde and stepped into the haze. Where the muck came up to Glissa's knees, it was almost at the chest of the short goblin.

"Raksha calls it the Dross," he said. He held his satchel up over his head to keep it dry. "Say it stick to you for days, huh?" It wasn't hard for Glissa to see he wasn't happy.

"Just move as fast as you can," she said. "They'll have to wade through it, too."

The two companions pushed their way through the muck. Glissa had to concentrate on her breathing to keep the bile from building up in her throat. After a while, her eyes stopped burning, and she could actually see a little better through the inky haze. There were several chimneys ahead of them. Now she understood why Raksha had given them that name. The dark wisps in the air seemed to be coming from their tops.

Unlike the chimneys outside the haze, these seemed to be active, almost alive. The black exteriors glowed with a purple energy, while clouds of black smoke belched from the tops. She could barely see strands of cable connecting the tops of the chimneys. She wasn't sure, but Glissa thought she saw a ball of purple energy run along the cable from one chimney to the next. An eerie hum in the air was starting to make her teeth ache.

"Why would anyone live here?" grunted Glissa as she headed toward the nearest chimney. It might provide a way to get them from the Dross, even if for just a while. The ground did begin to rise as they neared the chimney. The level of the thick sludge fell to Glissa's ankles. However, the hum intensified, and the ache in her mouth shot up into her temples.

Glissa looked behind. The nim were gaining on them. They seemed to glide right through the Mephidross. On the firm ground of the Glimmervoid, the nim's shambling strides had made them slow. Here in the Mephidross, their long legs kept them above the muck, and they used their long arms to push the liquid from the way. Glissa and Slobad could not outrun them, especially with Slobad's short, labored strides.

"Climb on my shoulders," she said to the goblin as she hunched down into the Dross.

"Huh?" asked Slobad.

"Ride on my shoulders, you stupid goblin!" she shouted. "I can carry you quicker than you can run."

Slobad handed Glissa his satchel and scrambled onto her shoulders. Glissa slung the satchel over her head and took off at a dead run around the chimney. She could see another chimney and headed toward it, trying to stay as much as possible on higher ground. She flitted from chimney to chimney. The elf was faster than Slobad, even with the weight of the goblin on her back, but still the nim gained on them. The combination of the liquid air in her lungs and the hum of the chimneys was wearing her down. She couldn't keep up her pace much longer.

"Don't they ever give up?" she gasped through deep breaths of acrid air.

"Slobad don't know much about nim, huh?" replied the goblin. "Raksha say they mindless. Never stop before reaching goal. Never stop. Never tire, huh? Mindless."

"If they're mindless, how do they know where to go and who to attack?" asked Glissa. "Could someone be controlling them?"

"Raksha sometimes sees humans behind nim in battle," said Slobad. "Don't know if they control." Slobad thought they just turning into nim, huh?"

"If they're being controlled," huffed Glissa as she ran, "they might stop if we can take out whoever is controlling them."

"What if they not stop, huh?" asked Slobad. "What if they not controlled at all? We stop; they not stop; we die, huh?"

"It's better than running ourselves to death."

They had come around another chimney. Glissa stopped. She hunched down so Slobad could slip off her back. "You continue on," she told him. "Climb a chimney for safety. I'll let the nim pass and try to find the controller."

Slobad looked as if he was going to argue, but Glissa cut him off. "It's our only hope. We can't outrun them, and we can't run all the way to the Vault of Whispers. Now go, and make sure they follow you."

Glissa handed Slobad his satchel and pushed him off into the Dross. He looked back at her, then shrugged before trotting off into the haze. Glissa turned and looked at the sheer side of the chimney. She pulled out her sword, made several notches, and began scaling the chimney, cutting holes for her hands and feet as she went. Fifteen feet above the swamp, she stopped and waited. She hoped the nim were as mindless as Slobad had heard. If even one turned after passing the chimney, she'd be trapped.

\* \* \* \* \*

From her perch on the chimney Glissa watched Slobad. He slogged through the Dross, holding his pack over his head. The humming intensified as she clung to the chimney, and her teeth were almost vibrating in her mouth. Below, the nim poured around the chimney. Glissa watched as row after row passed beneath her. Gas from the spouts on their sides wafted up, adding to the stench of the haze. Glissa closed her eyes and concentrated to keep the bile from welling up in her throat.

Once the nim passed, she opened her eyes, checking to see how close they were getting to poor Slobad. She couldn't see the goblin. The elf was sure he couldn't have gotten to the next chimney already, but there was no sign of battle in the ranks of the nim. Then, in the distance, she saw ripples in the muck. Slobad emerged from beneath the Dross just ahead of the nim army. The goblin screamed and waded as fast as he could away from the nim.

Glissa couldn't wait any longer. If she didn't attack them now, the nim would reach Slobad and tear him apart. No one seemed to be controlling them. She would just have to fight.

"Idiots!" came a voice from behind Glissa. "She's back here! Turn around, now!"

Glissa turned.

"I'm guessing you weren't talking to me," she snarled.

He was a gangly man nearly as tall as the shambling nim, and had the same dull purple skin half-covered in Dross. Like the nim, the man's mouth was like a gash across his face, but he lacked the exoskeleton and gas spouts of the nim. His features were almost humanoid—not human but not nim . . . at least not yet. Glissa could see the spark of intelligence in his eyes. It looked as if she had found the controller.

"Return!" he shouted.

Glissa glanced behind her. The nim turned around and began now slogging their way back toward her.

"I know just how long it will take them to get back here," she said. "Call them off and tell me why you're after us if you don't want to die."

The man looked over her shoulder and smirked. Glissa could hear the slosh of nim behind her.

"Who sent you?" she screamed. "Tell me or die."

"It matters not what you do to me," he said. His speech was slurred, as if his misshapen mouth couldn't form the words correctly. "You're as good as dead."

"So are you!" cried Glissa. She swung her sword with both hands. The blade caught the controller just below his shoulder, slicing through his upper arm on its way into the man's neck. The silver blade cut through vertebrae just as easily as it had cut into the iron chimney. The controller stood for a moment, the smirk frozen on his face, before his head rolled off to the side and he crumpled into the Dross.

Glissa jumped up onto the chimney again, grabbing the notches she had made and scrambling back up to her perch. She didn't know what the nim would do, but if they were truly mindless, they should continue past her, following their last orders. If not, the controller was right and she was as good as dead.

Glissa tensed and waited for the front line to get to her. They didn't seem to be paying any attention to her. Their eyes were locked forward. She worried that the nim might stop when they reached their dead master's body, but the corpse had all but disappeared under the Dross, and the horde continued on past the chimney, trampling him deeper into the muck.

She clung to the chimney until the nim had disappeared into the swirling haze, then dropped down again and ran off to find Slobad. He was standing where he had fallen, wiping muck off his pack.

"What happened, huh?" he asked. "Where did nim go? They coming back? You kill them? Huh?"

"They're returning," said Glissa, "just as they were told."

She told Slobad about the controller and about the nim's mindless march into the haze. The goblin looked horrible. The Dross hung off him like scabby skin. As she spoke, pieces fell off and plopped into the swamp.

"What happened to you?" she asked. "Did you fall?"

Slobad gave up on cleaning his pack. "Yes," he said. His eyes gleamed, and a smile spread across his face. "Something big under here. Big and metal. Tripped over leg or something, huh?

Fell on top. Something very big. Rolled off into Dross, huh? Think it some big machine, huh?"

"Machine? With legs? Like a leveler?" Her first instinct was to destroy it, but an idea occurred to her. "If it's a leveler, and you can fix it, could we ride it through this?"

"Slobad can fix anything, huh?" said the goblin. "Anything. Fix Raksha's doors. Fix cult's boiler. Take apart leveler once—"

"Okay, okay," said Glissa. "Let's see what you found." She reached beneath the Dross and felt around, then grabbed and lifted. With a huge effort, she pulled her find from the Dross. It looked like a metal boot at least two feet long from toe to heel, and it seemed to be attached to an enormous leg.

Slobad gasped, and Glissa dropped the boot. "What?" she cried. "What's wrong?" She spun around to see if the nim were coming back, but the haze was still. When Glissa looked at Slobad, she thought the goblin was going to explode.

"What?" she asked again.

"I've heard stories," said Slobad, "but never believed them. Myths. Not real. Always thought they just stories like Krark's journey into Mother's Womb. But we found one. We found one." He was practically jumping out of the Dross, he was so happy.

"What?" screamed Glissa.

"Come quickly," said Slobad. "We pull from Dross."

Slobad slogged to the nearby chimney and opened his pack. He pulled out some leather rope and a metal tool with a series of wheels and a handle. He tried to screw one end into the chimney but couldn't get it to go in. Glissa scanned the haze, looking for any sign of attack, but Slobad motioned for her to join him. She trudged through the muck to his side. The goblin screwed the contraption into a hole and looped the rope through the wheels. He gave one end of the rope to Glissa.

"Tie around foot," he said. "Go, go. Hurry up, crazy elf, before nim come back."

"Foot?" asked Glissa. She shook her head and trudged back into the Dross. She glanced around again, still wondering if the nim would ever return to look for their master, then worked on pulling the boot back up. She tied the rope around the boot, glanced around one more time, and headed back to the chimney. Slobad was trying to turn a crank, but it wouldn't budge.

Glissa took over for him. The rope went taut as she strained at the handle. She feared the rope would break, but then the handle began turning more easily and the rope started to move. She looked back and saw a large metal object coming from the Dross. It's a giant, thought Glissa. She could see a huge barrel chest, arms, legs, and a squat head coming toward them. As the Dross began to slip off the body, Glissa saw it was all made of metal.

"What the flare is that?" she asked.

"A golem," said Slobad.

# CHAPTER 9

# REAPER

Glissa hardly got any sleep that night. After hauling the massive golem into the chimney, she had trudged back through the Dross to make sure once and for all that the nim weren't going to return. When she got back, Slobad had the golem's chest open and had practically crawled inside. With his fire tube burning in one hand, the goblin peered into the chest cavity, making a racket with his tools.

The interior of the chimney was brighter than Glissa would have imagined. The purple energy that streamed through the walls of the chimney provided an eerie glow that illuminated the entire chamber. With light coming from all around her, Glissa cast no shadow at all inside. The structure was completely hollow except for a central tube that ran all the way to the top of the chimney. She could see no smoke, so she assumed it must travel through the tube.

Strands of the same cable she had seen connecting the various chimneys together also ran from the exterior walls to the central tube. Beads of energy ran along these cables, always going in the same direction—in toward the central shaft. As Glissa watched the strands, she saw some of the energy coursing along the walls transfer onto a cable and run across to the tube.

"I don't think we should stay inside these chimneys too long," she said to Slobad, but the goblin merely grunted in response.

Glissa didn't know what these chimneys did, but they were obviously spewing something toxic into the air outside. Was Slobad right? Did the Dross itself create the nim from humans? That controller certainly wasn't human any longer. Perhaps he never had been.

Halfway around the chimney, Glissa found a stairway cut into the exterior wall. It circled up and around the chimney. She climbed the stairs, ducking under cables periodically, and eventually came to a balcony that encircled the chimney. Holes were cut into the outside wall, and she could see out into the haze. It was growing dark, and she could barely see the outlines of the surrounding chimneys.

Glissa descended again and curled up by the door to get some sleep. It was not a restful night. Every hour or so, she awakened to the sound of the goblin swearing or a huge clatter of tools dropping. She knew that Slobad was too involved in his tinkering to notice anything important like an invading nim army, so she took these times to scout the area. She checked the windows on the balcony and patrolled the surrounding chimneys. There was no sign of activity, which bothered her more than if she had seen an approaching army. Surely the controller and his wayward nim would be missed.

In the dim light of early morning, Glissa awoke to find Slobad asleep next to the iron man. The golem's chest cavity was closed, and Slobad had wiped most of the Dross off the golem. As much as she wanted to let her friend sleep, Glissa knew now was the best time to begin their journey. None of the moons had yet come up, and the darkness should cover their exit.

"Slobad," she called to him. The goblin turned over and started to snore. "Slobad, wake up." She walked over to him and kicked him in the side. "Slobad!"

The goblin sat bolt upright, clutching the fire tube in his hand. "What? What? What is it, huh?" He flipped on his fire tube and looked all about. "What wrong, crazy elf? You not see me in dark? Go to sleep, huh? Slobad tired."

"It's time to go," said Glissa. "We should keep moving. I think that old tin giant is a lost cause."

Slobad looked at Glissa. Recognition of who she was and where they were slowly crossed his sleep-squashed face. "Yeah. We go," he said. "If had more time, could make it work again. Pity. Great machine. Never see anything like it, huh? Pity. Need more time—"

"Sorry," interrupted Glissa, "but we should go. You can't fix everything."

"Did fix everything," said Slobad as he gathered up his tools. "Cleaned inside and out. Should work, huh? Need more time to find what Slobad missed. Must have missed something. Should work."

"Well, it doesn't," said Glissa. "Now we should go before the nim come back." She went to the entrance and looked out into the haze. She couldn't see far, but she didn't hear anything and the Dross around the chimney was motionless. Glissa looked back at Slobad. He was still staring at the golem as if willing it to come back to life. "Come on, Slobad," she said. "It's time to let go."

"Elf not understand," said Slobad. "The golems from before-time. The golems here before goblins or elves or anything, huh? The golem was myth, but now real. Need more time."

Glissa came back over to the goblin and put her hand on his shoulder. "You said it yourself," she told him. "Those were just myths and legends—stories told to children—not real. This thing is probably just some old nim construct that got lost in the Dross. Leave it, and let's go before we're found by another nim patrol."

Slobad patted the giant on the chest and walked toward the door. Glissa followed him, and they headed into the Dross.

"Vault should be that way," said Slobad, pointing.

"Are you sure?" asked Glissa. "All these chimneys look alike to me. Is Ingle already up? I can't see any of the moons."

"No, Ingle not up yet, huh?" said Slobad. He pointed at another chimney just visible through the haze. "Elf fight nim controller there. We ran straight from the Razor Fields to here. Vault farther into Mephidross, huh? Come on. We go."

Glissa had no idea. All the chimneys looked similar. They were bluish-black and craggy. Some had large, reddish-orange patches of flaky metal that looked like the infection she'd had on her leg, but the differences were far outweighed by their depressing sameness amidst the inky haze and the ever-present Dross. Slobad seemed to have an innate sense of direction, probably from spending all his life crawling through tunnels.

As Glissa followed Slobad into the Dross, she stared at the chimney they had just left and tried to commit it to memory. Maybe they could come back for his golem later. When she looked forward again, she froze. What she had thought was another chimney ahead of them had just moved.

"Slobad," whispered Glissa. "Did you see that?"

"See what?" answered the goblin.

"That chimney," said Glissa. "It moved."

"Haze make crazy elf see things, huh?" said Slobad as he continued forward.

The dark shape in the haze moved again—moved toward them—and Slobad stopped short. "Now crazy goblin see things," Slobad said, rubbing his eyes.

The shape was moving faster now and heading straight at them. Glissa couldn't tell what it was through the haze, only that it was as big as a chimney. She looked left and right, but there was nothing but haze and Dross as far as she could see. They definitely couldn't outrun this thing, whatever it was.

"Back to the chimney," she shouted. "Quick!" Glissa grabbed Slobad around the waist and lifted him from the Dross. Holding the goblin under her arm like a vorrac carcass, she ran back toward the chimney.

The huge creature gained on them with every step. Glissa wasn't sure they'd make it to the chimney in time. The ground shook beneath her feet, and the Dross washed over her hips, slowing her down. Glissa pressed on, diving through the entrance into the chimney just as a wave of Dross slapped her in the back. She jumped to her feet and ran to the stairs.

"Get behind the golem," she called to Slobad. "Maybe it'll do something for you yet."

Glissa reached the balcony and looked out a window. The monster was right outside the chimney. It looked for all the world like a nim, but it was easily twenty feet tall. Its grayish-purple skin was emaciated. She could see every gigantic rib sticking out from the beast's chest. They must each be six feet long, thought Glissa. The cartilage along its back—what Glissa had thought was an exoskeleton on the nim—was easily three feet high and five feet across. There was something odd there, though. Its backbone looked different from the ones she'd seen on the nim.

The beast slithered around the chimney, peering back and forth as if trying to find its prey. It moved off toward the chimney where Glissa had fought the nim controller. As it wandered off, she noticed the creature held a long staff in its hands. The top of the staff curved over into a vicious-looking hook. If it went just a little farther, Glissa thought, they might be able to make it to the next chimney and hide until the monster left.

The beast stopped and whipped the hook end of its staff down into the Dross. When the hook came back up, there was something impaled on the end. It was the remains of the controller. Glissa watched as the huge beast lifted the hook over its back. The cartilage pulled away from its body with a terrible sucking sound to reveal some sort of chamber. The beast shook the staff until the body came loose. The carcass fell into the chamber with a sickening plop.

Glissa was frozen to her spot. She watched as the chamber closed and the beast turned and strode back through the Dross. It came up to the chimney, its face just a few feet from Glissa. She turned to run, but it was too late. The beast slammed into the structure, knocking Glissa from the balcony.

The elf screamed as she fell. There was nothing to hold onto, nothing to kick off from. She was plummeting straight to her death. Then she stopped. Something had caught her. She looked over and saw the squat face of the golem, its red eyes open and staring at her. Perched atop its shoulders was Slobad, grinning from pointed ear to pointed ear.

"What the flare?" exclaimed Glissa. "How—"

"Don't know how," said Slobad. "Just sit up and look at me, huh? Like I said . . . need more time."

Glissa fought to regain her composure. "Is it friendly?"

"Slobad think so," said the goblin. "Tell the golem to catch crazy elf, huh? It did. See? You caught, huh?"

"Great. Tell it to get us from here. Now!" The chimney shook as the beast slammed into it again. "Before that thing brings this chimney down on top of us!"

"Golem, walk," said Slobad, pointing toward the entrance.

The golem walked toward the door, holding Glissa under one arm. Slobad perched on its shoulders. The elf could tell they weren't all going to fit through the narrow entrance. It had been barely big enough to drag the golem through on its back. Now that she saw the construct standing, she realized it must be tall. When the golem reached the entrance, it thrust an arm out and smashed through the wall. Debris rained down on them, but they were through.

"Golem, run!" cried Slobad.

Glissa strained to look behind her. The huge creature was coming around the chimney. The golem broke into a trot, moving away from the creature, but even with its long legs it couldn't move through the Dross faster than the twenty-foot-tall beast. The creature gained on them with every stride.

"I need to slow it down," shouted Glissa. "Tell your golem to put me down."

"Golem," called Slobad. "Drop."

Glissa found herself facedown in the Dross. She pushed herself up onto her hands and knees and looked for the beast then had to dive back into the Dross to avoid its foot. After the monster passed, Glissa stood and followed, pulling out her sword as she ran. She dived forward, hoping to cut into the beast's tail, but it moved too fast and she couldn't reach it.

"Help," screamed Slobad up ahead.

Glissa looked up to see the goblin hanging by his pack on the end of the beast's hook. The chamber on its back was opening again, and Glissa could do nothing but watch in horror as it dropped Slobad into the chamber.

"No!" she screamed, rushing forward again.

The monster turned at the sound of her voice and moved toward her. Its hook came arcing down at Glissa, but she batted it away with her sword and ran on, trying to get inside its reach. She swung her sword back around at the beast's tail. The blade cut easily through the creature's pale skin and sinewy muscles, then stopped halfway through the limb. Glissa tried to pull the sword back out to swing again, but the blade was lodged in the bone and wouldn't budge.

Glissa looked up and dived from the way just as the hook came slicing at her again. She couldn't dance around this thing all day, she knew. The Dross limited her movement, and now she had no weapon. Glissa breathed hard, trying to catch her breath and think.

She dived under the Dross again and tried to swim forward as the beast swung the hook at her. The swamp was too thick to swim through. She came up for air right as the hook sliced down at her.

The weapon stopped. Glissa looked up. The golem had caught the beast's arm in mid-swing. The creature now turned its attention to the larger target. It slapped its hand against the golem. The golem strained to hold on to the beast as it slammed its palm into the metal man's chest. The golem looked at Glissa, its red eyes seeming to plead for help.

The elf warrior jumped to her feet and ran toward her sword. Instead of trying to pull it out, she jumped into the air and kicked both feet at the hilt, driving the blade through the bone and out the other side, slicing the tail in half. Glissa landed and dived forward again, following her sword as it flew through the air toward the Dross. Behind her, monster teetered, trying to keep its balance.

Glissa grabbed her sword as it went into the Dross and turned to help the golem. It seemed to be struggling with the hand holding the hook, but as Glissa approached, she heard something snap and saw the hook rise up again. Before she could scream, the hook came down hard, slicing through the emaciated abdomen of the giant monster. Pus and entrails exploded from the back of the beast, showering the Dross around Glissa with a putrid rain of gore.

Glissa watched as the beast fell into the muck, cut in half by one swing of its own hook. The giant metal man stood holding the weapon but looking as calm as when Glissa and Slobad had pulled it from the Dross.

"Golem," Glissa shouted, "pick it up!"

The golem moved forward and lifted the beast's torso from the Dross and turned it over. Glissa cut into its back beneath the cartilage and pulled open the chamber. A wash of acidic juice poured from the opening, along with Slobad and a number of partially digested bodies.

Slobad was covered in red welts, and the strap on his pack had completely dissolved. Glissa helped the goblin to his feet. "Are you okay?"

Slobad nodded. "Let's never do that again, huh? Huh?" He looked at his satchel. "Need new strap. Have to cut some rope. Get dagger . . ."

"Later," said Glissa. "Let's make sure you're okay first."

Slobad looked up at the severed beast in the golem's hands. "How did you . . . ?"

Glissa shook her head. "It was your golem," she said. "He may come in handy after all."

The golem dropped the half of the beast it was holding at the same moment Glissa saw something dart behind a chimney. "Golem," she said, pointing, "fetch!"

Slobad started to argue, but Glissa glared at him and he stopped. A few moments later, the golem returned, holding a man by the neck. The man's eyes and forehead were covered in a metal cowl that made him look more like a nim than a human. Glissa recalled the nim controller had a similar hood, but it had been pushed back at the time. The elf pushed the hood back from his face. His jagged mouth was contorted, and his bony body shook as he dangled in the grasp of the golem.

"Who are you?" she demanded. "What are you doing here?"

"Yert. My name is Yert," he sputtered, then began to cry. When the sobs turned to wails, Glissa motioned for the golem to drop him. Once he hit the Dross, the man rushed over to the hewn beast and bawled afresh.

"She killed you, my precious," he wailed.

"Is this your . . . monster?" asked Glissa.

The man looked up at her. "It's not a monster," he said. "It's . . . it was a reaper, the most feared enforcer in the Mephidross. Without him, I'm nothing. I'll never get another reaper. I'm nothing without him. Kill me now."

"Maybe later," said Glissa, shaking her head at the pathetic man. "First, you tell me who sent you, then maybe I'll let you die."

"Geth," said the man. He continued to sniffle. Glissa wondered how such a pathetic creature could gain control of a monster. "Geth said, 'Kill the goblin. Bring me the elf.' He never said anything about a giant metal man."

"Who is Geth?" asked Glissa. "What does he want with us?"

It was too late. Yert had begun sobbing uncontrollably again. Glissa would get nothing more from him until he calmed down. Meanwhile he draped himself over the body of the reaper.

Glissa looked at Slobad, who shrugged. She bent down next to the pathetic controller and put her arm around his shoulder.

"Look," she said, "take us to this Geth, and we'll help you. We'll force him to give you another . . . reaper. Okay? Just tell us why Geth wants us."

Yert shuddered, then wiped his eyes. He looked over at Glissa. "You would do that for me?"

Glissa nodded. "We're all just trying to stay alive here, right?" she said. "Following orders. Tell us why Geth wants us and we'll help you."

"I can't tell you," he said with a sniffle. "I don't know. Geth gave orders. Controllers don't question leaders. We follow orders or are banished to Dross. I can take you to him. You can ask him."

Glissa sighed. "Fine. Where is this Geth?"

"He's in the Vault of Whispers."

# CHAPTER 10

# VAULT OF WHISPERS

The dark moon—the "sun" Slobad called Ingle, where souls are stored—hung over the Vault of Whispers like a giant hole in the sky. The top of the huge chimney was shrouded in the ever-present haze of the Mephidross. A viscous purple and green liquid cascaded down one side of the Vault from somewhere within the haze. The rest of the Vault was etched, as if by acid, with a web of interconnecting lines and swirls. The Vault pulsed, much like the chimneys, throughout the etched webwork. Glissa felt a shudder travel down her spine as she stared at the forbidding edifice. She couldn't help feeling that the Vault was somehow alive.

"You sure you want to do this, huh?" asked Slobad again. "Look dangerous. Could be trap. Must be trap, huh? Very dangerous."

"That's why you two will stay out here," said Glissa. "If I'm not out by the time Ingle disappears behind the Vault, you and the golem come crashing in and get me."

Slobad nodded.

"Stay out of sight until I get back," counseled Glissa as she pushed Yert toward the chimney. The trip to the Vault of Whispers had gone quickly with Yert's guidance and the golem's long legs. Now the sniveling little man was going to walk them both into Geth's chambers.

"Here," said Glissa, passing her sword to Yert. "Take this. You were told to bring the elf to Geth. That's just what you're going to do."

She walked past him, unworried. The little man could barely hold the sword, let alone swing it. The two walked through the Dross up to the Vault. Yert guided her toward the disgusting waterfall, and her apprehension rose. The liquid would surely blind her as she passed through. Was Yert playing at something? As they approached, however, she saw the path led behind the falls to a dark opening guarded by two nim.

They passed inside. Glissa stared at the guards, ready to seize her sword should either of them attack. Neither nim moved an inch. They stared forward, waiting for an order. Glissa and Yert entered a great hall that seemed to stretch the entire length of the Vault. Glissa could see the walls disappear into the haze above her, which hung thick in the air just as it did outside. There were a few nim walking about, all apparently on errands. Most held objects stiffly in front of them and walked in straight lines back and forth, appearing from and disappearing into dark openings that lined the sides of the hall.

A few controllers also walked through the hall. They wore their cowls crumpled around their necks within the Vault, so Glissa could see their faces. Yet even without the cowls, these men looked more nim than human. Many of the controllers had nim escorts. Glissa even saw one leading a reaper. This controller stopped in the middle of the hall for a moment to stare at the odd duo. Glissa was just about to snatch her sword back from Yert, when the controller moved past them. She watched him until he left the Vault.

"Why does nobody question us?" asked Glissa. None of the controllers seemed to want to get involved in Yert's affairs, but Glissa knew her subterfuge couldn't be *that* convincing. She could hear her sword clanking on the ground behind her as well as Yert's occasional sniffle.

"As I said, we do what we're told," replied Yert. "We follow orders. To do less would invite Geth's wrath. To do more would impose on Geth's power."

The controllers weren't that much different than the nim or reapers, realized Glissa. They only did what they were told to do. "Hasn't anyone been told to guard against intruders? Doesn't Geth worry about his own safety?"

"Geth controls the most fearsome beast in the Mephidross," said Yert. "He has magical protections guarding against intrusion."

Glissa stopped. "When were you going to tell me about this?" she demanded. Some of the other controllers had stopped to watch the exchange, so she lowered her voice. "What protections? What creature?"

"There is a magical barrier that prevents enemies from entering his quarters bearing weapons."

"And the creature?"

"A vampire."

\* \* \* \* \*

They were almost halfway through the great hall. Nim and controllers meandered back and forth on either side of them. Glissa was too deep into the Vault now to battle her way out . . . at least not before confronting Geth.

"Fine," she said. "Where is Geth?"

Yert pointed at a doorway ahead of them, easily twice as large as all the others. Its edges glowed faintly. This, Glissa thought wryly, was what came of being clever. If Yert didn't make it through the barrier with her sword, she would have to face a vampire with no weapon. She had to risk it. She needed answers, and they were behind that door.

She passed through the doorway, but nothing happened to her or Yert. Before her was what must be Geth.

He was not at all what Glissa had expected. So far, all of the residents of the Dross had looked alike, emaciated with dull gray skin and carapaces or cowls of metal hiding their faces. Those faces she had seen had twisted features and gashes for mouths.

Geth looked nearly human. His skin still had some color and life to it. He wore no cowl, and the only hint of a carapace was a strip of metal that ran down the back of his head into the folds of a gray cloak he wore. He sat on a metal throne smiling and staring at Glissa as if he had expected her.

A large creature stood behind him, gray of skin, thick of neck, with a powerfully built chest. It wore long black robes, and Glissa could see little save the face. Deep-set eyes reflected no light at all. Its bare forehead glowed with a mystic purple emblem. Crimson tubes ran from the sides of its mouth down into its robes. As Glissa approached the throne, the vampire sneered, exposing yellow teeth that looked like sharpened pegs.

"Good, Yert," said Geth. "I did not expect you to return so soon . . . and so successfully."

"Not so successfully as you might think," said Glissa. In a single fluid movement, she twirled around behind Yert, snatched her sword, and snapped the edge of the long blade against the sniveling man's neck.

"Do you expect me to be afraid, little elf?" asked Geth. The ruler of the Vault had not even flinched or blinked at the sudden role-reversal.

"No. I expect you to tell me why you want me."

"And if I don't?" asked Geth, smiling again.

"If you don't start talking," replied Glissa, "I'll kill Yert."

Geth leaned forward in his throne and looked straight at Glissa. "Kill him. He is a boil on the surface of the Dross. I have hundreds of Yerts."

Glissa tried in vain to read Geth's eyes, but he was either telling the truth or merely cold and calculating. Either way, it mattered little. She stared for a moment more, then shoved the controller into the wall behind her. Yert's head bounced off the wall, and he slumped to the floor, unconscious. She turned back toward the throne. "How many Geths do you have?"

Geth slapped his hands. The vampire stood sneering behind the ruler. "Well done," said the ruler of the Vault. "A lesser being might actually be cowed by your display of mercy."

"He did ask me to kill him," replied Glissa. "I would have if he deserved it. Do you deserve death? Or will you tell me why you wanted me killed?"

"I did not want you dead," said Geth. "I had hoped to barter your life for a larger payment, but capturing you has proved too large an inconvenience. It will now be my pleasure to kill you. Do not expect mercy from me." Geth snapped his fingers, and the green-skinned vampire dropped its robe to the floor. The creature's chest was indeed broad, but its arms looked like skin stretched across bare bone. The tubes from the vampire's mouth ran back over its shoulders and wound their way down both arms, ending at metallic scythes on both wrists.

Without warning, the vampire leaped from behind the throne and barreled into Glissa, driving them both to the floor. It pinned her legs together with its knees and slapped at the blade when Glissa swung it at the creature. Before she could bring the sword back up for another attack, the vampire grabbed Glissa's wrist and squeezed until she dropped the silver blade.

"To answer your question," said Geth from his throne, "there is only one Geth, because there is only one vampire in the Mephidross. I control the Dross because I control the vampire."

The vampire raised its arm and slammed the scythe point down into Glissa's shoulder. The elf screamed in pain, then horror, as liquid rose up the tube toward its shoulder. The vampire was draining her blood!

Weakness flowed over her. She raised her free hand and hit

the vampire in the face, but it was like hitting the golem. She grabbed the vampire's wrist and tried to pull the spike out, but it was too strong. She grew cold, and her vision started to blur. She could see her life disappearing through the tube and could do nothing to stop it.

She flailed at the arm, but the creature was too strong and she was getting weaker. Then her fingers felt a small tube coming from the scythe's tip. She wrapped her claws around the tube and pulled. At first, the tube didn't move at all and Glissa lost hope, but after another moment she felt it shift a bit. She looked up into the vampire's eyes, but it was reveling in the kill too much to notice. Glissa pulled harder, focusing all her strength into that single task. Little by little the tube inched from the sheath. All at once, the tube sprang free. Blood sprayed over Glissa and the vampire as the tube whipped around in the air.

The vampire roared as the blood stopped flowing into its mouth. Glissa pressed her advantage. She wound the loose tube around her wrist and yanked on it like a rope. The tube snapped taut, pulling the vampire's head violently backwards. The creature toppled off Glissa, its spike slipping from her shoulder as it fell.

Glissa rolled over and grabbed her sword again. Rising to her knees, she brought the blade down hard on vampire's wrist. The spike snapped as the sword sliced through it on its way through the creature's wrist. Geth screamed, "No!" from his throne as the vampire roared in pain. The vampire's black blood spilled from the severed end of its arm, mixing with Glissa's red blood in a growing brown puddle.

Glissa stood up and stepped on the vampire's good arm. She felt a little unsteady but tried not to show any weakness.

"Now," said Glissa slowly, looking up at Geth, "tell me what I want to know or I will cut off its other arm. You said yourself, there is only one vampire, and I will not show it the same mercy I showed Yert."

"It's bleeding to death," gasped Geth, looking down at his vampire's severed arm.

"Then talk fast," said Glissa. "Why did you kill my family?"

"I didn't kill your family," said Geth. "I didn't even know your name until a few rotations ago. We were paid to attack you and that leonin ruler."

"Who paid you? What was his name?"

"I never knew," growled Geth. He glared at Glissa, then looked down at his bleeding vampire. "Let me bind his arm and I will tell you everything I know. If he dies, I will tell you nothing!"

Glissa shook her head. "The person who paid you," she said, recalling the figure she and Raksha had seen the night of the leveler attacks. "Did he wear gray robes and have a domelike head?"

"I don't know," snarled Geth. Sweat was pouring down his forehead. "I never saw him. My instructions and payment were delivered by flying artifacts—silver birds with globe heads and no beaks. I never met whoever controlled them. I was paid ten vials of serum for the attack on Taj Nar. I was to get twenty-five more for killing you. I thought I could renegotiate if I captured you alive."

"Why should I believe you?" asked Glissa. She pressed a little harder on the vampire's arm, and a fresh gout of black blood spilled onto the floor.

"The proof is in my throne," screamed Geth. "Now let me help my vampire, or I will call down the entire force of the Vault upon you!"

It was too late. The vampire stopped struggling, and the bleeding stopped. Geth jumped off his throne and ran forward. Glissa slapped the hilt of her blade into the human's face. There was a crack, and Geth dropped to the ground at her feet. Glissa kicked Geth in the chest to make sure he was truly unconscious, then, satisfied he no longer posed any threat, walked over to the throne.

What was this serum he had mentioned? A compartment in the

arm held a single clear vial of blue liquid, the vial no larger than her thumb.

"Hmmph," said Glissa. "You caused a lot of trouble for so small a price. I think I'll just take this, if you don't mind."

There was no argument from Geth. Glissa dropped the vial into the dagger sheath in her boot and stepped over the ruler of the Vault and his vampire. A trickle of blood still flowed from the vampire's severed arm.

I don't want to leave another enemy behind me, she thought. Besides, Geth had done no real harm to her. She kneeled beside the vampire. With her sword in one hand, and an eye on both Geth and his creature, Glissa summoned the power of the distant trees. A ball of green energy filled her palm, and she pushed it down onto the vampire's wrist. The wrist glowed green for a moment as the wound closed.

Glissa pulled the tubing free from the vampire's mouth and tied Geth's hands and legs behind his back. She walked over to Yert's inert form and prodded him awake. She held her sword tip to Yert's throat and placed a finger on her lips. Yert nodded his understanding. Glissa walked back over to Geth and slapped the leader's face a few times until he opened his eyes.

"I could have killed you," she said, "but I believe you didn't kill my family."

Fire raged behind Geth's eyes as he struggled against the bindings.

"I have healed your vampire, so you may maintain control of the Mephidross, but I suggest you remember who saved your life, Geth. Choose your allies more carefully in the future. Do we understand one another?"

The bound leader glared at Glissa, refusing to nod.

"Come here, Yert," said Glissa. "Yert here has lost his reaper. Either you agree to keep your nim inside your border, or I leave you tied up and Yert in charge when I leave."

Geth glared for another moment, then nodded his head. Glissa pulled the tubing from his mouth.

"I will not harm you or the leonin leader," he said.

"Fine," said Glissa. "I believe you. One more thing, though. You should find another reaper for Yert. He is your loyal servant."

Geth nodded his head. "You can trust me."

"I said I believe you," said Glissa. "I don't trust you."

She replaced the tube, then slammed the pommel of her sword into Geth's forehead, knocking him out once again. She handed her sword back to Yert and pushed him through the enchanted doorway. Glissa followed the controller into the main hall. The nim in the Vault of Shadows were still doing their menial tasks and took no notice of her. She snatched her sword from the young controller and ran for the entrance.

Shouts rang out behind Glissa as she reached the waterfall. The nim guards turned, but they were too slow. Glissa cut them in half without slowing. She dodged around the murky sheet of water and ran into the Dross. Each step took her closer to her friends and farther away from harm. As she neared the chimney, she dared to glance back and was surprised to see nobody pursuing her.

What she did see stopped her in her tracks. There, just at the far edge of the Vault of Whispers, was the figure from the Tangle. His domed head was reflecting the pale light of the pulsing building. Above him, two birdlike creatures flitted back and forth, the pale light glinting off their blue-domed heads.

"Slobad! Golem!" she cried. "Come here, quickly!"

Her friends appeared in the chimney doorway, but before they could reach her, Glissa felt an all-too-familiar darkness close in on her.

"Not now," she groaned as she fell face first into the Dross.

* * * * *

120

*When Glissa looked up, she was no longer in the Mephidross. Instead of purple slime and green haze, she saw brown dirt and green plants. Instead of scraggy chimneys around her, she was surrounded by great trees reaching up to a yellow moon . . . no, a sun. Yes, that was definitely a sun. Its brilliance hurt her eyes when she looked straight at it.*

*Glissa stood. She was back in the same forest of her flare. It looked just as she had remembered—green and gold, bright and warm. Water droplets clung to the moss and flowers at her feet, glistening in the bright rays of sunshine that filtered through the leaves. The metal covering her arms and legs was gone. Instead, she was draped in vines and leaves. She felt calm, the stress of the Dross melting away along with the memory of her other life. This was where she belonged.*

*She began walking. A voice inside her beckoned her. Her inner serenity was replaced by fear, but Glissa knew she could not turn back. Her destiny lay ahead of her. After a time, the trees gave way to a clearing. Within the grove, she saw many elves dressed in leaves and vines. More appeared at its edges and walked forward without speech or expression toward a bright light in the middle of the clearing.*

*Glissa felt a sense of doom overtake her as she stared at the globe of light. It didn't belong in the forest. It didn't belong in this world. Glissa tried to stop, to back away, but her legs would not obey her.*

*She raised her hands in front of her to shield her eyes and shouted, "No! Stop. Stay away!" but she was too late. The globe of light flashed, expanding out to engulf the entire clearing. Glissa was falling. The bodies of the other elves, silhouetted in the bright light, fell with her.*

\* \* \* \* \*

Glissa was back in the Mephidross, drenched in muck. She looked up to see the golem's face, with Slobad peeking around from behind. She was being carried through the Dross.

"Awake now, huh?" said Slobad. "Crazy elf pick funny time for nap. Fall facedown into Dross, huh? Not good. Slobad know, huh? Slobad know."

"It was a flare," said Glissa. "A vision we elves get." She looked over her shoulder to see where they were going but could not see the Vault of Whispers any longer. "Where are we? What happened to the figure?"

"We not see anything, but you fall into Dross," said Slobad. "Plop. Face first. Lucky you call us, or you still there, huh? The golem pull you out, and we head back to Glimmervoid."

Glissa struggled to escape the golem's grip. "No!" she said. "We have to go back. I saw the figure from the Tangle, the one in Ushanti's vision. He had silver birds flying above him, just like the ones Geth described." Glissa quickly told them what she had learned from the ruler of the Vault.

"Nim come swarming from Vault, after you fall," said Slobad. "Plop. Right into Dross. No robed figure or silver birds, huh? Just lots of nim and another reaper. Bad if we stay, huh? Had to leave. "

"You're right, of course," she said. "I'm sorry, Slobad. At least I have this." Glissa pulled the vial of serum from her dagger sheath and showed it to the goblin.

"What is that, huh?"

"I was hoping you could tell me. This was the payment Geth received for his attacks on Taj Nar. You've never seen it before? Geth called it serum."

As soon as that word left Glissa's mouth, the golem halted. Glissa almost fell from the sudden stop. She looked up at the golem's face. His eyes had narrowed, and he was staring at the vial in her hand.

"What's the matter, golem?" asked Glissa. "What is it?"

"Memnarch," said the golem.

Glissa stared up at the golem. "Did he just talk?" she asked.

"Yes," said Slobad.

"Has he done that before?"

Slobad shook his head. "No."

"What do you think 'Memnarch' means?" asked Glissa.

"I don't know."

"Huh."

# CHAPTER 1

# RISHAN

The trip to Taj Nar was quick and uneventful. Even laden with Slobad and Glissa, the golem moved twice as fast as Glissa could on foot. The metal man was tireless. By morning, they got to the edge of the Razor Fields, having met no resistance on their way out. Glissa saw groups of nim several times, only to see them change course and veer away. Perhaps Geth had gotten the message. Perhaps he was no longer being paid. Either way, Glissa was happy to avoid conflict.

Once out of the Dross, the golem moved even faster. The trip took only a single rotation. However, the golem remained mute after its single utterance, and Glissa was no closer to deciphering the riddle of the serum and the word "Memnarch" when they arrived at Taj Nar than she was when they had left the Mephidross.

"Maybe Raksha knows what serum is, huh?" said Slobad as they crested the hill surrounding Taj Nar.

"I'm more interested in talking to Ushanti," said Glissa. "This vial feels magical to me."

When they reached the base of Taj Nar, the gate stood open. When the guards saw Glissa and Slobad riding the golem, they came to attention and drew their weapons.

"Halt!" said one. "Proceed no farther."

Glissa jumped down from the golem's hands and bowed low. "I am Glissa of the Tangle and this is Slobad," she said, indicating the goblin still perched on the shoulders of the golem. "We have come from the Mephidross with information for Raksha."

"We know who you are," said the guard. "You are welcome. Raksha will see you immediately. But this creature is not known to us. It must remain outside the walls of Taj Nar."

Glissa furrowed her brow. "The golem?" she asked. "It's perfectly safe. In fact, this metal man saved our lives in the Dross. I will vouch for it."

"I apologize," said the guard. "However, our orders are clear. You and the goblin may enter. No one else."

"Look," said Glissa. "Do you think you'd even be standing here if the golem wasn't safe? It could tear you apart before you moved. . . ."

Slobad coughed behind Glissa, stopping her in mid-rant. She glared back at the goblin, while he motioned her to be calm.

"Not a problem, huh?" said Slobad as he winked at Glissa. "Slobad stay here with golem. You talk with Raksha, huh? No problem."

Glissa took a deep breath and nodded. As the guard led her into the city, she thought about how odd their trio must look—an elf, a goblin, and a golem running from some madman with a domed head. Perhaps she had been too quick to trust. What did she really know about Slobad and the golem? But they had both saved her life. Surely not everyone was an enemy.

Her musings came to an abrupt halt when the guard ushered Glissa into Raksha's throne room. She was duly impressed. The room was large and ornate. Bright shields lined both walls, each one carved with a different pattern. Shining suns were a common motif. Some depicted a proud warrior basking in the light, while others showed visions of Taj Nar or a great battle playing out beneath the bright orb. The sun pattern was displayed on the floor as well. A golden orb was inlaid upon a dais at the end of the room, its rays radiating out to each wall.

Instead of resting on the dais, the throne stood behind a large, silver table in the middle of the room. The table was filled with charts and papers. Raksha sat on his throne, staring at the papers. Glissa and the guard stood quietly waiting for the leader to finish his work. When he finally looked up, he motioned for Glissa to sit in a chair opposite him before going back to his work. All business, noticed Glissa. The leonin obviously did not believe in ceremony where their Kha was concerned.

"It is good to see you well," said Raksha in between scribbling notes. He sniffed the air. "It is obvious you have been to the Dross. You have brought much of it back with you. But you look well enough. Where is the little goblin? We know he must have survived the trip. Nothing on this world is capable of killing that one."

Glissa couldn't help smiling. Slobad had said that Raksha did not trust easily, but he certainly trusted deeply. "Slobad awaits below with our newest ally—a golem we found in the Dross. Your guards were wary. The golem is imposing."

Raksha waved his paw at the guard. "Bring the goblin and this golem to us immediately."

The guard's face looked pained. "Sire," he pleaded, "the golem is monstrously large. We cannot guarantee your safety."

Raksha looked at Glissa. "I will guarantee your safety, Lord Raksha," she said. "I would stake my life on it."

"Go. Bring them to us," Raksha said. After the guard left, the leonin observed, "They will hold you to that promise. Now, tell us what you learned in the Mephidross."

Glissa began her story. She told of the early attack and their discovery of the golem. She also told Raksha about the controllers and how she found out about their leader, Geth.

"We can behead their armies by killing these controllers," said Raksha. "We had often pondered on the question of who controlled the nim."

"There are problems, though," said Glissa. "The controllers look much like nim with their cowls up. The nim follow the last order given them, so they will continue to attack even if their controllers are dead."

"Still, this is useful information," said Raksha. "What of this Geth you mentioned?"

Before Glissa could answer, the throne room door opened and Slobad walked in, followed by the golem. Raksha looked them up and down.

"Great Dakan," he said. "It truly is huge." He pushed the massive throne back and strode around the table, circling the golem while Slobad looked on.

Seeing the large leonin leader dwarfed by the metal man made Glissa keenly aware of its immense power. What did they know about the golem? Its previous owner could be the one intent on killing her and Raksha.

Raksha studied the golem from all sides before retuning to his throne. "Perhaps it would be advantageous for us to find quarters for your metal friend," he said to Slobad. "We believe its presence could cause alarm." He turned to the guard, who had stood silent but was obviously ill at ease. "Find our guest suitable quarters."

The guard nodded and turned to leave.

Slobad said, "I stay with him, huh? Keep golem from trouble for Raksha. No problem. Keep from trouble." He led the golem from the room, following the guard down the corridor.

Glissa continued her tale, telling Raksha about her confrontation with Geth and her subsequent sighting of the dome-headed, robed figure. "I believe he was the one paying Geth to make the attacks," she said. "The robed figure paid Geth with vials like this." Glissa pulled out the vial of blue liquid. "It is called serum. Do you know where it comes from and what it does?"

"We have never seen such a thing," said Raksha. "Perhaps Ushanti can help us."

"Will she help?" asked Glissa. "I don't think she trusts me."

Raksha laughed. "That is true," he said. "But we have informed her that she must aid you in any way she can. Besides, if you have stopped the nim attacks, we all owe you a debt of gratitude . . . even Ushanti." He stretched. "The sun is almost above us. We shall feast first, then visit Ushanti."

* * * * *

The feast turned out to be part ritual and part meal. Raksha led Glissa and Slobad into the main courtyard, where a throng of leonin awaited. The Kha moved to the center of the courtyard and took his place next to the statue of Dakan. He raised his shield toward the yellow moon—their sun—and positioned it to reflect the light onto the flame Dakan held in his hand. The leonin warriors attending the feast encircled their leader and used their shields to reflect the moon's rays onto Raksha, bathing him and the statue of the first Kha in a pearly glow. Raksha tilted his head back and roared at the sky. The circle of warriors joined in, and the noise echoed across the Glimmervoid.

Afterward, leonin cubs and females brought out huge silver platters filled with meats. Glissa wondered about the role of females in the society. She had seen no female defenders, but she had also seen no male skyhunters or healers. Their society seemed to be highly rigid in its sexual caste system. She didn't feel she would be comfortable living with the leonin any more than Slobad had been when he lived here.

During the feast, Raksha made the mistake of asking Slobad about the golem. The goblin spent the rest of the meal telling the leonin how he had fixed the golem, going into minute detail about welding and reconnecting metal sinew. "I do everything, huh?" he said. "But blasted pile of metal lay lifeless. Even kick a few times, but nothing help. Not even kicking, huh?"

"But Glissa told us that you brought the metal man back to life just in time to save you both," said Raksha in between bites. He was obviously enjoying the tale more than Glissa.

Slobad beamed. Glissa thought he was going to jump onto one of the platters as he continued. "Amazing thing happen," said Slobad, waving his arms. "Amazing. I crouch behind golem. Reaper stomping around chimney. Slobad notice Dross oozing from golem's ear. Open golem's head; clean out Dross. Eyes snap open and look at Slobad, huh? Amazing. Just clean Dross. All there was to it."

"But," said Raksha, "Glissa informed us that it didn't speak until it saw this . . . this serum?"

"That's right," said Slobad. It say 'Memnarch.' We not know what it means, huh? Maybe golem's old owner. Maybe where it from, huh? Could be robed figure. We not know, and golem not say more, huh? Strange—"

Glissa interrupted. "Whatever 'Memnarch' means," she said, "it must have some connection to the serum. We need to find out what it is and how it's tied to both of us."

"We shall talk to Ushanti about it," said Raksha.

\* \* \* \* \*

Raksha led Glissa into the smoky chamber of the seer while Slobad retired to his room to tinker with the golem—at Raksha's gentle urging. The female healers met them at the door once again. Both bowed immediately when they saw Raksha. When they rose again, Glissa felt their steely gazes rest on her. Neither looked happy to see the elf. Glissa thought she saw a glint of something other than hate in Rishan's eyes as their gaze met, but it might have just been the smoke.

"Welcome, Kha, to the chamber of Ushanti," said Rishan, bowing low. "We are honored by your presence."

Raksha waved her up. "Rise, Rishan," he said. "We played in the square together as cubs. You need not bow to us."

Rishan straightened, but Glissa thought the young healer looked uncomfortable with the special treatment from her Kha. She turned abruptly and led them through the maze of curtains back to Ushanti's cauldron. Upon seeing her ruler, Ushanti dropped a handful of sand back into its bowl and hobbled over to greet them.

"Ah, Glissa," she said. "We knew you were coming. You have something to show us, don't you?" Ushanti held out her hand.

Glissa noticed Ushanti again showed no reverence to Raksha, and she did not trust the healer, but she had no choice. The serum was the only connection she had to the robed figure and the death of her family. She needed Ushanti's help.

"How did you know I was coming with this?" asked the elf as she pulled out the vial.

"Mother has been in a trance since you left," said Rishan. "She just returned from the fire this morning, saying you had come back."

"Did your vision provide anything that might help us against this new enemy?" asked Raksha.

"We have seen much but understand little of the events that are coming," said Ushanti. She took the vial from Glissa and held it up, examining it in the light of the brazier. "The fate of the world resides within these vials. We are caught up in a maelstrom we cannot control."

"Speak sense, woman," snapped Raksha.

"We cannot." Ushanti opened the vial and stared at the serum, as if looking into the depths of a blue sea. "The fire provides only glimpses of the truth." She dipped a claw into the blue liquid and brought it up to her lips.

Ushanti's tongue snaked out and touched the glistening claw. Suddenly her eyes widened and her dark pupils shrank to pinpoints. "We can tell you this, my young ruler," said Ushanti in a strange, stilted voice. "Your rule shall see the end of this world unless the elf dies. She may not destroy the world, but she will become the instrument of the one who does."

"Ushanti," said Glissa, looking straight into the old leonin's wide, white eyes, "I don't know that I believe your visions, but I do not wish to destroy this world. Is there any way I can stop this?"

"Die," said Ushanti. "Die before the end. It is the only way we see."

The room was heavy with silence.

"Is there no way to defeat this enemy?" asked Raksha at last.

"His power is older than the Glimmervoid, older than the Tangle and the Mephidross," said Ushanti. Her words began to slur. Her head rolled back until she stared at the smoky ceiling. "Only a power older than the world can stop him."

"What's his name?" asked Glissa. "Is it Memnarch? Does that name mean anything?"

Ushanti fell forward. Glissa caught the old leonin and grabbed the vial before it spilled to the floor. Raksha picked up Ushanti, lifting her as easily as he did his shield. Glissa replaced the stopper on the vial, while the Kha carried the healer through the curtains, followed by an agitated Rishan.

When the two leonin returned, Glissa asked, "Will she be all right?"

"She needs rest," said Rishan. She was wringing her paws and darting looks over her shoulder toward the back room. "Somehow that blue liquid brought on another trance. In her weakened state, she could not handle the strain."

"I need to know where this liquid came from," said Glissa, "and who she saw in that vision. Will she be able to help us?"

"So you believe her now?" asked Rishan, her eyes betraying her anger. Her eyes sought Raksha's and softened. "Come back tomorrow. Once Mother is stronger, I will ask her to help you."

Glissa was surprised by the young healer's change, but glancing from her to Raksha, she began to understand. The two young leonin had eyes only for each other.

\* \* \* \* \*

Shouts invaded Glissa's sleep. She was dreaming of the clearing she had glimpsed in her last flare. Elves were screaming as they fell into the pool of light. She could see them falling but couldn't reach them. The screams grew louder as they fell farther down into the white hole. She strained at the edge, trying to get her fingertips a little closer to the falling elves. Then she, too, was falling.

She awoke on the metal floor next to the soft bed, the blankets tangled around her body. The shouting continued. After a moment, she realized the screams came from outside her room. She stumbled to her feet, grabbing her boots and sword. When she opened the door, the elf was almost knocked down by a group of warriors rushing past, pulling on armor and shields. Glissa rubbed the sleep from her eyes.

"What's going on?" she shouted at a retreating soldier.

"We're under attack."

Glissa pulled on her boots and followed the soldiers into the main courtyard. Warriors lined the wall already, spears at the ready. Raksha stood in the center of the line, his battle mask covering his face. Glissa stamped her feet into her boots and ran to his side.

"Is it the nim?" she asked.

"No," came the booming reply. Raksha's voice seemed amplified through the mask. It was odd to hear his voice but not see his mouth move. "Our pteron riders skirmished with silver raptors before the first moon rose. Only a single rider returned alive. The beasts have followed. Look there!"

He pointed toward the rising red moon. Glissa saw specks in the halo of the moon's light. They grew as she watched. In a minute, she could see light glinting off their wings. A second later she heard an unholy wail that sounded like claws scraping against metal.

Glissa raised her sword and waited for the beasts to arrive. She tried to gauge their distance, but it was impossible to see the birds clearly by the light of the red moon. The hair on the back of her neck began to tingle just before a bolt of blue lightning streaked across the sky, hurled by the lead bird. The bolt blasted into the wall down the line. A leonin warrior screamed as metal ruptured in front of him, sending him to his death over the damaged wall.

Glissa's hair tingled again, and another bolt screamed through the air. The lightning struck a warrior, blasting a hole through his chest and continuing into the floor of the courtyard behind him. Bolt after bolt arced through the air, and the leonin soldiers scrambled away from the walls.

Glissa and Raksha held their ground. The elf felt another tingle on her neck and looked up. She saw a dot instead of a line. The bolt was headed straight toward her and Raksha. She dived to the side, knocking the leonin ruler to the ground and landing on top of him. The lightning exploded into the metal cobbles behind them, melting the silver and rupturing the floor.

Glissa rolled off Raksha and searched the skies for the attackers, but the silver-winged creatures had already flown by. She could see them now, but none were close enough for her sword. Their tails and wings looked as if they would be more at home in water than in air. Their serpentine tails ended in a vertical blade or barb that seemed to act as a rudder. As one, the flock flipped their tails to the side, sending them into a gentle turn. Their slender wings remained stiff, glinting in the red rays of the rising moon. But it was the creatures' heads that riveted Glissa. There were no eyes, no mouths, just a blue globe that seemed to pulse with energy.

She had seen these creatures before. They were the artifacts Geth had spoken of. They were the silver birds she had seen hovering over the robed figure in the Mephidross.

Raksha stood and called out, "Spears! Now!"

A dozen spears flew toward the retreating beasts. More than half hit their mark, piercing wings and tails, but only one of the winged horrors was brought down. The spear Raksha tossed struck one creature's bulbous head. The globe exploded, showering the courtyard with shards of glass. The body of the beast smashed into a wall, crashing through to the chamber beyond.

The silver creatures completed their turn and swept down for another attack. Glissa's hair began to tingle again.

"Look out!" she cried.

Bolts slammed into the ground. Glissa sheathed her sword and grabbed one of the spears. She aimed for the closest creature and threw, but the spear fell far short of the target.

The creatures veered off again, never nearing the ground. Raksha's troops threw their spears at the retreating birds. While their spears flew straighter, none of them had the strength to pierce the metal hide of their attackers.

"I cannot fight them from here!" shouted Glissa to Raksha. "I feel useless here on the ground. Where's that pteron that returned?"

"There," said Raksha, gesturing, "but take care."

Glissa ran around the courtyard to the stairs. She saw Slobad peeking out from a doorway. "Get the golem," she called. "Protect Raksha."

She bounded up the stairs three at a time. When she reached the pteron, she leaped onto its wing, slapped its beak back when it snapped at her, and climbed into the saddle.

She dug her feet into the bird's back as she had seen the riders do. The pteron walked off the ledge. As they plummeted, Glissa realized she had no idea how to pull from a dive. She pulled back on the reins, and the pteron's head lifted up. A moment later, the bird's wings flapped, and they leveled off.

Hoping she could control the pteron, the elf looped around toward the top of the tower in a wide arc. She scanned the skies for the blue-globed birds. The flock had turned and was heading back toward the tower. Glissa yanked on the reins and kicked the pteron's side again to spur it on. The great raptor flapped its huge wings. She was gaining but wouldn't arrive in time. The silver-winged creatures unleashed their blue lightning again toward the courtyard. Glissa saw a half dozen explosions. Leonin scattered.

Raksha stood his ground, spear in hand. At the last moment, he flung the weapon. It impaled a diving attacker just as the blue globe flashed. Lightning crackled along the surface of the globe and back along the creature's sinewy spine. The beast stopped for a moment in mid-air, engulfed in blue energy, then exploded. Shards rained down on the courtyard. Glissa saw the golem step in front of Raksha just as the debris reached the parapet. Glass shattered across the metal man's large chest.

Glissa spurred her mount on as she came up behind the ascending attackers. She leaned forward over the pteron's shoulder and swiped with her sword at the last flyer in the phalanx, cutting through its metallic wing and slicing into the tail. The injured beast spun out of control, and she pulled on the reins to guide the pteron up to the next one in line. Just as she came into range for another strike, the flock flipped their tails in unison and began a steep dive.

The metallic creatures shifted their silver wings and rolled over, turning back toward Taj Nar. Glissa yanked on the reins, but under her inexperienced control the pteron was too clumsy and slow to follow. The flock easily pulled ahead of her. As she dived after them, the silver flyers let loose another volley of lightning.

Only half of them fired, though. Before Glissa could wonder why, the other four broke from their dive and began climbing again. Glissa followed the rest of the flock but kept her eye on this new group. They rose until they were directly over her, then tilted their wings to roll and attack her from above.

Glissa kicked the pteron to spur it on, leaning forward to push its nose into a dive. She needed speed. She knew she couldn't out-maneuver those lightning bolts. She headed straight for Taj Nar at blinding speed. She had one chance, and she wasn't even sure she could get the pteron to do what she needed, but she had no choice. One bolt of lighting would shred the pteron *and* her if they got close enough to use it.

The elf maneuvered the pteron back and forth, cursing the creature every time it turned too far. Ahead of her she could see a small break between buildings on the far side of the courtyard. Behind her four sets of silver wings still followed. They were getting dangerously close. Glissa kicked the pteron one last time and flattened herself against the back of the beast. They hurtled toward a narrow gap between the buildings. At the last moment, Glissa pulled back hard on the reins and jammed her feet into the pteron's shoulders to force the beast to fold in its wings.

They sailed through the tight opening, the wingtips of the pteron just scratching both walls as it skidded through the passage. Glissa glanced back. The creatures following her frantically whipped their tales back and forth, trying desperately to avoid the walls. It was going to work!

Glissa looked forward again and screamed. Rishan had stepped from a doorway just ahead of the pteron.

"Get back!" she shouted.

It was too late. The pteron's wing knocked Rishan off her feet as they raced past her. Glissa rolled back over the tail of the pteron, but the bird's momentum carried her into the courtyard. She scrambled to her feet and ran back, but the globe-headed flyers were already in the passage. They bounced off the walls as they tried to fly through side by side. The lead beasts slammed into each other, shattering both globes in the impact.

The entire passageway exploded in a roar of blue flames that sent Glissa flying back into the courtyard. She slammed into the legs of Dakan's statue and rolled to the ground, stunned. Through the haze of her ringing ears she heard two more explosions. Her tactic had worked. She had killed all four beasts. But at what price?

Wearily Glissa pushed herself back up and ran to the doorway at the edge of the passage. Flames still licked at the walls, but the elf ignored them. She shielded her eyes with her metallic forearms and pushed her way past the flames. Her arms and legs felt like they were on fire, but she kept going, coughing as black smoke threatened to choke her lungs. She bumped into something soft in the smoke and dropped to her knees. It was Rishan. Glissa grabbed the young healer's shoulders and pulled her from the fire, but one glance as the smoke cleared told her there was no hope. All that remained of Ushanti's daughter was a charred corpse.

Glissa sat holding Rishan's blistered head in her lap. Tears welled up in her eyes and cascaded down her cheeks. She knew she should tell Raksha, knew there was still a battle to be won, but she couldn't move. She couldn't leave the young healer alone. She couldn't face Raksha now that she had brought death to Taj Nar.

A cheer erupted from behind her. She looked up to see the remaining beasts winging their way back into the crimson light of the red moon. Glissa knew the cheer would soon turn to tears, but she couldn't avoid her responsibilities any longer. The elf sobbed softly as she picked up the blackened body of Rishan and carried it into the courtyard toward Raksha.

# CHAPTER 12

# CHUNTH

"We believe you should leave now," said Raksha after the service. His shoulders were slumped, and his head hung low. He looked far less imposing than when Glissa had first met him at the gates . . . but that was a lifetime ago.

In a ritual of fire held in the courtyard, they had offered the body of Rishan and the warriors who died that morning to the yellow moon. The leonin howled while the bodies turned to ash, but the sound was not jubilant like the noon ritual the day before. These were wails of sorrow. Glissa, Slobad, and the golem stood in the burnt-out passage, well away from the throng of leonin crowded around the statue of Dakan and the ever-burning flame.

"I think you are right," said Glissa.

The Kha's eyes looked vacant, as if he were lost and looking for his way home. She was surprised he hadn't tossed them out the gate already.

"I am sorry for your loss." There was more she wanted to say, but she knew none of it would matter.

"Farewell, Glissa," Raksha said. "You will always be welcome here."

Glissa hesitated a moment, then hugged the large leonin. Raksha stood impassive. Glissa's tears welled up again.

"I shall not return," she said. "Not until the danger that follows me is gone. Not until I have found the one responsible for Rishan's death and made him pay."

Ushanti emerged from behind the Kha. "You are the one responsible, elf!" screamed the seer. She glared at Glissa with a rage the elf had never before seen in anyone's eyes. "You killed my daughter just as you will kill us all!"

She slapped Glissa across the face. Blood streamed from a long gash on the elf's cheek, mixing with tears. Ushanti raised her arm again, and Glissa saw blood dripping from the old seer's claws.

Ushanti's claws stopped an inch from Glissa's gut. Raksha held the seer's wrist and pushed her gently away from Glissa into the arms of a warrior.

"No," he said. "No more bloodshed."

Ushanti struggled against the grip of the warrior. "You!" she screamed. "You would welcome this elf back into your house? Death follows her like a plague. You'll see. You will all see!"

"We are the Kha here, Ushanti," growled Raksha. "You would do well to remember that." He motioned to the warrior holding Ushanti, and the leonin pulled the old seer back into her quarters.

"Don't blame her," said Glissa. She wiped the blood and tears from her cheek. "She has every right to hate me."

She looked at Slobad and the golem. "We should . . . we should leave. I'm sorry." She wiped her eyes and crossed the courtyard. Slobad followed with the golem. Neither spoke until they were out of sight of Taj Nar.

\* \* \* \* \*

"Where do we go from here, huh?" asked Slobad.

"I don't know," replied Glissa glumly. She had been walking aimlessly since they left. She had no idea if she was headed toward the Mephidross, Slobad's old lair, or somewhere else entirely. "The serum is our only link to the robed figure, but Ushanti won't help us with that now. I don't blame her, but we need to know where the serum came from."

"Krark cult have secret place, huh?" said Slobad. "We stay with them while I fix the golem. Fix the golem and he tell us what 'Memnarch' means. Maybe Memnarch make serum, huh? We find Memnarch, he tell us who robed figure is, huh? Maybe Memnarch is robed figure."

"Maybe Memnarch is the golem's name or a pet he used to play with," said Glissa sourly.

They walked on in silence. She stopped at the edge of a field of razor grass and glanced back at the goblin. He was perched on the golem's shoulder, staring at the ground. "Do you think you can get him to talk?" she asked, gesturing toward the golem.

"Just needs good cleaning," said Slobad, dully.

Glissa thought for a moment. "So, what do you need? Just some time to clean him?"

Slobad nodded. "'Dross muck up everything inside, huh? I think the golem actually fixing himself when we rest. Parts I clean fix themselves." He started to brighten. "Amazing, huh? Slobad never see machine like it. Fixes itself. Just can't clean self. Dumb, huh? But smart, too."

"You need time to clean," said Glissa.

Slobad nodded.

"Somewhere safe from the nim, the levelers, and globe-headed, silver birds."

Slobad nodded again.

"And I need answers from someone who knows as much about this world as Ushanti."

Slobad started to nod, then cocked his head and looked at Glissa. "You know place, huh?"

Glissa nodded. "Tel-Jilad, the Tree of Tales. It's impregnable. No leveler has ever entered—and many have tried. There are only two entrances. One is heavily guarded, and the other is a secret known only by the trolls—and me. Besides, it's time Chunth told me everything he knows about this destiny he's thrust on me."

Glissa almost smiled as she climbed into the golem's broad hands. "Slobad," she said, "I'm going home."

\* \* \* \* \*

It took them almost three rotations to get to the edge of the Tangle. Shortly after Slobad turned the golem around to head toward the Tangle, Glissa spotted silver specks circling in the sky ahead of them.

"We have trouble." She pointed at the flyers.

"They looking for us, huh?" said Slobad. "Bad if they find us. Very bad, huh?"

"We need to hide," said the elf. "I don't know if they're looking for us or not, but we can't fight or outrun them here. It's too flat and open."

Slobad guided the golem back over a small hill. Glissa and the goblin slid down to the ground and lay flat against the bare metal hill. The golem dropped to the ground next to them. Glissa peeked over the hill and watched the silver flyers. They did seem to be searching for something, snaking their way back and forth across the sky.

Their flight was bringing the flock toward the travelers. Glissa turned to Slobad. "They're coming closer!"

Slobad pointed down the hill. "Follow Slobad, huh?" he said. "We hide in old leonin lair." The goblin began to crawl, followed by the golem.

Glissa glanced back at the flyers again, then scrambled down the hill. They backtracked across the rolling terrain, keeping low to the ground and skirting hills until they came to a mound Glissa recognized as a leonin den. It looked like all the others she had seen—a rounded mound of metal topped by a patch of razor grass that protected an opening.

"How do you know it's abandoned?" she asked. "It looks like all the other lairs we've seen, and we never see any leonin when we pass anyway."

"Razor grass overgrown on top, huh?" said Slobad. "Crazy elf not see that?"

Glissa looked at the patch of sharp blades on the top of the mound. It looked like all the others to her. She shrugged and followed Slobad up the slope. At the top, she glanced around to find the silver birds. They were still making their way methodically across the sky. Glissa pulled out her sword and cut a path through the razor grass.

"No straight lines, huh?" said Slobad. "Leonin cut narrow paths through grass. Hard for enemies to attack. Look natural."

Glissa nodded. A wide swath through the grass would surely draw the attention of their pursuers. She began to cut a narrow, winding path through the grass toward the gash in the top of the hill that was the lair's entrance. It was slow work, and she did not have time to be careful. She cut her legs several times when razor blades fell in her path as she moved forward. The party finally reached the entrance and climbed down into the lair.

It did not gleam like Taj Nar had, but Glissa could see remnants of past splendor. The floor bore an inlaid pattern of the leonin sun, and a large table in the corner appeared to be made of gold. Most of the other furnishings had been removed, but there was a large fire pit beneath the opening with an odd, six-legged spit standing over it. The spit didn't look strong enough to hold a pot.

"Mirror-holder, huh?" said Slobad, pointing to the spit. "Leonin put mirrors over pit when sun up in sky. Lights up lair. Mirrors come off after sundown, huh? Light fire to keep dark away at night. They like dark less than you, huh?"

"Well, we need the dark now," Glissa grunted. "We'll stay here today and travel at night. I just hope those flying horrors can't see in the dark any more than I can."

Slobad nodded.

\* \* \* \* \*

For several rotations they made their way across the Glimmervoid under the stars, resting in abandoned lairs while the moons were up. Each morning and evening Glissa looked for the globe-headed birds. They circled the sky, snaking their way across the Glimmervoid, searching. As the travelers grew closer to the Tangle, however, they left the four moons and the birds behind. Glissa, Slobad, and the golem entered the Tangle well after the last moon set on the fourth rotation. They had walked most of the afternoon. Glissa was glad for the night. They would need the cover of darkness to smuggle the golem through the Tangle.

"Can he climb?" she asked.

"You know as much about golem as me, huh?" said Slobad. "He do many things. Maybe he can climb, too."

Glissa glared at the goblin and pointed to the Tangle tree beside them.

"Okay, okay. I ask him. Take it easy, huh?" From his perch on the metal man's shoulders, Slobad pointed to the tree and said, "Golem, climb."

The golem reached forward and grabbed the metal trunk. Spikes sprang out from his fingertips and feet, and he moved up the tree. He was almost as fast as the levelers, even with Slobad clinging to his back. The goblin clung tightly as the giant steadily mounted the tree. He eventually slung his pack over the golem's head and slipped his torso under the strap. Glissa used the holes left behind by the golem's passing to climb up behind the odd-looking duo.

Once in the trees, the elf led Slobad and the golem through the heights of the Tangle. She used unfamiliar routes, since she was unsure whether the narrower spires could handle the golem's weight. As well, she wanted to avoid terraces where elves tended to congregate after the evening meal. The result was that a trip that would normally have taken her an hour occupied most of the night. As the sky began to brighten she saw a patrol of Tel-Jilad Chosen pass beneath them. She ducked into the nearest opening and froze. She had come home.

The debris had been cleared, including the remains of the leveler she had destroyed, but Glissa could still see dark stains on the floor. She breathed hard and fell back against the wall behind her.

"You okay, huh?" asked Slobad.

The golem crawled through the entrance, and Slobad slipped off his back. "Out of breath? Want to ride golem? Slobad think he carry both of us, huh?"

"Check to see if the patrol has gone by yet," she said. "I'll be okay." Glissa closed her eyes and tried to keep the demons from her head. She was still panting when Slobad came back.

"All clear, huh?" he said. "See nobody in tree or below. You okay? We go now, huh?"

Glissa took a deep breath and blew it out slowly. She nodded and moved toward the door, keeping her eyes shut until she felt the cool air of the Tangle on her face. They didn't see anyone else the rest of the way to the Tree of Tales. By they time they reached the terrace above the secret entrance, the moons were cresting above the horizon.

"Down here," said the elf. "We're almost there. Any sign of our robed friend or his flying spies?"

"Slobad not see anything but blasted light fruit since we come here. Why live in such dark wood, then light it with crazy fruit, huh? No wonder elves can't see in dark."

Glissa chuckled. "I know you're tired, Slobad," she said. "I promise you a hard bed in a nice dark room is just beyond this terrace."

She jumped down to the terrace that held so many memories for her and jogged over to the trunk. The vorrac horn was still lodged in the knothole. The golem dropped to the terrace behind Glissa as she felt around for the catch within the knothole. After a few minutes, she heard a metallic click, then a grinding sound as the door opened. She slipped inside to the landing and waved Slobad after.

The goblin dropped off the back of his metal friend and led the golem through the door. It was a tight fit, but after some jostling, the golem crawled through the doorway. Glissa released the catch, and the door slid closed behind them.

"Stay here," she said. "I don't want to give the old troll a seizure."

She bounded up the tunnel to the chamber outside Chunth's bedroom. She was just about to knock on the wall that hid his room, when from behind her came shouts of trolls and the unmistakable sound of Slobad's fire tube igniting. She heard the metallic scrape of weapons being drawn.

Glissa turned back toward Chunth's door, but it was already open.

"Good morning, Chunth," she said as the stooped figure of a troll appeared in the doorway. "I've returned."

"In much the same way you left, I see," said the old troll, gazing down the tunnel. "Do come in. We have much to discuss, and each day brings the convergence that much closer."

"I brought friends," said Glissa, pointing down the steps. "I don't want them harmed."

"It will sort itself out, young one," said Chunth. He chuckled. "I will send word to put your friends into guest quarters." He moved as if to put an arm around her shoulders.

"Hold on there, old one!" growled Glissa. She evaded his embrace. "You don't get to play the doting uncle just yet."

She stalked into the room and dropped onto Chunth's chair facing the door.

"You kidnapped me and allowed my family to die. Before we discuss anything, you are going to tell me why that was necessary and who is trying to kill me."

Chunth called down the steps, "Stand down. They are guests. Give them quarters and anything else they need. I am not to be disturbed." He turned and entered the room, closing the door behind him. "I'm sorry, my girl," he said. "What did you say?"

"My parents. Why did they have to die?"

"I told you before, Glissa," the old troll said sadly. "You are the most important person on Mirrodin. We had to keep you safe. I am sorry your family was killed, but if you had been asleep when the levelers came, you would have died with them."

"You mean you hoped to fool the assassin into thinking I was dead," spat Glissa, "by letting my parents and sister get torn to pieces by those machines."

Chunth hesitated just long enough that the elf knew she was right.

"We were merely trying to save you."

"Liar!"

Chunth walked over to the table. The light from the gelfruit illuminated the leathery skin of the old troll's face. His eyes glistened in the light, and Glissa thought she saw a tear roll down one cheek. "Glissa," he said. "I am sorry about your family. I did what I had to do to save our world. The fate of all rests on you now."

Glissa shook her head. It was almost too much to take in. "Why? What's so special about me?"

"You need to know everything now."

"Yes," said Glissa slowly. "I do."

The troll sat across from her and poured them both a cup of water. "You are a nexus, Glissa," he said after taking a sip. "A nexus of great power waiting to be unleashed."

"What in the flare are you talking about?"

"Precisely," said Chunth. "Your flares. They have been unusual, haven't they?"

"How do you know that?"

"It is one of the signs of your power," said the troll. "Tell me about them."

Glissa shook her head angrily. "I don't have time for this. *Someone is trying to kill me!*"

"This is important," said Chunth. "No one can hurt you here. Tell me about your flares. Then I will explain what I can."

Glissa sighed. "Fine," she said. "Lately, they've been the same scene each time, but I've never seen this place before. I'm in a strange forest that's both soft and bright. There are no moons, but there is a large . . . sun—a word I'd never heard until I left the Tangle. My clothes are different. *I'm* different. My arms and legs are all fleshy."

"How does it end?" asked Chunth. He seemed unsurprised by her description. Of course, he had no metal on his body, either, so maybe it wasn't so strange to him.

"I'm drawn to a clearing. There is some strange energy glowing in the middle. Elves are all around me, walking toward the energy."

"Then it flashes?"

"Yes," said Glissa. She stared at the old troll. "How did you know? Trolls don't have flares."

"Those are racial memories, Glissa," said Chunth. "You are connected to the elves and to the mana of the forest at a primal level. Your flares show you visions not of your own life but of the life of your people . . . even of their life before the Tangle."    .

"Before the Tangle?" She laughed. "There was nothing before the Tangle."

"You know that is not true, don't you?" said Chunth. "You have seen the green forest, the bright yellow sun, and the vine-covered elves."

"So you've had these visions as well?"

"No," said Chunth. "The memories I have of the time before the Tangle are my own. I was there. I remember my forest. I remember the world of the trolls before the Tangle."

Glissa was silent for a moment as she fought to absorb this.

"And the energy?" she asked. "The flash of white light? Do you remember that?"

"Yes. It was different for the trolls but the same as well."

"Don't start talking in riddles again, old one," she scolded. "Speak clearly, or I swear I'll go live with the goblins."

"I do not know what the ball of energy was," said Chunth, "or how it worked. It changed the world of the trolls. We exchanged our world for his world . . . this world."

Glissa caught the swift change. "*His* world?" Glissa remembered something Slobad had said about the golems. They were from before the time of elves and goblins. She looked at Chunth. "Do you mean Memnarch's world?"

Chunth stared back at Glissa, the cup of water halfway between the table and his mouth. "Where did you hear that name?" he asked at last. "Did it come to you in one of your flares?"

"No," said Glissa. She had finally wrested control of the conversation back from the troll and felt an odd sense of triumph at having done so. "The golem said it when he saw this." She pulled the vial from her boot sheath and placed it on the table. "Who or what is Memnarch? Is that who's trying to kill me? Whoever made this serum used it to make the nim attack us."

Chunth dropped his cup on the floor and picked up the vial of serum. "I never should have let you go into the world alone," he said softly. "Listen, Glissa. You possess a power—a gift—within you that some wish to use for their own ends. If you are not careful—"

"Yes, I know," interrupted Glissa. "End of the world, death to us all. I heard the same thing from an old leonin seer. I expected a more direct answer from you. Why save me from the levelers if all I can bring to this world is death?"

"Death is not your gift," said Chunth. "I told you, you are a nexus of power. You must learn to harness that power before the convergence or it may well *be* the end of the world."

"Then teach me, O wise one," said Glissa. "Show me how to use my power, and I will save the world. That's what you want, isn't it?"

"It is not as easy as that," said Chunth. An urgency in his voice made Glissa suspend her sarcasm and listen. "You may not know the right thing to do when the time comes. You don't understand."

"Help me understand," said Glissa softly. "Look, I know you sent me out with this sword to try to save my family. I'm grateful for that. But I need some answers. Who is Memnarch? What is the serum? Who is trying to kill me? How do I stop all of this?"

Chunth took a deep breath, settled down into the chair, and closed his eyes. "All right. No more riddles," he said. "I will tell you what I know. The person behind this must be a vedalken."

"Vedalken?"

"They dwell on the Quicksilver Sea, past the Mephidross. The vedalken harvest the serum you have there. They crave power and are willing to do anything to gain it."

"Even kill," said Glissa.

"Oh yes," replied Chunth. His thick lips curled in an unpleasant smile. "The vedalken have killed millions over the years . . . maybe more. This vial of serum alone cost the lives of a score of blinkmoths."

"What are blinkmoths?"

"They are what you see at night. You imagine they are the stars above and the fireflies that roam the Tangle. They are living creatures, lighting the sky with their serum-filled bodies, raining water down upon the land. For hundreds of cycles the vedalken have harvested them."

"Why?"

"The vedalken drink the serum to gain knowledge of the world and knowledge of Memnarch," said Chunth. His eyes grew distant. "I, too, drank the serum, once. Long ago, when the Tree of Tales had but a few runes etched into its base, I learned of the blinkmoths and many other secrets of this world. It is an amazing liquid. It unlocks the knowledge of the world, its creation, and its creator. A taste provides visions of the mysteries of the cosmos. A vial such as this can begin a journey toward unlocking those mysteries."

"That sounds wonderful," said Glissa. "Why not use the serum to help us live better lives? We could learn to control the levelers, make it rain more often, begin to master this planet. . . . Oh! I see."

"Yes," said Chunth. "You see. Where does it end? Even the most altruistic among us would eventually use the power for personal ends. That path inevitably leads to ruin. Power and greed together are always destructive, and the price for the power is too high. The vedalken have murdered blinkmoths by the millions to attain their current stature."

"Are these vedalken a tall, robed people with domes for heads?"

Chunth nodded. "They were not always as you see them now. Their race has evolved far beyond any of the others on Mirrodin."

"Because of the serum?"

Chunth nodded again.

"But why do the vedalken want me dead?" the elf persisted. "If they have all this power, what do they want with me?

"That I do not know," said Chunth. "They are playing at being gods. They have the knowledge of the ancients but not the power to wield it. Perhaps they fear your power. Perhaps they wish to harness it. I do not know."

"Or perhaps they just want to stop me from destroying the world," said Glissa drily. "If Ushanti of the leonin had the power, she would kill me. What of this Memnarch? Is he the leader of the vedalken?"

Chunth looked weary. His eyes were closed and he was rubbing his temples with his fists. Glissa wasn't sure he'd even heard her questions. Perhaps she should let the old troll rest and begin again later. At last he spoke.

"For many hundreds of cycles now, I have tried to keep the elves and trolls safe in the Tangle. I kept knowledge of the blinkmoths a secret to prevent our races from falling victim to the allure of their power. I erased all mention of the old world from the histories so the elves and trolls would not search for their pasts. But you need to know of Memnarch. You need to know the truth."

The metal door scraped across the floor behind Chunth, and the old troll turned. Glissa looked up. Another troll stood in the open doorway. It was not one of the guards. He wore the robes of an elder.

Chunth barked, "I left instructions not to be disturbed. What is so urgent?"

The troll in the doorway did not speak. Instead he lifted his metal-clad arm and turned his wrist over. Glissa could see something cupped in his fist—a blue orb that gleamed in the dim light of the gelfruit.

"What is that?" demanded Chunth. "What are you doing?"

"She must die," responded the elder in a faint voice. He opened his fist, and the orb flashed. A bolt of blue lightning streaked across the room. Glissa dived off her chair as Chunth jumped to his feet in front of her. The lightning slammed into the old troll's chest, knocking him back onto the table.

He crashed to the floor, taking the table, cups, and gelfruit with him. The vial of serum flew from his hand. Glissa tried to move, but her foot was pinned beneath the broken table. She stared helplessly as the elder in the doorway held the orb out again, his palm facing Glissa.

Nothing happened.

He shook the orb, trying to make it work. His eyes strayed to the floor and widened when he saw the vial of serum. Glissa pulled frantically on her foot but could not free it. The elder smiled a toothy grin, scooped up the vial of serum, and turned and fled down the tunnel. Glissa looked from the empty doorway down to Chunth, sprawled atop her leg. A huge hole penetrated his chest, and he was gasping for air.

"Glissa . . ." he wheezed. "I must . . . tell you. . . ."

Glissa lifted the old troll's fleshy head and cradled it in her arms.

"Don't speak," she said. "I'll get help." With an agonizing jerk, she pulled her foot free.

"No time," he rasped. "You need . . . to know."

"What is it?" said Glissa. She could feel tears on her face.

"The world," said Chunth. Blood trickled from his mouth as he spoke. "Not . . . what it seems. It . . . is . . ."

"What?"

"Hollow."

Chunth's eyes closed, and his head sagged into Glissa's arms.

# CHAPTER 13

# ASSASSIN

Glissa laid Chunth's head down and stood, testing her ankle. Chunth was gone. Another in a growing line of deaths meant for her. There was only one person who could tell her why. She sprinted down the tunnel after the assassin, screaming.

"Guards, guards," she shouted. "Chunth has been murdered."

When she reached the secret door, guards surrounded her. "Chunth is dead," she gasped. "An elder with a blue orb . . . did any of you see him come past you?"

Glissa turned and looked at the wall, searching for the catch that opened the secret door. Behind her, one of the guards was barking orders.

"You four, get the elders to safety," he snapped. "The rest of you escort the elf to her friends."

"No," screamed Glissa as she patted the wall. "We must find the elder. He killed Chunth. I told you. An elder killed Chunth, then ran down here."

The guard spun around to face her. "How do we know you didn't kill Chunth? You have attacked us before."

Glissa stared at him. He could have been one of the guards she had locked in Chunth's room the last time she was here. They all looked alike to her.

"Because if I had," she said slowly, "I wouldn't be screaming about it . . . and you would all be dead by now."

The guard swallowed hard and released her arm. "What did this elder look like?"

Glissa turned back to the secret door. She found the catch, but the door refused to open. "He was an old troll," she said over her shoulder. "He was carrying a blue orb that shoots lightning." She slammed the catch with the butt of her sword and swore. "Flare! Why won't this open?"

The guard reached over her shoulder. "The release is jammed."

Glissa bashed the hilt of her sword into the catch again, but it didn't budge. She slammed her shoulder into the door and even tried to slice through the tree with her sword. It was reinforced throughout. Nothing seemed to work.

"He's gone through here," she cried. "I need this open, now!"

The guard turned to the remaining guards. "Go out the main entrance. Climb the tree and open this door."

Glissa felt a scream welling up inside her and fought to keep it down. "That will take too long." She had a thought. "Where's the goblin?"

"A little ways down the tunnel," replied the guard.

"Slobad!" Glissa screamed as loudly as she could. "Golem! I need you!"

After a moment, she heard booming footsteps coming up the tunnel. When the metal man appeared around the bend, Glissa gasped. He was missing an arm.

"What happened?"

"That's what I ask you, huh?" said Slobad. "I cleaning the golem arm, then hear screaming, huh? What do you need? I thought this quiet place. Time for cleaning and sleeping." He paused and looked at Glissa. She was fuming and her face was stained with tears. "What wrong?"

"Chunth is dead," said Glissa quickly. "The assassin went through this door. Now it's stuck. Open it!"

The golem moved forward, and Glissa backed up to give him

room. The golem walked up to the door, pulled his arm back, and slammed his hand into it. The secret door flew away, landing on the terrace twenty feet away.

Glissa ran through the door, shouting at the guard. "The goblin will fix it later. Go to the elders. Protect them. Find out which one is missing."

\* \* \* \* \*

The elf looked around the terrace. Trolls were great climbers, but they weren't as agile as elves. Glissa was sure the elder wouldn't have jumped as she had so many nights ago. He either climbed onto the next terrace or took to the trunk. She checked the trunk first.

Recent claw marks led off the terrace around the trunk. Glissa curled her fingers and dug her claws into the tree, pulling herself around the tree as best she could. She was a decent climber but had never scaled the Tree of Tales before. She leaned in and sniffed the claw marks left behind by the elder to get his scent. She might not be as good a climber as a troll, but she was the best hunter in the Tangle.

Halfway around the tree, Glissa lost the scent. There were no claw marks above her, so the troll elder must have descended. The elf pulled her feet away from the tree and pressed in with her claws. They couldn't hold her weight, and she began to slide down the tree. Glissa dropped her head to see where she was going. It was a straight drop all the way down the tree. No terraces or spires impeded her path to the floor of the Tangle.

How unusual, thought Glissa. A troll escape route, perhaps?

She pulled her claws halfway from the grooves they were making and sped up. Nobody in the Tangle but me would be stupid enough to try this, she thought wryly.

As the elf neared the ground, she was nearly free-falling. The trunk was a blur as it flew past her. Glissa waited as long as she could, then dug her claws back in and slammed the soles of her boots into the trunk to slow her descent. Twenty feet from impact, she kicked off hard and released her claws to send her body flying away from the tree.

She timed the kick perfectly and flew straight toward the end of a curving spire. She grabbed, dug in her claws, and twirled around the tapering spire several times to bleed off momentum. She dropped the last ten feet to the Tangle floor and looked around for movement.

Footsteps sounded behind her, and she twirled, drew her sword, and swung. Kane dropped to the ground before he lost his head.

"Fine way to greet your best friend." He tried to turn over and get up, but his slagwurm-plate uniform made it impossible for him to bend at the waist.

"Kane, what are you doing here?" cried Glissa. She sheathed her sword and helped him to his feet.

"I was on guard duty at the main entrance. What are you doing here, and what in the flare is going on inside the Tree?"

"No time to explain, but I'm glad you're here. Did you see an elder pass by in the last few minutes?"

"Yes," said Kane calmly. "It was High Priest Strang."

Glissa looked at Kane. "How do you tell them apart?" she asked, then shook her head. "It doesn't matter. Help me find him."

"He was headed toward the Radix."

"Follow me," said Glissa. She trotted off toward the center of the Tangle. "We can't let him get away."

Kane ran to catch up with Glissa. "Why? What happened?"

"Strang killed Chunth," said Glissa, "and he stole something from me that I want back."

"Chunth?" gasped Kane, running beside his friend. "I thought he was a myth. The troll elite guards speak of him sometimes, but I've never seen him."

"How do you know Strang?" asked Glissa.

"I've been assigned to him a few times during rituals. It's a great honor to serve the High Priest. Strang practically runs Tel-Jilad."

Glissa and Kane dodged around either side of a rain barrel. Kane continued, "I can't believe Strang would kill anyone! He's the most respected elder in the Tree. He presides over the most important rituals. Why would he kill Chunth?"

"I don't know," said Glissa as they neared the Radix. She said nothing to Kane of Strang's attempt to kill her as well. The orb he had used made her neck tingle just like the spy-birds' attacks. Was Strang, like Geth, working for the vedalken? Chunth said he had kept the serum a secret from the trolls and the elves. How did Strang know about it? She turned these questions over in her mind as they ran.

"Power," she said at last. "It always comes down to power. Chunth had it and Strang wanted it."

* * * * *

Glissa stopped. They were at the edge of the Radix. She dodged behind a Tangle tree, pulling Kane close to her. She breathed in his musky scent as his face came close her hers. She had forgotten how good he smelled.

"Kane," she whispered, "I need your help. If Strang sees me, he'll run. Go in there and distract him. I'll take care of the rest."

Kane hesitated, his eyes darting to the ground. "He's an elder. The High Priest. Shouldn't the council take care of this?"

"They're not here," hissed Glissa. "Listen, you have to trust me. After he killed Chunth, Strang stole a vial from me. We can't let him drink what's in it. Believe me, after I get it back we'll take him back to the Tree of Tales and turn him over to the council. But we have to get him *now*."

Kane straightened his armored jerkin and looked at Glissa. For a moment she thought he was going to salute.

"Okay."

"Keep him occupied for a minute or two," said Glissa, "and be careful. He's a cornered animal."

Kane nodded, then turned and walked around the tree. Glissa climbed the trunk. She passed two sets of spires before moving around to the other side of the tree. She looked down into the Radix. Kane was talking to Strang. Glissa couldn't see the blue globe or the vial.

She dropped onto another spire that curved over the edge of the Radix and sprawled onto her stomach. Cautiously she inched her way out over the Radix, marveling, as she always did, at how barren it looked. The clearing was perfectly round and devoid of trees and gelfruit. She had never once seen a vorrac or any other animal inside it. The elves shunned the area as well, using it as a dump. Anything left on the ground there was gone the next morning.

Strang must be getting rid of his evidence, thought Glissa. Well, we'll see about that. As she inched out closer to the elf and the troll, Glissa could hear them talking.

"What is wrong?"

"It seems there has been an attack," said Kane. "That rogue elf, Glissa, attacked the Tree of Tales. You must come with me to safety."

Good, Kane. Glissa inched ever farther toward the end of the spire. Make him feel at ease.

"I will return as soon as I am finished here, Chosen one," said Strang. "You may return to your post now."

"My orders are to escort you to safety, High Priest," Kane insisted. "Please come with me now. Your life may be in danger."

He turned and walked away from Strang, leading the way. Glissa tensed, watching for the troll's reaction. He'd killed once already. He might do it again to cover his tracks.

Strang hesitated. Glissa saw him reach into his robes. Then the old troll followed Kane, who had stopped to wait for him. The pair came right toward her.

Come on, Kane, thought Glissa. Just a little bit farther.

As Kane passed, Glissa dropped off the spire, landing on Strang's hunched back, knocking him to the ground. She rolled to the side, jumped to her feet, and drew her sword, but Strang was just as fast. He regained his footing and sprang back a step. Glissa moved in on him, but the old troll surprised her again. With a quick swipe of his claws, he knocked the sword from her hand.

"Don't just stand there, Chosen one!" he shouted to Kane. "Defend your elder against this rogue elf!"

Kane jumped forward to cut off Glissa, pulling out his own blade as he moved in front of Strang. "I don't want to hurt you, Glissa," he said, "but you must be brought to the council to pay for your crimes."

Momentarily taken aback, Glissa saw him wink at her. "You know you're no match for me, Kane," she shouted at him. "Even without my sword I could always kick your Tel-Jilad Chosen face across the Tangle. Get out of my way."

Glissa lunged for Kane, and he brought his sword arm up to block her. She batted aside the arm and barreled into him. Kane staggered backward. He slammed the hilt of his sword into Strang's face, knocking the old troll back to the ground.

The troll assassin grabbed for the sword, but Kane rolled off just as Glissa dived on top of the elder, pinning him to the ground.

"Hold his arms down, Kane."

Strang clawed at Glissa's face and neck, but she held him down between her knees while she slapped away his attacks.

Kane grabbed for the elder's arms. He finally caught them both and slammed them onto the ground. Glissa reached inside the troll's robes and found the vial, still full of blue liquid, as well as the blue orb.

She brandished her find before the troll's staring eyes. "I don't need vedalken magic to kill, Strang," she said.

Fear and recognition sprang into Strang's eyes as she said the name. She had been right about where the troll had gotten his little toy. It was a blue globe, just like the heads of the silver birds that had attacked Taj Nar, like the birds she had seen with the robed vedalken at the Vault of Whispers.

"Nothing would make me happier than to snap your neck with my bare hands," she growled. "But I've promised your Chosen guard here to turn you over to the council. It's up to you: You can walk back to the Tree of Tales peacefully or die at my hands here in the Tangle. Which is it?"

"I am dead either way," said Strang finally.

"Fine by me," said the elf, reaching for his neck.

"No!" he cried.

Glissa rested her palms on either side of the troll's thick neck. "Tell me who paid you to kill me, and I might ask the council to let you live in exile."

There was another long pause before he said, "You were right. It was the vedalken."

"I want a name," snapped Glissa.

"He never said his name," muttered Strang.

"Then you can draw me a picture when we get back to Tel-Jilad. Now get up."

She climbed off the elder troll, making sure to kick him in the ribs as she rose. He'd be doubled over in pain all the way back to the Tree.

Kane pulled Strang to his feet, his sword pressed against the elder's back while Glissa retrieved her sword. "Why, Strang?" Kane asked as they moved through the Tangle.

"Chunth was too old to lead us anymore," said Strang. "He thought he could insulate the elves and the trolls from the entire world, but the world has much to offer to those willing to take a chance. What was one dead elf compared to a new golden age of power for the Tangle?"

"Their power comes at too high a price," said Glissa. "Chunth knew that."

"I don't understand," said Kane. "You were trying to kill Glissa? Why kill her if Chunth was the one in your way?"

"The vedalken said that she is a problem," said Strang. "She came too early. He needs more ti—"

The hair on the back of Glissa's neck began to tingle. She dived, knocking Kane over with her, just as a bolt of blue lightning shot across the Tangle. It streaked right through where she had been standing. Strang dropped to the ground beside them a moment later. A charred stump smoldered between his shoulders where his head used to be.

# CHAPTER 14

# ASSAULT

"What the flare was that?" shouted Kane.

"Don't talk!" replied Glissa. "Just run." She jumped up and pulled Kane to his feet.

The two elves raced into the Tangle. Rounding the next tree, they came face-to-globe with four of the flying constructs that had attacked Taj Nar.

"Split," shouted Glissa. She broke to the right. The tingling came again, and she dived to ground and rolled. Two blasts singed the ground next to her. Glissa came up, sword in hand, and swung at the first movement she saw. Her blade caught the silvery tail of one beast, slicing off the barbed end. The second creature banked left to avoid a Tangle tree and come back around, but the one she had cut couldn't make the sharp turn. It flipped its shortened tail to the left and lifted its right wing, but that wasn't enough. The beast smashed globe-first into the tree. An azure explosion nearly drove Glissa to the ground.

She turned to see how Kane was faring against the other two. He had dodged behind a tree. Glissa could see two scorch marks on the trunk but couldn't see the metallic birds anywhere.

"If you feel a tingle on your neck, dodge!" she shouted as she scanned for the returning flyer.

"Got it!" he called back. "More friends of yours come calling?"

"Just watch yourself," she replied. "This isn't a game. It's a hunt, and we're the prey."

The all-too-familiar tingling returned. Glissa dropped and rolled around the trunk, but the bolt didn't come. She heard two loud cracks from the other tree and knew the flyers had gone after Kane. The elf jumped to her feet and scrambled up the tree to the lowest spire. She crouched there and surveyed the forest again.

The the two flyers that had strafed Kane disappeared around another tree. He was still on the ground. Glissa scanned the trees and found the third flyer. It was heading straight for Kane. She screamed and launched from the spire toward the flying beast as it flew past her, but the silver-winged creature was faster than she realized. She had hoped to drive it to the ground, but instead she fell past. Desperate, she stretched out a hand and caught the beast by the tip of its tail.

Elf and flyer slammed into the ground. The creature's tail slipped from her grasp as she hit, so she dropped her sword and caught it with her other hand. Glissa rolled over with the beast and got both hands on it. It flailed in her grasp, flapping its wings and flipping its tail, trying to wriggle free. She wanted to slam it into the ground but was afraid it would explode. Instead, she fought to get to her feet while controlling the creature.

When she got to one knee, the beast flipped its tail again. Glissa lost her balance and stumbled back to the ground. When she looked up, Kane was standing beside her. His sword was raised, ready to stab the beast.

"Not the head," she screamed, but she was too late. Kane's sword slammed down into the beast's bulbous head. Glissa rolled to the side and covered her face as the globe exploded in a shower of electric energy.

She was spared the brunt of the blast, though her arms and legs were bloody from shards of glass. The elf scrambled to her feet and searched for her friend. She found him sprawled beneath a nearby tree, his sword lying in pieces nearby.

As she bent over his body, she felt the tingling return. The beasts were coming in fast, much faster than she had ever seen. They had evidently tired of playing with the agile elves and intended to end it once and for all. Glissa dodged away from her fallen friend and sprinted toward another tree just as twin bolts of lightning slammed into the ground behind her.

She had no idea how long until the next bolts would come and hoped she could reach the tree. The flyers gained on her with each step. She could hear their wings flapping behind her. They were ten feet back . . . eight . . . six. As Glissa reached the tree, she could feel the tingling build on the back of her neck. The blasts were coming.

Glissa jumped high into the air. Behind her the beasts spat bolts of lightning. She grasped a low-hanging spire and swung her legs up from their path. Her momentum carried her around the spire. She pulled her legs in to gain speed, then kicked them back out as she came around. Her feet slammed into the backs of the flyers, sending them careening toward the ground.

Glissa dropped and ducked behind the tree as both flyers hit the ground and exploded. She could hear glass shattering against the trunk. Her arms and legs quivered as the released energy washed past her. She peeked around the tree to make sure both creatures had crashed, then jumped up and ran back to Kane, picking up her fallen sword as she went by.

As she approached Kane's prone body, all the missed opportunities of her life flashed through Glissa's mind. Kane had been her best friend, the only person outside her family she remembered after her first rebuking ceremony. Over the past hundred cycles they had grown even closer. Now she might have lost him without telling him how she truly felt. A hole opened in her heart.

As she approached, Kane moaned and grabbed his head with both hands. Glissa smiled broadly and wiped the tears from her eyes and cheeks. She ran to his side and hugged him as he tried to sit up.

"What the flare was that for?"

"I thought you were dead," said Glissa. "I'm . . . I'm just happy you're okay."

"We'll see about that," he grunted. "My head is throbbing."

Glissa helped Kane to his feet, then smacked his cheek. "Well, it should hurt, you thick-headed elf!"

"Ow," said Kane. "You . . . Oh, never mind. What *were* those things?"

"That was the power Strang sold us out for," said Glissa. "Constructs. Tools of my enemy. They attacked me once before and dogged me all the way back to the Tangle. I saw two of these things with a robed figure Chunth called a vedalken—some evil race that wants me dead. And no, I'm not being paranoid. That's who Strang sold us out to. Look, I doubt he only sent four of them. We should get back to the Tree of Tales. Can you run?"

"I think so," said Kane. He looked around. "My sword!" he cried suddenly. "What happened to my sword?"

"What almost happened to your head. Come on. We'll get you a new one. You're lucky that's all we have to replace."

\* \* \* \* \*

As the two elves ran back through the Tangle, Kane asked the questions Glissa had been asking herself. "Who are these vedalken? Why do they want you dead?"

"I wish I knew," said Glissa. "But I intend to find out."

Near the Tree of Tales, Glissa slowed and grabbed Kane by the shoulders, pulling him behind a tree. He opened his mouth, but Glissa held up a finger.

"Do you hear anything?" she asked.

"No. It's quiet."

"That's what worries me," said Glissa.

Kane thought. "It's still pretty early."

"Yes," she replied, "but if there were more of those constructs attacking Tel-Jilad, we'd hear sounds of battle. If not, don't you think there would at least be some commotion over Chunth's death?"

"Maybe," said Kane. He looked unconvinced.

"Humor me," said Glissa. "Let me check this out. You stay here—and be careful this time."

"Okay," said Kane. "I'll watch your back."

Glissa hesitated. After everything that had happened in the last few days, she didn't want to wait another moment before telling Kane how much he meant to her. But now was not the time. She needed to concentrate on staying alive. She gave him a quick kiss on the cheek.

"What the flare was that for?"

"That was for later," said Glissa, smiling.

She slipped around the tree, sword drawn, and surveyed the small clearing in front of the Tree of Tales. There were no guards at the main entrance. Kane should have been missed by now. The council would have reinforced the entrance with a squad of Tel-Jilad Chosen or troll Elite Guards. Something was definitely wrong.

Glissa crept toward the entrance, her sword in front of her. She waited for the tingle in her neck to announce the approach of the silver-winged constructs but felt nothing. The Tangle remained quiet save for the dull sound of her own footsteps. Midway across the small clearing she stopped and listened again. Something rustled above her, but it could have been the wind moving through the spires or a vorrac racing along a terrace.

The elf scanned the trees and spires, watching and waiting. She was just about to call Kane from his hiding spot, when they appeared from behind the Tree of Tales. A dozen or more globe-headed flyers swarmed from either side of the great tree. They must have been clinging to the trunk out of sight, waiting for her to return. Glissa ran for the entrance.

The flyers swept around the tree, two curved lines of death winging their way toward her. The tingle ran down her spine as the air around the silver birds began to crackle with building energy. One after another, they unleashed blinding arcs of lightning. Glissa dodged back and forth as bolts slammed all around her. She dropped to the ground as one bird screamed right at her. She rolled twice, then pushed off to the side as another bolt tore a hole in the ground where she had been.

The agile elf landed on her feet in a dead run and zig-zagged toward the entrance to Tel-Jilad. She leaped through the open doorway just as three more bolts hit the tree around her. Inside, Glissa rolled to the side and put her back up against the wall. A single silver bird flew through the opening. Glissa whipped her blade straight up, slicing through the beast's wings and spine.

The blue globe continued on, slamming into the back wall of the entrance chamber. Glissa shielded her eyes from the resulting explosion. Dropping to one knee, she leaned around the edge of the entrance to see if any more would try to enter the Tree. What constructs she could see were heading from the little clearing.

Preparing for another attack run, thought Glissa. She'd seen their tactics and knew it would take them a few moments to turn around for their next assault.

"Kane," she called out. "Move it now! Before they return. You can make it!"

He raced from behind the tree. Glissa was ready to run out and distract the silver birds if they came back. What she saw instead made her shudder with fear. A robed figure stepped out from behind another tree. It raised an ornate staff and pointed it at the Chosen guard. Glissa screamed, but with a quick flick of his wrist the mage sprayed azure energy that streamed toward the running elf.

The bolt slammed into Kane's back and enveloped him. He screamed in agony and dropped to the ground. As Glissa raced from the Tree toward him, she could see his face twisted in pain. The muscles in his neck bulged, and his arms flailed uncontrollably as the energy cascaded up and down his body.

Glissa stopped, horrified. The metallic parts of his body—his arms, thighs, and shoulders—were melting away! Glissa dropped to the ground next to his writhing body. She was afraid to touch him as the energy continued to crackle across his body and could only watch. Now half the warrior's body, had turned to liquid, pooling around the remaining flesh. Kane stopped screaming, but his body continued to twitch until there was nothing left but his head and a bloody torso.

\* \* \* \* \*

Glissa stared at Kane's remains as the mage approached. She glanced up as he drew near. What she had mistaken for a gleaming head was actually a globe like the heads of the silver flyers. Inside the globe she could see a misshapen, bald face with bulging cheek bones and an over-large skull. The robes concealed an extra set of arms she had not noticed before. He stood holding his staff and smiling at her.

"I thought that would bring you from hiding," he said. "Now it is your turn." The vedalken—so Glissa assumed he must be—raised his staff over his head.

The mage began to mumble, and the tip of his staff glowed with blue light. Glissa stared, motionless, and thought how easy it would be to let the vedalken win. She glanced down at her friend's bloody remains, and something snapped inside. All the feelings she had for Kane over the past two hundred cycles—

the slow progression from simple friendship to something more—boiled over and turned to rage.

"Nooo!" she screamed at the mage. Her sword slashed up and around in a blindingly fast arc. Tendrils of green energy licked at Glissa's hands as she slashed the blade through the mage's staff, sundering the weapon just above his upper hand. Blue energy coalesced around the top of the staff as it fell toward the ground, exploding in front of the mage's domed head. The force of the explosion slammed Glissa to the ground and sent the vedalken mage flying backward into the trees.

Glissa scrambled to her feet. The tendrils of energy flickered up and down her battered and bloodied arms. Her face was flush from the explosion and the rage that seethed within her. She wanted to stain her sword with the blood of the murderer who had stolen every piece of her life from her, but he was nowhere to be seen. She could hear him laugh. The sound echoed through the trees.

"A point to you, Glissa," said the laughing voice, "but my aerophuis will soon bring this game to a close."

"This is no game," muttered Glissa. "It's a hunt." She headed off toward the surrounding trees, but then her neck began to tingle again. A dozen aerophuis dived toward her. They had spread out and now streaked toward her from every corner of the clearing. She had nowhere to run. The green strands of energy enveloped the elf's arms and chest, but in her blind rage she took no notice. She thrust into the air, ready to spear the first hawk that got too close.

She knew it would never come to that. The tingling warned her, but she didn't budge. Bolts of blue lightning erupted from the silver-winged aerophuis. A primal rage welled up inside the elf warrior, and she screamed at her attackers.

Twelve bolts of lightning raced toward her.

The cascading energy surrounding her body rushed up her

arms into the hilt of her sword. The sword glowed brighter than the yellow moon at noon over Taj Nar. The bolts of lightning curved toward the tip of the glowing sword as if drawn to the power. When the bolts hit the sword, blasts of emerald energy raced back up the blue lines and slammed into the aerophuis.

One after another, the silver-winged beasts exploded as the energy from Glissa's sword smashed into their blue-globed heads. Shards of glass, shredded silver wings, and tails cascaded around Glissa as she collapsed on top of Kane's dead body. With all of the energy drained from her body, she sprawled across her best friend's remains and wept.

# CHAPTER 15

# CULT OF KRARK

Glissa lay in the clearing in a daze. The Tangle was still and calm. The battle was done, and the commotion inside Tel-Jilad couldn't reach her. The trolls were apparently either dead or frightened off. The elves had disappeared. She had the entire forest to herself. But for the first time in her life she felt alone and out of place within the Tangle.

Glissa had never had many friends, but she had had a home, a family, and Kane. Now she had nothing. No, she amended to herself. Now she had a destiny . . . a destiny and a legacy of death. She stared at the ground, hardly aware of her surroundings. She heard Slobad's voice calling her, echoing as if she stood at the edge of a great abyss.

She looked down. There was no chasm. Just blood and melted copper. Her eyes fell on something else on the ground next to her. It was a finger and thumb lying next to the shards of the mage's staff, blue-gray and emaciated. They weren't elven. Glissa snatched them from the ground and held them hard in her fist, rocking back and forth.

"Glissa," called Slobad. He sounded far off. His voice echoed all around her. "Glissa. Where are you, huh?"

Was she lost? thought Glissa.

"Pick her up," she heard someone say from a great distance. "We get her to safety, huh? Then find out what happen here."

Glissa fell into the depths of the huge hole. The lip of the chasm passed her by, and she fell into nothingness. Her only companion was the wind rushing past her ears. Swirling shapes danced in front of her, then disappeared into the blackness. She saw her mother and father. She saw Lyese. They were reaching out to her, their mouths open as if screaming in terror. She couldn't move. She couldn't reach them.

There was no sound but the wind. Their screams were silent. Glissa tried to scream, but she had no voice. She saw Chunth, serene but dead. His eyes were closed. She could see the scorched hole in his chest. The charred body of Rishan floated by, writhing in agony. The elf warrior tried to run toward it, but she was running in air. She saw Kane. He was running as well, running toward her, a smile on his face. Then he was gone, a look of astonishment in his eyes just before the darkness returned.

Glissa had no idea how long she had been falling. Time had no meaning anymore. There was only the darkness and the wind. Was this her destiny? An endless fall into darkness? Or was this a punishment? Perhaps she couldn't be killed because she had a destiny. Everyone around her paid for her destiny with their lives. Her punishment was to live in the darkness with the memories of her failure.

Next she saw Slobad and the golem in the darkness. Slobad was calling to her. She could see him mouthing the words, "Glissa, Glissa," but she couldn't hear him. There was only the wind. Something was different, though. Slobad wasn't dead, at least not that Glissa remembered. The golem wasn't really alive. What were they doing in her personal purgatory?

She concentrated on Slobad, trying to make him come closer . . . or go away. As she concentrated, she began to hear his words.

"Glissa," he said. "Glissa. Are you in there? Come back, huh? Glissa!"

He seemed concerned, as did the golem. Somehow the metallic

man's ever-stoic face seemed furrowed, his eyes narrowed. He looked at Slobad and opened his mouth.

"What now?" asked the golem.

\* \* \* \* \*

That raspy voice jarred Glissa back to reality. The golem had spoken. Glissa opened her eyes slowly to see the goblin and the golem standing before her just as they had in her dream. Or had it been a flare? Glissa didn't know. The blackness dissolved into a dark red behind her two companions. Where was she? What happened to the Tangle? When did the golem learn to talk?

Glissa opened her mouth to ask these questions, but all that came out was a gurgle. She coughed and tried again.

"Slobad," she said. "Where are we?"

The goblin smiled and slapped the golem on his iron knee. "She's back, huh?" said the goblin. "She's back."

"I see," said the golem.

A thousand questions circled around Glissa's brain. "Where was I?" she asked at last.

"You tell us, huh?" said Slobad. "Glissa shut down in forest after aerophins attack. Not say a word in three rotations. The golem carry us to safe place."

"Aerophins? Three rotations?" The words hurt her throat, and her mouth was dry. "Water?"

Slobad looked at the golem, who walked away. "We go to mountains," he said. "To cultists I tell you about. To Dwugget. We safe here now."

"No," said Glissa. "We're not safe. They're not safe. Nobody is safe, not with me around."

The golem returned with a jug of water. Glissa took it and drank deeply. "I should go," she said. "You should have left me in the Tangle."

"Trolls tell us to go, huh?" said Slobad. "After Slobad fix secret door. They say better for you to leave forest. Say with lot more words, lots of bowing and smiles. Could tell trolls afraid. Slobad see that look before, huh?"

"Then you should have left me in the Glimmervoid," said Glissa. "It's not safe here. It's not safe anywhere. That vedalken mage has spies everywhere. He bought off Strang, and now Chunth is dead. He paid Geth to attack us. I wouldn't be surprised if he didn't get to Ushanti. She recognized the serum. I could tell. We can't trust her now. We can't trust anybody."

"We trust Dwugget, huh?" said Slobad. "Cultists never even see other races. They outcasts like us, huh? Outcasts."

"Perfect targets for treachery," said Glissa. She rose from the pile of hides where she had been lying and tested her legs. They were in a small cavern lit by a fire inside some metal contraption in the corner. She walked unsteadily across the room to look at the fire sconce. "Even if the robed mage didn't get to Dwugget, I bet those foul birds have been stalking us since we left the Mephidross." She felt like a caged animal. "We led them right to Rishan and Kane. Now you've put the cultists in danger. You say we're safe? We'll never be safe."

Gently the golem guided Glissa to the hides. He sat her down and held her shoulders. She scratched at a spot on her leg for a while, scraping the molder off the copper, then picking the green rot out from under her claws. There was something in her fist. She hadn't realized that her other hand had been closed all this time.

The elf opened up her hand. What she had been clenching was the thumb and finger she had picked up after the battle. They were even more shriveled and gray than she had remembered.

"I cut these off the robed figure," she said. "I'll keep these until I can unite him with his dead fingers." Glissa ripped a strip of leather from the hides beneath her. She stabbed her claws through the severed digits, threaded the leather strip through the holes, and tied the gruesome band around her neck.

"Listen, crazy elf," said Slobad. "You acting crazier than usual, huh? You need rest. Get strength back. Don't worry about Krark cult. Dwugget keep them hidden for fifty cycles. Nobody find us here, huh? Nobody. Tomorrow we talk. Pick what to do next, huh? Like Bosh said. Then we leave. We leave, and cult stay safe."

The golem gave her more water. Her body shook as she drained the mug. The water helped calm her a little, that and the gentle kneading of the golem's hands on her shoulders. Somewhere down deep, she knew she was being foolish. Not everyone was trying to kill her. But until she found that mage and finished what he had started with her, nobody would be safe.

Something nagged at the back of her brain as she fingered her gruesome pendants. "Bosh?" she asked. Was this some new enemy she needed to add to her growing list? "Who's this Bosh, and what did he say?"

"Golem is Bosh," said Slobad. "His name Bosh. He tell me on trip, huh? Bosh."

"He . . . Bosh . . . talks?" asked Glissa. "How?"

"Slobad clean rest of Dross in Tangle and one trip, huh?" said the goblin. "One morning he start talking."

Glissa drank another cup of water. She was tired. She realized that. Three days asleep, but she hadn't rested. That was all it was. She looked at her friends. They were good friends. She could see the concern on their faces. It was time to come from the darkness and rejoin the world.

Glissa took a deep breath and looked up at the golem. "So, you can talk now?" she asked.

"Yes," said Bosh.

Glissa looked up at him, waiting for more, then looked at Slobad and raised her eyebrows.

"I say he talks," said Slobad. "I not say he talks a lot, huh?"

Glissa laughed. She was starting to feel better, but the doubt and fear that had enveloped her and sent her hurtling into that abyss still lingered in the shadows of her mind. The sooner she left the cultists, the better, she thought—for them, anyway. Perhaps she *should* leave Slobad and Bosh as well—at least until the danger passed.

Later, after Glissa had gotten a little dream-free sleep, she told Slobad and Bosh of the events of the Tree of Tales: of what she had learned from Chunth and his murder. She told them that the vedalken were the source of the serum. She told them of Strang's treachery and the robed figure in the forest. She told them of Kane's death. That was the hardest of all.

"I'm sorry," said Slobad. His head fell forward. "We couldn't keep up. Slobad put golem back together, huh? We got from Tree as fast as we could. Sorry."

"Doesn't matter," said Glissa. She began rocking back and forth and realized that she was playing with the severed fingers again. She pushed the necklace under her tunic and shook her head and arms to put away the darkness that threatened to consume her.

"Better you weren't with me," she said after a while. "You'd be dead, too."

"Maybe," said Slobad. "Maybe no. Still sorry. Would give life to save friend, huh?"

"No!" snapped Glissa. "No more deaths. Not because of me. We leave here now. We'll go to the cult and end this." Glissa pushed herself up off the hides again. Her legs and arms ached from two days of inactivity, and she almost fell. Bosh stuck out his arm and caught her by the shoulder.

"We leave soon, huh?" said Slobad. "Soon as you able. Eat. Rest. Then we go, huh?"

The elf sighed. "Go where? We can go to the cult and talk to them, but we don't even begin to know how to find the vedalken."

Slobad gave a short cough, as if clearing his throat. "Slobad hear of vedalken before, huh? Not much, no. But some things."

"What?"

"Vedalken live around Quicksilver Sea. That long way from here, huh? Slobad never been. Long walk for crazy elf, Slobad, Bosh. But we can do it."

"Do what?"

"Find vedalken at Quicksilver Sea, just like I tell you." The goblin was plainly growing impatient with Glissa's limited intelligence. "Maybe we go there after see Dwugget."

There was a table in the middle of the room with bowls on it. Glissa realized she was famished. With the golem's help, she walked to the table, where she found some stew. She gulped it down, then served herself more from a large pot. She didn't even worry about the odd chunks of meat that she couldn't identify.

Glissa wondered if she should tell Slobad and Bosh about Chunth's last revelation, about the hollow world. They might think she had dreamed that part of the conversation. She wasn't even sure if it was real anymore. But it reminded her of something Slobad told her about Krark. He had seen the inner world.

"Tell me about this cult again, Slobad," she said. "Why are they hidden? What did Krark see?"

Slobad sat down and poured himself some stew. "Krark was goblin shaman, huh? Krark branded as heretic for violating Steel Mother," he said in between gulps. "Executed for violating Steel Mother. But Krark story spread. Cult formed to follow his words, follow him, search for Mother's Heart."

"The Steel Mother?" asked Glissa as she poured herself a third bowl of stew.

"The world," said Slobad. He thought for a moment, then continued, as if reciting a litany learned as a child. "Goblins come from Steel Mother, keep Great Furnace burning for her in life, and return to Steel Mother in death."

"And this Krark violated the Mother?" asked Glissa. "He found her Heart? How did he do that?"

"Krark entered the Womb of the Steel Mother."

"The Womb?" asked Glissa. She was interested in the story despite the disturbing imagery.

"Slobad never seen it," said the goblin. "Cult say Womb is wondrous place—a huge dark tunnel straight down into the Steel Mother. All goblins live around the Womb."

"A hole?" asked Glissa. "A huge hole in the world?"

Slobad nodded.

"Tell me about this Heart Krark found," the elf said. "It was inside the Mother's Womb?"

"Yes," said Slobad. "Krark say he found Heart of the Mother, huh?" Hhe continued, reciting from memory again. "'I stood in sloping chamber with no roof, surrounded by ancient towers of coral. A giant sun hung above me, glowing like Sky Tyrant, and Bringer, and Ingle, and Eye of Doom. I had found Mother's Heart.'"

"Those are the moons, right?" asked Glissa. "This Krark found a chamber inside the world with a fifth moon?"

"Sun," said Slobad. "Only shines in all colors. That what cult says, huh? Slobad never really believe. But they give me home, so Slobad listen. Every day, Slobad listen."

"Memnarch," said Bosh.

Glissa and Slobad both turned and stared at the golem.

"What?"

"Memnarch," the golem repeated. He paused as if straining to remember something important. ". . . Lives inside the world."

Glissa and Slobad stared at each other.

"Bosh," said Glissa, "is Memnarch a vedalken?"

Bosh concentrated again and stood mute for at least a minute. Glissa worried that she might have overtaxed the metal man. Finally, he looked at her and said, "I do not know. I have never heard of vedalken . . . before today."

"Do you remember anything else about the serum or Memnarch?"

"No," said Bosh. "Not yet."

Glissa tapped her chin thoughtfully. "I need to speak to the leader of the cult."

"Why?" asked Slobad.

"Something Chunth said before he died. He said he'd been keeping a secret. He said the world is hollow. The cultists believe Krark went down a hole into a world with a single moon . . . sun . . . and Bosh remembers that Memnarch lives inside the world. We need to jog Bosh's memory. Maybe the cultists can tell us something of Krark's journey that helps Bosh remember."

"So we not go to Quicksilver Sea?" asked Slobad.

"Not yet," replied Glissa. "We don't know if it's the vedalken or Memnarch after me. Flare, Memnarch might even *be* a vedalken." Glissa remembered something. "Bosh, did Memnarch have four arms?"

"Four arms?" asked Slobad.

Glissa nodded. "The robed figure in the Tangle had four arms and a bald, misshapen head."

Again Bosh stood silent, for several minutes. Glissa was sure she had broken him this time. Finally he focused on her again and said, "I do not remember."

Glissa sighed. "We need to see the leader of the cult."

"It wait until first moon rises, huh?" said Slobad. "You sleep for three rotations, but Slobad need rest. I take you see Dwugget after breakfast, huh? Sleep, food, Dwugget."

The elf nodded. "I could use some rest as well. I wasn't exactly relaxing on the way here, either." Actually, she felt renewed. Her heart was pounding, and she felt completely awake. This changed everything. If Memnarch was below her and there was a hole in the goblins' lair, they might not have to leave the mountains to leave the mountains.

\* \* \* \* \*

Despite her excitement Glissa was asleep moments after she lay down, a sleep mercifully devoid of dreams. When she heard Bosh's voice calling to her and opened her eyes to darkness, she felt a momentary panic, as if she had fallen back into the abyss.

"Slobad, Glissa," said the golem again. "Wake up. Something is wrong."

"What is it?" said Glissa, glad to hear her own voice in the darkness. She sat up and squinted, trying to pierce the gloom. She could see two red dots high above her that could only be Bosh's eyes.

"A battle approaches."

Glissa heard something that sounded like a small explosion, and the hairs on the back of her neck stood up. "Aerophuis," she said. "Bosh, grab Slobad. We're under attack. We have to get to the cultists."

Bosh lifted the goblin, who snorted sleepily.

"Wake him," hissed Glissa. "I need light."

Glissa crept along the wall toward the door. She could barely see its outline. From down the corridor came a flash of light.

"I'm going to take a look," she whispered. She inched down the corridor, her back against the wall, and peered around the edge. Pools of light from goblin fire tubes dotted the next corridor. In the dim light, Glissa saw a score of goblins running toward her.

They were being chased by what looked like large, walking aerophins. The creatures had the same blue, bulbous heads, but their silver bodies were much larger—man-sized. Each had two massive arms connected to barrel-shaped bodies. Their legs were mere stubs jutting from the base of the barrels, yet they moved amazingly fast.

One of the silver assassins pointed an arm at the retreating goblins. It had no hands, but a huge metal arrow shot out, impaling, two goblins. Their bodies knocked down several in front of them. A second barbed missile shot out from another creature, taking down a third goblin. Then the goblins were past Glissa, running down the hall. A bolt of lightning came from another beast, blasting the mass of fallen goblins.

Glissa fell to her knees. "No!" she screamed. "Not again!" The silver attackers stopped and searched for the source of the screaming then moved forward. They glided down the corridor, their stubby legs never touching the iron flooring.

She could do nothing but watch in horror as they drew near. In the pile of goblins she saw only the faces of Kane, Rishan, Chunth, and her family. Her grief paralyzed her. Two hovering attackers reached the corner and peered into the darkness. Glissa curled into a ball, half-hoping they wouldn't see her, half-hoping they would.

Something struck her, hurling her back down the corridor to fall in a heap. She looked up in time to see one of the silver men point its deadly arm at her. The bolt flew toward her. She made no attempt to dodge.

Inches from her face, the harpoon stopped, snatched from the air by Bosh.

The golem flipped the spear over in his hand and flung it back down the corridor. The huge missile slammed into the hovering beast's crystal head. The resulting explosion knocked the headless creature to the floor and slammed its companion through the wall of the corridor.

"Pick her up," said Slobad. "Follow. I get us out, huh?"

Bosh snatched Glissa from the floor, cradling her in his arms. The hair on her neck tingled, but she couldn't even cry out. Bolts of lightning struck the walls and floor behind them as they ran. Bosh stumbled and almost fell. Glissa felt a surge of energy run through her body. The golem regained his balance and kept running.

They raced through dark corridors, twisting back and forth, followed by sounds of lightning cracking and harpoons clanging. At last they halted, and Bosh set Glissa down. She looked up to see Slobad wrestling with a plate on the wall. The goblin grunted as he tried to pry it open with one of his tools. Bosh came forward, pushed two thick fingers behind the cover, and ripped it off the wall.

"In here," said Slobad. "Quick, huh?"

Glissa crawled into the cramped tunnel.

"Keep moving," hissed Slobad.

Glissa obeyed. The darkness of the air duct called to her. She welcomed it back into her mind.

Slobad pulled out his fire tube, lit it, and tossed it into the ductwork. Glissa grabbed the light and inched forward. She could see now, but still the darkness closed in on her. The abyss was near, and she could do nothing but crawl toward it. She heard the clanging of harpoons again, as if through a fog, then Bosh's voice.

"I cannot fit," said the metal man. "Proceed without me. I will safeguard your escape."

There was silence. Glissa looked back to see Slobad hug the giant golem's leg.

"Goodbye, Bosh," he said.

"Farewell, friend," said Bosh.

Bosh turned. Two harpoons stuck from his back beside a huge scorch mark. He lumbered down the hallway into the darkness.

"Keep moving, huh?" said Slobad after a deep breath and a stifled sniffle. "Keep moving."

Glissa crawled through the ductwork, following Slobad's directions. The farther she went through the maze of cramped tunnels the closer she came to the abyss. After a while, she could hardly hear Slobad's commands through the fog in her mind.

She saw light up ahead. A few more turns and they reached the end of the tunnel. The yellow moon was rising in the distance. Glissa fell to the ground in a heap. She heard Slobad drop to the ground behind her, but she stared in silence at the moon.

# CHAPTER 16

# THE GREAT FURNACE

"What now, huh?" asked Slobad from behind Glissa.

She glanced up at the goblin. "What did you say?"

"What now, huh?" he repeated. "We get away. What we do now?"

Glissa stared at the goblin. She had no idea where they were or what was going on. She had heard that same question before, but it wasn't Slobad who had asked it. It was . . .

"Where's the golem?"

Now it was Slobad's turn to stare at Glissa. "What you talking about, crazy elf?" he asked. "We left Bosh back in the cult caves." Glissa could see tears streaming down the goblin's face. When she didn't respond, he continued. "Cult was attacked, huh? Remember? Flying silver men with blue heads. Goblins die. We run. Bosh stay behind so we can escape. Remember? Any of it? Bosh save Glissa's life—again."

"Bosh is the golem?" asked Glissa, more to herself than to Slobad. "And he speaks now. . . ." Bits and pieces of the last few days swirled around inside her head. Kane's death. Her descent into the abyss. Bosh's voice pulling her back. The attack. The dead goblins. Bosh taking a lightning bolt in the back that was meant for her.

"You left him there?" she demanded.

Slobad wiped the tears from his eyes and nodded.

Glissa backed away from the goblin and drew her sword. "The vedalken got to you, too, didn't they?" she demanded.

"What?" said Slobad. "No! Bosh my friend, huh?"

"Just like the cultists were your friends," sneered Glissa. "You left *them* to die with Bosh. All this time you told me you were cursed, but you're the one who always lives when everyone around you dies. How does that happen, Slobad? Hmmm? You're good at getting away, at leaving your friends to die. You left the cultists to die once before. You told me yourself."

"Stop it, huh?" snapped Slobad. "You talking crazy. You don't know what you say."

"Don't I? My life has been a disaster since I met you."

"Slobad didn't kill your family, Glissa," said the goblin gently. "Didn't kill trolls or elf friend. Didn't attack Taj Nar."

"Then who did?" screamed Glissa. "I have to blame somebody. If not you, then who? Me? Is that what you're saying? It's all *my* fault?" Glissa's face flushed as she continued. "I have a destiny, Slobad. A destiny. Do you hear that? And that destiny is to watch everyone I love die one by one." Her breathing came in gasps. "Is that *my* fault? I say it's *your* fault. It's your flaring curse that has caused all of this!"

Glissa stopped suddenly. She was clawing for breath. Then she was crying. She tried to wipe the tears from her eyes and cheeks with her palms, but they kept flowing. She balled her hands into fists and jammed them into both eyes, as if to cork the flow of tears.

"It *is* my fault, isn't it?" she whispered after a time.

"Attacks not your fault," said Slobad, dropping down beside her. "Not Slobad's fault. Not curse's fault. Not destiny's fault. It was globe-headed mage, huh? Memnarch. Vedalkens. Someone trying to kill you. Stop your destiny."

"But look what I've done to your only family. It's dangerous to be around me."

"You my family, now, huh?" said Slobad. "Listen. I live alone for long time. Not happy, just surviving, huh? Then crazy elf drag Slobad from hole and into danger. Show Slobad how to fight for life, not hide from it. Give Slobad purpose, huh? Make me feel part of family."

"Get Slobad killed," sighed Glissa.

"Maybe." The goblin shrugged. "But die for cause, huh? Die fighting evil. Die fighting beside friend. Better than living in hole, safe and alone. I leave cult first time to save Slobad, huh? I leave this time to save friend. Come. We find vedalken mage. Or Memnarch. Whoever behind attacks. We find, huh? Make him pay for Glissa's family, friends, Slobad's cult family, Bosh."

Glissa nodded her head. The little goblin had a way of cutting through to the truth. She saw plots and deceit everywhere. He saw life and truth. The truth was that someone really *was* trying to kill her, and it wouldn't stop until she made it stop. She owed it to Slobad to save his friend and his family. Glissa reached out and hugged her companion, squeezing until he pushed her away.

"Crazy elf."

"Come on, we have work to do." She jumped to her feet and headed back toward the tunnel.

"Where you going, huh?" asked Slobad. "Quicksilver Sea that way." Slobad pointed across the craggy hills that surrounded them toward the open lands of the Glimmervoid.

"The vedalken can wait," said Glissa. "Our friends cannot. First we save Bosh and Dwugget, then we make Memnarch pay."

* * * * *

Glissa and Slobad made their way back through the ductwork to the Krark cult lair. Slobad led the way with the fire tube doused. Glissa followed blindly, holding onto Slobad's satchel so she didn't lose him in the winding tunnels. After crawling through the dark for some time, Glissa nudged Slobad.

"Did it take this long on the way out?"

"No," said the goblin. "Taking us to secret part of cult lair, huh? So secret, even they don't know about it."

"Another one of your personal improvements?" asked Glissa.

"Yes. Hiding spot, huh? See most of lair. Hide there when shaman's warriors attack long ago. No time to get others to safety. We go there now. Check for danger, huh?"

"Good plan," said Glissa. "That should bypass any guards they may have left at our escape tunnel."

"That, too," said Slobad. "Now, be quiet, crazy elf. We under lair right now."

The two crawled on in silence for a while. After a few more turns, the goblin stopped. Glissa could hear him grunting. A moment later, she heard metal scraping. Then Slobad began moving again. His satchel pulled her upward until she grabbed the lip of a hole.

The elf pulled herself up into a large room. She could barely see anything, but light seeped from small openings near the floor all around her.

"Slobad," she hissed. "Where are you?"

"Over here, huh?"

Glissa felt her way through the dark toward the goblin's voice, bumping into what felt like a table, then a chair, along the way.

"We spy on lair from here, huh?" said Slobad. "Kneel down. Look through hole. Hole shows hall where attack start, huh? Look."

Glissa knelt and looked through the opening. It was the same size and shape as the cover Slobad had to remove to get into the tunnels, which she suspected were air ducts. Ingenious little goblin. Through the hole Glissa saw an intersection of two corridors. The hallway across from her was dark. That must have been where we slept, she thought. To the right was where the goblins were attacked. Glissa could see the scorch marks on the floor and the blood, but otherwise the corridor was empty.

"Where are the bodies?" she whispered. "At least five goblins were killed there. Where'd they go?"

"Good question. Maybe silver beasts take them."

"Maybe," said Glissa, "but why? Dead goblins wouldn't help them find me. That has to be the right corridor, though. I saw the blood."

"Check other holes, huh?" said Slobad.

Glissa and Slobad circled the large room, checking each peephole in turn. There were several on each wall. Through each, they saw the same thing. Deserted corridors, scorch marks, and some blood. There were no sign of goblins, hover beasts, or Bosh.

"Where in the flare is everybody?" asked Glissa

"I think I know," said Slobad, "and it not good. Not good at all. Very bad, in fact."

"What do you mean?"

"Look at this, huh?" said the goblin.

Glissa followed the walls around the room until she bumped into Slobad, then bent and looked through the hole. The corridor outside looked much like the others. Scorch marks on the walls and some blood on the floor. "What am I looking at?" she asked.

"See symbol?" asked Slobad.

"No. What symbol?"

"Look at black mark on wall, huh?" said Slobad. "Something drawn there. Symbol. See? Huh?"

Glissa looked at the scorch mark again. Sure enough, there was an odd symbol scratched into the wall. The black soot from the lighting bolt almost obscured it. Even after Slobad pointed it out to her she could barely make out the image. It looked like an eye above a mountain.

"What does that mean?"

"It means goblin shaman here again," said Slobad. "Come and clean out lair. That Eye of Doom mark. Shaman carve to mark unclean lairs."

"That can't be a coincidence, Slobad," said Glissa. "You said the cult had stayed hidden for fifty cycles. There's no way those vedalken beasts and the goblin shaman found this place at the same time. The shaman must have sold out to the vedalken just like Geth and Strang. But why did the goblin shaman take the dead bodies?"

"Take everyone to Great Furnace. All metal must be returned to clan."

"They're going to burn them in the furnace?" asked Glissa, a note of panic in her voice as the realization sunk in. "Oh, flare! Bosh!"

"We hurry," said Slobad. "No time for sneaky elf." The goblin lit his fire tube and ran back to the hole in the middle of the floor. He dropped into the tunnel before Glissa could even move. The sudden light had blinded her. Through the dots floating in her vision, Glissa stumbled to the hole, which glowed with the light of the torch below.

She followed Slobad back into the ductwork tunnels but could barely keep up with the little goblin. She might be able to outrun him on land, but her long legs were not made for this environment. They traveled for over an hour through the twisting tunnels. With the fire tube lit, Glissa could tell that even the straight passages weren't all that straight or smooth. It looked as if the rusty metal had been banged into shape by hammers.

The two passed many openings. Most of the time, Glissa could see nothing in them but darkness. Sometimes a fire tube beyond the duct would illuminate an open cavern or a small room filled with metal and tools. She saw goblins hard at work heating and banging metal or cutting away walls and floors of caverns. It looked as if they were mining metal from the mountains, then fashioning it into whatever they needed.

After more than two hours, Glissa had to stop. A cramp shot up her calf into the knee, and she dropped to the floor of the tunnel. Hearing her groan, Slobad stopped several feet on. Glissa straightened out her leg, but in the small tunnel she could not reach down to massage the muscle. Worse, the passage was getting warmer.

"Not much farther," said Slobad. He came back and sat in front of her. His head was jammed up against the top of the tunnel, and he looked at her from an odd angle.

At least he can turn around and sit, thought Glissa. "I'll just be a moment," she said. "Why is it getting so hot?"

We close to furnace, huh?" replied Slobad. "Ducts take hot air to goblins. Cool furnace and heat homes. Smart. Goblins good with machines."

"Will the ducts take us all the way to the furnace?"

"No," said Slobad. "We can't get to furnace by duct. Air too hot at Furnace, huh? Goblins replace ducts above furnace every cycle. Melt away. Furnace very hot."

"Then where are we headed?"

"Holding pens," said Slobad. "We find Dwugget, maybe. Cultists. Pens close to furnace. If not there, we too late."

Glissa's leg was still sore, but she could move. "Lead on," she said.

Soon after, Slobad stopped at an opening on the floor of the tunnel. He pushed the cover out, then pulled it through the opening, placed it in front of him, and shut off the fire tube. Glissa could just see the silhouette of his head as he leaned over and stuck it through the opening.

"Nobody here," he said. "Safe. Come on, huh? Hurry."

Glissa followed him through and landed in a corridor lined with rusty cages. Fire tubes at the end of the corridor provided dim light. Most of the cages were empty, but one held about a dozen goblins cramped together. The companions crept to the packed cell.

"Dwugget," called Slobad. "You in there, Dwugget?"

"Here," came a hoarse reply. "All here, my son. Is that you, Slobad?"

"It me," said the goblin. "Come to get you out, huh? Set you free."

"How did you get away, little Slobad?" asked the cult shaman. He pushed his way out to the rusty bars. Dwugget wore what Glissa assumed must be shaman robes. For goblins that amounted to a leather jerkin that hung to his knees instead of a simple loincloth.

"Why did you come back? It's very dangerous here for you, huh?"

"I tell you," said Slobad. "We come to get you. Me and Glissa. My friend. Golem help us get away. Now we set you free, huh? This all that lived?"

"Yes," said Dwugget, "The dead were already taken to the Great Furnace, may Krark lead them to the Mother's Heart."

"What about Bosh?" asked Glissa. "The golem—where is he?"

Dwugget looked over at Glissa. "I am glad to see you awake," he said. "Slobad was worried about you, huh? You were in a dark place. Now you have returned to the light. It is the Mother's will that you live."

Does everyone know more about my life than I do? wondered Glissa. She smiled and nodded at the shaman. "The golem?" she asked again.

"Of course," said Dwugget. "Sorry. Your metal man was taken with the dead to the Furnace. We are next for the fire."

Slobad turned and started toward the other end of the hall.

"Slobad!" called Glissa. "Where are you going?"

"Save Bosh," said Slobad. "Be back, huh?"

Glissa ran after Slobad and grabbed him by the shoulder. "We can't leave them here," she said. "They'll be killed."

"Won't let them melt him down, huh?" cried Slobad. "They not make boiler or ductwork from Bosh!"

Glissa released him and patted him on the back. "Go find Bosh," she said. "I'll get Dwugget's people into the duct, then come find you."

Slobad opened the metal door, which creaked horribly as it moved. He peered out the doorway for a moment then slipped through. Glissa turned back toward the cell, pulled out her sword, and moved forward.

"Stand back," she said.

The mass of goblins inched away from the bars as best as they could. They huddled against the wall, whimpering. Glissa stepped back and gauged the distance. She swung her sword hard toward the iron bars. It sliced through four bars, coming to rest just inches from Dwugget's head. Glissa swung the sword again, aiming low. The iron bars clattered to the floor, leaving an opening large enough for the goblins.

"Quickly," she said. "This way."

The remaining Krark cultists scurried to the opening in the duct. Glissa lifted Dwugget into the hole and held him there as he scrambled through. One by one, she aided the rest of the cultists.

"Replace the cover and move down the tunnel," she said to Dwugget. "Wait for us to return—and for flare's sake stay quiet."

The elf ran down the hall, grabbed the fire tube, and opened the door a crack to look out. The heat from the next chamber slammed her in the face like a stiff wind. She fought for breath in the stifling heat as she slipped through the door. Glissa scanned the chamber beyond the cells. All the lair areas she had seen so far had been goblin-made. They were small, square rooms made of hammered metal fused together.

This chamber was altogether different. It was a huge circular cavern hundreds of feet across. The walls were made of iron but had not been hammered. They looked almost like intertwined Tangle trees. Tubular veins of rusty iron grew from the floor up to the ceiling high above her, snaking back and forth through each other. Fire tubes were jammed into crevices between the veins here and there, but the majority of light—as well as the blasting heat—came from the furnace in the center of the room.

The furnace looked like a massive knot of iron tubes growing from the floor of the chamber. Hundreds, if not thousands, of the iron tube-veins came from the floor, intertwining, branching, and reaching up at least thirty feet. It was as big around as Tel-Jilad, the Tree of Tales. Smoke and fire belched from the tops of the tubes at irregular intervals. Most of the room was bathed in a red glow from the fire and the rusty iron, but the ceiling was pitch black from flare knew how many cycles of fire.

Glissa stood above the floor of the furnace chamber. The door she had come through was carved right into the tube wall. There was a hammered path in the uneven floor leading down to the furnace. Paths had been leveled throughout the chamber. Some of the paths looked like ledges or bridges spanning a dark trench. She could see goblins moving about performing tasks, but it was almost impossible to distinguish Slobad from any other goblin working around the furnace.

That's one advantage Slobad has here, thought Glissa. He can blend in. She dropped to her knees to avoid being spotted while searching the cavern for her friend. She spotted a goblin with a satchel amidst a large pile of debris near the back of the chamber. Many of the goblins had satchels, so she couldn't be sure. They all looked so much alike. But this goblin seemed to be looking for something in the pile. She moved around to get a better view.

As she got closer, Glissa saw the figure lift some debris and toss it aside. Underneath, she could see something large. The goblin tossed shards of metal aside to uncover more. Glissa crept even closer until she could see that the large object was Bosh's chest.

The elf looked around for a way down. A path led to the furnace floor over near the pile, but Glissa decided to stay hidden and not draw attention to Slobad. She would watch for danger from above. With any luck, Slobad could activate the golem and ride it out before the other goblins guessed what was happening.

By the time Glissa arrived at her new vantage point, Slobad had uncovered most of Bosh. Glissa realized the golem was in pieces. Worse, several goblins seemed to have taken an interest in Slobad and were heading toward him.

# CHAPTER 17

# ESCAPE

Glissa crouched and watched the approaching goblins. They didn't seem in a great hurry and weren't brandishing any weapons. Unless they recognized Slobad, he was probably better off if she stayed hidden. She slid her sword from its sheath and readied herself.

Slobad looked up as the trio of goblins approached. His hand slipped inside the satchel. Take it easy, thought Glissa. Smile and stay calm. Just get rid of them and get back to work. We don't have much time before someone notices the cultists are missing.

All the goblins in the chamber were busy with other tasks. One large group worked on a ruptured duct, while several smaller groups hauled metal toward the furnace or picked through similar debris piles strewn about the chamber. Glissa looked back at Slobad and saw that he had moved down the pile away from Bosh's body to meet the approaching group. They were talking. Slobad pointed at something, and the trio scrambled over the debris in that direction. Two of them lifted a goblin body off the pile and began hauling it back down the pile. The third goblin patted Slobad on the shoulder, then followed the other two.

Slobad sauntered up the pile toward Bosh. The three goblins moved off toward the furnace, burdened by the weight of the body.

As they crossed one of the bridges, the lead goblin tripped and lost his grip on the body. The dead goblin dropped onto the path and almost bounced over the edge, pulling the second goblin with it. The clumsy goblin caught an arm, diverting the disaster, but the third goblin ran up, smacked the clumsy one in the head, and shouted at him.

Slobad, meanwhile, had gotten Bosh's head and body put back together and was now working on the legs. As Glissa watched him attach the golem's leg, she wondered how they were going to get out of there. Slobad had to lead the cultists through the ducts, but Bosh wouldn't fit—a fact that had gotten the metal man in this predicament in the first place.

Glissa glanced back toward the door to the cells and saw a group of goblins heading up a ramp toward the holding area. They looked different from the ones working around the furnace, clad in long leather shirts much like the one Dwugget wore. The one in the lead had an ornate fire tube that looked more ceremonial than functional. It seemed to have several iron tubes twisted around each other and welded together, reminiscent of the look of the walls and furnace.

Something told Glissa these were the shamans. They must be coming to escort Dwugget and the cultists to their trial . . . or perhaps straight to their executions. Either way, Slobad and Bosh were out of time. As soon as the shamans found the empty cage, the alarm would be raised.

The elf left her hiding spot and ran down the ramp toward Slobad and Bosh, hoping nobody would see her. The last thing she needed was to draw attention to Slobad, but it looked as if their luck had run out. The goblin who had dropped the body earlier was now walking backward with his load. Glissa glanced at the trio just as the lead goblin looked up. Their eyes met.

"Flare," muttered Glissa as the three goblins turned and started back toward the debris pile, pulling out their fire tubes as they ran. Glissa hurried, but the pathways were narrow, and one misstep would send her flying to the rough floor, or, worse, down into a pit.

The alarm sounded just as she reached the floor of the furnace chamber. The shamans ran from the holding area, screaming and banging the iron walls with their fire tubes. The noise echoed through the cavern. All around her, goblins hammered the walls and floors in response. It was an odd alarm system, but it certainly was effective.

Glissa veered toward the goblin trio to divert attention away from Slobad for a little longer. The three goblins were too busy running to hammer the floor. They seemed intent on taking the intruder on their own. Bad decision, thought Glissa as she noticed where they were standing. She sheathed her sword and sped up as much as she dared.

The goblins did just what she hoped they would do. They stopped where they were and took up a defensive stance—right in the middle of a bridge. The leader of the group pushed the two carriers in front of him. As Glissa neared them, she dived forward into a roll. She stuck her elbows out as she moved through the front two, swiping their stubby legs out from under them. Both goblins flew off the side of the path into the darkness. Glissa barreled on past them into the leader of the group. He toppled over backward from the impact, and Glissa rolled to her feet over him. She casually kicked him over the side and watched his fire tube fade into the inky blackness.

The elf turned and ran back to the debris pile. The clanging echoed around her as she scrambled up and over the pile to hide behind it.

"I'm back," she called to Slobad.

"I noticed," huffed the goblin.

"How much longer?"

"A while," said Slobad, grunting. "Stupid goblins. Tear apart amazing machine like Bosh. . . . Not know what they have. . . . Stupid. . . . Take a while to fix. . . ."

"We don't have much time," Glissa reminded him. She peeked over the top of the pile to see Slobad pressing on a tool wedged into the golem's knee joint.

"Working . . . as fast . . . as I can, huh?" grunted Slobad. "Much to fix. . . . Stupid goblins—"

"Less talk. More work," interrupted Glissa. The hammering continued around them. Glissa glanced up toward the pens. The shamans were descending toward the furnace floor. "Maybe I can give you more time. They won't notice you if they have to chase me."

"How you get out?"

"Send Bosh for me when he's ready," said Glissa. "You lead Dwugget's people back through the ducts. They're waiting for you."

You don't know way out, crazy elf," snapped Slobad. He'd finished securing one leg and was pulling the second leg into place.

"I do," said Bosh.

Glissa stared at the golem. She wasn't sure who surprised her more—Slobad or Bosh but both were remarkable. "Fine," she said. "Bosh will get me out of here. You get Dwugget out. We'll meet at the cult lair."

Slobad shook his head. "Not safe there."

"We'll figure that out if we get that far," replied Glissa.

She followed a path behind the debris pile toward the rear of the furnace, trying to get as far away from Slobad and Bosh as possible before she was spotted. Most of the workers were around the front and sides, so the way was clear. When she came to a fork in the path, she moved closer to the furnace. It would help block her from view, and she hoped it would take her where she really wanted to go.

As Glissa wound her way around the structure, she saw a lone goblin ahead of her banging on the path with his tube. He saw her as well and immediately changed the cadence of his beat. The general alarm first raised by the shamans was slow and steady. As soon as this goblin saw her, he quickened his tempo into a steady stream of bangs. All other banging in the chamber ceased.

He's signaling the shamans, thought Glissa. Not yet. She drew her sword and ran up to the pounding goblin. When she swung, the worker didn't even block but kept signaling until the sword slashed through his side. The dead goblin dropped to the floor on top of his fire tube, which ignited his leather clothes and skin.

"Oh, flare," muttered Glissa, as she jumped over the burning corpse. "They know where I am now."

The elf continued around the furnace and saw what she was looking for—the air duct that was being repaired. Most of the workers were scouting for intruders. Several were heading her way already, while a half dozen remained behind. When they saw her, they began banging the "I found her" rhythm. Worse yet, Glissa was on the wrong path, and the closest bridge to the duct was past the workers. She didn't have that kind of time.

She stepped off the path and screamed. The tubes in the floor were scalding hot. Now she understood the need for the paths, but goblins were converging on her. She had no other choice. She jumped as far off the path as she could, landed on her toes, and jumped again. The leather soles of her boots burned away, and pain shot up her legs. Two more jumps and she made it to the right pathway.

Two goblins headed toward her, fire tubes in hand. The flames from the tubes were long and white-hot. Glissa had never seen Slobad's tube produce such an intense flame. The first goblin came in swinging. Glissa threw her arm out to block, and the flame burned hot against her metallic forearm. She slammed the pommel of her sword down on the goblin's arm, shattering the bone. He dropped the fire tube. She bashed him in the face. The force of the punch broke the goblin's nose and knocked him off his feet into the creature behind him.

Glissa twirled, whipping her sword out in an arc. As she came back around, she grabbed the pommel with both hands and swung it hard at the stumbling goblin. The sword cut through both goblins' necks without slowing. Glissa twirled around once more before she could stop.

The move had cost her. Glissa's feet screamed at her. She looked down to see the tattered remains of her boots, held on by the straps alone. The sides and soles of her feet were bare. Blisters were forming from the intense heat of the furnace room floor. She had no time to heal, though. Glissa pressed on toward her goal, gritting her teeth against the pain of each step.

A few moments later, she reached the broken duct. The workers had scrambled over the metal to face her, waving fire tubes in front of them. The first one came in. Glissa sliced through the first tube jabbed at her. A great gout of flame erupted from the side of the tube, singeing her arm. The sudden eruption also jerked the tube's goblin around. He lost his balance and fell off the path onto the hot tubes.

Glissa left him screaming and scrambling on the tubes as she stepped up to the next two goblins. They hesitated, and the elf used their indecision to her advantage. She swung her sword ahead of her to make them pull back, then rushed in low. She slammed into both goblins with her shoulder. Two fire tubes went flying back over the duct. The goblins flailed their arms, trying to regain their balance. Glissa kicked her leg out to one side as she punched the other way. Her foot slammed into the knee of one opponent just as she smacked the other goblin with the pommel of her sword. She could hear the knee pop as her punch shattered the other goblin's jaw. Both goblins fell away onto the furnace room floor.

Glissa straightened up, but the next goblin was already on her. He swung his fire tube at her gut, burning away a line of leather and cutting into her skin. Glissa swung the sword straight up, almost on instinct, then watched in horror as the goblin split apart in front of her. The two halves toppled off either side of the pathway. His blood spilled on the ground and boiled away.

The last two goblins looked at Glissa, dropped the tubes, and ran. The elf looked down at her gut, but the flame had cut across her ribcage and had done little more than burn away some skin. Glissa scooped up the tubes and turned them off as she walked up to the duct. The metal box came from the furnace and ran across the chamber and up the wall. A steady spray of steam issued from the other side of the duct where the goblins had been working. She climbed over the duct, pressing on the flat of her sword to keep her hands off the hot metal.

Glissa stared at the duct and tried to decide how to do the most damage. She glanced up toward the holding area and could see a few shamans still lingering there. She needed a large distraction to lure everyone toward her and give Slobad a clear path back to the holding area. When she looked back at the duct, the elf saw one of the goblins she had shoved off the path creeping toward her. She swung her sword in a flash across the top of the duct and sliced through the creature's ribs. He fell back, but others were coming, including the rest of the shamans.

Glissa was out of time.

"This is going to hurt."

She took the two fire tubes she had scavenged and slapped them down on top of the duct, side by side. Raising her sword over her head in both hands, she tilted her head to the side behind her arms and slashed through the tubes and into the duct.

The tubes exploded in twin balls of flame. The force of the blast went down into the duct through the gash made by Glissa's sword. The elf was flung up and away from the duct. She landed hard on her back on the edge of a nearby bridge, and her sword clattered from her hands. Groggy and disoriented from the blast, she stood up just as the joints to either side of the hole in the duct tore apart.

Steam erupted from the severed duct. A great gout of hot air hit Glissa in the face and knocked her backward. Her feet left the edge of the path. She threw her hands out blindly and grabbed the path. Her claws dug into the rusty metal, and her muscles flexed as she swung under the bridge. She could see nothing but blackness beneath her. For all she knew, she could be hanging over the Mother's Womb. If she let go, she thought she might fall right down into the center of the world.

"Not today."

She tried to claw her way back up onto the bridge, but the rusty metal flaked away under her claws. She decided to swing her legs up to get a foot onto the bridge, but before she got her feet up high enough, Glissa heard footsteps above her. She let her legs drop underneath her and slowed her breathing.

It was too late. The footsteps stopped right above her. Glissa heard metal scraping against metal and looked up to see the head priest standing above her. In one hand he had his ceremonial fire tube, Glissa's sword in the other.

"You have damaged the Great Furnace," said the shaman. "For that alone you should die, huh? Are you also the one who freed my prisoners?"

"What prisoners?" spat Glissa.

"I think you know. I'm sure it is no coincidence, huh? An intruder destroying the Great Furnace as prisoners are free? Two are connected."

"I don't know what you are talking about," gasped Glissa. She tried to swing her leg up onto the bridge again, but the shaman swatted at her with the flat of the sword.

"Tell me where cultists are. I'll let you live, huh?"

"Give me back my sword," replied Glissa, "and *I'll* let *you* live."

"This sword?" shrieked the shaman, brandishing the weapon. "I found this on the bridge! It belongs to me now!"

"Help me up and I'll show you where your prisoners are."

"I have seen you fight, huh?" said the shaman. "I believe I am safer with you there. Now, you tell me what I want to know. I have upper hand here."

"Maybe," grunted Glissa, "but I have your foot."

She dug her claws in with one hand and grasped the ankle of the shaman with the other. With a quick yank, she pulled the shaman's leg over the edge. Unbalanced, he dropped unceremoniously on his back above Glissa. She yanked on his leg again and pulled him off the bridge.

The shaman swung below Glissa, upside down at the end of her arm. She held on tight but could feel her grip on both his ankle and the bridge slipping. The goblin grabbed her sword in both hands.

"You want this sword so much," he said. "I give it to you, huh?"

"Do that and we both die."

Glissa heard the lesser shamans scrambling above her. "Stay back or I'll drop your chief priest into the bowls of the Mother," she shouted.

The scrambling footsteps receded.

The shaman glared at her, a defiant look in his eyes. "Drop me, and you lose sword."

"I don't have time for this," muttered Glissa.

More footsteps, heavy ones. The goblins above her screamed. One by one, they fell over the edge. Glissa saw a massive club swinging back and forth above her, knocking goblin after goblin off the bridge. She looked back down at the shaman and smiled.

"My ride is here. It's time to go."

The goblin shaman screamed and swung the sword at Glissa,

but the elf was too fast for him. She kicked her feet at his hands and knocked the sword up into the air, then released her grip on the goblin's ankle and grabbed the pommel as it dropped past her. The shaman fell down into the blackness, screaming and flailing his arms. A moment later, Bosh's massive hand reached over the ledge and pulled Glissa up onto the bridge.

Bosh bent over to pick up his club. It was the golem's other arm. He grasped his own hand in a weird handshake and stood up. "No time to finish reconstruction," said Bosh. "You required help."

"Thank you," said Glissa. "Slobad make it out okay?"

The golem nodded.

"We'd better leave as well," she said. "We can't let him beat us there."

\* \* \* \* \*

Glissa climbed onto the golem's shoulders. Bosh ran straight through the furnace cavern, only using the paths when he needed to cross a chasm. Any goblins who dared come near were greeted by the golem's massive, iron arm. Bosh swung the improvised club back and forth in front of him as he ran.

Once out of the furnace room, they went through several goblin-made passageways. Glissa could see other caverns to the sides as they ran, though none as large as the furnace room. The golem stopped, and Glissa peered over his shoulder. They stood at a doorway into a cavern that dwarfed the furnace room. Glissa couldn't see the other side or the ceiling of the huge cave, but she could see a massive hole in the center. She had been wrong. The furnace didn't sit on top of the Mother's Womb. It was right there in front of her.

Hundreds, even thousands, of goblin-made buildings of all sizes surrounded the hole. A small army of goblins had left the city on the edge of the Womb. They marched up the path toward the entrance, heading straight for them.

"Why have you stopped?" demanded Glissa.

"I know this place," replied Bosh.

# CHAPTER 18

# THE INNER WORLD

"Is that the way out?" asked Glissa. She pointed toward the approaching goblin army.

"No," said the stoic golem.

"Tell me about the hole later," screamed Glissa, "and get us out of here."

Bosh turned from the Mother's Womb cavern and ran down the hall. Soon the hammered walls gave way to natural metal formations. Tubes ran up the walls and across the ceiling. The hammered floor continued for a while longer but eventually gave way to the rusted iron tubing that seemed to run throughout the goblin complex. The corridor had turned into a cave, and Glissa could finally see the entrance ahead. Light from the red moon washed over the floor like blood.

They emerged from the cave in the middle of a mountain range. Tubular metal formations spread out ahead of them in every direction. The mountains looked much like the furnace. Iron tubes sprang up from the ground and intertwined with one another around a central core to form metal buttes that dotted the landscape. Many of these tubular mountains were larger than Taj Nar. The ground was a twisted mass of iron tubes. A layer of rust coated everything, giving the mountains a dull red appearance.

Glissa glanced back at the entrance to see if they were being followed, but Bosh's long legs and tireless pace had left the goblin army well behind. The mountain behind them was enormous. It dwarfed the surrounding buttes. They were about a quarter of the way up the side and yet the top was obscured from view, fading into the sky and stars above. The entire mountain was made of the same tubular metal Glissa had seen inside the caverns. In fact, all the formations around her looked like they were connected through an endless iron pipeline.

"What the flare formed all of this?" she asked out loud.

"Memnarch," said Bosh.

"Memnarch made all of this?" asked Glissa. "The mountains, the furnace, the big, flaring hole?"

"He shaped the world to create homes for everyone."

"What is he?" asked Glissa. "A god? A planeswalker?"

"I cannot . . . remember."

"Well, don't hurt yourself." Glissa slapped him on the shoulder. "It will come back. Give it time. For now, tell me about that big hole—the Mother's Womb."

"I ascended a hole similar to the . . . Womb," said Bosh. "I recall the inner world that Slobad described. I remember emerging from such a hole and seeing the stars and moon above."

"Wait a minute. You said 'a hole similar to that one.' Are there others?"

"Yes," said the golem. "I believe so."

"How many?"

"Three," said Bosh. "Perhaps four."

"Do you remember anything else?" asked Glissa.

"No."

* * * * *

Bosh ran on in silence. Glissa turned around and watched the red moon disappear behind the mountain. She examined herself in the dim light of the blue moon, the one the goblins called the Eye of Doom. The wound over her ribs had closed, but her feet had swollen in the hours since the battle on the furnace floor. She summoned mana from the distant Tangle and let it pulse in her palms. She rubbed her feet lightly with the energy. It soaked into her blistered flesh and soothed the pain. She would need new boots, but her feet would heal. She had been lucky.

Glissa glanced up at the Eye of Doom again. They must head toward the Eye next, which always seemed to hover at the horizon. Chunth said the moons were heading for a convergence. Each moon, she knew, would rise over its own land. During her time with the leonin, she had seen the yellow moon—what the leonin called a sun—rise high above Taj Nar. The red moon—Slobad's Sky Tyrant—was almost directly overheard when they emerged from the goblins' lair. She was sure the Eye of Doom shone most brightly over the Quicksilver Sea. That was where they would find the vedalken. That was where she would find her answers.

Eventually, Bosh slowed down. "We are near the entrance to the cult lair," he said.

Glissa glanced about. The only light came from the distant blinkmoth stars. While her eyes were poor in pitch dark, they worked well enough in the dim twilight. She spotted a faintly illuminated rectangle outlined in a tubular outcropping.

"There," she said, pointing to the disguised door.

Bosh pressed on a tube next to the door to open it, and they slipped inside. Glissa dropped off the golem's shoulders and led the way through the halls. She didn't know the layout of the lair, but she was sure she could find the inner wall that housed Slobad's secret scrying room. She watched for duct covers. After twisting and turning through the lair she found a long hallway that had duct openings placed at regular intervals, each across from an intersecting corridor.

"This is the spot," she said. "I don't know how to get in there, though."

"I can get us through the wall," said Bosh.

"I don't think Slobad would like that much," said Glissa. "We'll just wait for him."

A portion of the wall opened up behind them, and Slobad peeked out. "You right, elf," he said. "Secret room not very secret with hole in wall, huh?"

"Slobad!" shouted Glissa. She ran over and dropped to her knees to give the little goblin a hug. "You made it out."

"Of course." He pushed the elf away and brushed himself off. "Slobad always survive. It what he do best, huh? You okay?"

"I could use some new boots and a good night's sleep," replied Glissa. "How are Dwugget and the others?"

"Alive," said Dwugget, coming up behind Slobad, "thanks to you, my girl."

"Thank Slobad. He got me there. He put me back together just as he did Bosh."

Slobad looked at Bosh. "I need to finish job. Do better work on elf, huh?"

The goblin led the golem and Glissa into the secret room and began to work on the golem's arm. Bosh held his limb in place while Slobad climbed onto the metal man's shoulders to work. Glissa sat across from them and pulled off the tattered remains of her boots. She set the boot sheath aside and laid out the scorched leather to see what she could salvage.

Dwugget took the leather from Glissa. "Let us help," he said. "We repair before we leave."

"Thank you, Dwugget," she said. "I'm going to need them. I have a long trip ahead of me this time."

"Where will you go?" asked Dwugget. "What great mission take you and Slobad all across Mirrodin, huh?"

Glissa almost laughed. "I plan to go to the Quicksilver Sea," she said. "I'm going to find the person responsible for the attack last night."

"We thought it was the goblin shamans," said Dwugget, "come to purify the Krark cult once and for all."

"They probably helped," said Glissa. "But those silver beasts belonged to someone who's been trying to kill me. I've seen similar creatures before."

While Slobad fixed Bosh's arm, Glissa told Dwugget her tale. She explained how Slobad saved her from the leveler and how they had found Bosh in the Dross. She told him of the deaths of her friends and family.

"Those deaths not etched in your metal, huh?" said Dwugget. "They not your fault. Do not blame yourself for the corrosion of others."

Glissa nodded. "We plan to cut away the corrosion so it cannot taint our metal any longer," she said. "That's why we go to the Quicksilver Sea, to find the person responsible."

"Slobad tell me your destiny has something to do with Great Shaman Krark and our Mother's Heart," said Dwugget.

"I don't know," said Glissa. "It may all be connected somehow. My shaman, a troll priest named Chunth, told me of a world within our world. He believed it was very important to my destiny. What can you tell me about the inner world that Krark found?"

"Krark keep journal during trip," said Dwugget. "Goblin shamans destroy, but not before I copy most, huh? We call it *Book of Krark*. I let you read."

"Thank you."

Dwugget took her boots over toward the cultists, who were resting on the other side of the chamber. Glissa turned to Slobad, whose hand had disappeared into the joint between Bosh's arm and his shoulder.

"Where can we take Dwugget's people where they can be safe?" she asked.

"We take to leveler lair as soon as Bosh fixed," he replied. "Should be safe there again, huh?"

"You and Bosh take them there," said Glissa. "I'm going to the Quicksilver Sea."

"Leveler lair not far," said the goblin. "We all go. Slobad know way. Bosh get us there fast, huh?"

Dwugget returned with a dark leather book. The cover was curved, leather wrapped around a piece of mountain iron. Inside, leather pages were bound together by straps laced through the iron half-tube. Glissa took the book as she had seen trolls handle religious objects during ceremonies. Touching it filled her with a sense of wonder and purpose she had never before experienced.

She bowed her head to Dwugget, then turned back to Slobad. "You two are staying," she said. "It's not safe."

"That why we go," grunted Slobad, pushing against some tool inside Bosh's shoulder. "Keep crazy elf safe."

"You will require our assistance," said the golem.

Bosh's commanding voice seemed almost comical as he sat holding his own arm in his lap while Slobad perched on his back, grunting and poking inside the golem's shoulder. Glissa wanted to argue the point. She knew it would do no good. In the end, they were as stubborn as she was. For now she began to read the *Book of Krark*.

> *The Great Mother called to me again last night. She sent me a vision of her Heart. I floated down through her Womb into an inner world. Her Heart hung low in the sky, glowing with the might of the four suns. I reached for it, but the Heart was just out of my reach. It hung there, filling the inner world with power and light. I felt warm, as if I were standing before the furnace. I felt content, like I had found my true home.*

\* \* \* \* \*

*Glissa looked up from the book to see an alien landscape. She stood on bare metal. The ground around her was featureless: flat, smooth, and gray as far as she could see. The* Book of Krark *had disappeared from her hands, but she remained in her own metal-clad body. Huge plantlike formations of crystalline material dotted the metal plains around her. The crystal plant towers reached hundreds of feet into the air toward a huge ball of energy that dominated the sky. They glittered and reflected the light of the Heart in every direction, creating rainbows of color that swept across the sky and collided with one another.*

*Glissa knew this was a flare, though she had never before recognized one while she was in it. How could this scene come from her life or from some racial memory? The elves had never been to the inner world. Or was she reliving Krak's journey? Yet she was in her body, not some ancient elf or goblin body.*

*The vision began to dissolve around her as she pondered its reality.*

*"No!" she cried. The sound echoed strangely across the plains. It bounced back and forth among the crystal towers, multiplying into hundreds of noes winging their way across the inner world. The vision came back into focus as Glissa concentrated on the echoes.*

*She walked among the crystal towers. They seemed to reach into the sky toward the central moon . . . or was it a sun? High above her, Glissa could see white specks floating in the air. Blinkmoths? She couldn't be sure. They seemed to glow, but perhaps it was the light of the orb passing through them. The orb pulsed like a beating heart inside the breast of the world. Each pulse sent a different color cascading around the orb—blue, red, white, black, green.*

*The specks began to swirl. The light pulses within the Heart cycled faster, and the tiny motes twirled faster as well. The effect was dizzying. Glissa's knees buckled beneath her, and she fell to*

*the ground. She stared up at the Heart. The colored lights sped
across the Heart so fast they became a blur. The cloud of white
specks turned into maelstrom, twisting around and around above
her like a tunnel to the Heart.*

*The Heart turned bright blue for a moment at the other end
of the storm, then burst in a shower of color. A blue orb of energy
hurtled down the twisting tunnel like a bolt of lightning. A huge
thunderclap shook the ground and tossed Glissa into the air.
When she landed, the elf glanced up and screamed just before
the blue ball slammed into the surface of the inner world . . . and
her.*

\* \* \* \* \*

Glissa awoke with a start. The *Book of Krark* clattered to the
floor. The room was dark around her. A single fire tube burned in
the far wall above the cultists. They were asleep on the floor.
Glissa picked up the book and set it on the table.

She rose and walked around the room. Bosh sat in a corner, his
red eyes glowing in the darkness. Glissa could see Slobad curled
up on the golem's legs. He was snoring again.

"Are you all right?" whispered Bosh.

"Yes," she said, "but why do they always have to end with my
death?"

"I'm sorry?"

"Nothing," said Glissa. "Just had a bad dream."

"You should sleep," the golem said. "I will guard until the
suns set."

Glissa chuckled. "You've been listening to Slobad," she said.
"The elves call them moons."

"Why?"

"I don't know," she said. "They just feel like moons to us.
They never rise above the Tangle, and they give us precious little

light. A sun should burn bright above you and warm your face when you look at it."

"You should sleep," said the golem again. "We leave after the . . . moons set."

Glissa watched the cultists sleep. Her repaired boots stood on the floor near Dwugget. She picked them up and sat at the table to put them on. Glissa glanced down at the *Book of Krark* again, then at the remaining cultists. There weren't many of them left, but they still clung to their beliefs—even though that belief had nearly cost all their lives. These goblins gave up their former homes, their former lives, and risked everything because they believed in something larger than themselves. Could she do no less?

Something bad was happening to their world. Chunth knew it. Ushanti dreamed it. Glissa had seen glimpses of it in her own flares. She was fighting for all of them now. Whether she wanted the mantle or not, she had become the champion for the goblins as well as the trolls and elves—perhaps even for the leonin, nim, and everyone else on this world. There *was* an inner world. She knew that now. Somehow she also knew that she had to reach it to face her destiny.

Bosh had been right. She needed Slobad and the golem in this battle. The stakes were too high. It wasn't just her against some killer. It was her battling for the future of their world. Bosh had information locked in his head about the inner world and Memnarch. She needed it to make the right choices, to avoid Ushanti's vision. Slobad knew how to survive. He had an instinct for living, an instinct she would need in the coming days. Bosh was right. She needed them. If not for her, then for the Krark cultists, for the leonin, the elves, and the trolls.

Glissa picked up the *Book of Krark* and carried it over toward Bosh. She lay down and curled up beside the metal man, holding the book to her chest. Bosh patted her head with his newly replaced arm. She fell asleep with the golem's arm wrapped around her like a blanket.

\* \* \* \* \*

They left after the red moon set behind the mountains. The terrain flattened somewhat as they made their way toward the Glimmervoid. Rust-colored outcroppings of metal still surrounded them, but the iron tubes no longer ran through the ground beneath their feet. Those had given way to flat metal slabs that seemed slammed together in a huge red tile mosaic. The slabs often shifted under their feet, making the descent slow and torturous. As they skirted between the rusty buttes, Glissa could see the rolling metal plains of the Glimmervoid glittering in the starlight in the distance.

Bosh and Slobad scouted ahead during the night and returned just as Glissa saw the top edge of the yellow moon between two outcroppings. The goblin and his golem led Glissa and the cultists to an abandoned cave they had found.

That night, Glissa read more of the *Book of Krark*. As a shaman who received visions from his deity, Krark set himself apart and made an enemy of the shaman elder, who seemed more concerned with his own power than imparting any sort of wisdom to the goblins. One passage stood out to her:

> *I have asked the shaman elder to let me enter Mother's Womb. I told him of my visions and my desire to seek her Heart. He cursed me for spreading lies about the Mother and promised to send me to the furnace if I spoke such heresy again. He cannot see the glory of the Mother. I must make him see. I must see the Heart. She calls to me.*

The next night, Glissa came to the passage Slobad had recited to her in the cult lair before the attack.

*I stood in a sloping chamber with no roof, surrounded by ancient towers of coral. A giant sun hung above me, glowing like Sky Tyrant, and Bringer, and Ingle, and the Eye of Doom. I had found Mother's Heart. The Heart beat in the sky, giving life to the world. The stars danced around the heart, happy to live in her divine glow. Her heat warmed my face and my heart. I was home.*

On the next page was a sketch showing the scene Krark described. Glissa recognized it, both from Krark's description and from her own flare two nights before.

"Look at this, Bosh," she said. "It's an image of the inner world. Dwugget must have copied this from the original journal. Do you see the specks rising up from those . . . towers? Krark says, 'It rained upward toward the heart from them.' I saw these in a dream the other night. Are they blinkmoths? Chunth told me that the rain comes from the blinkmoths—the stars we see above us."

Bosh looked at the picture in the book. His eyes narrowed, and Glissa could tell he was trying to remember anything else about his life within the inner world. His eyes opened wide as if he'd had a disturbing vision.

"Myco . . . mycosynth. Those are mycosynth spores, not blinkmoths. The mycosynth crystals produce spores. Blinkmoths are eternal. Mycosynth arrived later."

"What do you mean?" asked Glissa. "Memnarch created the mycosynth but not the blinkmoths? I thought you said he made everything."

"Memnarch shaped the world to his desires. He did not create it," said Bosh. "Blinkmoths predate even Memnarch. Mycosynth arrived later like a plague. I believe I may have been created to battle the mycosynth infestation, but I lost the battle. That is all I remember. Everything else is blank until you and Slobad found me in the Mephidross."

Glissa left Bosh alone with his patchwork memory and returned to the book. They were less than a night's travel from the leveler lair, and she was almost finished with the *Book of Krark*. It read like a flare. Krark had been drawn to the Womb and the Heart as if by destiny. He entered the massive hole and walked down its length into another world, a world inside the world, that curved up and away in all directions.

> *It is like being in a valley surrounded by hills that stretch up to the sky. In that sky, Mother's Heart hangs like a single sun that never moves.*

Chunth was telling the truth. Krark had seen it. Bosh had lived it, and Glissa had dreamed it, but what did it all mean? If there were huge holes leading to this inner world, why had nobody but Krark ever descended? Bosh said the mycosynth were a plague, but if they were so pervasive, why had no one ever seen them in the outer world? They were pieces of a puzzle, but Glissa had no idea how to put them together.

Glissa pulled out the vial of serum. Were the answers in there? She thought about drinking the serum to gain the knowledge of whatever ancient power had created the blinkmoths. But Chunth had kept his secrets to protect the elves and the trolls from the serum. He'd died protecting his secrets—and her. She would only use the serum if she had no other options.

\* \* \* \* \*

They arrived at the leveler lair well before the moons rose the next morning. Glissa and Slobad went in to investigate, while Bosh remained to guard the cultists. Slobad lit his fire tube as they entered the dark chamber that had been his home. The place had been ransacked. The table, chairs, and workbench had all been destroyed. When Slobad checked the passage to the leveler lair, he found it blocked off.

"You were right," said Glissa. "Whoever takes care of those monsters found your home. Aren't you worried they'll come back?"

"Only if some crazy elf destroys more levelers, huh?" said Slobad. "You not going to do that, huh?" He smiled.

"I was thinking about it," said Glissa. She looked around. "There's not much space here."

"More chambers there and there, huh?" said Slobad, pointing to the walls on either side of the small room. He pushed the remains of his workbench out of the way and opened a panel then moved across the room and opened a second panel. "They survive."

The other chambers were untouched, and Glissa crawled out to get the cultists. "It's not much," she said to Dwugget, "but you'll be safe here. The shaman elder will never send anyone here. When this is over, maybe Slobad can clear out more chambers for you."

"Thank you again," said Dwugget. "You have done much for us, huh? We follow Krark and Glissa now."

"Well, I'm not sure I'm planning to follow Krark down that hole," she said.

"You will," said the cult leader. "All answers are within the Mother's Heart."

# CHAPTER 19

# BRUENNA

They left for the Quicksilver Sea immediately. There was still a few hours of dark before the yellow moon rose over the Glimmervoid. Slobad rode atop Bosh, and Glissa had taken her normal seat in the crook of the golem's iron arm. They backtracked up into the mountains for a while before turning and heading in a new direction. Glissa could see the Glimmervoid off to her left through the mountains.

"We're going to need information about the vedalken," Glissa said to the goblin. "Do you know anything at all about the Quicksilver Sea?"

"Know that humans live on edge of sea, huh?" said Slobad. "Wizards, mostly. Have no need for goblin repairs, so Slobad leave alone. Never go back, huh?"

"Wizards?" said Glissa. "The robed figure was a wizard, but he was vedalken. At least we assume he was. At the very least, he definitely was not human—not with four arms. If these humans live near the sea, though, they may know something about the vedalken. It's as good a place to start as any. We'll find ourselves a wizard and ask some questions. How far is the sea?"

"Not far," said Slobad. "Not on Bosh's shoulders, huh? Be there one rotation, maybe less."

\* \* \* \* \*

The next day, Glissa, Slobad, and Bosh emerged from the mountains. Small outcroppings of tubular iron dotted the slope ahead of them, but beyond those lay a flat valley that led to the shores of the sea. Glissa looked up and down the mountain range. To her left, the range flattened out to meet with the Glimmervoid off near the horizon. The valley and the sea snaked in and out at the edge of the mountains. To her right, she could see that both the mountains and the sea ended abruptly in a curtain of green haze just at the limits of her vision—the Glimmervoid.

Glissa searched for signs of habitation. She didn't know if the humans lived in the mountains, in the valley, or on the sea. She hoped they didn't live in the Dross. Her gaze kept wandering back to the Quicksilver Sea. It glistened in the light of the moons, seeming almost alive. From her vantage point in the hills above the valley, she could see its silvery surface swirl and ripple in a hypnotizing pattern of blue, red, yellow, and black shadows.

The ripples were chaotic. As children, Glissa and Kane would toss small bits of metal in rain barrels to watch the tiny waves build and move across the surface and break against the edges. The Quicksilver Sea, though, undulated at random, as if something just below the surface, or the sea itself, were alive.

Glissa tore her gaze from the sea and concentrated on the valley. As they moved past the last of the iron formations, she saw at the edge of the sea a town of some sort. Shelters had been built in circles around a central structure much larger than the rest. A series of large planks stuck out from the shore at the edge of the town. In between these planks Glissa saw transports of some sort that must be used to cross the sea.

"There," she said, pointing to the human town. "We'll find our answers in that settlement."

"You think they talk to goblin, elf, and golem?" asked Slobad. "Never see elf this far from Tangle. Nobody ever see the golem before, huh? And goblins and humans never get along, huh?"

Glissa thought about it. "You may be right," she said. "We won't get any answers if they think it's for the goblins, and Bosh will just scare the flare from them."

"We capture one?"

"No. If the humans aren't working with the vedalken, we don't want to alienate them. If they are, capturing one might expose us."

"What we do, huh?"

"Glissa can impersonate a human," said Bosh. "Just conceal her ears."

"And her claws, huh?" added Slobad. "They scary, too." He smiled.

Glissa stopped and looked back at her companions. "Are you serious?" she said. "I've never even seen a human. How can I pretend to be one?"

"You have better plan, huh?" asked Slobad. "Wait for hover birds come back and follow them?"

Glissa considered that one for a moment. "No," she said. "Okay. We'll try deception. It might work if I don't stay too long. Just ask some questions and get out. I'll need something to cover my ears. I can't just tie a sword belt around my head."

"Leave to me, huh?" said Slobad.

\* \* \* \* \*

After the moons set, Slobad slipped into the town while Glissa and Bosh skirted around to the docks, heading for several large buildings near the ships Slobad said were used for storage. Glissa wandered around the storage shed. Several dismantled ships from the docks sat inside. Glissa didn't know if they were being built, destroyed, or fixed. From their appearance, though, she could tell they weren't vedalken. These ships were crude compared to the hover beasts she had fought. They looked more like something Slobad would build. The sides were hammered, and the connections were visible. The hover beasts had been sleek and self-contained.

Glissa climbed up on the deck of one of the ships. It was nothing more than leather hide stitched together and strapped across a metal-and-bone frame. Two large tubes of iron supported the leather deck. Glissa suspected these had been taken from the mountains. No wonder they don't get along with the goblins, she thought. The humans have been stealing goblin metal.

She heard a noise and dropped to the deck, but it was just Slobad returning. The elf clambered down from the ship and took the bundle he handed her. She unwrapped the package to find a dark, hooded robe and matching blouse and boots.

"Where'd you get those?" she asked.

"Borrowed them, huh?" said the goblin, grinning.

The clothes were like nothing Glissa had ever seen before. They smelled like leather but were supple and flowed like water in her hands. She looked closely at the material. It appeared the leather had been cut into fine strips and woven together.

Glissa stripped off her jerkin and pulled the new blouse from the bundle. Slobad spun around and Glissa thought the goblin's neck turned an even darker shade of red.

"No time for modesty, Slobad," she said as she slipped the new shirt over her head.

She pulled off her tattered boots. The cultists had done a wonderful job repairing them, but they wouldn't last much longer. She pulled on the new boots. They were a little large, so she tied them around her leg with a few strips of leather from her old boots, slipped the dagger sheath into her new boots, and stood up.

"I found out leader's name," said Slobad, still facing the wall. "She female named Bruenna. Live in big building, huh? Middle of town. Big building, huh?

"You can turn around now, Slobad," said Glissa. She pulled the cloak around herself. "I'll go pay Bruenna a visit."

"Wait until the first sun is about to rise," said Bosh.

"Why?" asked Glissa. "She'll be alone now. This will be the best time to talk to her privately."

"She will not expect a guest at night," replied Bosh. "She will be suspicious. Go while she breaks her fast. You avoid the crowds but do not raise suspicion."

"Fine," said Glissa. "This is your plan. I'll wait." She pulled her hood over her head and walked to the back corner of the shed to lie down. "Wake me when it's time."

\* \* \* \* \*

Bosh shook Glissa awake. "The blue sun rises," he said.

Glissa looked at the metal man through bleary eyes. "What?" she asked.

"The blue sun," he said again. "It will crest over the Quicksilver Sea momentarily."

"Oh. Fine."

She walked to the door, readjusting the hood to cover her ears and most of her face. She then folded her arms inside the folds of the cloak to hide her claws. Those parts of her skin that were still visible she covered with mud, hoping no one would notice her green hue. Slobad opened the door, and Glissa peered out.

"Most of the ships are gone from the docks."

"Fisherman, maybe? They early risers, huh?" said Slobad. "All leave while you sleep."

"What's a fisherman?" she asked.

"A man who fishes, huh?" said Slobad. He continued as Glissa stared at him with a blank expression on her face. "You crazy again, elf? Humans catch fish—food—in sea. Bring home to eat, huh? Man who catches fish is fisherman."

Glissa nodded. "Well, find yourselves a good hiding spot until I get back," she said. "In case someone comes back needing parts."

She slipped through the door and crept to the side of the shed. She saw nobody walking about in the lanes between the shelters. It looked as if Bosh was right. She turned the corner and began walking slowly and deliberately toward the center of the town, keeping her head down and her hands tucked inside the cloak.

She passed a few humans heading toward the docks on her way through the ring of homes surrounding the main town building. She nodded at them as they passed, but they mostly ignored her. Glissa didn't know what a fisherman would look like, but these people were all dressed in robes like her own and had an air of magic about them. She wondered if they used magic to catch the fish.

She found Bruenna's home easily enough. It was the largest building in the town, larger than two storage sheds. While the shelters surrounding it were simple metal boxes with leather curtains for doors, this building was ornate. Metal columns supported the roof, and symbols had been etched in the wall above polished double doors. Glissa climbed the wide steps that led to the doors and knocked.

The door opened, and an old human female stood before Glissa. She had long white hair, and her face was almost as wrinkled as a troll's. The old woman wore dark clothing similar to that which Slobad had stolen for Glissa, but her robes were dyed blue, and strands of silver ran through the woven leather. The dress glittered in the light of the blue moon rising behind Glissa.

"Bruenna," began Glissa. "I—"

"Are you here to see Mistress Bruenna?" the woman interrupted.

"Yes," said Glissa. "Tell her a messenger brings news from the vedalken."

"Right this way," said the woman. She showed the elf to a chair. "Wait here while I tell Mistress Bruenna of your arrival. May I take your cloak?"

"No!" stammered Glissa. "I—I am cold from my journey through the night. I will keep it for now."

"As you wish." The old woman left the room.

Glissa glanced about the room. It was bare. Taj Nar had been resplendent in gold and silver trinkets. The entire city gleamed in the moonlight from all of the polished metal. This house, though, which seemed so grand on the outside, was plain within. Bruenna's home had few furnishings of any kind and no ornamentation on the walls or tables. For a leader of her people, Bruenna lived a simple life, thought Glissa.

The old woman returned. "Mistress Bruenna will see you now."

Glissa followed the woman down a short corridor. They entered another room, where a beautiful young woman sat eating, long blonde hair curling around her face. She wore the same blue garment as the older woman, but hers had gold fibers woven throughout the garment instead of silver.

Bruenna was looking through a leather scroll. The table was strewn with piles of scrolls. It looked as if the leader of the humans hardly ever left this room.

"Yes? What is it?" asked Bruenna without even looking up at Glissa.

"I bring an important message from the vedalken."

"What do they want now?" asked Bruenna. "More wizards? More goblin ore? Well, I don't have any more wizards to send them, and the next shipment of ore isn't due for days. Go tell them that, and leave me to my work."

"They wish an audience with you, Mistress Bruenna," said Glissa. "To discuss . . . schedules."

Bruenna looked up at Glissa. "I—I've been called before the Synod?"

"Yes," said Glissa. "I am to take you there myself." She was amazed at how well Slobad's scheme was working. Could she really get Bruenna to take them to the vedalken?

Bruenna was obviously agitated. She slammed the scroll down, almost toppling a plate of food. "I have done everything demanded of me. What more can they want?"

"Perhaps more serum?" ventured Glissa.

The human gave her a cold stare. "Who are you?" asked Bruenna. "Who sent you?"

"I told you," said Glissa. "I am but a simple messenger of the Synod."

"Did Lord Xauvrer send you?"

"Why yes," said Glissa. "I believe it was Lord Xauvrer himself who dispatched me."

Bruenna smiled grimly. "There is no Lord Xauvrer. Anyone— any human—would know that is not even a vedalken name. Who *are* you?"

With a quick wave of her hand, Bruenna released a ball of blue mana into the air. It expanded and washed over Glissa like a cold wind, pulling her hood back and ripping the cloak from her body. Glissa pulled out her sword and leaped onto the table.

"I'm no human," she said, "but you *are* coming with me to this Synod of yours."

Bruenna waved her hand again, and a stiff wind tossed Glissa and the table back against the wall. Glissa fell to the floor amidst a rain of scrolls. Her sword clattered to the floor beside her.

"What in the winds are you?" demanded Bruenna.

"I am an elf," Glissa replied. "An elf who doesn't want to kill you, but I will if I have to." She snatched her sword from the ground and jumped to her feet.

"Let's see you try." Bruenna waved her hand again.

"You'll need more than a little wind to stop me," growled the elf. Another blast of wind slammed into her, but Glissa braced her back foot against the overturned table and held her ground. When the wind subsided, she dived at Bruenna, carrying the human to the floor beneath her.

"Perhaps your old servant will be more willing to take me to your vedalken masters," Glissa gasped, pinching her legs together to hold Bruenna in place.

"You leave my mother out of this," shouted Bruenna. "I won't let you harm her."

The human brought her hands up between her and Glissa. Glissa tried to grab the mage's wrists to keep her from casting any more spells. The two women scrambled on the floor, but before she could get Bruenna's arms secured, Glissa felt a strange tingling on the back of her neck. She threw herself off Bruenna and rolled into the corner of the room.

The wall erupted behind the human, showering the room with scraps of metal. Electricity danced across the remains of the tattered metal wall. A moment later a second bolt of lightning screamed through the hole and blasted the upturned table.

"Aerophuis!" shouted Glissa. "I knew you were in league with the vedalken. How did you call them here so quickly?"

"How did *I* call them?" demanded Bruenna. "Look what they did to my wall." She scrambled to the other corner of the room and put her back up against the wall. "You must have brought them with you!"

"Your master's assassins, come to help you defeat me," snorted the elf. "Well, I've fought aerophuis before. They don't scare me."

"They scare the wind from me," retorted Bruenna.

"Why would they attack you?" asked Glissa. "Aren't you allied with the vedalken?"

"Allies? No. We're little more than slaves."

Glissa considered Bruenna for a moment. She didn't know if she should trust the human at her word. The aerophuis made up Glissa's mind for her. The tingle returned to the back of her neck.

"They're coming in for another pass," she shouted. "Come on."

The elf scrambled to her feet and ran from the room, slicing through what was left of the table with her sword. She could hear Bruenna running behind her. Glissa dived to the ground in the front room just before the next impact. When she glanced down the hall, all she could see was smoke and lingering electricity where the corridor wall used to be.

Bruenna's mother ran into the room, screaming. "They're back, they're back, they're back! Why are they back?"

The human ruler ran to her mother and wrapped her arms around the older woman. "I don't know, Mother. We must have displeased the Synod."

Glissa stood and sheathed her sword. "It's my fault," she said. "They're after me. If you'll help me, maybe I can help you."

Bruenna looked at her mother, then looked down the corridor at the wreckage. "That would be dangerous for me and for my people."

"More dangerous than staying here?" retorted Glissa. She felt a familiar tingle. "Decide now. The aerophuis are returning."

Bruenna and her mother shook in fear, but the young mage found the courage to reply. "Defeat the aerophuis and save my people. Then we'll talk."

"Fine." Glissa ran for the front doors. "Once I'm outside, they should leave your house alone. I could use your help, though."

The elf emerged into the blue dawn and ran down the steps. She felt rather than saw the human mage behind her. The pair sprinted toward the ring of shelters surrounding Bruenna's home. Glissa heard the aerophuis roar over the house behind them.

"See if you can slow them down with that wind of yours," she shouted as she ran.

"I'll try."

Glissa's ears popped as the air pressure dropped suddenly behind her. She looked back and saw two aerophuis tumbling end over end backward toward Bruenna's home.

"Well done!"

"You still haven't defeated them," shouted Bruenna.

"I have friends down by the docks. They'll be able to help us if we can get there."

The two women ran side by side through the town. People rushed back and forth looking for protection from the attacks. Some villagers called to Bruenna for help. Between strides she ordered them to return to their homes.

Lightning bolts flew behind them, but Bruenna's spells kept them safe long enough to reach the docks. The elf banged the door open to the storage shed and ran inside, slamming it behind Bruenna.

"Slobad, Bosh," she called. "Where are you? We need you. Now!"

Nobody was in the shed. One ship was missing. Glissa frantically searched the shed.

"I'll go find them," she said. "You stay here."

Bruenna didn't argue. Glissa opened the door and changed her mind about leaving. At least ten of the silver assassins were arrayed just over the docks. They hovered there, facing the door. She slammed the door shut.

"We have a small problem."

# CHAPTER 20

# QUICKSILVER SEA

Glissa beckoned Bruenna to the door. "Aerophins," she said. "Lots of them, and my friends are missing. We're on our own."

"Why didn't you sense them?" asked Bruenna.

"I don't know," replied Glissa.

Bruenna paced back and forth, her eyebrows furrowed. "You can sense their mana buildup. They have to charge their attack before releasing the lightning. That's why it takes so long between blasts. Someone's figured out you can sense that, so the aerophins haven't charged up yet."

"Then why are they hovering out there?" asked Glissa. "They have us trapped in here. Why not attack?"

Both women stared at each other.

"Because they have us trapped in here," said Glissa slowly.

Bruenna nodded. "They're holding us here until something—or someone—else arrives."

"We have to get away from here. Any suggestions?"

"Run," said Bruenna.

*"That's* your plan?"

"Look," said Bruenna, "it will take the aerophins time to charge their attack. That gets us out the door. I'll slow them down with a gust of wind, and we run."

Glissa shook her head. "They'll follow us wherever we run. Where do we go?"

"I don't know," the human mage answered. "Away from town. Into the mountains. Anywhere. Staying here is suicide and puts my people at risk."

"Fine." Glissa nodded. "You're right. We'll run into the mountains. That's the most likely place to find my friends. Anyway, maybe I can destroy some of these beasts. I've done it before."

"How did you do that?" asked Bruenna.

"I have no idea," said Glissa as she moved back toward the door. "It just happened. You might have to die first, though. Ready?"

Bruenna walked to the door, crossed her arms in front of her, and nodded. Glissa pulled the door open, and the mage flung her arms wide. Glissa felt a blast of wind whip by her. The doorframe rattled from the force. Bruenna ran out the door, and the elf followed.

The aerophins scattered, tumbling in the sudden wind. Bruenna ran along the shore, Glissa beside her, glancing back to keep an eye on their pursuers. Two of the aerophins crashed into the sea. The quicksilver was thick and buoyant. The aerophins didn't sink, but they couldn't pull themselves free, either. Behind one of the aerophins a sleek neck broke the surface of the quicksilver with hardly a ripple. It looked like a giant serpent. Its head snaked five feet into the air and opened its jaws wide, revealing rows of shiny teeth, then slammed back into the sea, snapping its mouth shut around the tail of the silver creature. The predator disappeared under the surface.

As they cleared the dock area, Glissa heard screams from the village. Young children ran screaming through the streets while adults tried to catch and calm them down. A little boy ran right toward Glissa, crying, followed by a gray-haired man. "Riley, come back here! It's not safe," shouted the man.

"Get indoors!" shouted Glissa as she ran on. "Hurry."

She doubled her pace. The man caught Riley at the shore just as the aerophins roared over their heads.

"We have to get away from town!" shouted Bruenna. "Then we'll head toward the mountains."

"There's not much cover in the valley."

"I'm counting on you to tell me when to dodge."

"Great," said Glissa. She felt a familiar tingling sensation. "Now would be a good time. They're charging."

Bruenna broke away from the sea's edge and dived to the ground. Glissa thought about plunging into the quicksilver but remembered the sea serpent.

The aerophins held their charge. Either they had gotten smarter or something was controlling them. Glissa's foot slipped into the quicksilver and slid out from under her. She landed flat on her face—an easy target.

The aerophins were almost on top of her. She rolled back away from the sea and went for her sword. They came in fast and low, their globes glowing and crackling with lightning. She had nowhere to go. Lightning streaked over Glissa's head and slammed into the dirt and quicksilver around her.

Glissa glanced around, looking for Bruenna to thank her for blasting the aerophins. Instead she saw a human boat speed through the flock. Slobad stood at the front of the boat, staring intently at a board in front of him, with Bosh right behind him. As the boat sailed through the low-flying aerophins, Bosh swatted at the silver birds, knocking two into the sea with a single swing of his large, iron hand.

The rest of the flock flew up into the sky. Glissa scrambled to her feet and ran after the boat, hoping the goblin could turn it before the aerophins returned.

Bruenna ran over. "What was that?" she asked.

"My friends," replied Glissa. "Come on."

The two ran back toward the docks, following the boat. Slobad was not completely in control, and it swerved back and forth next to the shore. The little boy, Riley, screamed as the boat sped toward them. The old man grabbed the boy and dived out the way. Slobad veered away from the shore and skidded sideways into the docks.

Glissa glanced behind her. The remaining aerophins had regrouped. "Get inside!" she shouted at the old man. "It's not safe out here." The old man stared at her, shaking. Glissa sprinted for the boat.

She heard Bruenna behind her. "It's all right, Jerryl. She's a friend . . . I think. Get your grandson to safety."

"Hurry up!" shouted Glissa. The tingling began on her neck. "We're out of time."

The elf took two steps into the sea. The quicksilver pulled at her feet. She stretched her arms out to grasp the side of the boat and missed. Her fingertips scraped the iron tube on the side as she saw the quicksilver coming up toward her face. A hand shot out from the boat and grabbed her wrist. Bosh pulled on Glissa's arm, but her momentum carried her into the side of the boat. Her stomach slammed into the rusty tube and knocked the wind from her.

Bosh pulled Glissa onto the boat and dropped her onto the leather deck. She curled up into a ball and wrapped her arms around her stomach. Glissa fought for breath so she could speak. "Protect . . . Bruenna," she gasped.

"I have her," the golem said calmly.

"Slobad . . . go!" Glissa wheezed.

She heard the wings of approaching aerophins. She tried to stand but was thrown to the deck as the boat lurched away from the dock. Glissa looked up to see Bruenna wave her arms at the beasts. Her ears popped as the wind rushed from Bruenna's hands above her.

"Did it work?" asked the elf. She pushed herself back up again. Her gut hurt, and she had trouble balancing in the moving boat.

Bruenna shook her head. "Most of them dived under the gust. It slowed them down, but they're still coming."

Glissa saw the aerophins behind them, skating just above the sea. "I have an idea," she said. "Blast 'em again, but aim at the quicksilver. Do it quick. My neck is tingling."

Bruenna tossed her hands out and spread her fingers wide. Glissa watched the energy leap from her hands as the mage released a blast of air. The wind hit the sea and sent a wave of quicksilver up into the air behind the boat.

"Pour it on," called Glissa.

Bruenna fed more mana into the wind. The wave grew and spread away from the boat. The aerophins tried to rise above the incoming wave but couldn't climb fast enough. The quicksilver wave slammed into the flock, engulfing the lead birds before they could get out of the path. One by one, the aerophins disappeared into the receding wave until only two were left. They rose up away from the sea and sped toward the boat.

"Can this thing go any faster?" called Glissa.

"Don't ask me, huh?" grumbled Slobad. "I just learn to work it."

"I can get more speed from it," said Bruenna. She walked to the front of the boat, hooking her feet under an iron tube that ran the length of the leather deck as she moved. She pushed the goblin from the way. Glissa saw two more iron tubes sticking up from the deck at the front of the boat, bent in toward one another about level with the goblin's head. Between them sat a large ball of quicksilver. Bruenna summoned mana into her palm and grabbed the ball. The boat lurched forward again, much faster than before.

Glissa hooked one foot under the iron rail and grabbed Bosh to steady herself. Slobad, with nothing to hold onto, slid toward the back of the boat. Glissa stuck out her free foot and caught the goblin as he went past.

"You might want to stay low," called Bruenna. "I'm going to try to lose them in the crystal islands."

Glissa reached down and pulled Slobad over to the foot rail. The goblin grabbed the iron tube with both hands. His little body bounced up and down on the leather deck as the boat sped across the quicksilver. Glissa bent down into a crouch and grabbed the iron tube to steady herself. She glanced back to check on the aerophins. Twin gusts of wind sprayed from the end of the iron pontoons that supported the leather deck. Quicksilver sprayed into the air behind them as the boat skipped across the sea. The aerophins dropped back behind the spray but kept pace with the speeding boat. Glissa had no idea how fast they were going, but since Bruenna had taken control of the ship the shoreline had disappeared.

The boat swerved violently to the left, and Glissa snapped her attention forward again. They were coming up fast on the crystal islands, which looked more like towers than islands—giant, silver spires flowing from the sea.

The islands twisted and snaked their way into the sky like the quicksilver serpent Glissa had seen earlier. There was a group of ten ahead, but Glissa saw more dotting the sea in the distance. The towers were mesmerizing. They looked like crystallized quicksilver. The light of the two moons in the sky reflected off the spires as well as the surface of the water, turning the air between the islands into a cascade of color.

They whipped around the first island, skimming between two silver buttresses that curved down from the tower above them. Glissa looked up as they sped underneath. Dozens of rounded terraces jutted from the spire high above. Two silver bridges connected this tower with the two nearest islands in the group. Glissa thought she saw people on the bridges and terraces as they sped toward the next island, but she couldn't be sure. They were too high, and the boat was moving too fast.

Bruenna swerved sharply around the next island and continued through the chain. Glissa noticed an opening in the base of the island large enough for the boat to enter. She peered inside as they sped past and saw a glittering cave with a number of human boats moored within.

"Can we hide in one of those caves?" shouted Glissa as they raced toward the next island. The aerophins swung wide around the silver spire but were still close behind.

"Maybe, if I can lose them," snapped Bruenna. "If they follow us in, we'll be trapped."

Glissa pushed her hair from her eyes. "Slow down," she shouted.

"Are you crazy? They're charged and ready to attack if they get close enough. One bolt of lightning could sink us."

"Just a little closer," said Glissa. "Lure them in, then accelerate into the next cave. They can't turn as tight as you can. Trust me. This will work."

Bruenna shook her head. "Sounds crazy."

"Crazy what she do best," called Slobad from where he clung to Glissa's leg.

Bruenna moved her hand back on the quicksilver control orb, and the boat slowed. Glissa kept an eye on the aerophins as they sped toward the next island, looming closer and closer. The tingle on the back of Glissa's neck returned. They would fire any second, but the island was still some distance ahead.

"Full speed!" she shouted. "They're close enough."

Bruenna rolled her hand up on the orb, and the boat lurched forward. The aerophins were still gaining slightly but hadn't attacked yet.

"Cut as close as you can to the side of the cave."

Bruenna maneuvered the boat around a crystal island, which had a single spire growing straight from the water. As they sped around the other side, Glissa saw a silver arch curving out from the tower into the sea ahead of them. Bruenna twisted the boat to the right, just missing the arch as they skided into the cave.

The first aerophin slammed into the leg of the arch, exploding and sending debris into the sea. The second made the turn, but its momentum propelled it straight for the far side of the cave.

"Everybody down," cried Glissa. She dropped to the deck right as the aerophin slammed into the cave wall and exploded in a shower of electricity and glass. When the elf looked again, the boat was still speeding through the cave, heading straight for a row of docked boats.

"Bruenna," she screamed.

The mage stood and slapped her hand back on the quicksilver control. The boat slowed down, but Glissa could tell it wasn't going to be enough. Bruenna twisted her hand, and the boat slid sideways. They came to a stop, bumping the last two boats in the line.

"She learned that from me, huh?" said Slobad. "I did that first, huh? Remember? I did that at docks."

Glissa ignored the goblin. "Is everyone okay?"

Slobad and Bosh nodded. Bruenna looked concerned.

"What's wrong?"

"I'm fine," said Bruenna, "but we're not safe. The vedalken will send someone down here to investigate those explosions."

"Is there somewhere safe we can go?" asked Glissa. "We need to finish our talk."

"Yes, we do." said Bruenna. "Before I agree to do anything else for you, I'd like to know who you are and what trouble you've brought to my people."

"So," said Glissa, tapping her feet on the leather deck. "Where can we go?"

"I know a place," said the mage.

\* \* \* \* \*

Bruenna made her way through the islands in the chain and sailed into the middle of the sea. Glissa watched behind to make sure nobody followed. While the human piloted the boat toward a set of distant spires, Glissa told Bruenna of her adventures, starting with the death of her parents and ending with Kane's death and the description of the four-armed mage who killed him. She left out references to the goblin cult and the inner world.

After a time, they came upon a lone island jutting from the sea near the intersection of the mountains and the Mephidross haze. The island was a simple spire that corkscrewed up from the sea. Glissa noticed that it did not glitter like the towers in the crystal island chain. In fact, the silver spire looked almost dirty.

"The vedalken abandoned this island long ago," explained Bruenna as she guided the boat into the cave at its base. "It was too close to the Mephidross and was being infected by the necrogen mists—that green haze hanging over the Dross. We should be safe here."

The cave seemed to take up the entire base of the spire. A central stairway spiraled up from a landing in the center. They docked at the far side of the landing so the stairs blocked the boat from view, and ascended the spire. The interior of the crystal island was dull and greasy from the necrogen, but still it fascinated Glissa. Light from the moons came through the walls, but the walls bent the light in odd ways, stretching and distorting the world outside. If she stared at it too long, her eyes blurred and her head began to hurt.

"Would we not be more secure near the boat?" asked Bosh.

Bruenna stared at the golem. "It talks?" she asked.

Glissa smiled. "I forgot to mention that," she said. "Sorry."

Bruenna grunted. "You have some strange servants."

"They aren't servants," said Glissa. "They are my friends."

"Thank you, Glissa," said Bosh.

Bruenna stared at Glissa and shrugged. "We're going up to one of the terraces," she said. "We'll be able to see anyone coming from there."

They emerged onto a terrace that completely encircled the spire. Bosh and Slobad patrolled it while Bruenna and Glissa continued their talk.

"You were right," Bruenna said. "The mage who killed your friend was a vedalken. Why do they hunt you? I've never seen so many aerophins used against a single person before."

"I don't know," said Glissa. "I was hoping you could help me find out."

"Why should I help you?" asked the mage. "I brought you this far to get you away from my village. If I help you further, the Synod will order the destruction of my town."

Glissa sighed. "Look," she said, "you don't trust me and I don't trust you, but I have no choice. The vedalken want met dead, and I need your help. Just give me some information and you can walk away if you want. What is this Synod?"

"The Synod is the ruling council of the vedalken," replied Bruenna. "If they find you, they will know I helped you. It must be a member of the Synod after you. Only they have access to that many aerophins."

"Then help me defeat them so they don't find out," pleaded Glissa. "Look, they've already attacked my people twice. If I don't stop this, a lot more people will die, including the people of your village. Help me, and I'll try to stop that."

"With what?" asked Bruenna. "A rusty construct and a filthy goblin?"

"Fine. Don't help us. Take us back to land, and we'll find another way." Glissa turned and stared out over the vast expanse of the Quicksilver Sea. "You can go back to your forced servitude to the vedalken. Just tell me one thing—why do you work for them? You humans seem to be a fairly intelligent race, and you have magical powers. Why not work for yourselves?"

"That is exactly what my father said," said Bruenna. "They killed him for it."

"What happened?" asked Glissa.

Bruenna stared off across the gentle rippling sea. "We used to be like the other human settlements," she said. "We worked with the vedalken . . . or at least we thought we did, but our lives never improved, and they kept everything we helped to create. My father had enough. His life's work was complete, and those bastards in the Synod stole it from him. He led our town in a revolt against the vedalken. We refused to work for them any more. That's when they sent the aerophins . . . fifty of them. Those silver assassins ravaged the town and killed everyone who dared fight back. So, yes, we still work for the vedalken, but we have no illusions as to our role anymore. We are their slaves, and nothing can change that."

"I can," said Glissa.

"How?"

"I have a power," said the elf. "I don't understand it yet, but I can destroy the aerophins. With your help, I can learn to control it. If you help me, I will protect your village."

"I don't know," said Bruenna. She wiped her eyes on her sleeve. "We've lived in peace with the vedalken for almost thirty cycles."

"You mean you've lived in slavery. What would your father do?"

Bruenna stared at Glissa for a long moment. Tears streamed down her face. At last she asked, "What do you need?"

# CHAPTER 21

# PREPARATIONS

Glissa grabbed Bruenna's shoulders with both hands. "Thank you," she said. "I need to find out who is trying to kill me and why."

"I don't know anything about their motives," protested Bruenna.

"Maybe not," said Glissa, "but you know how they operate."

"I know a little about their magical research," said the human mage, "at least those projects my people are working on. Not much more. I have no idea what they're thinking, and I don't know anything about the inner workings of the Synod."

"Something pretty big is going on here," said Glissa, tapping her chin thoughtfully. "The vedalken have made deals with the nim and the goblins. They've attacked the leonin, the trolls, and the elves. It has something to do with some deep, dark secret about the world the vedalken have uncovered. There must be *someone* who knows something about this."

Bruenna shrugged. "The vedalken are a lot smarter than humans. They treat us as if we are no better than beasts. It wasn't always like that, though. I've heard tales from long ago of a time when humans and vedalken worked as equals, but the serum changed all that. It changed the vedalken."

Glissa nodded. "I've heard about the serum, too. It expands your mind and gives you insight into the creation of the world."

"The serum does more than that. It expands all your senses.

You become aware of the connections between all living things. I have heard it can even unlock racial memories. You can learn everything your ancestors ever knew. Unfortunately the effect is only temporary, so the vedalken need a steady supply. Much of their research goes into finding faster ways to refine the serum."

"I've also been told it comes at a terrible price," muttered Glissa.

"It certainly did for the vedalken," replied Bruenna. "They turned cruel and used the knowledge they gained from the serum to take control of the sea and everything in it."

"It has another drawback as well," said Glissa. "The vedalken have to murder millions of blinkmoths to maintain that steady supply."

"That I did not know. I am glad I never took the serum."

Glissa looked at her companion in some surprise. "How do you know of the serum if you've never taken it? Do the vedalken ever give it to humans?"

"Winds, no!" exclaimed Bruenna. "It is forbidden to humans. The vedalken keep it all for themselves. My father once worked refining the serum. Later he became a research assistant and was able to learn more about the serum."

"Yet they trade small quantities to their allies," said the elf. She pulled the vial from her boot sheath. "I got this from the leader of the nim. It was to be his payment for killing me. The vedalken probably assume a few vials won't do any harm if the effects wear off so quickly."

"You have a vial of serum?" asked Bruenna. She reached eagerly for the vial, but Glissa pulled it back.

"I'm loath to use it," she said, "but it is my only link to the mage who killed my friend."

Bruenna drew back her hand, a sheepish look on her face. "Sorry," she said. "I don't really want it, either. I gave up wanting to be like the vedalken long ago. However, there may be a way to get your answers with that vial."

"Do I have to drink it?"

"Yes," said Bruenna, "but not here. Not now. First, we have to get you into Lumengrid."

"What is Lumengrid?"

"Lumengrid is the crystal fortress of the vedalken. It is where the Synod sits. It is where they keep their most prized possession—the Pool of Knowledge."

"A pool of knowledge?" Glissa was skeptical. "I bathe in it and I magically get all of my questions answered?"

"Something like that," said Bruenna, smiling. "I am not sure how it works. My father told me tales of it before he was killed. He even tried to use it once."

"Did it work?" asked Glissa. "Did your father learn the knowledge of the vedalken? Is that why they killed him?"

"He only got flashes of images," said Bruenna sadly. "It was enough for him to realize how horrible the vedalken are. That is why he tried to lead our village from under their control."

Glissa ran her fingers along her jaw. "How is that going to help me?"

"I did some research of my own when I was younger," said her human companion. "After the revolt, I took my father's place as research assistant. I think the vedalken wanted to keep an eye on me. After a few cycles, I became nothing more to them than a piece of research equipment, but I never forgot what they did to my father. When my vedalken master wasn't watching I went through his journals and personal research notes. From what I learned, I believe the Pool of Knowledge will only work correctly for someone who has taken serum."

"That's why you wanted the serum?"

"Once," said Bruenna. "I planned to gain the knowledge my father sought so I could use it to exact my revenge on those responsible for his death. But I learned—over time—that there are more important things than vengeance. I dedicated the last ten cycles to my people and to my mother."

"Vengeance is a great motivator," said Glissa drily. She reached out and touched Bruenna's shoulder. "If there's anything I've learned over the past week or two, though, it's that it must be tempered by reason or it will consume you."

The pause in the conversation grew uncomfortably long. Finally Glissa said, "So, I just down the vial and jump into the pool? That sounds easy enough."

"It won't be," said Bruenna. "Lumengrid is impregnable, and the Pool room is closely guarded."

"You have a plan, right?"

"I do," agreed Bruenna. "I planned for a long time after my father's death. First, we need to go back to the village."

"What's there?"

"My father's legacy."

* * * * *

Bruenna controlled the boat while Glissa, Slobad, and Bosh crouched in the stern, talking.

"You think we can trust her, huh?" asked Slobad.

"I don't know," said Glissa. "I think so. She lost her father to the vedalken."

Slobad crossed his arms. "She don't like goblins, huh?"

"Neither do you," replied Glissa. "Her people have feuded with the goblins over mining rights forever. That's all she knows of the goblins."

"She could be leading you into a trap," said Bosh.

"She could have turned us over to the vedalken as soon as we destroyed the aerophins," said Glissa. "She didn't. Now she's risking her life and the lives of everyone in her village—

including her mother—to help us. I think we can trust her."

Bruenna whistled softly. "We're almost there," she said. "I'll land the boat away from the town."

Glissa joined her. "Then what?"

Bruenna looked nervous. "I built a copy of my father's diver," she said. "It took me five cycles to complete, but I never found a power source strong enough to make it work. I know the vedalken constructs, especially large ones the size of that golem—she gestured to Bosh—have a powerful mana source inside of them, usually a crystal or a stone of some sort. I thought we could deactivate the golem . . . Bosh . . . and use its power source in the diver."

"Out of the question," snapped Glissa. "I won't kill my friend to get revenge on the vedalken."

"I would be willing to make this sacrifice," said Bosh. "My mana battery should be sufficient." He opened up a cavity in his chest and began to reach inside.

"No," said Glissa. She put a hand on his arm. "I know you are willing to die for me. You've proven that already. But I need you fighting by my side. I need you to remember your past. We will find another way to get into Lumengrid."

"There is no other way," said Bruenna. "We need the diver to get into Lumengrid. The diver needs a power source."

"You just get us back to town," said Glissa. "We'll think of something."

"I have idea, huh?" said Slobad. "If anyone want to hear what goblin has to say."

\* \* \* \* \*

"Are you sure this will work?" asked Bruenna later.

"Simple goblin solutions often best, huh?" said Slobad as he worked on the diver. "Goblins no need magic to make machines work. Goblins smarter than magic."

Glissa chuckled. She left the mismatched pair to their work and wandered around the storage shed. After they landed the boat, the group had made their way to Bruenna's personal shed. The human leader had hidden the diver behind several boats in various stages of repair.

It didn't look like much. In fact, it looked more like a goblin artifact than anything else. Bruenna explained that she used her father's plans but had to substitute goblin iron for the sleek, silvery vedalken metal. The diver was a huge cylinder of rusty iron. It ran from one side of the shed to the other and was just slightly taller than Bruenna. It looked for all the world like one of the tubes in the walls of the goblin tunnels, but it was much larger around and capped at both ends.

Slobad was busy working with his fire tube at one end of the diver. A thin white line of flame came from the tube, just like the flame Glissa had seen the goblins using on the duct by the Great Furnace. Bosh held a loop of iron against the front of the diver while Slobad melted a bar of silver above the loop and the diver. They had already affixed a similar loop on the opposite side of the front end.

"Come up here," called Bruenna from on top of the diver.

Glissa scrambled up the side. The mage stood next to a circular opening on top of the diver.

"We'll ride inside the diver," she said. "I'll use my wind magic to fill it with air and keep the quicksilver out. Once your golem . . . I mean, once Bosh gets us inside Lumengrid, we can make our way to the Pool of Knowledge."

"Won't the vedalken stop us?"

"It will be difficult to get inside the Pool of Knowledge chamber, but getting to it shouldn't be a problem. The vedalken don't even notice humans walking about inside their towers unless we are performing some task for them. Then we're tolerated at best or punished if we're too slow or the vedalken is in a foul mood."

Glissa rubbed her head. "Surely there are mages in other villages who feel the same way that you and your father do about the vedalken."

"Some do, but most are content to work for the vedalken like beasts and pick up what little power they can. You learn very early to do what you are told. Subservience is rewarded with easier work and better working conditions. Defiance is punished by forced labor in the serum processors or by the hoverguards.

"That's horrible," said Glissa.

"Yes," said Bruenna, "but that means once inside Lumengrid, we'll be able to walk around freely. Humans are discouraged from talking to one another, and the vedalken won't even notice us. Just keep your hood up."

"You think this diver will get us inside undetected?"

Bruenna nodded. "I had planned to pilot the diver in through the waste tubes below Lumengrid, but with no power, it is little more than an iron tube now. That is why I will have to provide air. I will have to concentrate the whole time we are under the sea."

"How long can you do that?"

"Long enough," said Bruenna. "We will tow the diver most of the way. Then Bosh will take us down to the bottom."

Glissa called down to Slobad and Bosh. "Are you two sure Bosh won't have any trouble under the quicksilver?" she asked. "Didn't the Dross get inside of him and clog his gears?"

"That took long time," said Slobad. "Maybe hundreds of cycles. Bosh okay for short trip."

Glissa looked at Bruenna. "He grows on you after a while."

"He would have to."

\* \* \* \* \*

Bosh cleared a path through the shed while Bruenna opened a chest and pulled out a large coil of braided leather. Glissa had seen these attached to the boats and the docks outside. Bruenna tied the two ends of the rope to the iron rings and handed the coils to Bosh.

"Wrap this around your torso," she said to Bosh. "I will levitate the diver. You just pull it with the rope. Glissa and Slobad, you will need to guide the diver on either side."

Bosh looped the rope around his body a few times, then walked toward the door. Glissa moved to the back of the diver. It floated into the air and began moving. It was a slow process. Bruenna couldn't move very quickly while keeping the diver in the air, and Glissa and Slobad had trouble controlling it. Several times, Glissa pushed too hard and sent Slobad diving to the ground as the diver swung over his head.

It was easier once they tied the diver to the boat. Slobad navigated it out from shore while Bruenna kept the diver aloft. Once the diver was over the sea, Bruenna eased it down. It sank about halfway into the silvery sea but remained afloat. The mage guided the boat and diver away from town.

"Can't we go any faster?" asked Glissa.

"We are straining the power of the boat as it is," said Bruenna. "I am afraid to push too hard. I might burn out the mana orb. Then we would be stranded until my villagers head to the crystal islands in the morning. We should be able to make it to the abandoned island before the blue sun rises."

"What do we do from there?"

"Submerge."

*     *     *     *     *

Both the blue and red moon had risen by the time they pulled into the cave beneath the abandoned tower, but Glissa was sure nobody had spotted them.

"How far is it to Lumengrid?" she asked.

"Not far by boat," returned Bruenna. "I think it will take most of the day in the diver."

"Why not get closer, huh?" asked Slobad. "Not spend so much time trapped under silver water. Seem dangerous to Slobad."

Glissa answered. "Because someone might see the abandoned boat and get suspicious." She turned back to Bruenna. "Can you keep the quicksilver out that long?"

"I will not have to," said the human. "The Quicksilver Sea is actually quite shallow. We should be able to ride on top most of the way to Lumengrid."

"Let's do it."

Slobad helped secure the rope around Bosh. "If see trouble," said Slobad, "pull this rope to untie, huh?"

"Fine," said Bosh. He turned to jump into the sea.

"Be careful, huh?"

"You as well," said the golem.

Bosh stepped off the boat and sank into the quicksilver. Glissa could just see the top of his head as he walked away from the boat. The quicksilver swirled around him, covering and uncovering his iron head as he moved.

The other three scrambled onto the diver. Bruenna dropped through the opening, and Glissa and Slobad followed her down. The diver was cramped and dark inside. Glissa could barely stand up straight and then only if she stood underneath the hole. Slobad was more at home in the cramped space. He immediately crawled into the back of the diver next to the provisions Bruenna had packed and curled up to sleep.

"How do we see where we're going?" asked Glissa.

"Like this," said Bruenna. She waved her hand in an arc around her body, and the iron cylinder disappeared. Glissa could see the quicksilver rippling against the invisible diver but couldn't see anything past that edge, including Bosh. She mentioned this to the mage.

"The quicksilver is completely opaque," said Bruenna. "You normally cannot see through it at all. That was the hardest part of the diver program. My father and the vedalken he worked for perfected this spell, though."

She waved her hands again, and it looked as if the sea had parted around them, well out past Bosh—at least where he was supposed to be. Glissa still couldn't see him. The golem had disappeared along with the quicksilver. She could see the rope. It was wrapped several times around something no longer there.

"Where's Bosh?" she asked.

"Invisible," said Bruenna. "It's a bubble of invisibility. Bosh and the sea are still there. We just can't see them anymore."

"Will that work on us?" asked Glissa. "It would make getting into the Pool of Knowledge chamber a lot easier."

"No," said Bruenna. "It only works on metal. Take a look at your arms."

Glissa glanced down at her hands. She couldn't see them. The human robes covered her forearms. It took her a few seconds to get used to where her invisible hands were so she could pull up the sleeves. When she did, Glissa gasped. Her arms stopped just above her elbows. She fumbled for her sword. It was invisible also.

"We don't want to walk around like this," she said. "It would be pretty hard to fight when I can't see my hands or my weapon."

They traveled across the Quicksilver Sea most of the day. The rope remained taut, and Glissa could see the horizon move above the surface of the sea when she stood up. Periodically, Bruenna climbed up on top and pulled on the ropes to get Bosh to turn one way or another. The scenery was boring. They were in an open expanse of sea. Glissa could barely see the mountains in the distance past the endless silver sea. She wondered how Bruenna even knew where they were.

Early in the journey a group of silver eels attacked Bosh. Somehow they could sense where he was. They obviously weren't made of quicksilver—at least not entirely—because Glissa could see them. She would have jumped from the diver to help her friend, but the eels couldn't harm the metal man. They tried to bite him and wrap themselves around his invisible body, but they didn't seem to be doing any damage and eventually turned away from the golem and headed for the diver. It was odd to see them swimming through the invisible quicksilver. It looked as if the eels were flying toward them. Glissa recoiled when the eels opened their mouths to attack. But the attacks stopped well short. They banged off the wall of the invisible diver. The eels attacked a few more times, then flew off through the quicksilver wall.

While the blue moon set in the sky behind them, Lumengrid rose up ahead. It looked like an immense mushroom sitting on the sea. The central tower was larger around than the entire crystal island chain. It quickly dominated Glissa's view. The dome top spread out from the central tower on either side, seeming to reach out to the horizon.

Sitting atop the dome was a massive orb. It looked like a fifth moon—a silver moon—in the sky. Electricity arced out from it, filling the sky with a network of lightning that stretched to the surrounding islands—several dozen smaller towers clustered around the fortress. A system of bridges connected the lesser towers together. The lightning, towers, and bridges looked as if they were all joined together like a giant spider web.

# CHAPTER 22

# DESCENT

"Time to dive," called Bruenna. "The sea gets deeper around Lumengrid. Bosh will pull us under any time. I need to start my air spell."

Bruenna sat in the back of the diver and began moving her hands in an intricate pattern. Her palms danced around each other as she twisted her wrists and slid her arms over and under one another in a sinuous rhythm.

Glissa felt the pressure build around her as the mage's arms wove their spell. It felt uncomfortable at first, and she found it hard to breathe.

"Relax!" called Bruenna. She spoke slowly and precisely. "Breathe normally. Close your eyes. Lie down. It will help."

Slobad came over to Glissa and helped her lie down on the bottom of the diver. "Why . . . aren't you . . . having . . . trouble," gasped Glissa.

"Underground, undersea," said Slobad, "no different to goblins, huh?"

He massaged Glissa's temples. After a few minutes, she was able to breath almost normally again. The elf sat up and looked back at Bruenna. Her arms continued to weave in and around each other. The mage's eyes had glazed over.

"Are you well?" asked Bruenna. Her voice seemed distant, as if she weren't really in the diver anymore.

"I'm fine," Glissa said. "Thank you. Thank you both."

Glissa turned around to see where they were headed, but she could no longer see Lumengrid. She saw the taut rope coiled around the invisible the golem ahead of them, but they had completely submerged. All she could see above her was swirling quicksilver at the edge of the invisibility bubble.

"Does he know where to go?" she asked Bruenna, pointing toward the end of the rope.

"Hard to miss, huh?" said Slobad. "Lumengrid huge. Bosh not need eyes to walk straight."

"Let's hope so," said Glissa, speaking so the goblin alone could hear her. "I feel trapped in here. What if something happens to Bosh or Bruenna? We should have a plan."

"If plans make you happy," said Slobad, "plan away. I sit and rest for both of us, huh?"

Glissa stared out the front of the diver and watched the rope bounce up and down. As the minutes wore on and the diver moved through the invisible quicksilver, Glissa became increasingly aware that she was completely out of her element here. She must rely on her friends. It was a strange sensation.

A swarm of the eels slithered from the opaque quicksilver, nipping at the invisible golem again. At first, the attack went as before. Glissa could see their open mouths stop short and bounce off when they hit what must have been Bosh's legs. One wrapped itself around what must have been the golem's neck or head—it was well above the ropes and narrower than his chest. It was strange watching the eel try to squeeze something that Glissa couldn't even see. None of the eels seem to bother Bosh at all. At least, he wasn't doing anything about them. The ropes continued to bounce up and down and the diver kept moving forward.

Glissa wondered how long it would take for the eels to give up again. Several more creatures joined the first one around Bosh's neck and head area. They seemed to merge together and grow longer. Once four or five had wrapped themselves together, Glissa could see the golem's head and neck outlined in the bodies of the silver eels. The eels striking at the golem's feet also merged together and wrapped around both of his legs. Glissa almost laughed as she looked at the strange golem with a silver head and legs but no torso.

Bosh came to a halt, unable to move his legs any longer.

Glissa jumped up. "Slobad, Bruenna!" she called. "Bosh is in trouble."

"I cannot help him," said Bruenna, her face pale. "I must concentrate on the air."

"What matter, huh?" asked Slobad groggily.

"He's being attacked by those silver eels," said Glissa. "They've wrapped up his legs. He can't move."

"What can we do?" asked Slobad. "Bosh out there. We in here, huh?"

Glissa watched as Bosh's eel-wrapped head bent down. The sea creatures around his legs began to pull away. The golem was trying to pull them off. Glissa knew how hard it must be, since Bosh couldn't even see his own hands. The eel around the golem's head peeled away slightly and swam upward, yanking Bosh's head back straight. The eels around his legs tightened their grip again. Several more eels merged together and began coiling around the middle of the golem.

"They're wrapping up his arms now," cried Glissa. "He needs help! I must get to him."

"You cannot," said Bruenna. "No air out there."

"You control the wind," shouted Glissa. "Make some air!"

Two eels broke away from the attack and headed toward the diver. Glissa didn't flinch this time as the eels slithered toward her. She thought they might merge and attack the diver. Instead, they cut across in front of the diver and bit through the ropes tethering it to Bosh. The diver began to drift up and away from Bosh.

"Flare!" shouted Glissa. "We're heading for the surface."

"Wait," said Bruenna. "Let me try something."

She increased the speed of her hand-dance and muttered a few more words. The pressure Glissa had felt on her chest since they dived under the quicksilver decreased. The diver dropped to the bottom of the sea. The sudden jolt startled Glissa. She forced herself to take a few slow deep breaths to relax.

"Extended air bubble . . . out to Bosh," gasped Bruenna. "Quickly. Cannot . . . hold it . . . long."

"Slobad," called Glissa. "Come with me!"

The elf dropped her cloak and scrambled from the diver. It took her several tries to grab the lip. She couldn't see her hands or the diver. She had to feel around for the opening, then pull herself up. Getting Slobad out proved even harder. She couldn't see his hands, and he couldn't see hers. He finally held his satchel up, and she grabbed at it, pulling the goblin through the hole.

Glissa jumped off the diver to the sea floor and sank up to her ankles in muck. Slobad dropped beside her, but his wide feet kept him from sinking as far. Glissa tried to lift her legs, but her feet were stuck fast. She pushed her hands down into the muck to pull them free. An invisible claw skewered her boot and scraped her leg as she struggled. When she finally pulled that foot free, Glissa could see her hands again. The muck had coated them. She pulled her other foot free, then drew her sword and spread mud on the blade.

She turned toward Bosh. He was almost completely covered in thick eels. They didn't seem bothered at all by the air surrounding the golem. They writhed around him. Glissa could see his entire shape now. Those eels caught swimming when the wave of air expanded now slithered across the seabed toward the golem.

Slobad stood staring at his hands. Glissa couldn't tell what he was doing until a jet of fire sprang forth from his fist. His fire tube was invisible as well, but she could see the flame.

Slobad fiddled with the tube until flame turned into a bright white blade of fire, then moved up to an eel slithering on the ground and jabbed it with the flame-blade. The thin flame sliced through the eel, cutting it in half. The heat from the flame scarred and blackened the edges of each half as it cut. The two halves flopped uncontrollably. The blackness spread along the silvery eel's body. After a moment, there was nothing left but a pile of ash atop the muck.

Glissa moved in slowly behind the goblin, walking on her toes to keep from getting stuck again. "Use your fire on the eels covering Bosh," cried Glissa. "I'll keep the others off you."

Glissa stabbed an eel slithering toward the goblin's foot, slicing it in half. She skewered a second and third eel as Slobad burned away the writhing mass attached to Bosh. She glanced at Bosh and Slobad. The goblin had cleared off most of the golem's legs, which were covered in ash. The rest of the eels continued to squirm around Bosh. They bulged around his torso, as if Bosh was trying to break free from the inside.

Glissa scanned the surrounding quicksilver to see if any more eels might swim into the air bubble. She saw a few eel heads poke through the silver curtain, but they disappeared a moment later. The elf looked back toward the diver to check behind them. She saw the wriggling halves of the eels she cut inching their way across the muck. Each half had grown a new end. Where there had been three eels, Glissa now had six to contend with.

Several more creatures poked their heads from the quicksilver behind the diver. They didn't push all the way through, yet Glissa noticed the ones trapped in the air pocket with them continued to attack. It was odd. They must react on instinct, thought Glissa. They could survive in the air, at least for a time, but they weren't willing to leave the quicksilver on their own. Glissa stepped up to the first half-eel and kicked it toward the side of the bubble. It landed short of the quicksilver wall but bounced into it. Once it hit the quicksilver, the eel retreated into the liquid and didn't return.

Glissa kicked three more times, sending the eels flying through the air bubble into the quicksilver wall. It was sort of fun. Two left. She turned. The last two merged back into one large eel. She kicked at it anyway. But it had enough mass and length to collapse around her foot. When the two ends met behind her ankle, the eel began to constrict. Her foot went numb as blood stopped flowing past her ankle. She fell down into the muck. She couldn't cut the eel for fear of slicing her own leg. The creature's mouth opened up and snapped at her hands as she tried to grab it. She needed Slobad.

"Glissa!" called Slobad.

"What?"

"We got problem, huh?"

Glissa glanced over her shoulder at Slobad and Bosh. The goblin had burned most of the eels off of Bosh. The golem's ash-covered hands pulled at the remaining eels wrapped around his head. Glissa couldn't see what had spooked Slobad. Then she saw the quicksilver beyond Bosh move towards them. She thought Bruenna was losing her concentration until the mass of quick-silver grew tentacles.

"What the flare is that?" cried Glissa.

She had no time to deal with the eel on her leg now. Glissa reached down. When the eel snapped at her, she slammed her fist down its throat. The eel slammed its jaws shut, digging its teeth into the invisible metal of Glissa's forearm. She spread her claws inside the beast, puncturing through its neck. Gritting her teeth against the pain, Glissa pulled her arm up and away from her legs. The eel ripped apart, but the mouth continued to chew on her arm. Glissa scrambled to her feet and kicked the squirming mass at her feet into the quicksilver wall. She ran toward Bosh, half an eel still attached to her arm.

The quicksilver monster loomed in front of Bosh. It was a huge blob of silver at least ten feet tall with tentacles waving out in front of it. She could see Bosh and Slobad reflected in the silvery skin of the creature's body. The ends of the tentacles disappeared as it moved forward. The air must extend past the invisibility bubble, thought Glissa. She'd better attack it before it disappeared completely. She slogged through the muck as fast as she could.

Slobad wavered behind Bosh. He looked as if he wanted to run, but he wouldn't leave the golem's side—his self-preservation at odds with his love for Bosh.

"Slobad," she called. "Come here." She moved forward, waving her eel-clad arm at the goblin. "Burn this off and I'll take care of that thing."

As she approached, the monster lashed out with its tentacle arms. Bosh was still pulling at the eels wrapped around his head. He didn't see the attack coming. Neither could Glissa. The tentacles disappeared before they reached the golem. But the tentacles didn't retract. Glissa saw Bosh's ash-covered arms pulled away from his head. Then the golem was moving forward, only his legs weren't moving. Bosh dug his feet into the muck and tried to pull back.

Glissa screamed. She looked down to see Slobad burning away the remains of the eel attached to her arm. Ash mixed with blood from dozens of puncture wounds on her invisible arm. More tentacles snapped out from the quicksilver beast and disappeared into the invisible air surrounding Bosh. Glissa slogged forward to attack, but the monster stepped back through the silver curtain and from the air bubble.

A moment later, the beast pulled Bosh out of the area covered by the invisibility spell. He was completely wrapped up in tentacles. They encircled the golem's torso like the leather rope that tied Bosh to the diver. The golem waved his bound arms, trying to free them, but more quicksilver poured into the tentacles, thickening the ropes around the golem. Before Glissa could even scream, the tentacles pulled the golem through the quicksilver wall, leaving a furrow in the muck behind him.

Glissa looked down at Slobad. He had followed her and was now staring up at her. She could see tears streaming down his cheek.

"I couldn't save him," said the goblin dully. "I saw it, and I couldn't move, huh?"

"I know," said Glissa. She looked at the wall of silver. "I'll get him."

"How?" asked Slobad. "Can't see in there, huh? Can't even breathe. How you survive?"

Glissa pulled the vial of serum from her boot sheath. "This will help me see." She uncorked the vial.

"You need serum, huh?" said Slobad. "Need it for Learning Pool."

Glissa smiled. "Bosh is more important."

"How you breathe, huh?"

"I'll hold my breath," said Glissa.

"How long you hold breath, huh? How long?"

"Long enough."

Glissa brought the vial to her lips and poured the thick, blue liquid into her mouth. It tasted sweet, salty, bitter, and sour all at once. The serum activated all of her taste buds as it spread through her mouth. She felt the liquid seep down her throat, coating and burning like a smooth hot drink.

As the heat spread through her body, it seemed to coat every inch of her in a warm embrace. Glissa became acutely aware of everything around her. She could feel Slobad standing next to her, his heart beating quickly, his breath shallow in the compressed air of Bruenna's bubble. She could sense the mage in the diver behind them. Her hands continued their intricate rhythmic dance, but sweat poured down her face. The area just outside the bubble teemed with eels squirming around each other. Ahead of her, Glissa could "see" Bosh and the monster, just outside the bubble. The quicksilver monster had completely enveloped the golem.

"Hand me your fire tube," she said to Slobad. She could hear her own voice both in her head and reverberating through the air bubble. It was disorienting. "Take my sword back to the diver. Tell Bruenna to collapse the bubble."

"What you do, huh?" asked Slobad.

"Get Bosh," said Glissa as she took the invisible fire tube from Slobad. "I'll be back."

The elf moved off toward the quicksilver curtain. She could sense the soft spots in the muck and avoided them. She held the fire tube in front of her as she reached the edge of the air bubble. The flame burned a hole in the swirling surface and caught the eel Glissa knew to be squirming inside.

She took a breath and followed the fire tube into the quicksilver. She had to push her body into the viscous liquid. It enveloped her like water and pushed against her like a stiff wind. The sensation was far more intense than the sudden rush of air from Bruenna's spell. Her entire body felt compressed by quicksilver. Glissa fought back an urge to gasp for air. Her ears felt as if they would pop. Her chest tightened.

She focused on the eels and the monster. The fire tube cut an ashen swath through the quicksilver in front of her, melting any eels that dared swim near. She could feel Bosh kicking and punching inside the beast but knew the golem's attacks were having no effect on the monster. It simply stretched and reformed after each assault. The monster was just a few feet farther, but Glissa was moving in slow motion. The creature stayed just out of reach. The elf began to drift up away from the sea bottom as swirling currents pushed her body around.

She tried to swim forward, waving her arms and kicking her legs in the quicksilver, but all that did was create an intricate pattern of ash with the fire tube. The current seemed to have a mind of its own. It shifted Glissa back and forth and turned her around. She twisted back around, then concentrated on the currents between her and the monster. She could sense it ahead of her. The sea floor was close beneath.

Glissa shoved her legs out to push against the sea floor. She jetted up a few feet into a current she detected above her. The current swept her along toward the monster. She lifted the fire tube above her head and pointed her toes as she approached. The current dragged her deadly fire across the shoulder of the beast. The quicksilver quaked as the monster screamed in pain. Glissa heard the scream more inside her head than through her ears. The vibrations resounded through the sea.

The current threatened to sweep her past the monster. Glissa reached out and grabbed a silver tentacle. Glissa could sense where the sea ended and the beast began. It had a solidity of being the amorphous sea lacked. She held on and brought the fire tube back around to drive it into the monster. It howled again. Glissa's head began to ache from the pounding echo of the monster's wailing and the lack of oxygen.

The quicksilver monster spat out Bosh and poured quicksilver into a dozen tentacles. Arms flailed at Glissa through the sea. With her enhanced senses, Glissa saw the monster's attack almost before it came. She swung the fire tube in a slow arc through the quicksilver and cut off three tentacles before they reached her, but she was too slow in the thick liquid to bring the fire back around, and the other tentacles wrapped around her.

She bounced off Bosh. The golem grabbed at Glissa, but she knocked his hand away. They couldn't escape the beast, not in its element. She had to kill it. She had to do it now. She allowed herself to be drawn toward the beast's silver body.

The monster squeezed her mercilessly, constricting her chest and forcing the air from her lungs. Bubbles escaped from Glissa's mouth and combined around her head in a small pocket of air. The beast squeezed even tighter, making it impossible for Glissa to draw another breath, and pulled Glissa closer.

Now was her chance. Glissa fought to bring her arm up. Tentacles slid, little by little, up her body. She got her elbow free and jammed the fire tube deep into the chest of the monster. The creature screamed and tightened its grip around Glissa. The pressure in her chest mounted, while the creature's screaming pounded in her head. The monster tried to slide its body away from the fire. Glissa pushed back. She held her hand—and the fire tube—inside the beast.

The melting fire spread through the beast's body. Glissa watched the beast's torso turn to black ash. The Quicksilver Sea flowed in to displace the ash. The creature's head soon followed, which finally silenced its head-splitting wail. The fire spread into the tentacles last, which dissolved around Glissa, releasing their hold on her.

With the pressure gone from her chest, Glissa's instincts betrayed her. She immediately tried to draw in a breath of air. Instead, she drew quicksilver into her lungs. She choked uncontrollably. Every choke ended in a gasp, forcing more liquid into her lungs. She dropped the fire tube and grabbed her neck. But there was nothing she could do. Glissa's enhanced senses closed down around her. The world began to go black. The last thing she saw was a looming dark form above her.

**CHAPTER 23**

# LUMENGRID

*Glissa walked through the forest, basking in the warmth of bright sunshine filtering through the leaves. A squirrel skittered up a tree as she passed and shouted at her from the lowest bough. She felt free and alive. The morning dew squirted through her toes as she walked, barefoot, through the grass and moss.*

*Rays of light glinted off dew-moistened flowers, turning into rainbows that jumped from blossom to blossom. Her life was perfect. The forest provided everything the elves needed and protected them from the wars and ravages of men and gods. Her people existed to protect the forest. She knew that now. When had she forgotten? The forest existed to protect the elves. It was a truly symbiotic relationship. The elves would have it no other way.*

*A cloud drifted across the sky, blocking the sun and casting a shadow over the forest. She glanced up to watch for the warm light to return, but the cloud darkened and began to grow. Soon a charcoal mass of roiling storm clouds threatened to blot out the entire sky. Lightning played across the bottom of the turbulent cloud. The air became charged with raw power and lightning crackled across the sky. Glissa could feel the forest's energy surge as the storm built. Was the storm feeding on the mana of the forest or bleeding off excess energy into the forest? She didn't know.*

A bolt of lightning shot down from the cloud into the forest ahead of her. The thunder deafened Glissa, and the force of the shock wave knocked her to the ground. She jumped to her feet and ran toward the impact. Lightning often brought fire to the trees. The forest must be protected. That was the law of the elves. Nothing else mattered.

She ran through the dark forest. No rain fell from the storm clouds, and the lightning seemed content to stay in the sky for now. Glissa smelled something burning ahead of her, but the odor was not wood turning to charcoal. It was more primal, more powerful. She broke into the clearing where the lighting had struck and was surprised to see a large body of elves already gathered there, as if they had all been drawn to this spot by the lightning.

In the center of the clearing, Glissa saw a black patch of grass at least twenty feet across that had been turned to ash by the lightning. A glowing sphere of energy hovered above the ash. The elves who crowded around seemed to be hypnotized by the sphere. They didn't move closer to investigate, but neither did they make any attempt to flee from it. She wanted to look away from the sphere and knew she would be lost if she didn't escape the clearing, but she couldn't make her body move.

The sphere flashed, engulfing the gathered elves in a bright white light. Glissa screamed. It felt like her skin was burning, as if the light was consuming her. She fell but didn't hit the ground. She couldn't see anything but light and sparkling motes flying past her eyes as she fell into a white nothingness. Then she was on the ground, crumpled into a fetal ball, hugging her knees to her chest. Her eyes were closed, and there was a blessed darkness behind her eyelids.

After a time, Glissa dared to open her eyes. She expected to find black stalks where the trees had once stood. She feared there would be dozens of burnt and misshapen corpses surrounding her.

*She wondered whether she was truly still alive or had passed onto Gaea's reward. Nothing she could have imagined, though, prepared the elf for what she saw when she opened her eyes.*

*Elves lay all around her. Most curled up as she had been. None were burnt or scarred from the flash. A few had pushed themselves up off the ground or sat and surveyed the damage to the forest. But the forest was gone. The trees, the flowers, the sun, even the black cloud had all disappeared. Glissa looked down to see bare metal beneath her. She looked up and saw great towers of twisted metal surrounding the elves. In the sky, there was nothing but stars, but even those were unfamiliar.*

*Glissa felt sick inside. The metal world swirled around her as she tried to get to her feet. A wave of nausea overtook the elf. She rested on her hands and knees, and closed her eyes to make the world stop spinning around her. She hoped it was all a dream that would be gone when she opened her eyes. The elf looked again, but the metal world was still there. She dropped her head down between her arms and vomited.*

\* \* \* \* \*

Glissa kneeled on the bottom of the diver, puking. Her chest and neck convulsed as a torrent of silver liquid erupted from her stomach and lungs. The spasms stopped a few moments after the last drops of quicksilver dribbled from her mouth and nose. She stayed there, hunched over a silver puddle, and just breathed, spitting excess quicksilver into the puddle every so often. Finally she crawled toward the front of the diver, feeling her way along the invisible metal, and sat down.

"I think that's the last of it," she said as she wiped her mouth and nose. "What happened?"

"You tell us, huh?" said Slobad. "Bosh dump you in diver. Think it was Bosh. Couldn't see him. You not breathing. Not breathing at all. Human make spell and you start hacking. Spit up entire sea, huh?"

Glissa looked back at Bruenna. The mage was still concentrating on her air spell. "You saved me?" she asked.

"I put air in your body," said Bruenna. "Bosh saved you."

"Thank you," said Glissa. She looked around. "Where's Bosh?"

"Out there," said Slobad. He pointed past Glissa. "Pulling to Lumengrid, huh? Just start pulling again like nothing happen, huh?"

Glissa looked out the front of the diver. She could see the severed ends of the ropes hanging over the sea floor, right above Bosh's muck-covered feet, which continued to trudge through the sea.

"Any sign of eels or other monsters?" asked Glissa.

Slobad shook his head.

"We are near Lumengrid," said Bruenna. "I feel it."

Glissa nodded. There was nothing to do now but wait. She sat and thought about the flare she had experienced while she was . . . dead. It had been so intense, so real. She had seen things she'd never seen before. Had the serum opened up her mind to a different time and place? Or was it just a hallucination caused by flirting with death? With Chunth dead, her only chance to find out the truth was the Pool of Knowledge, and now she had no serum to activate it.

Her musings were cut short by a loud clang from ahead of them. Glissa looked around to see what happened, and was worried when she saw the ropes floating down to the bottom of the sea. But then she noticed the golem's feet trudging back toward the diver. The feet banged into the side of the invisible diver, then climbed the side, leaving muddy smears behind. The elf heard Bosh's voice boom from above her. He must have climbed up the iron tube and stuck his head through the opening.

"I am glad you have recovered, Glissa," said the golem's disembodied voice.

"Thank you, Bosh," said Glissa. "I owe you my life."

"As I owe you. I believe we have arrived. I have struck a metal wall. How shall I proceed, Bruenna?"

"Pull us around the base," said Bruenna. "You will see a tube. Take us in there."

"How will he be able to see the tube?" asked Glissa.

"Good question," said the human mage. "I haven't worked out all the problems with the diver yet."

The two women looked at each other blankly.

"Why not use air bubble, huh?" said Slobad finally. "Like before. Saw metal monster past golem."

Glissa nodded. "Good idea, Slobad." She turned to Bruenna. "Can you control the size of the invisibility bubble?"

Bruenna moved her hands through their spell dance. "How much control are you talking about?"

"Collapse the invisibility bubble to just around the diver and extend the air bubble out past Bosh's ropes. Then we can see him and he can see the fortress wall."

"I can do that. I do not know how long I will be able to hold it, though."

"Just do your best."

Glissa watched as Bruenna muttered a few words and changed the pattern that her hands followed. The quicksilver rushed toward them for a moment, and Glissa gasped, then the air pressure dropped and the quicksilver washed away from them past the ends of the ropes. A silver wall appeared in the bubble, extending out past the edges and down into the mud.

Glissa heard Bosh climb off the diver then saw him appear in front of the transparent wall of the diver. He picked up the ropes and began moving around the edge of Lumengrid. Glissa watched the walls slip past them. She was amazed at the size of the place. She could only see a small part of the vedalken fortress at the edge of the bubble, but it seemed to go on forever.

She looked back at Bruenna. Bruenna's hands were a blur. Her face had turned red and sweat dripped off her chin. Finally Glissa saw the tube Bruenna had mentioned. It was enormous. Only the bottom of the tube was visible within the air bubble. It curved up at the edges and disappeared into the silver curtain around them.

Bosh pulled them into the tube. After a short time, Glissa could feel the diver rising. She fell backward as Bosh pulled them up a ramp. Eventually they leveled out again, and the tube they were in began to get smaller. She could see the sides of the tube rise up around the diver until they met at the top, just above Bosh's head.

Bruenna said, "Stop. We must stop here."

Glissa turned and banged on the walls of the diver, wrenching a finger as she misjudged the distance between the two invisible objects. Bosh looked back and Glissa waved her hands, but then she realized he couldn't see them. She grabbed her sword sheath and pointed at the top of the diver. Bosh dropped the ropes and walked back toward the diver, but he couldn't fit between the top of the tube and the diver. Glissa looked back at Bruenna.

"What now?" she asked.

Bruenna pointed at a panel in the top of the tube, above Bosh. "We must go through there."

Glissa waved her sheath at Bosh and pointed it up at the panel. The golem nodded his head. He grabbed the ropes and pulled the diver forward. The panel disappeared as the diver moved under it. Bruenna collapsed the invisibility sphere. The diver reappeared around Glissa. She moved to the center and looked up.

The panel came into view above the opening, and the diver stopped. Bruenna said a few words, and the diver rose up toward the panel. Glissa picked up Slobad and set him on her shoulders. The goblin pulled a tool from his satchel and began working on the panel. After some grunting, Glissa heard metal scrape against metal. Light spilled into the diver through a hole above Slobad.

"Help me out, huh?" called Slobad.

Glissa pushed Slobad through the opening and turned to Bruenna. "You next," she said.

Bruenna walked over to Glissa. She continued to move her arms through their intricate pattern as Glissa grabbed her around the waist and hoisted her through the opening. Slobad leaned down and grabbed her by the shoulders as Glissa pushed from below. With Bruenna safe above, Glissa grabbed her cloak, which she had dropped before the eel attack, and clambered through. Once above, she tossed the cloak aside, leaned back down, and knocked on the diver again. Bosh pushed it back away from the tube opening, then climbed through the hole.

They were inside Lumengrid.

\* \* \* \* \*

Glissa looked around, worried someone might have spotted them crawling up through the floor, but they had come into the corner of some sort of storage area. Nobody was around. They were surrounded by silver crates. The crates and the walls were made from the same silver material as the towers. Glissa guessed the vedalken had found some way to turn quicksilver into a more durable material. It was the only metal they seemed to have access to. She opened one of the crates. It was filled with empty serum vials.

Bosh moved a stack of crates out of the way, and Glissa immediately pulled out her sword. Three constructs stood against the wall. They were similar to the ones that had attacked the cultists. Glissa advanced on them, then noticed one of construct was missing an arm, while another was headless. She examined the constructs. All three were covered in dust.

When she turned around, the elf gasped. The rest of the room was enormous, larger than Bruenna's entire house. Crates littered the floor around her, and a thick coat of dust covered everything. The center of the room was dominated by a large mechanism. Glissa walked over to it. The machine ran almost the entire length of the room and was packed tightly with intricate parts.

"What is this place?"

"It is an old serum processing room," said Bruenna. She walked over to the machine, reached out her hand toward it, but then pulled away. "Father worked down here in his youth. He kept this processor running." Bruenna wiped her eyes. "He even made some improvements to the system. That is how he got noticed. Soon after, he began working with the top vedalken researcher."

Glissa stared at Bruenna. The human mage had been quiet since they entered the room. Now Glissa knew why. The place was full of ghosts for her, full of memories.

Bruenna evidently misinterpreted the elf's thoughts. "I did not know about the blinkmoths," she said defensively. "Not before you told me. Father never mentioned where the serum came from."

"Maybe he ashamed," said Slobad. "Ashamed of killing for vedalken, huh?"

"Maybe," said Bruenna. "Just like them to make us do their dirty work. But that has changed. They have not used this facility in twenty cycles. The vedalken do not trust the humans with the serum anymore. Not after my father got as far as the Pool of Knowledge."

Glissa left Bruenna to deal with her personal demons, opened another crate, and looked through the vials inside. After a time, Bruenna came over. Glissa glanced up. The tears were gone and a steely determination had returned to her eyes.

"Do you think there's any serum left in any of these vials?" Glissa asked Bruenna. "We're going to need more before we get to the Pool."

"What happened to the vial you had?" asked Bruenna.

Glissa looked over at Slobad, who shrugged his shoulders. "Oh," she said, "I thought Slobad would have told you. I used the serum when I went into the quicksilver to save Bosh."

Bruenna's face turned red with rage. "Why in the winds did you do that?" she shouted. "We *needed* that serum. Without it, I . . . we'll never get the information you need!"

"I had no choice," said Glissa calmly. "If I hadn't used the serum, we would have lost Bosh."

"So?" shrieked Bruenna. "Without the serum, all you will get from the Pool is random images. The trip is worthless without the serum. Did you think it would be as easy to replace as finding a stray vial in a crate?"

"No," said Glissa. "I made a decision to value the life of my friend over the value of the serum."

Bruenna was hardly even listening anymore. "Getting more serum will be impossible. If I could have found my own serum, I would have come here long ago. I've waited thirty cycles—*thirty cycles*—for this chance! All I lacked was a vial of serum, and you threw it away to save the life of a construct. He's not even alive, for wind's sake!"

"Stop this!" Glissa glowered at Bruenna. "I know you see him as just a construct, like these lifeless things here. But he is my friend. And that is more important than serum, or knowledge, or even power. Maybe that's what the vedalken have forgotten in their rush to rule the world. Maybe that's why humans are now slaves and not equals to the vedalken."

Bruenna slammed her hand down on the crate. The vials jumped and clinked together inside. "This was my one chance," she said weakly. "My last chance to finish what my father started." She looked over at Bosh. Tears streamed down her face. "I am sorry. Glissa. Slobad. Bosh. I am sorry. This room. The vial. I thought we could really do it this time. I'm sorry. I did not mean what I said. Without Bosh, we would not even be here. I know that, but there is no way to get another vial. I have tried."

"Yes," said Glissa, "but you didn't have a goblin and a golem to distract the vedalken for you." She put her arm around Bruenna and led her away from the crates toward the door. "We can still do this. You have to believe me. You have to have faith in your friends."

Bruenna shuddered within Glissa's embrace, but she didn't argue. Glissa stopped at the door and turned to Slobad. "You know where you're going?" she asked.

Slobad nodded his head. "You not be disappointed, huh?"

"I'm sure I won't," said Glissa. "I'm sure I won't."

Bosh opened the door. Slobad ducked under the metal man's arm and glanced into the hall. He nodded to Bosh but then hesitated and turned back to Glissa. "Glissa," he said. "I . . . how we get off this rock, huh?"

Glissa looked at Bruenna. "There are vedalken transports at the sea level. Meet us there."

"Good," said Slobad. He looked at Glissa again, nodded, then slipped through the door.

Glissa grabbed Bosh's arm. "Don't wait for us too long," she said.

"We will not," said Bosh as he stepped through the door. "If you are delayed, we shall retrieve you." The door closed before Glissa could argue.

\* \* \* \* \*

Glissa turned to Bruenna. "Are you ready for this?" she asked.

Bruenna nodded and tossed Glissa her cloak. Glissa donned the cloak and pulled the hood up over her ears. "You know," she said, "this didn't work very well the last time I tried it."

"Don't worry," said Bruenna. "As I said, the vedalken do not even notice humans walking around. We are less than beasts to them. In fact, humans probably outnumber vedalken here in Lumengrid."

"I hope you're right," said Glissa. "You were smart enough to see through my disguise."

"Do not worry," said Bruenna. "You did not have a friend who knew what to say if challenged. As long as we look like we are supposed to be here, nobody will bother us. Just let me do the talking."

Lumengrid looked nothing like the deserted tower they had visited the day before. The walls were completely opaque. Glissa could see her own reflection in the silvery surfaces but couldn't see anything else through them. Perhaps they were thicker, or perhaps there were just more walls between her and the outside world. Glissa didn't know. The walls glowed, providing ample light. There seemed to be no seams between the walls and the floors. The metal looked fluid—almost alive, like the quicksilver monster that attacked Bosh.

The Tangle trees, the mountain ridges, the leonin mounds, and even the chimneys in the mephidross looked and felt organic from the outside. But all showed signs of being worked and shaped on the inside. Glissa had seen elves cut chambers within the Tangle trees for new homes. The floors and walls in the goblin tunnels were pounded into shape. The leonin inlaid tiles of gold and silver throughout their city. Even Geth had a door that had been cut and placed to seal him off from intruders.

But the chambers and corridors inside Lumengrid flowed from one to another and reflected the light everywhere at once. If Glissa stared too long at one spot, she began to see multiple copies of herself in the wall. Maybe it was a trick of the light but she felt like she could pass her hand right through the walls and touch one of her infinite selves.

The main difference between Lumengrid and the other towers, though, was size. The corridor they walked down seemed to go on forever ahead of them. It curved slightly in the distance, but it never seemed to end. They passed doors every so often, but the view never changed.

After walking for a while, Glissa saw something in the distance. They had yet to see anybody else in the complex, and this was the first indication that they weren't just walking in a circle around the base of the fortress. Bruenna explained that most of this level had been used for serum processing and was now largely abandoned. The thing in the distance turned out to be stairs up to the next level.

Bruenna led them up the stairs. "Pull your hood forward more," she cautioned. "We will see humans and vedalken on this level."

When they reached the top of the stairs, Glissa was almost disappointed to see yet another long, curving corridor ahead of them, devoid of any people. She wondered if all of Lumengrid was nothing more than a warren of spiraling passageways. At this rate, it would take them forever to get to the Pool of Knowledge, and Slobad's surprise would come too soon.

"Why is this taking so long?" asked Glissa, as they trudged down another endless, curved corridor.

"There are no direct routes though the center of Lumengrid," said Bruenna. "I do not know why. It is a secret closely guarded by the vedalken. It must have something to do with the Pool of Knowledge. That room, I know, is in the center of the fortress on the highest level. We will make better time as we get higher, but we will also encounter more vedalken."

"Or any," muttered Glissa. She was apprehensive about actually seeing a vedalken. She feared they would somehow see right through her flimsy disguise. They had seemed to know her movements every step of the way. Why shouldn't they know she was here now? But more than that, Glissa worried that the vedalken weren't behind the attacks, that the four-armed, robed figure was something else, something even more sinister. Somewhere deep down inside, Glissa still believed the one truly behind the attacks was the fabled Memnarch Bosh had spoken of.

After a while, they began to pass humans walking the hall. Some hurried past them, perhaps on an errand for their master. Others walked in pairs or groups and talked or laughed as they walked the halls. Obviously, not all the humans were as troubled by their enslavement as Bruenna. As they passed each group of human mages, Glissa would drop her head slightly to help hide her elven features, while Bruenna would greet them with a smile and a nod of her head.

About halfway back around the tower, the corridor opened up into what looked like a large marketplace. Hundreds of humans walked about or stood next to tables. It was enormous. Glissa couldn't even see the other side of the room, and the ceiling, which had been twenty feet high in the corridor, rose to at least three times that height within the market. She felt like she had stepped outside, but they were still within the fortress.

As they entered the market, Bruenna explained. "We humans make everything the vedalken need," she said. "In turn, the vedalken let us sell the excess to ourselves. The whole thing makes me sick."

"Why?" asked Glissa. They passed some of the stalls. They were filled with food, crockery, cutlery, cloth and linen, woven leather clothing like Bruenna wore, and even fine leather boots. "These are well-made items. You could trade with other races, like the leonin, and improve your life."

"Only that is not allowed," said Bruenna. "We make the items. We sell them to each other, but the vedalken are the ones who benefit. Each of these stalls is owned by a vedalken. They pay us to work for them, then we pay them back for our own necessities. It is little better than slavery."

As they passed through the market, a small group of human mages approached. They weren't purchasing but didn't seem to be in any hurry to complete a task, either. Glissa wondered where all the vedalken masters were for these wayward workers. One of the humans, an older male, smiled as the group approached Glissa and Bruenna. He moved ahead of the rest and stopped in front of Bruenna.

"Bruenna," he said. "It's been so long. How are you?"

Bruenna extended her hand and grasped the man's arm with it. "Hello, Daven," she replied. "It goes well."

Daven grasped Bruenna's arm in return. "What brings you to Lumengrid?" he asked.

Bruenna hesitated for only a second before responding. "Business with the Synod, actually."

Daven was clearly impressed. "I had heard your moon was rising. Following in your father's footsteps, I see."

Bruenna smiled. "You could say that."

Bruenna tried to pull her hand back and move on, but Daven held her there. "Who is your friend?"

Bruenna looked at Glissa, then back toward Daven. But before she could respond, they all heard a commotion coming from the side of the chamber. Glissa looked over. The sea of humans was parting like a wake, creating a wide path through the market. Glissa swallowed hard when she saw the force that could move people as easily as quicksilver. A robed figure strode through the market, and it was coming right at Glissa.

Glissa felt a wave of panic. It was definitely a vedalken. Its domed head towered over the surrounding humans, and its voluminous robes swayed back and forth, covering and uncovering its extra arms as it strode through the crowd. Not a single human came close to the vedalken as it moved quickly through the crowd, and it barely seemed to even notice the throng of humans as they scrambled to stay from its way.

Glissa tensed and reached inside her robe for her sword. Was this the one who had killed Kane? She couldn't tell and didn't really care. She was willing to kill them all just to make sure she got the right one. Perhaps if someone showed these humans they could fight back, they would revolt. Bruenna must have sensed her intent, for she grabbed Glissa's arm and shook her head. Glissa released the pommel of her sword and turned slightly as the vedalken strode up behind Daven.

"What is going on here, Daven? I sent you out an hour ago to retrieve the timebend phial I need for my experiment, and yet I am forced to leave my experiments and come searching for you, only to find you talking in the market."

Glissa could see the horror in Daven's eyes as he released Bruenna's arm. The human path behind the vedalken closed, but everyone around Glissa's group seemed to melt away into the crowd, even those humans tending stalls. Daven dropped his head and said, "I have it, my lord. I was on my way to bring it to you."

"Then do so now, for if you and the phial are not within my quarters by the time I return, your pay will be docked for an entire phase," said the vedalken.

Glissa dared not turn around. The voice had the same deep resonance as the one she had heard in the Tangle when Kane died. The commanding tone and the lingering memory made Glissa freeze. She hardly dared breathe. The voice must have had the same effect on the humans, for Daven still hadn't moved.

"Take it to the lab," said the vedalken, "and be quick about it."

Daven and his friends disappeared into the crowd around Glissa and Bruenna. Bruenna tried to follow Daven away from the vedalken, and Glissa followed. They had only taken a few steps, though, when the voice boomed behind them.

"Halt," said the vedalken. "I do not recall dismissing you yet, Bruenna, or is your business so pressing that you cannot spare a moment for your father's old employer?"

Bruenna turned around. "We are on business for the Synod, Lord Pontifex."

"I had not heard you were coming to Lumengrid, but if you have business with the Synod, I am headed toward the upper levels myself—you may accompany me."

Bruenna nodded. "Thank you, lord. We appreciate your time."

"What are you doing?" whispered Glissa, but Bruenna didn't answer.

Pontifex turned and headed back through the crowd. Those nearest to the vedalken must have been watching him, for they immediately moved to the side to give Pontifex room. The humans in the market parted once again for the vedalken, and Bruenna and Glissa followed in his wake.

"I have never had a chance to tell you how sorry I was to hear about your father's death," said Pontifex as he led them from the market and back into a long, curving corridor.

"Thank you, my lord," said Bruenna.

Glissa couldn't read vedalken speech patterns well enough yet to tell if Pontifex was earnest in his sympathy, but Bruenna's answer had a definite edge to it.

"I have kept an eye on your career for many cycles, and I see you have done well for yourself since his death, though," continued Pontifex.

"I live to serve, my lord," she replied.

There was a definite edge to their conversation. Glissa could tell there was bad blood between these two, and there was more going on here than a chance meeting between old friends. So why were they following him? They were making better time, as the vedalken had access to more direct routes between the stairwells. But Glissa knew that Slobad and Bosh would be ready soon. They needed to make a break for it. Glissa watched for an opportunity, but there were a lot more vedalken on the upper floors. She was just about ready to stab the vedalken, when he stopped in front of a door.

"I must make a short detour on our trip that won't take long. Wait here, won't you?" Pontifex passed his hand over the door, and it dissolved in front of him. He stepped through, and the door appeared again behind him.

"What are you doing?" asked Glissa again.

"Playing along," said Bruenna. "How could I refuse? It would have looked suspicious. Besides, he could lead us right to the Pool."

"I don't know," said Glissa. "You two have history going on that I don't like. Who is this Pontifex, anyway?"

"Pontifex is the vedalken's most respected researcher," said Bruenna. "He was my father's master. He . . . was also responsible for Father's death."

"Then why are we following him?" asked Glissa. "Let's go now, while we can."

"I think . . ." The door opened again in front of them.

Both women looked up to see a trio of guards emerge from the door and surround them. Glissa whipped back her robe and pulled out her sword. But as soon as she got it free of the sheath, the sword was ripped from her hands by some unseen force. The silver blade flew past the guards into the waiting hands of Pontifex.

"Please be more civil, my dear Glissa," said Pontifex, lowering a staff, "for you are my guest now."

# CHAPTER 24

# PONTIFEX

Pontifex marched them down the corridor. Glissa and Bruenna were held firmly in the grasp of two guards behind the vedalken. Their feet swayed above the floor as the guards flew through the endless corridors of Lumengrid. The third silver guard hovered next to Pontifex, carrying Glissa's sword.

The elf looked at Bruenna. The guard had its arms wrapped around her, holding her arms against her sides. From what she had seen, Glissa didn't think Bruenna could cast spells without her hands free. Instead, Glissa concentrated on her own hands. She tried to summon the power she'd used to destroy the aerophins in the Tangle. But control over that power still eluded her. She stared at her sword just out of reach. She couldn't wait for Slobad and Bosh. They seemed overdue. She needed to distract Pontifex and get her hands on the sword.

"Where are you taking us?" she asked.

"Why, to the Synod, of course," replied Pontifex. "For you, my dear—and I must thank you, Bruenna, for delivering her to me—will finally buy me a seat on the council."

Glissa glared at Bruenna. The human mage shook her head.

"No," she said, "I never meant—"

"Of course you didn't mean to," said Pontifex, "but I knew it was only a matter of time. Bruenna has longed to enter the Pool of Knowledge ever since her father died for his indiscretions."

"If you've known about her treachery for so long, why not just kill her?"

"Because it's so much easier to keep an eye on her in that big house of hers," said Pontifex. "Think of it as an experiment—an experiment in human nature. My hypothesis—and it appears that the data has proved it correct—was that given enough time, Bruenna would provide me with what her father couldn't."

"A seat on the Synod," stated Glissa.

Pontifex turned to Glissa and smiled. "You're intelligent, especially for a warrior. It might prove interesting, once all of this is over, to study *your* race for possible use."

Glissa ignored the threat. Instead, she probed for more information. The vedalken seemed all too easy to draw out.

"You exposed her father," said Glissa. "You had him killed to gain favor with the Synod."

"Actually, it was the Synod's decision to have Donal killed," said Pontifex, "which was a shame, and I was sorry to see it happen, as he was an able assistant and brilliant—for a human. You see, I was more interested to find out what a taste of the Pool would have done to his abilities."

"You sent him in there," accused Bruenna. "He respected you, said you were different from the other vedalken, but you sent him into the Pool just to get a seat on the Synod."

Pontifex stared at Bruenna for a moment, then smirked. "You humans never cease to amaze me. Your vision is so limited that you can't see the larger ramifications of your own actions. Your father's death was not the path to the Synod—as you can see, since I am still searching for that position. No, I had much larger plans for your father after his trip into the Pool. But I've always been patient—that's why I am such a respected researcher—and that patience has paid off. By delivering Glissa, my seat on the Synod is assured."

"Why am I so important?" asked Glissa.

They were ascending a curving stairway, and Pontifex fell silent again. Glissa wondered if the vedalken didn't know or just didn't want to tell her. Then she saw another vedalken coming toward them down the stairs. They had passed many human mages on their way, but none had even glanced up at Glissa and Bruenna as they went by, and Pontifex hadn't even noticed the humans when they passed.

Evidently Pontifex *did* care if another vedalken knew what he was doing. Glissa half-hoped a dispute might erupt over who got to deliver her to the Synod. It might giver her a chance to get to her sword. However, the other vedalken didn't give Pontifex or the guards a second look. Apparently, disciplining humans was an ordinary occurrence.

"Do you mean to tell me that you haven't figured out why you are important, my dear?" he asked. "Perhaps I was wrong about your species, after all."

"I know it has something to do with the serum," said Glissa. "Are you afraid I'll expose your extermination of the blinkmoths?"

The vedalken's laugh grated against Glissa's back teeth. It sounded like someone scraping a vorrac tusk against a Tangle tree. "Who could you tell who would believe you and have enough power to stop us?"

"Memnarch?" asked Glissa.

Pontifex stopped at the top of the stairs and turned, towering over Glissa. "What do you know of Memnarch?" he asked.

"I now know that you fear him," said Glissa, undaunted by the vedalken's presence.

"Fear him?" snorted Pontifex. "Memnarch is our god. We revere his name and serve at his command. If Memnarch commanded your death, it would be my pleasure to carry out the deed."

Had Memnarch not commanded her death? Glissa didn't understand. She remembered something Strang mentioned right before he died. He said Glissa was in the vedalken's way.

She could use that.

"Memnarch didn't order my death, did he? Someone has. It was the Synod, wasn't it? Why have the vedalken forsaken their god, Pontifex?"

Pontifex took a step down the stairway toward Glissa and pointed his staff at her face. "I will kill you myself for even suggesting such a thing."

Before the vedalken could unleash his spell, Glissa heard a rumbling from far below. It was time. Bosh and Slobad had started the diversion. The rumbling grew louder, and Pontifex stumbled a step as the floor beneath him began to shake. Explosions rocked the base of Lumengrid. The tower swayed back and forth around them. The guards bumped into each other as their thrusters tried to compensate for the moving floor and walls.

Another, larger explosion shook the tower. Pontifex lost his footing on the unstable steps and pitched forward down the stairs. The falling vedalken barreled into Glissa and the guard. Pontifex grabbed for the guard, but Glissa kicked him away. He dropped his staff and tumbled down the steps. The force of her kick slammed the guard into the wall. He lost his grip on Glissa, and she fell to the steps. The elf kicked out at the guard holding Bruenna, sending it into the opposite wall, where it dropped the female mage.

"Bruenna," shouted Glissa. "My sword. Quick."

Bruenna waved her hands at the third guard and muttered a quick spell. The guard flew up into the air and smashed its crystal globe into the ceiling. Glissa covered her face as the guard exploded. When she opened her eyes, the sword was in front of her. She grabbed the sword and swung it at the guard behind her, slicing through the guard's silver arm as it reached forward to grab her again. A second swing cut off its head. The guard's body fell to the ground, and its head rolled down the stairs past Pontifex. The researcher was reaching for his staff.

Out of the corner of her eye, Glissa saw the last guard raise its weapon arm and point it at her. She dived past the advancing vedalken just before the guard shot. She rolled to a stop and looked back. The vedalken was pinned against the wall of the stairs, a harpoon jutting from his robes. Before the guard could get another shot off, Bruenna waved her hands and tossed it down the steps with a blast of air. The resulting explosion told the women they were now alone with Pontifex.

The vedalken had all four arms on the harpoon and was trying to pull it out. His arms were thin and frail. Glissa wondered if vedalken bodies were as pathetic under those robes. She picked up his staff and watched him struggle.

"I'm guessing those spindly arms can't do much beyond hold this staff," she said to the pinned researcher. "All of your power is right here, isn't it?" Glissa snapped the staff over her knee and tossed the broken pieces down the stairs.

"Your only hope of getting out of this alive," continued Glissa, "is to do exactly as we say."

"Kill him," said Bruenna, coming up behind Glissa. "If you won't do it, then get out of my way." Bruenna waved her hands at Pontifex and sent a blast of wind at the vedalken. He slammed back against the wall and the harpoon barb.

Pontifex screamed in pain. Luckily, his scream was just one of many echoing through the corridors. Human mages ran up and down the stairs as explosions continued to reverberate throughout the complex. Nobody seemed to know what was happening or what they should do. Their little tableau on the stairs was just a minor drama amidst the chaos of Lumengrid.

Glissa wheeled on Bruenna. "We need him alive," she said.

"He killed my father. He deserves to die."

"Then your father died for nothing," said Glissa. "Pontifex can get us into the Pool chamber. He can probably get us the serum we need. We can enter the Pool together. Use the man who betrayed your father to realize your father's dream."

"Why should I help you?" moaned Pontifex.

"Because I will let you live if you help us."

"Why exactly should I trust you, you who blaspheme our god and come here to destroy us?" asked Pontifex.

"You can't," said Glissa. She grabbed the harpoon and wrenched it to the side. Pontifex screamed again. "But your only other choice is to die right here."

"Fine," said Pontifex. "I will take you to the Pool chamber, and I'll even get the serum for you, but you'll never get out of here alive."

"We'll see," said Glissa. "But for now, shut up. You talk too much." She turned to Bruenna. "Hold his arms still."

Bruenna cast a spell, and a vortex of wind surrounded the vedalken, pinning all four arms against his side. Glissa reached up just outside the swirling vortex and grasped the harpoon. With a quick twist of her wrists, she snapped the shaft off. She then took her sword and sliced through the head of the harpoon behind Pontifex.

Pontifex slumped forward, perhaps weak from loss of blood. The whirlwind kept him from falling. Glissa put her hands up near the wound and summoned her own mana. Her palms glowed green and she grasped the broken shaft again. She fed enough healing energy down the harpoon to close the wound around the weapon.

"I'll get that out after you deliver the serum," she said. "Until then, it'll be a reminder of who's in charge here." Glissa twisted the shaft before letting go, then pulled his robe over the broken end of the harpoon to hide it. "Lead the way."

They followed Pontifex through the chaos and panic of the tower. Glissa held her sword ready under her cloak and told Bruenna to keep a reserve of mana ready should she need to bind Pontifex again. Most of the humans they saw rushed past the trio, giving the vedalken a wide berth. Luckily, the group didn't see any other vedalken.

After a while, the explosions stopped, but the chaos didn't. The tower continued to sway, and the humans seemed intent on getting out as quickly as possible. Pontifex had trouble walking through the rocking tower. It seemed to be a lot harder for him than for Glissa or the humans. He kept falling into the wall as he moved. She hoped that was what was keeping the other vedalken holed up in their chambers.

They reached another stairway, but it was jammed with people pushing their way down toward the lower levels of the swaying tower. When the humans saw Pontifex, though, they fell silent and parted in front of him, just like in the market. The sea of people closed much more quickly behind the vedalken as panic made the humans reckless, even around one of their masters. Bruenna and Glissa had to jostle their way through to keep up.

As they walked down yet another curving corridor, Glissa saw another vedalken coming toward them. He was having trouble walking as well. "Who is that?" she hissed.

"Iapetus," said Pontifex.

"Synod?" asked Glissa.

"No," said Pontifex. "A minor researcher."

"Get rid of him," said Glissa.

Pontifex stopped in front of Iapetus. Glissa motioned to Bruenna to stay behind Pontifex, while she moved up beside him to keep an eye on the exchange.

"What is happening, Lord Pontifex?" asked Iapetus.

"I do not know," replied Pontifex, "though I have heard rumors of an invasion of some sort, and I think you should get to the lower levels and secure the humans." Glissa shot Pontifex a glance and prodded him with the butt of her sword from underneath her cloak. Pontifex continued more succinctly. "I will secure the upper levels."

Iapetus turned to pass them, but Pontifex stopped him with a hand on the younger researcher's shoulder. "If you see Janus . . ." he began, but Bruenna bumped into him, jarring the harpoon lodged inside his body. Pontifex moaned. "Tell him I have the situation under control here. Now go. Hurry."

Iapetus trotted down the corridor and out of sight around a curve. Glissa prodded Pontifex again with her sword. "Watch your mouth," she said. "Who is Janus?"

"Lord Janus is the leader of the Synod, who will—"

Glissa pushed Pontifex forward. "That's all I need to know," she said, and fell in behind the vedalken as they made their way on down the corridor. "Sounds like someone I should like to meet."

"I believe you already have," said Pontifex, "and the next time you two meet, I don't think you will be so lucky."

"Just keep moving," said Glissa. "How much farther to the Pool chamber?"

"It is just ahead," said Pontifex. As they continued around the curve a door came into view. Two guards stood to either side of the door. Pontifex broke into a run and screamed, "Guards. Attack the humans!"

"Flare," said Glissa. She whipped off the cloak and brought up her sword. She ran after Pontifex, using his flowing robes to shield her from the guards. Two harpoons flew past her on either side of the running vedalken. She heard a whoosh of wind from behind her. Glissa thrust her sword down between the vedalken's legs to trip him and dodged to the side as he fell.

Another harpoon came directly at her, but Glissa rebounded off the wall from its path. The large missile skidded off the wall, gouging out a chunk of the silvery metal before clattering to the floor. Glissa stepped on Pontifex and leaped at the nearest guard. She flew through the air, leading with her sword, and embedded the blade into the chest of the metal creature.

Glissa dropped to the floor and lifted the guard into the air on her sword. It was amazingly light. The guard tried to propel itself sideways with its hover thruster. Glissa was pulled over and began to lose her balance. She adjusted and used the extra momentum to toss the impaled guard at its partner. It smashed into the second guard just as that one unleashed a blast of lightning. The guards crashed to the ground in a pile, and the bolt flew high, scorching the wall above Glissa's head.

"That was too close," the elf snapped. She thrust her sword over her head and jumped into the air above the prone guards. As she came down, Glissa swung her sword down through both guards, cutting one in half and taking the head off the one underneath. After she landed, Glissa beheaded the second guard just to be sure, then kicked both heads down the corridor away from Bruenna and Pontifex.

She turned around to find Bruenna holding their hostage to the ground with a wall of wind.

"You looked like you had everything under control," said Bruenna.

Glissa smiled. "Looks like you were right," she said. "Let him up. It's time he opened that door."

Glissa grabbed Pontifex by the shoulder and pulled him to his feet. She kept one hand on the harpoon shaft hidden under his robe in case he tried anything else. She pushed him toward the door. "Open it," she said.

"I'm sorry, but that may be a bit of a problem . . ." began Pontifex.

Glissa jostled the harpoon, causing the vedalken to moan in pain. "Why?" she asked.

"Without the guards to verify my identity," he replied, "the door will only open for a member of the Synod."

"Try anyway," said Glissa.

Pontifex waved his hand over the door and muttered a few

words. Glissa saw mana streak from his hand to the door and another bolt of mana streak back and spread across his fingers. But nothing happened. The door remained closed. He can do some magic without his staff, Glissa realized. I wonder how helpless he really is right now?

"Only a member of the Synod can open that door for you now." He smirked at them. "Too bad your father wasn't more help to me, my dear Bruenna, or I might have the power you so badly need right now."

"Let's see you smile after I crack open your dome," said Bruenna. She advanced on Pontifex, waving her hands in front of her. Mana built up in her palms.

"Wait," said Glissa.

"Why?" asked Bruenna. "He's no more good to us."

"He may yet be," said Glissa. "I have an idea."

Glissa reached up and yanked on the leather strap she wore around her neck. The leather snapped and Glissa pulled the remnants of the strap from underneath her blouse. A shriveled thumb and forefinger dangled on the end of the leather. If Pontifex was telling the truth about her previous encounter, these belonged to Janus, the leader of the Synod. Glissa tossed the leather strap to Pontifex.

"Hold these in your hand and try again," she said.

Pontifex looked at the severed digits and shuddered. "Where did you get . . . ?"

Glissa twisted the harpoon shaft again. "Don't worry about that. Just do as you're told."

Pontifex curled his thumb around the severed ends of the digits and held his palm up toward the door again. His hand shook as he performed the door-opening spell, but this time, when the energy spread across his fingers, it seemed to linger on the extra finger and thumb for a second. The door disappeared in front of them.

"Inside," said Glissa. She pushed Pontifex through the door

and followed him into the room. The Pool chamber was perfectly round and larger than the central courtyard at Taj Nar. The ceiling overhead was domed, giving Glissa the feeling that she was standing in an upside-down bowl.

The entire room was made of the same shimmering silver as the rest of the complex, but the light from the walls seemed to flicker around them. At first Glissa thought there might be a problem, that perhaps Slobad's explosions had somehow affected the chamber. But then she realized it was just the reflection of the Pool on the walls.

The Pool of Knowledge itself dominated the center of the large room. But it was difficult to see where the floor ended and the Pool began. It looked very much like the Quicksilver Sea—silver like the surrounding floor, but alive. Ripples moved randomly across the surface, going in several directions at once, often colliding with each other and starting anew. The only way to see the edge of the Pool was to watch the ripples hit the side and bounce back toward the middle. Light from the walls reflected off the ripples and bounced all over the room.

Glissa moved to the edge and looked down into the pool. Unlike the Quicksilver Sea, she could see down into the Pool of Knowledge. But her vision was distorted by fleeting images. They almost looked like reflections, but the images moved and changed as the ripples washed over them. Glissa saw herself walking around the room, even though she never moved from the Pool. It was hypnotic and a little scary.

She moved away from the edge and shook her head to clear her mind. Across the pool, Glissa saw another door. "Where does that lead?" she asked.

"That is where we keep the serum," he replied, "which, as you know, is necessary to activate the Pool. Without the serum, you cannot control the Pool, cannot tune into the visions you wish to view. You are at the Pool's mercy, and—"

"Be quiet already," said Glissa. "Bruenna, go with Pontifex and get two vials of serum. Be careful."

Pontifex moved around the pool to the other side, followed closely by Bruenna. Glissa watched them but kept an eye on the door to the corridor as well. Pontifex waved his hand over the door and it disappeared. Glissa glanced over and saw that the room beyond was larger than just a storage room.

"Look out!" she shouted. But it was too late. Pontifex dived to the side as a harpoon flew past him. Bruenna tried to jump from the way, but the missile slammed into her thigh. The impact spun the mage around. She fell hard on the floor beside the door. The head of the harpoon, and part of her bone, stuck out from the back of her leg.

A squad of guards glided into the room in front of another vedalken.

"Hello, Glissa," said the vedalken. "I am pleased to see you again."

# CHAPTER 25

# JANUS

"Janus," said Glissa. She pointed her sword at the vedalken across the Pool. "I've been looking for you."

The guards broke into two groups of four and glided around both sides of the pool.

"Save your bravado," said the vedalken leader. "It does not frighten me or my guards."

Glissa waited. Janus seemed content to let his guards take care of her. His mistake. She waited until the groups were halfway around either side of the Pool, then made her move. Glissa ran toward one group. The guards raised their weapon arms and fired. Glissa dived forward underneath the harpoons. She rolled and came up running, barreling into the guards before they could fire again.

Glissa tumbled to the ground atop one of the guards. Her sword fell from her hand and skittered across the floor, out of reach. The guard wrapped its arms around Glissa and held her fast. She pushed against the ground, trying to break free, but the guard's grip was too strong. Maybe she had made the mistake. The hair on the back of her neck began to tingle. The other guards had recovered. She pushed hard with one hand and rolled over, pulling the construct over on top of her. A bolt of lightning slammed into the guard, knocking it off Glissa. But now she was exposed, and the tingling had not subsided. Glissa rolled across the floor as two more bolts impacted behind her.

She grabbed her sword as she rolled over it, and swung it at the nearest guard. The blade bit into the base of the construct and stuck. Glissa rolled over again and spun the impaled guard onto the floor. Its weapon arm snapped off as the guard slammed into the floor. Glissa jumped to her feet, yanked her sword out, and kicked the helpless guard across the floor toward its two companions.

As the two guards glided from the path of the skidding construct, Glissa glanced at the other group. They had reached the other door. They would be in harpoon range soon. She was running out of time. Glissa got an idea. She scooped up a harpoon from the broken weapon arm and hurled it at the head of the closest guard. The missile smashed through the creature's globe top. Lightning crackled back along the shaft. Glissa dived to the side as the guard's head exploded. Shards of glass and metal shredded the guard standing next to it. The tattered remains of both guards dropped to the ground and fell into the Pool of Knowledge.

Glissa scrambled back to her feet and moved around the Pool, away from the second group of guards. Janus moved.

"Aren't you afraid of Memnarch finding out about your campaign to kill me?" she asked Janus as she closed on him.

The vedalken didn't seem cowed by her words or her quick disposal of half his guards.

"I don't know what you think you know," he said, "but the truth of this world would make you want to curl up in the crook of one of your Tangle trees and cry yourself to sleep. Why don't you leave the running of Mirrodin to your masters?"

Glissa continued to stalk around the Pool, just out of range of the oncoming guards. Pontifex was backing away as well, but the vedalken leader held his ground. "So now you're my master?" she asked. "Hardly."

"Ah, but I do know how to control you, as I proved in that dark little forest of yours," said Janus.

Pontifex stepped past Bruenna. The female mage had pushed herself into the wall. She was now tying a strip of her cloak around her thigh to stop the bleeding. "Pontifex," said Janus, "grab the human traitor and bring her to me, if you please."

"Leave her out of this," said Glissa. She broke into a run.

"Stop," said Janus, "or I will kill her, and you know I can do it—I proved that in the Tangle as well."

Glissa stopped. "Don't you people ever tire of hearing yourself speak?" she taunted. The guards continued to move toward her.

Janus smiled. "You brought her into this—bound her to your destiny," said Janus, "so don't blame me if you cause her death."

Pontifex moved in on Bruenna. But when he bent down to grab her, she thrust her arms up and released a huge blast of wind. The vedalken researcher flew into the air, riding Bruenna's vortex. He slammed into the ceiling above the Pool. Then Bruenna released the spell and let him fall. A huge wave of silvery liquid washed across the chamber, drenching Glissa's legs and pushing the guards back into the wall. Glissa watched Pontifex sink from sight, pulled down by the weight of his robes.

"I'm not dead yet!" spat Bruenna. But the backwash began pulling her across the slippery floor toward the Pool's edge.

Glissa started forward, but the hair on the back of her neck began to tingle. She looked at the approaching guards. Their heads glowed with crackling energy. She twirled and flung her sword at the group. All four guards flew back a few feet and shot their beams of lightning at the sword. The energy disappeared into the blade as it clattered to the floor.

Glissa glanced back at Bruenna, but Janus rushed forward and grabbed her by the neck. He lifted the mage off the floor and flung her back against the wall. Bruenna crumpled to the floor, unconscious.

The guards advanced again, their weapon arms raised. Glissa needed to rid herself of them quickly so she could confront Janus without further interruptions. She raced toward the guards, dodging back and forth to avoid harpoons. As she reached the first, Glissa threw up an arm to block its attack. Metal clanged against metal and pain shot up her arm, but she got inside its reach. Glissa grabbed the construct around the torso and twisted it around to keep its weapons pointed away from her. She spun to face the other guards. With no clear shot past her hover shield, the guards hesitated.

Glissa took the opening and rushed forward. She slammed her shield guard into the next guard in line and shoved them both over the lip of the Pool. They fired their thrusters over the glistening liquid, but that did little more than create large ripples that splashed over the edge. Both guards dropped into the Pool of Knowledge, firing their harpoons wildly before sinking from sight.

Glissa stood between the last two guards. They raised their arms to fire. Glissa kicked out at the one behind her as she ducked under the harpoon arm of the one in front of her. Its shot flew over Glissa and slammed into the reeling guard behind her, sending it over the edge of the Pool as well, where it sank down next to its companions. Glissa grabbed her sword as she straightened up, and whirled completely around, swinging the sword in a blazing circle. Electricity still crackled up and down the blade as it sliced through the last guard, just below its domed head.

Glissa turned and glared at Janus. The vedalken stood over the unconscious Bruenna, holding her head up by the hair with one hand while pointing his staff at her face with another. His second set of hands clapped very slowly.

"Impressive," he said. "But ultimately futile. I don't think you want another death on your hands. Give yourself up to me and I will spare the human's life."

\* \* \* \* \*

Janus shifted his hand on the staff and it flashed. The doors on either side opened. Six more guards flew into the room through each door and moved to surround Glissa. She was trapped and her arm ached from the guard's blow. She couldn't handle another dozen guards. Glissa thought for a moment about diving into the Pool, but if she left, Bruenna would surely die.

"How do I know I can trust you?" she asked.

"You do not," said Janus, "but you have no other choice, do you?"

"You will release all of my friends?" she asked.

"Yes."

"And leave the other races alone?"

"You have my word."

The guards lined up on either side of Glissa. She could feel their energy pulsing across the hairs on the back of her neck. She truly had no choice. "Then I surrender," she said.

"Take her," said Janus. Two guards moved in and grabbed Glissa's arms. Pain shot up her sore arm when the guard wrenched it up away from her. The other ten guards circled around her. "Now hold her so she can watch as I melt another one of her friends!"

"No!" screamed Glissa. Janus began his spell. Mana built up around the top of his staff. Glissa's rage and fear triggered something inside, just as it had after Kane's death. In an instant, green tendrils of energy enveloped her body and coursed up and down her arms and legs. Without even thinking, Glissa unleashed the power.

The tendrils coalesced around her hands and flashed to the guards holding her. Both guards went rigid and began shaking as energy spiraled around and through their bodies. A moment later, tendrils shot from the two guards holding her out to the ten surrounding guards. A spider web of emerald energy pulsed around Glissa as the guards shuddered and broke apart under the magical onslaught.

Then it ended, as quickly as it began. All twelve guards disintegrated into piles of fine silver powder around Glissa. The entire incident happened before Janus could finish summoning mana. Glissa slumped to the floor, spent. Her arms and legs felt dead. Her heart was racing, and she couldn't catch her breath. She rested on her hands and knees and stared at Janus across the Pool.

The vedalken didn't speak. He merely dropped Bruenna's body and began moving around the pool toward Glissa. The end of his staff pulsed with energy.

"Why?" asked Glissa as she continued to gasp for air. "Why do you want me dead?"

"Because you threaten our way of life, our mastery of this world," said Janus. "Because Memnarch will use you to destroy Mirrodin, and it is our duty as the master race to protect the other races—from you!"

"Liar!" someone screamed.

Pontifex rose up from the Pool behind Janus. He floated above the liquid, his wet robes matted against his body, glistening in the flickering lights of the room. "Liar!" he screamed again. With a flip of his hand Pontifex flew toward his leader. Liquid sprayed from his robes behind him like a wake as he slammed into Janus and pushed him back into the wall of the chamber. Pontifex grabbed Janus's staff and tossed it to the floor behind him. The leader of the Synod grabbed at the researcher's wet robes and tried to push him away. But Pontifex grabbed the leader's domed head in two hands and flung it against the wall.

Glissa heard a loud crack. Liquid begin oozing from the dome covering Janus's head. The leader let go of Pontifex and grabbed at his headpiece with all four hands, frantically trying to find the source of the leak. Pontifex, still holding Janus, turned to look at Glissa, who was still kneeling on the floor watching the strange spectacle.

"He convinced the Synod to destroy the champions of each

race," explained Pontifex, "and told them it was to safeguard our power, told them we would lose our power if Memnarch succeeded."

"It's true!" screamed Janus. "Memnarch will destroy the world. We will all be lost."

"All but you—isn't that right, Janus?" Pontifex turned to accuse his leader. "I have seen all of your lies, hidden deep within the Pool of Knowledge. You would usurp our god and take his place, dooming us and everyone on Mirrodin—all for your own glory."

Janus's robes darkened from the liquid draining from his dome. The level inside the dome had fallen past the top of the leader's head. Janus began to shake uncontrollably. Glissa glanced over at Bruenna. She still lay unconscious where Janus dropped her, but she was dangerously close to the edge of the Pool.

"You were right, Glissa," continued Pontifex. "Memnarch doesn't want you dead, for he needs you alive for the final phase of his grand experiment. Janus ordered you killed because you arrived too soon and upset his own plans, for, you see, this snake planned to take Memnarch's place in the grand design. But he wasn't yet ready to move against our god, so you needed to be eliminated."

The liquid was now below Janus's flattened nose. Glissa could hear him gasping for breath. His eyes, which had been dark and sunken, now protruded from their sockets. He struggled against Pontifex, obviously desperate to get away from the researcher and fix his cracked dome. The two vedalken pushed against one another. Their arms flailed for purchase on each other's wet robes.

Janus whipped his head forward and slammed his cracked globe into the front of Potifex's own dome. The researcher's head snapped back, and he lost his balance. Pontifex fell away from Janus. He tried to grab the leader's robes to steady himself, but Janus knocked Pontifex's arms away and pushed him to the floor.

"I will kill you for this insolence, Pontifex," screamed Janus. His voice warbled as the liquid sloshed around his mouth.

Janus stepped over Pontifex and headed for his staff, which still pulsed with summoned mana. Glissa scrambled forward and dived for the staff. Janus reached for it but fell to the floor just short. Glissa grabbed the staff and rolled over. Pontifex grasped his leader's robe again, pulling him away from the staff. Glissa scrambled to her feet and lowered the head of the staff to touch Janus's cracked dome.

"Leave him to me," said Pontifex, "and I will make sure Janus pays for his lies, pays for his crimes against the vedalken and our god."

"I think not," said Glissa. "He needs to pay for his crimes against my people—my family."

She flicked her wrist as she had seen Janus do that night in the Tangle. She wasn't sure the staff would work for her, but Janus hadn't spoken when he activated the staff's power earlier. It all seemed to be in the hands.

A stream of blue energy streaked from the staff and enveloped Janus. The vedalken screamed and clutched at his chest. Pontifex released the leader's robes and rolled back toward the wall. Glissa held the staff steady and poured more mana into the effect. The remaining liquid inside the dome began to boil. Bubbles filled the dome and popped against the cracked glass.

Smoke rose from Janus's robes as he tore at the fabric with his hands. Glissa kept pumping mana from the staff into the spell. The skin on the vedalken's arms blistered and peeled away. Layer after layer of skin sloughed off until the vedalken's muscles were exposed. These melted off the bones, leaving a sticky goo on his smoldering robes.

It was a gruesome sight. Memories of Kane welled up inside her as Glissa watched Janus melt before her. Tears streamed down her face, but she didn't turn away. She had to see this through.

Exact her revenge. The glass dome on Janus's head shattered and Glissa could see his eyes, almost pleading with her to let him die. After all that, the leader still lived. Glissa could have ended his pain with a quick swing of her sword, but she didn't. He didn't deserve a noble death at the end of her sword. He deserved pain.

Finally, there was nothing left of Janus except robes, bones, and a skull rattling around inside the shattered dome. Glissa broke the vedalken's staff over her knee and dropped it on his robes. She glanced at Pontifex, who was curled up against the wall. She shook her head and walked over toward Bruenna's crumpled body. Glissa sat down next to Bruenna, lifted the unconscious mage's head, and cradled it in her lap.

"It's over," she said.

"Not exactly, my dear," said Pontifex. He had risen and walked over to the door that led to the corridor. The researcher passed his hand over a dark circle on the wall, and an alarm began ringing out in the corridor. "For you see, I am loyal to Memnarch, and I plan to deliver you to him for the final phase of his glorious experiment."

# CHAPTER 26

# THE POOL OF KNOWLEDGE

Bruenna moaned. Her skin was pale and her breath shallow. Glissa laid the mage's head down on the floor and bent over to check her leg. The leather strips Bruenna had tied around the wound were soaked with blood. The barbed head of the harpoon stuck out the back of her thigh, along with the jagged end of a bone. Glissa had to get the harpoon out so she could set the leg. Only then could she apply any forest healing magic. But pulling on the harpoon would do more damage. The barbed head was lodged behind the bone. She couldn't push or pull on the weapon without ripping the broken bone from Bruenna's leg.

Glissa looked up at Pontifex, who was moving around the Pool toward her. "Help me," she said. "She'll die if we don't get this harpoon from her."

"Perhaps you didn't hear me," said Pontifex as he came closer. "You are my prisoner now. Leave her. She is not important."

Glissa stared up at Pontifex. "She is important to me," she replied. "Besides, I just saved your life. You owe me this."

"And I saved yours," said Pontifex, "so I owe you nothing."

"Fine," said Glissa. "We'll call it even. Now, help her and I will go with you peacefully."

"I don't believe you, but you will go with me, peacefully or not, for as we speak, several squads of guards are on their way." Pontifex moved up beside Glissa. "With Janus's death and my knowledge of his treachery, my place on the Synod is now assured. So tell me, why should I bargain with you, you who have nothing more to give me but your life?"

Glissa swept her sword out. She slapped the flat of the blade against the vedalken's legs, knocking him to the ground. Pain shot up into her shoulder from the impact. Glissa gritted her teeth and sprang on top of the researcher. She pressed her blade against his neck and stared into his eyes. "I can give you your life," hissed Glissa. "Or I can take it away, long before your precious guards open the door."

"Which would gain you nothing," said Pontifex, his expression stoic even in the face of death, "for your friend would still die, and the Synod would either kill you or send you to Memnarch."

Bruenna's body shuddered next to Glissa. She didn't have much time. Glissa pressed the edge of her sword into Pontifex's neck. It was her only advantage and she had to hope the vedalken's survival instinct would override his humongous ego. Blood seeped out around the blade and ran down to the floor. Glissa pressed harder. Finally, Pontifex's calm demeanor cracked slightly.

"I will help you save your friend," he said, "but only if you pledge to lay down your sword and accompany me to Memnarch. By delivering you to Memnarch myself, I will not only gain a seat on the Synod, I shall rule it."

Glissa looked at Bruenna and thought of Slobad and Bosh waiting for her somewhere far below. She had started this journey alone, driven by her fear of the unknown. She had lost family and friends searching for her destiny but had gained a new family in her new friends. She depended on them and trusted them far more than she had ever thought possible before. But now it was time to continue her journey alone—for their sake.

She pulled the sword away and climbed off Pontifex. "I so pledge," said Glissa. "I will go with you, but only after all of my friends are safe and far from here. Until then, I think I'll keep my sword." Glissa dragged Pontifex to his feet, then pushed him down next to Bruenna. "Now help me pull this harpoon out."

"There is no need for such barbaric measures," said Pontifex, "when all one needs is a simple application of magic." Pontifex grasped the harpoon. He concentrated for a moment, and Glissa could see the mana build up around his fingers. She held her sword ready, should the researcher try to harm her friend. But Pontifex simply said a single word and the harpoon vanished.

Blood began pouring from Bruenna's leg. Glissa slammed her palm down on the wound and grabbed the protruding bone gingerly with her other hand. She summoned as much mana as she could. The Tangle was far away, past the goblins' mountains, but she could still feel its power. Green tendrils of energy danced around her fingers. She willed them into the wound as she pushed the bone back through the skin. She willed the wounds to close and tried her best to mend the broken bone inside.

After a time, the blood stopped flowing. Glissa untied the leather strips from around Bruenna's thigh and tossed them aside. She checked the wound. It had closed completely. The skin was red and cracked, but it would hold. The bone would need time and more healing magic to mend properly, but at least her friend would not die. She turned toward Pontifex.

"Thank you," she said. "Why didn't you do that when you were struck in the hall?"

"I did," said Pontifex. "Eventually." He opened his own robe. The harpoon that had impaled the researcher through the shoulder was gone.

"Why?"

"I wanted you to feel in control," he said. "You never would have trusted me unless you thought you had complete control over me."

"So you orchestrated all of this?" she asked, waving her hands at the carnage in the room. "Why?"

"I merely took advantage of an opportunity," said Pontifex. "I've suspected Janus for a long time, but he was too powerful to confront. I needed proof. . . . I needed to get into the Pool—just as badly as you did—and your attack provided me with that chance."

"How do you know I won't kill you now?" asked Glissa. She pointed her sword at the vedalken.

"Because you still need answers," said Pontifex. "You want to know why you are so important—what is so special about you. You want to know the secrets of this world, and you can only get those answers from Memnarch. Besides, you gave me your pledge, and I suspect that means more to you than even your own life."

Glissa held the sword steady, ready to plunge it through the vedalken's faceplate. "The only thing that I value more than my own life is the lives of my friends," she said. "You will keep your word—you will free Bruenna and let my friends leave here alive—or I don't get my answers and you don't get your prize."

Pontifex nodded.

"How do I know I can trust you?"

"You have no other choice," said Pontifex. "Any second now, fifty guards will come through those doors, and they can either capture you and kill your friend, or escort her and the others home. Which will it be?"

"How about choice number three, huh?"

\* \* \* \* \*

Glissa and Pontifex looked up at the same time. Bosh stood at the edge of the Pool. Glistening liquid dripped off his iron frame and pooled at his feet. The golem's chest stood open. Slobad climbed from a chamber within the iron man's chest and slammed the chest panel shut.

"Grab him, Bosh," said the goblin.

Pontifex stood and turned. Glissa saw a ball of mana building in his palm.

"Watch out, Bosh!" she warned.

Pontifex raised his hand to cast a spell, but the golem was already on top of him. Bosh grabbed the vedalken's wrist and lifted him off the ground by his arm. Pontifex screamed. Glissa heard a pop as the researcher's shoulder broke. Blood stained his robes from the spot where the harpoon had speared him. The mana in Pontifex's hand dissipated as he lost concentration on the spell.

"Kill him, huh?" said Slobad. "Then we go."

"No," said Glissa. She stood and faced Bosh. "No more killing. No more death today. He saved my life . . . and Bruenna's. Let him live."

Bosh tossed Pontifex into the wall. The vedalken slammed against the side of the chamber and slumped to the floor. Glissa ran over to check on him. His eyes were closed, but she saw no signs of cracks in his dome. She turned back to Bosh and Slobad.

"How did you get here?" she asked.

"Long story, huh?" said Slobad. "After we leave you, we look for vedalken power source. Bosh and I wander—"

"There's no time now," interrupted Glissa. "Can we get out through the Pool?"

"Yes," said Bosh.

"You won't believe what we found, huh?" said Slobad. "Amazing. Under the Pool—"

"Later," said Glissa. "Bosh, grab Bruenna. We're leaving."

"Back into Pool?" asked Slobad.

"Yes," said Glissa. "Guards are coming. Lots of guards."

Slobad nodded. He opened the chamber in the golem's chest and climbed in again. Bosh picked up Bruenna and turned toward the Pool.

"Hold your hand over her mouth and nose," said Glissa. "I'll follow you."

Bosh wrapped his massive palm over the unconscious mage's face and walked to the edge of the Pool. He stepped over the side and dropped into the swirling liquid. The doors opened on either side of Glissa. She glanced up and saw a horde of guards outside the chamber. She ran for the edge of the Pool and dived toward the liquid. She heard the loud snap of harpoons launching, but the next moment she was in the Pool. Harpoons splashed into the Pool all around her as she swam toward the bottom.

\* \* \* \* \*

Glissa could see Bosh. He was walking along the bottom of the Pool toward a doorway in the side. But then another image replaced the scene in Glissa's vision. She saw the golem striding across the grounds of a palace. There were no moons in the sky, but the light from millions of stars bathed the landscape in a pale glow. It was Mirrodin. Somehow Glissa just knew. But it was a different Mirrodin than she had seen these past few weeks. It was perfect. It was beautiful.

The trees had metallic leaves and branches instead of twisted spires and uneven terraces. There were flowers surrounding a fountain. Everything gleamed and glittered in the starlight. The silvery surface of the palace reminded Glissa of Lumengrid. But the palace was built on land. It didn't flow from it. Each block fit with precision and reflected light and images in perfect proportions. The mirrored walls of Lumengrid twisted and distorted everything caught in their surface.

The silver man turned toward Glissa. He opened his mouth to speak but then disappeared. In his place, Glissa saw a new figure. This one was silver, like the last, but something was wrong with him. The new figure's forearms were made of flesh, as was part of his face and neck. He appeared to be in great pain. His fleshy mouth was open and twisted as if screaming. But the figure's metallic eyes seemed dispassionate, cold. He was reaching out to Glissa. Behind him Glissa saw crystalline spires dotting an oddly curved landscape.

Light seemed to come from above the figure. Glissa looked up into a bright, multi-colored moon, hanging impossibly close in the sky. The light blinded Glissa, and when she looked down again, she was in the Tangle. The afterglow of a bright light lingered in her eyes. Elves lay on the ground all around. They were unconscious or asleep. Glissa looked down at an elf girl at her feet. The girl had an angelic soft face and long flowing hair. She wore a green tunic tied on by leaf-covered vines. It was the girl from Glissa's flares.

"What are you doing here?" Glissa asked.

The girl looked up and screamed.

Glissa glanced up and screamed also. A horrible creature was above them both. It had the face of a human or perhaps a vedalken, but the rest of the body looked like a horror from the Mephidross or some enormous leveler. It was all legs and spikes and pincers, with a human head floating in the middle of it all. Glissa turned to run, but the creature grabbed her in its pincers and placed her in a large chair. She looked down to see that she was already strapped in, her arms and legs held in place by metal bands. Another band descended toward her forehead. The horrible, human-faced insect loomed over her. Glissa opened her mouth to scream, but nothing came out except bubbles.

\* \* \* \* \*

Glissa was back in the Pool. Bosh was dragging her through the doorway at the bottom. He passed his hand over a circle on the wall, and a door appeared, closing them off from the rest of the

Pool. A moment later, the liquid in the little room drained away. Glissa looked up at Bosh.

"Thank you," she said.

The golem nodded. "Are you all right?" he asked. "You appeared to be in trouble."

Glissa wrung the liquid from her hair. "I'm fine," she said. "I saw images. Disjointed, fleeting images. Without the serum, I couldn't control them. Just like Bruenna's father. It was like the images were controlling me."

Bosh continued to stare at her. "I'm okay. Really." She looked around the small chamber. "Where's Bruenna?" she asked.

"In the next chamber," said Bosh. "I placed her in Slobad's care. She is safe."

Bosh passed his hand over another circle on the far wall. Part of the wall disappeared, creating a doorway from the little room. An odd glow emanated from the room beyond, but Glissa couldn't see anything past the door. Bosh moved through the doorway. But as he did, the golem's body tipped forward. It looked like he had fallen into a hole, head first. But Glissa could still see the iron man's back, and he seemed to be walking down, away from the base of the door.

Glissa walked to the doorway and peered through. The small room opened into a tunnel that descended straight down into Lumengrid. Luminescent moss grew on the sides of the tunnel, providing light. But what Glissa saw made her stomach flip over. Bosh stood on the side of the tunnel beneath her. Next to him sat Slobad, who was cradling Bruenna's head in his lap. They were all below her, standing, sitting, lying on the side of the tunnel.

"Is this safe?" asked Glissa. She could see the three of them there, somehow attached to the moss-covered wall, but Glissa's brain refused to believe she wouldn't fall as soon as she stepped through the doorway.

"It is," said Bosh.

Slobad nodded. He was stroking Bruenna's hair. Glissa suppressed a chuckle. She was sure that if the human mage were awake, she would not enjoy the attention she was currently receiving from a goblin. Glissa took a deep breath and stepped over the edge. Just like Bosh, she rotated over the bottom edge of the doorway as she stepped through. Her foot came to rest on the side of the tunnel, but Glissa's stomach tried to leap from her throat. She fell down next to Slobad and threw up.

"Helps if you close your eyes, huh?" said Slobad.

Glissa closed her eyes for a moment and let her stomach settle back down into her gut. When she opened her eyes, the world looked normal around her. She felt like she was in a long tunnel . . . a long tunnel with a door in the floor.

"Where does this tunnel lead?" she asked.

"Down," said Bosh, pointing away from the door.

"How far?" asked Glissa.

"Past bottom of Lumengrid, huh?" said Slobad. "Found entrance below. Amazing. Tunnel wide as Mother's Womb down there. Go on forever."

"That must be why all of the corridors go around the center of Lumengrid," said Glissa. She looked at Bosh. "Is this one of the other holes down into the inner world? You said there were more like the Mother's Womb that Krark used in the mountains."

Bosh nodded. "We should proceed," he said. He picked up Bruenna and began walking away from the doorway. Slobad and Glissa got to their feet and followed the iron golem.

"What happened to you?" asked Slobad as they walked.

"Visions," said Glissa. "Like Bruenna's father experienced. Random visions I couldn't control."

"Anything useful?" asked Slobad.

"No," said Glissa. "Maybe. I don't know. It was all a jumble." Glissa kicked at the moss that covered much of the silvery surface of Lumengrid's inner core.

"Flare!" she muttered. "We came all this way for nothing. Bruenna almost died . . . and for what? The vedalken may no longer want me dead, but this Memnarch plans to use me to destroy the world. I don't even know where to find him, let alone how to stop him. We're no closer to figuring out Chunth's great mystery than we were when we left the Tangle."

"The trip was not completely without merit," said Bosh.

"What do you mean?" asked Glissa.

"The Pool aided me in recovering my memories," said Bosh.

"That's great," said Glissa. She ran down the side of the hole to catch up with the golem. "What do you remember?"

"Everything."

# Tales of Dominaria

## LEGIONS

**Onslaught Cycle, Book II**
**J. Robert King**

In the blood and sand of the arena,
two foes clash in a titanic battle.

## EMPEROR'S FIST

**Magic Legends Cycle Two, Book II**
**Scott McGough**

War looms above the Edemi Islands, casting the deep
and dread shadow of the Emperor's Fist.

## SCOURGE

**Onslaught Cycle, Book III**
**J. Robert King**

From the fiery battles of the Cabal, a new god has arisen,
one whose presence drives her worshipers to madness.

## THE MONSTERS OF MAGIC

**An anthology edited by J. Robert King**

From Dominaria to Phyrexia, monsters fill the multiverse,
and tales of the most popular ones fill these pages.

## CHAMPION'S TRIAL

**Magic Legends Cycle Two, Book III**
**Scott McGough**

To restore his honor, the onetime champion of Madara must
battle his own corrupt empire and the monster on the throne.

*November 2003*

Legend of the Five Rings.

# The Four Winds Saga

## Only one can claim the Throne of Rokugan.

### WIND OF JUSTICE
**Third Scroll**
**Rich Wulf**

Naseru, the most cold-hearted and scheming of the royal heirs, will stop at nothing to sit upon the Throne of Rokugan. But when dark forces in the City of Night threaten his beloved Empire, Naseru must learn to wield the most unlikely weapon of all — justice.

### WIND OF TRUTH
**Fourth Scroll**
**Ree Soesbee**

Sezaru, one of the most powerful wielders of magic in all Rokugan, has never desired his father's throne, but destiny calls to the son of Toturi. Here, in the final volume of the Four Winds Saga, all will be decided.

*December 2003*

**Now available:**

### THE STEEL THRONE
**Prelude**
**Edward Bolme**

### WIND OF HONOR
**First Scroll**
**Ree Soesbee**

### WIND OF WAR
**Second Scroll**
**Jess Lebow**

# The Hunter's Blades Trilogy

*New York Times* best-selling author
R.A. SALVATORE
takes fans behind enemy lines in this
new trilogy about one of the most popular
fantasy characters ever created.

### THE LONE DROW
#### Book II

Chaos reigns in the Spine of the World. The city of Mirabar
braces for invasion from without and civil war within. An orc king
tests the limits of his power. And *The Lone Drow* fights
for his life as this epic trilogy continues.

October 2003

*Now available in paperback!*

### THE THOUSAND ORCS
#### Book I

A horde of savage orcs, led by a mysterious cabal of power-hungry
warlords, floods across the North. When Drizzt Do'Urden and
his companions are caught in the bloody tide, the dark elf ranger
finds himself standing alone against *The Thousand Orcs*.

# R.A. Salvatore's
# War of the Spider Queen

## Chaos has come to the Underdark
## like never before.

### *New in hardcover!*
### *CONDEMNATION*, *Book III*
### **Richard Baker**

The search for answers to Lolth's silence uncovers only more complex questions. Doubt and frustration test the boundaries of already tenuous relationships as members of the drow expedition begin to turn on each other. Sensing the holes in the armor of Menzoberranzan, a new, dangerous threat steps in to test the resolve of the Jewel of the Underdark, and finds it lacking.

### *Now in paperback!*
### *DISSOLUTION*, *Book I*
### **Richard Lee Byers**

When the Queen of the Demonweb Pits stops answering the prayers of her faithful, the delicate balance of power that sustains drow civilization crumbles. As the great Houses scramble for answers, Menzoberranzan herself begins to burn.

### *INSURRECTION*, *Book II*
### **Thomas M. Reid**

The effects of Lolth's silence ripple through the Underdark and shake the drow city of Ched Nasad to its very foundations. Trapped in a city on the edge of oblivion, a small group of drow finds unlikely allies and a thousand new enemies.
October 2003